A BATTLE PLAN

Rebecca's fists pounded on Edward's powerful chest. "I will forever hate you," she cried, "if you don't let me fight this battle. Danger be damned. I will not sit back like some blithering sap of a woman and do nothing."

He held her wrists still, in one hand, and his eyes filled up with a mirthful light. He pushed her shirtsleeve up to her shoulder, then offered his arm, releasing hers. "Roll up my sleeve—do it!" he ordered.

Rebecca pushed up Edward's sleeve; he put his arm next to hers. Even in the dim light, the contrast was obvious. Edward's arm bulged with taut muscles. Hers, although well-shaped, looked like a thin spindle in comparison.

"What I lack in strength," she said, "I have in wit."

"And in passion. Before you started to pound on me," Edward said, "I was about to tell you that I want you by my side. Use you passion to help us defeat the Kirkguards."

"And if one of us fails to return from the battle?"

Edward smoothed her hair with his large hand. "We'll not fail," He said. "We'll live to see our children's children."

Rebecca stretched her arms around his neck and found his lips with hers.

Edward growled playfully, then landed Rebecca on her back in the soft pine needles. Her lips never left his. . . .

BOOK YOUR PLACE ON OUR WEBSITE AND MAKE THE READING CONNECTION!

We've created a customized website just for our very special readers, where you can get the inside scoop on everything that's going on with Zebra, Pinnacle and Kensington books.

When you come online, you'll have the exciting opportunity to:

- View covers of upcoming books
- Read sample chapters
- Learn about our future publishing schedule (listed by publication month *and author*)
- Find out when your favorite authors will be visiting a city near you
- Search for and order backlist books from our online catalog
- Check out author bios and background information
- Send e-mail to your favorite authors
- Meet the Kensington staff online
- Join us in weekly chats with authors, readers and other guests
- Get writing guidelines
- AND MUCH MORE!

**Visit our website at
http://www.zebrabooks.com**

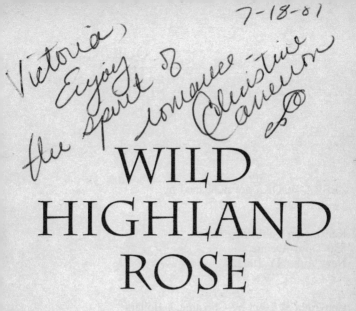

Victoria,
Enjoy
the spirit of
romance
Christine
Cameron
7-18-01

WILD HIGHLAND ROSE

CHRISTINE CAMERON

Zebra Books
Kensington Publishing Corp.
http://www.zebrabooks.com

ZEBRA BOOKS are published by

Kensington Publishing Corp.
850 Third Avenue
New York, NY 10022

First Printing: January, 1999
10 9 8 7 6 5 4 3 2 1

Printed in the United States of America

ONE

"Try not to look so disgusted. What else did you expect from our wedding night?"

Rebecca caught her breath. How much must a chieftain's daughter suffer? Her warrior spirit took hold. "You can do what ye will with me, but you canna tell me what to feel. We marry for our clans, that is all."

Ruppert's face turned a shade of purple. His fingers dug into her shoulders as he lifted her from the bed. Pain seared into her mind. Squeezing her eyes closed she tried to separate her soul from her body. Her head snapped back as he shook her.

"Open your eyes and look at me." He forced her to stand.

Her legs buckled, but her eyes remained closed. The force of his anger thrust her across the chamber. The taste of her own blood as it flowed from her nose sent her instincts into action. Her eyes opened to see Ruppert's fist headed her way. Lifting her arms up into his, she deflected the blow.

I canna do this. Rebecca tried to escape him before he could claim her bitterly and without feeling. Her back slammed against the wall. Gasping for breath she tried to see past the blackness that threatened to overtake her. He advanced on her, his face distorted.

As she clawed the wall behind her, her hand came in contact with the cold steel of Ruppert's sword. Suffering another blow, she clutched the sword handle and swung it around, striking him with the blade. His body slumped to the floor.

She threw down the offensive weapon. Its clatter sent shock waves through her body. Shuddering, she watched the blood streaming from his body. *What have I done?* Running to the bed she took a cloth and kneeled next to Ruppert, pressing it onto his wound.

If I stay—they'll hang me. Leaving his side, she struggled to clothe herself. Her fingers fumbled with the ties. She trembled. Sobs escaped her lips. A warm sensation crawled up her back. Now her family would be in great peril. There would be no alliance between the clans. Her actions would bring the Kirkguard army to Cavenaugh castle's door, and they were strong enough to take it from her clan.

She would have to flee for her life. Even a life in exile held more appeal to her than returning to Cavenaugh castle to face her shame. Self-loathing crept into her stomach and twisted it into knots. She'd killed the Kirkguard laird. The stiff white gown taunted her. Blood spotted its purity.

Climbing the stone window ledge, Rebecca was knocked back into the chamber by a man launching himself in through the window. When she fell to the hard floor, the large man nearly landed on top of her.

He wore clan colors . . . she tried to place them. Her father's enemy. She knew him. Rebecca's body heated and went weak. She watched him survey the scene. Willing her body to move again, she scrambled to her feet and leapt to the sill. Caught in mid-flight she stumbled backward, her back bumped against his firm body. He held her there. Then she heard, for the first time, the noise of a castle under attack.

"What's wrong? Wasn't your new husband satisfactory?" His deep resonant voice and breath fell on her ear. "It seems ye have the same opinion of Ruppert as I do. Come with me."

In an instant, he scooped her up in strong arms and took her to the window. He climbed the sill with ease and they finally left the repulsive chamber behind them. She looked up at the man and his long black hair caressed her face.

"Edward MacCleary." *God in heaven!*

"Ah, you do remember!"

Edward carried her to the balcony edge where a rope dangled to the ground. He helped her climb down onto the rope, following closely behind as she descended.

She thumped to the ground and lost no opportunity as Edward landed beside her. Deftly, she plucked a knife from his belt and pointed it at the surprised face of the MacCleary chieftain.

"And now, I'll bid you farewell." She sidled toward his waiting mount.

In one swift move Edward had the knife and threw Rebecca, stomach first, onto the saddle of his horse. He bounded up behind her.

"You'll have to work on that, Rebecca." He grabbed the reins and the horse jumped into action.

Rage clouded her reason. She started to kick and scream, causing the horse to rear. "Dirty MacCleary swine! Let me go—"

"Stop it—whoa!" Edward worked to get control of the horse. A sharp slap to her backside ended her tirade.

Her face on fire, as well as her temper, she tried to control herself. Her body trembled with the cold, and the events that bought her to this point.

Edward slowed the stallion to a walk, and helped her to sit upright. Pulling a tartan out of his saddlebag, he draped it over her shivering body.

She thrust her arms out, refusing the offer. The plaid fell between them. "I'd rather freeze than wear a MacCleary tartan."

Edward's deep laugh didn't ease her ire. "Spoken like a true lady."

An uproar, approaching from behind, drowned out Rebecca's response. She turned to see who approached and looked at Edward's face.

He halted the horse. "My clan approaches."

"You're sure?" Her teeth chattered with the cold.

"Aye. Rebecca Cavenaugh, or is it Kirkguard now? Swallow your stubborn pride and don this tartan. Unless you'd like me to knock you senseless and don it for you?"

Knowing Edward to be a man of his word, she quickly pulled on the warm plaid. The clan clamored through the bushes on horseback. She caught sight of the burly, wild-faced men before hiding in the folds of the tartan amid shouts of: "Well done. Ye got the lass!"

They rode into a large clearing a safe distance from Ruppert's castle, before stopping. Dismounting, Edward looked up at Rebecca.

"I wouldn't do that, if I were you." Edward's deep highland brogue assailed her senses.

How did he know she was about to kick the horse's flank? He hauled her off the saddle and she landed heavily on her feet. Rebecca clenched her hands into fists.

"Are ye going to stay put?" Edward ducked his head to look into her eyes and answered his own question. "I think not." He grabbed a rope from his saddle and turned her around, securing her hands under the tartan and behind her.

She struggled, but Edward's large hands had no difficulty controlling her protests. He finished by tying her legs together and sitting her on a large rock.

"What good could I be to you? Let me go."

"I'm surprised you have to ask." The lusty gleam in his eyes sent a rush of heat coursing through her. "Or maybe I'll avenge my father's death and give your father his due."

While Edward gathered wood Rebecca sat brooding. But she filled his ears when he returned. "Edward, untie me and let me be on my way. Surely you don't want the wrath of the Kirkguard clan on you."

"You're stayin' put. I already have the wrath of the Kirkguard and the Cavenaugh clans. When all I would have is the love of this wee one." He chucked her under the chin and smiled a devastating smile.

Her head felt light and the darkness nearly overtook her

again. The thought of her helpless situation roiled in her mind. "Let me go. Untie me, and let me go to my fate."

"No." His answer echoed in her head, strong and final.

"You'll not have my love. I would rather die than be touched by a MacCleary. You do naught but treat people false."

"Close your mouth." His voice sounded tight and controlled. Now she took every opportunity to insult the Clan MacCleary. Her tongue lashed his family and all its previous and future generations.

Edward MacCleary did his best to ignore Rebecca, but each word dug deeper at his heart. He could see his men looking at her with murder in their eyes.

"If ye don't take care of that caterwauling, I shall." Nathaniel, Edward's second in command, appeared to be speaking for the other men as well.

"I'll handle it." Edward sent him a scalding glare.

"Oh, aye, you're good at hurtin' women. Why don't you handle me?" Rebecca stared into his eyes.

Something snapped inside him. He knelt in front of her. His eyes glared into hers as he worked the knots at her feet free. Knowing Rebecca, he decided a duel would settle their differences, as it had in the past. She never blinked. Moving behind her, he untied her hands.

He pulled her to her feet and picked up Nathaniel's sword. Thrusting the sword hilt into her hands, he took up his own. Rebecca slipped the tartan from her shoulders and sliced the blade through the air. He could see sparks of excitement in her eyes as she glared at him, waiting for his first move.

He lunged forward and she met his sword with Nathaniel's. The force of her parry surprised him. The sound of metal on metal echoed in the still night air. The clansmen watched in amazement.

"It's a twist of fate, Edward." She spoke quickly, her face the very study of determination. All the while she met his blade in true style.

"Fate, Rebecca?" Edward retreated and met her thrust with his own. Moving forward again, he forced her to retreat and parry.

"They'll blame you for my husband's murder." Rebecca's voice was becoming breathless. "Just as my father was falsely blamed for your father's death."

"You lie to save your own skin."

Her sword sparked off his, adding a deadly accent to her words. "I'm—not—lying."

Finally Edward found a defect in Rebecca's swordplay, just enough to send her sword flying and pin her to the ground. His blade to her neck.

"Before you die, woman, tell me the real truth."

"I've spoken the only truth I know." Gritting her teeth, Rebecca closed her eyes.

Edward stood, returning his sword to its sheath. He stared down at her. The sight of her wildly curling hair against her fair complexion made his blood course hotly through him. Her eyes flickered open and glistened with unshed tears . . . eyes the color of blue heather.

He shook his head to clear it. "Did you see who killed my father? Can you honestly say, without a doubt, that your clan is not responsible?"

She stared at him, not speaking. Her tears streamed.

"I thought not. You best stay in this camp, unless you wish to feel the full force of my wrath." Turning, Edward walked away.

He'd won the duel. She'd have to honor his wishes.

After sitting beside the fire eating dried meat and bread, Rebecca approached Edward. "Shall I simply squat here in front of all these men, or are you going to provide me with some privacy?"

Edward did not look amused. "Pardon me, my lady. Allow me to help you." He took hold of her arm and dragged her through some bushes. "You still can't bring yourself to ask for help nicely, can you?"

Rebecca yanked her arm out of his grasp and used all her self-control to keep from striking out at him. "Turn around."

Edward turned. "I have extremely good ears, so don't try anything."

What a comforting thought. Rebecca watched Edward as she tried to relieve herself . . . quietly. His tall, well-built body had always set her blood boiling. Like wine, he'd become finer with age. She could not believe the path her thoughts were taking.

"Done," she sang out, relieved that at least one discomfort had been taken care of.

Edward had the dignity not to look back at her but walked straight ahead, expecting her to follow. She thought about running but realized she could never outdistance the highlander.

Removing his belts, he set his tartan on the ground next to a small fire. He wore only his shirt and breeches. A man brought an extra tartan over to him.

Rebecca's stomach shrank into a knot. Would this farce never end? "Why don't you just kill me and get it over with?"

"Ach, Rebecca, don't be so dramatic." Edward walked over to her with a rope and started to put it around her waist.

She stepped away. "Go to the devil."

"I probably will before this night's o'er." He grabbed her and tied the rope around her waist.

She wished she could kick him, but the situation was far too uncertain. Tying the other end of the rope around his waist, he leaned closer to her. She breathed in his musky scent, accidentally brushing his neck with her nose and lips.

Edward turned his head to look into her eyes. She swung her face away so he wouldn't see the desire she knew must be evident there. He laughed and touched his lips to her neck. She turned toward him ready to attack.

"You started it." Edward grinned.

She reacted quickly, slapping his face. Instantly he slapped her back.

"You better control that temper of yours. You'll find I've a temper to match."

Rebecca's eyes filled with hot tears. Edward pulled her down beside him, tossing the tartan over them both. As they lay there she tried to think of anything but his body touching her own.

Her thoughts circled dangerously around the events in her wedding chamber, but she forced them away too. As her sorrow flowed from her eyes, she became aware again of his body heat warming her.

She tried to ignore the emotions coiling around her senses, melting her body against his, and sending her pulse racing. Her strong will fought the feelings and finally allowed her to fall into an exhausted sleep.

Edward lay beside Rebecca breathing in her sweet scent. She was a handful. He'd always known that. They'd been reunited for such a short time and already they'd come to blows.

He thought about her father, MacKey. How could he give his own daughter to the Kirkguard tribe? Her regally shaped jaw sported a dark bruise. *That Kirkguard swine.* He watched her sleeping face for a long time.

Morning dawned slowly. Edward saddled his horse and led it to where Rebecca sat by the fire. "Get up." He stood beside the horse.

When Rebecca didn't move he advanced on her.

She crossed her arms and shook her head. "Is there no spare horse for me? I ride well, and it'll tire your horse less."

"Get. Up." He moved closer to her, willing himself to remain calm. Thankfully, Rebecca complied, climbing onto the saddle. He mounted behind her.

Edward rode in brooding silence, the words she'd spoken weighing heavily on his mind. How could he know if she'd spoken the truth? Had he been wrong all these years? A feeling deep within him tried to tell him that indeed he had been wrong.

He remembered Rebecca when she was little more than a child. Unlike most girls he'd known, she was full of life. She made his senses hum. As her body bumped against his with each step the horse took, he found it impossible to control his body's reaction to her. His breeches became unbearably tight.

Edward called for another horse, helped Rebecca onto her new mount, and warned, "Stay near at all times or I'll have your reins."

She nodded, her smug look making him want to strike her. He held his temper in check. For now, he would be calm, but let her try to escape and she would be very sorry.

Rebecca glanced over at Edward as they rode. "Where is it you're takin' me?"

"MacCleary castle."

"Why?"

"Because, I'm going to get to the bottom of this misunderstanding, if there is one. If there isn't, I will use you to my best advantage."

"Your best advantage would be to let me travel to my home, so I can explain Ruppert's demise to my father and my clan."

Edward laughed. "Do you take me for a fool?"

His high color and warning glare told her to stop trying to bargain. As they rode Rebecca's mind worked frantically. She realized now that she had to get away to face her parents and warn them. A letter would never do. She feigned downheartedness and rode automatically, but her mind stayed crisply aware of every opportunity.

She saw her chance when the men stopped to discuss which would be the safer route. She urged her horse into some trees and stealthily made her get-away. Suddenly a piercing whistle split the air. Her horse's head snapped up and it swung around, heading back toward the men. Rebecca struggled just to keep her seat. She could not persuade her mount to stop or turn back. Purposely, she slid off the animal and landed heavily on her feet, stumbling to her knees.

Edward lumbered through the trees, his face dark and threatening. *He's going to kill me.* Rebecca sprang to her feet and swung her fist toward him. He caught her arm and lifted her up over his shoulder.

"Put me down." She pounded on his back with her fists.

"You best stop that!" He gripped her legs tighter.

Rage roared in her ears, nearly drowning out the snickers from Edward's men. He dropped her down onto the hard ground where she bounced a few times on her buttocks.

Springing to her feet, she stuck her face close to Edward's. "I need to warn my clan."

Edward spoke quietly, holding her arms. "We'll discuss this later. My clansmen need to get back to the castle. We've been on the road for many days. No harm will come to you."

Rebecca took a deep breath, disappointed that she'd weakened. Edward helped her back onto her mount and climbed back onto his horse, tying her rein to his saddle. The men finished their discussion and the clan continued on their journey.

"Do you imagine a woman could merrily travel on her way in these troubled lands?" Edward gave her a sideward glance.

"Many women could not, I could."

"You're the woman of a clan with many enemies. You think you can protect yourself. I've proved that you can't. At least you've found your match in me."

Rebecca shrugged and urged her horse as far ahead of Edward's as the rein would allow. He whistled and the horse fell back into step with his.

"You may not lead this party. You best remember the proper behavior of a woman to a chieftain."

"Edward, when have you ever known me to be proper?" She smiled sweetly.

He laughed. "Such a rivalry we've had. Have you been keeping score?"

"On last count, you're ahead by one."

Edward smiled. "Of course."

The journey continued, more peacefully than before. Rebecca watched for opportunities to leave the MacCleary's company, but found none.

Day in and day out they journeyed across the steep land, sometimes barren and other times thick with forest. A week was far too long to ride and sleep next to Edward without a fever growing within her.

She almost gasped as his castle came into view. Set on a foothill amid the great mountains, the castle possessed a natural beauty. A large wall skirted the top of the hill and the castle within rose majestically with many peaks and turrets. Ivy grew on its walls creating a soft tapestry-like effect.

As the party approached, two guards at the top of the wall trumpeted and the large gates opened. A courtyard full of trees and flower gardens spread before them. Carpeted with grass, it smelled fresh and clean.

Rebecca gazed around, appreciating the sights. Out of the corner of her eye she noticed Edward observing her closely. "Quite lovely," she said to him.

"Thank you, m'lady." He looked proud. "Perhaps I could persuade you to stay."

"Surely, you jest." Rebecca grinned, trying to hide her astonishment at his words. A pleasant sensation tightened her stomach.

They dismounted and entered the main hall followed by Edward's clansmen. The hall lacked the musty smell that most castles possess. It sparkled with pride, as did the clan members who poured from every room to pay respect to their returning forces. Wives, husbands, and children embraced.

Each addressed Edward in turn, but no wife or child greeted him. Admiration showed in their eyes with curiosity evident when they looked at Rebecca. Whispered exclamations of, "Cavenaugh," could be heard now and then.

For the first time, Rebecca thought of what she must look like. She imagined her blond hair wildly framing her face, and her dress torn and dirty. But still, she held her head high.

Edward began to give directions. He instructed a young girl to take charge of Rebecca. She led her up the right side of a branching stairwell, onto a grand balcony and down a large hallway. They entered the last chamber at the end of the hall. Rebecca walked into the room and over to the window. The view of the mountains took her breath away.

"My name is Gwen, I'm the sister of Edward's cousin, Nathaniel."

"I am Rebecca, of the Clan Cavenaugh." Rebecca turned to face her.

"Aye, m'lady, I've been warned." Gwen's face turned a shade of pink.

"Warned you, did they? Don't worry Gwen, I have no quarrel with you."

"I'll bring some water up for a bath."

"That would be fine."

Gwen curtsied and left the chamber.

Rebecca sat on the window seat leaning against the sidewall. She watched the sun creep closer to the mountains. The beautiful spectrum of colors almost made her forget her problems.

Turning, she surveyed the room. A large bed stood to her left with wooden steps leading up to its soft surface. A lush canopy and curtains tied back made it look private and inviting. Suddenly, she longed to be fast asleep on its softness. Only a gritty feel on her skin stopped her.

Had Edward not married? To her right a fire in an ancient fireplace heated a kettle of water, a large tub sat beside it. Next to the bed stood a washstand and a dressing table with an urn of flowers on it. Rebecca stood and walked over to the bright flowers. Their fragrance drifted to her nostrils, bringing back memories of her childhood.

Abruptly the door opened and Edward walked in. "Have your bath and dress for evening meal. I'll come for you and we'll walk down together so I can properly introduce you to my people."

Rebecca swung around. "Don't you knock before entering a lady's chamber?" She hated to be caught unawares. "I am more tired than hungry, so I will not be joining you for dinner."

Edward frowned, his eyes narrowed, but his voice remained calm. "Forgive me for my rudeness. You're quite right, I should have knocked. However, you will need some nourishment after living on dried meat for a week. You *will* join me, even if I have to drag you down kicking and screaming."

It wouldn't be the first time. Rebecca cursed herself for showing her anger and curtsied prettily, "As you wish, m'lord." She knew her eyes gave away her true feelings.

Edward nodded and turned to leave the room. He swung around to face her again, as if to speak. Instead he turned toward the door as Gwen came in with buckets of water. "Mind yourself around this Cavenaugh." Edward wagged his finger at Gwen as he left the chamber.

Rebecca stuck her tongue out at the retreating MacCleary. Gwen's blue eyes seemed to laugh and her face lit up with a smile. Rebecca helped her fill the tub, adding the heated water. "Just right, m'lady, I'll leave you to your bath." After handing Rebecca a small bottle of lavender oil, Gwen left the room.

Rebecca dribbled some oil into the water, stirring it with her fingers. She placed the bottle on the mantel. Leaving her clothes in a puddle at her feet, she slid into the tub. The warmth seeped into her skin, making her feel delightful. She breathed in the wonderful smell of lavender, and her sore muscles relaxed. It always amazed her how sumptuous a bath could feel.

Resting in the tub, she faced the window and watched the sun set behind the mountains as the gloaming began. Darkness would still be a long way off. She ran her hands through her long hair working out the dirt.

She carefully stood and twisted the water from her hair. Her thoughts flitted dangerously to Edward, warming her even in the cool air. Finding a blanket, she wrapped it around her body. A gentle knock sounded at the door, making her jump nearly out of her skin.

"Who is it?"

"It's Gwen, I've brought you some clothes."

Rebecca opened the door and Gwen walked quickly inside and shut the door. "I was wondering what I would wear . . . " Rebecca gazed at the MacCleary colors Gwen held out to her. "I don't belong to this family, Gwen, how can I wear these plaids?"

"My apologies, but Laird Edward insists. Either these or your all-in-all, if you know what I mean." Gwen laid the gown across a small couch before the fire, and with deft fingers began to comb and plait Rebecca's hair.

"Very well, we mustn't anger the chief." Rebecca realized that wearing the clan colors would keep her protected from any bitter MacCleary who might choose to rid the world of a Cavenaugh.

"Here, let me help you a bit." Gwen fussed until Rebecca stood fully clothed. "The colors become you. Much more so than the Lady Mary."

"Lady Mary?" Just at that moment another knock sounded at the door. Rebecca and Gwen looked up. "Would you open the door please, Gwen?" Annoyed with the interruption, Rebecca finished straightening her cuff.

Gwen nodded.

Edward walked in and his mouth dropped open when he saw Rebecca. "Ah, it does my heart good."

"You best guard your heart when my sword is around." She tried to hide her discomfiture with words.

Gwen looked scandalized and Edward let out a hardy laugh. "She's all talk, Gwen. She would never run me through."

Rebecca laughed. "You think not?"

Edward's expression darkened. "Aren't you too tired and hungry to continue these games?" He walked toward Rebecca, causing Gwen to inch out of the room. "I'm afraid that I must insist on your best manners. There is only so much a clan will do for their chief if they think he's bewitched by a Cavenaugh."

"Very well." Rebecca held her arm out for Edward to guide her from the room. As they entered the hall she noticed the guards stationed at her door. She looked up at Edward. "Guards?"

"You'll be considered a guest of this clan, a means for peace. The guards are for your protection, and for the protection of my best interests. I've sent for your father to negotiate peace. You are his incentive." Edward smiled pleasantly, tightening his hold on her.

Her face grew hot, her teeth clenched. "My father always wanted peace."

Edward motioned her silent. They had reached the staircase. The crowd below became quiet and looked up at Edward and Rebecca.

"Ladies and Gentlemen of the Clan MacCleary," Edward's voice sounded loudly. "I present to you Lady Rebecca of Northumbria, and the Clan Cavenaugh." Gasps of surprise could be heard throughout the crowd. Weapons clanked as the men came to full attention.

Edward and Rebecca climbed down the stairs toward the hall full of people. Curious eyes observed them. He held Rebecca possessively and even as her core melted at his closeness, her uneasiness grew.

"Why wears she the colors of MacCleary?" said a large man as he stumbled towards them. Instantly, the strong smell of a highland brew drifted to Rebecca's nose.

"She wears these colors because she is under the guard and protection of myself, this clan's chief, and will be held here until some details can be discovered about my father's death."

"There're no details to discover. Let us take her life as her clan took our chief's." He drew his sword.

TWO

"She'll not be harmed or you'll have me to answer to. Heed my words, Duncan, harm a hair on her head and you *will* pay." Edward moved in front of Rebecca to block her from Duncan's wrath.

A hush fell on the hall. Rebecca wished her sword and belts were flanking her side instead of this woman's garb. Surveying the crowd from behind Edward, she saw their expressions held only warmth and trust toward their chieftain. The people looking at Duncan narrowed their eyes.

"There are many among us who disagree with you."

"Many? Then let the many leave these tables for I will have a peaceful meal, if I have to draw blood to gain it." Edward drew his sword.

"Aye, I'll give you that. All who would join me rise." Duncan paled when he realized no one joined his cause. He sheathed his sword, turned unsteadily, and left the hall. In his wake the hall erupted with lively conversation.

Watching Duncan leave, Rebecca shivered. Surely, they'd not heard the last of him. But Edward made her feel safe as did the friendly faces that greeted her. The heady scents of fresh food assailed her senses.

They sat down to a tasty meal of swan and heron. The meat melted in her mouth. Wonderful spices brought out its flavor.

"Lady Rebecca, how wonderful to see ye again. I, for one,

am happy to see a Cavenaugh at our table." A woman across from her spoke.

"Thank you." A haze seemed to surround Rebecca as she listened to their voices. Looking around, she recognized some of the MacClearys she'd known. It surprised her that the ties of warmth and family would surface after the long years of feud.

Edward spoke her name a few times before she thought to answer him. "Have you eaten enough? I'll take you to your room."

She nodded and bid good night to those around her. He pulled out her chair and helped her up. Glancing shyly at Edward, she realized that he was sensitive to her needs. The corners of his lips curved up in a satisfied smile. He looked far too dashing for comfort. Could he be happy to be saddled with her in these hazardous times? Her body reacted with a wave of warmth that swelled through her. They walked toward the stairs.

Rebecca lifted her gown carefully, watching her steps as Edward led her up the long stairway. Only when they reached the hallway was she able to look up at him again.

He stood tall with his long black hair waving lavishly past his broad shoulders. His dark eyes and thick brows always showed his feelings. Rebecca thought back to her earlier days with Edward. Her heart still quickened at the sight of him. But as yet, she could not figure out if it was from a feeling of adversity or romance.

Those lips. She remembered how he'd kissed her once. What would have happened if Edward's father had not been killed? There had been talk, they were to be promised.

Edward glanced at Rebecca as they walked down the hall. She flushed, her high cheekbones looked so becoming. Her blond hair always found its way out of its binding, much like the lady herself. What would it look like flowing free? How would it feel if he ran his fingers through it?

He had waited a long time to see her again. When he got word of her wedding, he rushed his men on an unplanned raid.

He'd been obsessed with reaching her before she married Ruppert. He drove his men hard, but still hadn't arrived in time.

Edward bent his head down closer to hers as they reached her room, holding her arm. The guards at her door sobered him.

"Rebecca—be wise and ride this out. I'm a very stubborn man. I always get what I want." He spoke heatedly because he knew he wouldn't be getting what he wanted tonight.

As the door closed behind Rebecca, he bid the guards good night and knew they could be trusted. Years ago, these men had been most loyal to the Cavenaugh clan.

The next day dawned beautifully. In her room she ate freshly baked bread with butter and a delicious brew she hadn't tasted before. Feeling refreshed, she dressed in a MacCleary plaid skirt that swept to her ankles, and a soft blue linen shirt that matched the plaid nicely.

Did someone fill the wardrobe with various clothing, in her absence? Who was Lady Mary? And were the clothes hers? Rebecca's face heated.

She opened the door and was met by two unsmiling guards. "Excuse me, I wish to take a walk this morning."

"I beg your pardon, m'lady, Laird Edward orders that you not leave your room. He regrets he has business to catch up on and will escort you 'round the grounds on the morrow."

"I see." Rebecca hid her sour look and stepped back into the room, closing the door. *We'll see about that.* Clenching her hands into fists, she fought to control herself. Being a creature of habit and free will, and regardless of her situation, she refused to be forbidden to enjoy her early walk or ride. She didn't enjoy *anyone* ordering her about.

Her confusion and restless feelings could only be dealt with in the saddle of a good horse. Nothing calmed her better than a brisk gallop in the open air. Today looked to be the perfect day. Rarely, did the sun shine so early through the mountain mists.

A knock sounded at the door. "Come in." Rebecca looked up as Gwen entered the room.

"Lady Rebecca, good morning." Her eyes narrowed as she quickly continued, "Laird Edward gave orders for you to stay in your chamber and rest today."

"Ach, Gwen! Have you ever seen such a fine morning? Surely, we could go out for a walk or a short ride?"

"Nay, that would not be wise."

"Please Gwen, I promise you, I'll not attempt to leave. I just have to get some fresh air to clear my head. A good ride is the only way I know to do that."

"I can't disobey a direct order," Gwen said, "and the guards would never let you pass."

"Gwen, I grew up in a castle. I know how to get around the guards. We'll switch clothes, your cap will cover my hair and face. I'll be back before mid-meal, no one the wiser."

Gwen's eyes grew wide—it was working. "But . . ."

"I'll return before you know it, and you would have helped me gain back my wits. This has been a trying time for me . . . please Gwen?"

Gwen agreed, and they switched clothing. Before Rebecca knew it she was gliding past the guards, her head low. Buckets in her hands, she hurried down the hall and outside to the well.

Laying the buckets beside the well, she went out to the stables. With no one about, she saddled and bridled a black mare. Her heart pounded in her chest. She walked her mount out among the people coming and going through the castle gate, which stood open wide for the daily activities.

Indeed, this would be the perfect escape. What would she escape to? She had killed a man. She felt a panic rise within her. She had to get back home—but she would not betray Gwen. Having given her word, she would keep it.

She galloped down a foot hill and across a green field.

Gwen's cap fell to her shoulders and her hair flew free in the wind. She savored the free feeling and slowed the horse to enter a path in the outlying forest.

* * *

Edward, discussing supplies with his clansmen, stood up from his chair at the table and stretched. He looked out the window at the clear sky. The corner of his eye glimpsed a horse and rider. He looked closer and saw it was a woman with blond hair blowing in the breeze. He startled as he recognized the rider's style. "Rebecca."

He stormed out of the room and ran the length of the castle to Rebecca's chamber. He gave the guards a disgusted look. "Go and help in the kitchens. You're of no use to me here."

The guards looked puzzled, but did as he commanded.

Edward entered the room and found Gwen pacing nervously back and forth. She stopped when she saw him.

"What have you done?" He grabbed Gwen's shoulders and shook her. Her face drained of color.

"She promised to come back. She just needed to clear her head."

"And you believed her? Stay put until I get back. God help you if any harm comes to her." He pushed her roughly onto the window seat.

Edward stormed down to the stables. He grabbed the first haltered horse he could find and galloped to the entrance of the woods. Leaving his mount, just inside the wood and off the path, he continued on foot.

He found Rebecca sitting on a large rock making a flower wreath. He held back, watching in amazement. *She hasn't even got a sword.* Edward crouched nearby and watched her long graceful fingers tie together the delicate flowers. Her face looked smooth and held a glow of pinks and golds, no longer tainted by the bruises dealt to her by Ruppert. She lifted the flowers to her nose and closed her eyes.

Suddenly her face lost its glow and became a mass of worried lines. *She'd better worry.*

Rebecca felt in control of her life again. She said a prayer holding the sweet moist flowers to her lips and nose. Her mind a mass of thoughts fighting each other for her attention. She just wanted to forget. Forget that horrible night in Ruppert's chamber. She wanted to be back in that sunlit pasture of her childhood, before all the madness.

A sudden foreboding invaded her sense of well being. She realized she should be getting back. Her heart started pounding again, she hoped Gwen had kept quiet. Rebecca gracefully rose and mounted the horse. She placed the wreath of flowers around her neck, a present for Gwen. Pulling the cap onto her head she stuffed her hair back into it. She started to feel guilty for putting Gwen in such a compromising position. Leaving the woods she galloped back.

Dismounting, she walked the horse to the stables, fetched the water, and went to her chamber. Her eyes keenly aware of who did or did not see her. Why would her heart not stop pounding—where were the guards?

Rebecca opened the door and entered the room. She put the water buckets down and went to Gwen who looked ill. She pulled the flower wreath over her head, and held it out to her. "Look, Gwen, I brought you flowers . . . " Gwen didn't move but stared behind Rebecca with a stricken face.

"Do you enjoy leading my kin to do treason?" Edward's voice sent Rebecca reeling around. The flowers fell to the floor. He walked slowly toward her until he towered over her. Holding a crop, he circled her like a large cat circled its prey.

"Hardly treason. She just allowed me a little fresh air to clear my head. As you see I've not even tried to escape." Rebecca's hands turned sweaty and her knees shook, but she stared boldly at Edward's outraged face. She stood in front of Gwen, shielding her.

"Step aside, Rebecca, *now.*" When she didn't move Edward pushed her away. "Come here, Gwen." He pointed to the floor in front of him with the crop he held in his hand. Gwen knelt before of him. "Not only did Gwen put the peace of my clan at risk, but also your life."

"Nay, don't punish Gwen. It was my fault." Rebecca lunged forward to protect her.

Edward pushed her away again and lashed Gwen's back with

his crop. Rebecca lunged forward. Getting in between, she received the last lash.

"There will be no more treachery." Edward struck Rebecca once more and left the room.

Kneeling on the floor, she held the sobbing Gwen, trying to comfort her. "Gwen, I'm so sorry. Please forgive me." She glanced at the trampled flowers on the floor.

"The pain is not so much in my back, as it is in my heart. I should never have betrayed my kin. But I have to thank you for returning. If you hadn't come back, I would have been killed for treason."

Rebecca hung her head. How had she been so thoughtless? Gwen quietly left the room. Rebecca rubbed her hip where it still stung from Edward's crop. She had shamed herself and Gwen. Her abashment caused her anger to raise its ugly head.

Storming over to the door, her reason abandoned her with the force of her anger. Heat spread through her blood as she pushed the guard aside. The guard, stunned, didn't move fast enough to stop her from entering the chamber next to hers. She closed the door in the guard's face.

"I thought that this would be your chamber . . . " Rebecca lost her voice as she took in the scene before her.

Edward sat upright at her entrance, the water from his bath sloshing over the sides.

The guard entered the room. "I beg yer pardon—"

"Leave," Edward ordered.

The guard ducked back out of the chamber.

"You had better turn around and get back to your room before I forget my manners, as you have, and do something we'll both regret." Edward spoke slowly and measured. He looked as if he would stand at any moment.

Rebecca stared, transfixed. Time stood still. She wasn't at all sure she would regret what Edward had in mind. Seeing him about to rise she whirled around and heard the telltale sounds of the water as he stood. She reached for the door handle and did not turn around. "I'll say what I came to say. If I ever see you strike Gwen again I'll challenge you to a duel, to the death."

Feeling a total fool, she left the room. Edward's laughter followed her.

Restless and upset with her own actions, and Edward's, Rebecca tossed and turned in her bed, snatching sleep here and there but not substantially.

Gwen woke Rebecca the next morning. "The chief wants you at the hall for morning meal."

Rebecca groaned. "Couldn't I . . ." She saw a look of fear rush onto Gwen's face and changed her mind. "Would ye comb out my hair so I'll not be late?"

Looking relieved, Gwen combed out Rebecca's hair. "My lady, if I were you I would not cause any more problems in the Mac-Cleary house. It is only by Laird Edward's insistence you're alive. He is a fair and just chieftain, but he's also short of temper."

"Aye, I've noticed." Rebecca dreaded the thought of facing Edward. There was a knock at the door. She frowned at Gwen as she put the last tie in her hair and went to open the door. She curtsied as Edward entered.

"That will be all, Gwen." Edward held the door open and shut it behind her. He turned to Rebecca, frowning. "Has your temper cooled or do you need another lesson?" He tapped his crop on the side of his leg.

"I beg your pardon," Rebecca's face grew hot, "I had no intention of causing all that trouble. It won't happen again." Rebecca curtsied. "However, the use of that"—she pointed to the crop—"is—"

Edward interrupted with a warning glare. His hand tightened on the crop. "Will you join me for breakfast?"

"Aye, m'lord." Rebecca was amazed that no sarcasm slipped from her lips or actions. Somehow, she would see that he never used that crop again.

Edward nodded and offered his arm. She took it as he led her from the room. They walked quietly to the great hall.

Edward thought he might have seen sarcasm in Rebecca's eyes, but decided not to look for trouble. He understood she was an only child, used to getting her own way. There's a lot she needed to learn about the harshness of the real world.

Edward hated to lose his temper. He often lost control of his anger and it made him feel sorry after he raged. But he could not tolerate Rebecca coaxing his kin to be disloyal. Loyalty was how his Clan survived to the turn of the sixteenth century. Edward always kept his eyes open, and rid his land of many would be problems.

When they reached the table he pulled out a chair for Rebecca. She must be hungry after missing meals the day before. They sat, rinsed their hands, and began to eat. Aye, and she did eat heartily.

Edward looked at Gwen sitting down the table from them. "Gwen, ye better curb your contrary ways," he turned to Rebecca who looked as if she would choke, "Lady Rebecca has promised a duel to the death if I take you to task again."

The clan members had a hardy laugh.

"Maybe I should just follow Duncan's advice," Edward added. He smiled at Rebecca, daring her to speak.

Her high cheekbones turned a rosy red and became more pronounced. He could see her teeth clench tightly together.

I'll see you get yours, Edward MacCleary. Rebecca could not remember ever keeping her temper under such teasing. Still, she kept her tongue from wagging. When morning meal finished, they walked from the hall together.

"We'll see the gardens now, I believe today is as fair as yesterday." His eyebrows rose as he looked at her.

His request surprised her into smiling, glad she would not have to endure the day in her chamber. Rebecca nodded and followed Edward to the north side of the hold.

Before her a beautiful world unfolded between the castle and its wall. Land with a garden in full bloom and apple trees spread before her. In the middle stood shrubs taller than Edward.

As they walked Rebecca took a deep breath, enjoying the fragrant flowers. "Is that a maze?"

"Aye. If you promise not to get into mischief, we'll see who can make it through first."

Rebecca nodded, still a little embarrassed from her behavior the day before. "You ought to give me a head start. You must know this maze."

"All right, are you ready?"

"Aye." Rebecca's sporting blood began to boil. Not usually good at walking mazes, she formed a plan. Edward motioned for her to go and she walked calmly into the maze. As soon as she was out of his sight, she hiked up her skirts and took off running.

Rebecca hid in the first dead end she found, and waited for Edward to pass. Then she followed cautiously behind him. He led her to a round area with two sheathed swords on a stone table.

Edward picked up one of the swords and went to the far end. He pointed the sword at her hiding place. Rebecca came out of hiding, feeling sheepish. Taking the other sword in her hand, she wielded it through the air.

She savored the power of the weapon in her hands. Her muscles reacted in kind, thrilling to the feel of a good match.

He swung his sword in a salute and pointed it at her once again, standing ready. Rebecca did the same and waited for his first move.

Suddenly, she decided to make the first move herself. Swinging the sword to her far right in an arch, she made a direct cut toward Edward. He countered. Their swords clanked together. Rebecca swung her body and sword around, creating momentum and strength and almost knocked the blade from his hands with her next attack. Her near victory caused her to drop her concentration. She lost her sword.

Edward landed her on the ground. The length of his body lay on top of hers, his blade to her throat.

"Haven't we done this before?"

Rebecca thrilled to the closeness of their bodies. She breathed in gasps, trying to control her reactions.

"While I have your attention, let me ask you a question. Why do you think you were ordered to stay in your chamber?" Edward removed the sword, but stayed on top of her.

Rebecca rolled her eyes.

He grabbed her chin in one hand roughly, forcing her to look into his eyes. "Your father may have let you get away with disrespectful gestures, but I'll not stand for it."

Rebecca lowered her eyes.

"Look at me."

It took pure will to look at Edward's glaring eyes again. They seemed to look into her soul, and she could see his. The intensity made her eyes tear. She'd missed this man for ten long years.

"Answer my question. Why do you need to stay in your rooms?"

"For my protection."

"Don't ever forget that. You're always in danger from my clan and Ruppert's clan. Leaving the castle's wall is foolish. And you, not even sporting a sword. Don't you dare do it again." His hand gripped her chin harder. "Do you understand?"

"Aye, Laird Edward." The sound of his station sent a chilling dread through her. He's a chieftain now. No longer just a rowdy boy of fifteen.

Edward finally released her chin. She still watched his eyes and saw a fire kindling within. Desire. For her? She had to look away. Her body burned with her need for him, ignited by the fire she had seen in his eyes. Chieftain or no, when it concerned her, she'd have to keep him in his place.

Edward stood and put his hand out to help her up. Not wanting to lose this match entirely, she smiled brilliantly at him and as he helped her up, she watched for him to be off balance . . . a wee bit . . . and with both hands she pulled down on his arm as hard as she could. He rolled forward with an oath. She moved out of his way just in time, jumping up. Grabbing up her skirts she ran. She heard Edward's laughter.

"No more cheating, Rebecca!" he yelled after her.

Weaving this way and that she met a few dead ends but ended up surprising herself by finding her way out of the maze in good time. She looked around. No Edward. Periodically glancing back at the maze exit, she ran over to an apple tree, picked an apple, and sat down against the tree trunk, acting as if she'd been waiting forever.

Leaves rustled above her and an apple core landed in her lap. She screamed and brushed it away as Edward jumped down from the tree branches.

"What took you so long?"

Rebecca launched her half eaten apple at Edward's head. He ducked, and then offered her a hand up.

"The problem, Edward, is that we've only known each other as summertime chums." She brushed the leaves from her skirt.

"Our problem, Rebecca, is that I didn't have time to teach you manners in the space of a summer." He shook his finger at her.

"Oh, I see, and pushing a young lady into a loch is manners?"

A castle guard interrupted at that moment and told Edward he was needed in the castle.

"Please excuse me, m'lady." Edward nodded to her. "See that Lady Rebecca returns to the castle and remains within."

Edward's eyes narrowed as he looked back at her.

"Thank you, m'lord. I'll enjoy the reprieve from my chamber." She curtsied.

Edward walked to the library and spoke to his men. As he took care of matters at his desk, he remembered the summer he'd spent in Rebecca's company. They had sported much the same as they did today. Her energy and craftiness amazed him. They continually played pranks on each other, and kept score.

The first time he saw her wild beauty, it astounded him. She dueled with her mentor each morning and he joined her classes. He learned a lot that summer, about swordplay and horseplay. In their free afternoons Rebecca showed him around the foothills and got him into quite a few scrapes. When he tried to get revenge he ended up in trouble with his father.

After a few long afternoons of the worst duties for punishment, he sought out Rebecca. Finding her standing by a loch, his anger clouded his judgment. Letting out a loud war cry he lunged for her, knocking her into the loch. He stood laughing at her floundering as she tried to swim in her cumbersome skirts.

Finally he held a branch out to her and pulled her to shore. Her language surprised him, as well as her father, who rode up on his horse just at that moment. Once on shore she pounded on Edward with her fists.

"Is that any way to treat someone who just saved your life?" Rebecca's father dismounted and grabbed her away from Edward, her fists fell on the air.

"He pushed me into the loch," Rebecca accused as her teeth chattered from the cold.

Edward acted quickly and blurted out the whole story, from the beginning.

"Perhaps Edward's father and I should arrange a marriage for the two of you." Her father walked away laughing. From then on, Edward remembered, the two did not bother either parent with any complaints.

"Have ye nothing better to do?" Rebecca spoke to the guard, after she realized he was trailing her.

"Pardon me, my lady, Laird Edward has ordered me to see . . ."

Rebecca turned and ignored the guard's answer. She would get away from him later. Making her way to the kitchen, she looked for a drink. Edward's sister, Madeleine, stood discussing the meals with the kitchen ladies.

"Madeleine, how are you?" Rebecca walked up to her. They hugged.

"Thank you, I'm very well. And you?"

"I could be better."

One of the cooks handed Rebecca a cup of apple cider and she sat down at a table. Madeleine joined her.

"I still remember your kindness when I was feeling ill." Rebecca also remembered visiting Madeleine with fresh fruit and flowers. Madeleine talked about the castle, giving Rebecca bits and pieces of information.

"To whom do I owe my thanks for these fine dresses?"

"Ah, they belonged to Lady Mary. Edward's late wife. You hadn't heard?"

"No, I hadn't." Rebecca was shocked at the emotions that coursed through her. Her blood froze, leaving a numb trail where it flowed.

"We're not to speak of her." Madeleine got up from the table and started directing the activities again.

Rebecca stood up and followed her, grabbing her arm. "Certainly you can tell *me* of her." She spoke softly so the other ladies would not hear.

"No, I cannot."

Rebecca was becoming bored with Madeleine. She turned to leave.

"Join me on the terrace, Rebecca. You can help me with my embroidery."

"I'm sorry Madeleine, I don't sew."

"You don't . . . oh that's right. Just sit with me then."

"Perhaps I will . . . a little later."

"Good." Madeleine hugged Rebecca again.

Rebecca turned to leave. She pushed away the unpleasant thoughts of Lady Mary. Her mind turned to getting rid of the guard.

She wandered around the castle, enjoying the winding stairways and large rooms. The guard did not seem pleased with her exploring. She disregarded his feelings for her love of learning unknown castles. Edward's castle. She worked to discover some secret passages. She thought of how she'd learned all the passages in her own castle by the time she was six years old, by herself.

Her sharp mind took in and remembered all the staircases, memorizing the lay of the castle and telltale signs of secret passages. Generally, she didn't feel safe unless she knew some

ways to get out. Finding a hall next to a narrow back stairway
she stopped to admire the tapestry hanging there.

Rebecca watched until the guard looked away and slipped
quietly down the stair. Moving quickly she found herself in the
kitchen. She continued down a hallway and out a door to the
terrace. Laughing when she spotted Madeleine.

Madeleine looked up at her and smiled. "I know that laugh.
It was usually followed by a description of how you had bested
Edward."

They laughed together. Rebecca sat down on a bench beside
her and caught her breath. "I slipped away from my guard."
She winked at Madeleine.

"You've not changed a bit. I used to love watching your an-
tics. The best one was when you tricked Edward into a briar
patch. Ach, how he screamed."

Rebecca laughed. "Aye, but he got me back. He tied me to
a tree and left me there until evening meal, threatening death
if I told."

"Aye, and if I remember you did tell. Father had quite a talk
with him." Madeleine's head bowed as she concentrated on a
small stitch.

The day passed pleasantly. Rebecca enjoyed the cool breezes
and the fresh smell in the air. They walked around the castle,
chatting and catching up on each other's lives, ending up on the
terrace as the gloaming began.

Rebecca was surprised the guard had not caught up with her
by then. Movement on the field beside the terrace caught her
eye. Edward and another man walked out onto the grass to
practice swords. She walked to the terrace wall to get a closer
look. Boosting herself up and onto the wall, she dangled her
feet over the other side.

"Do be careful, Rebecca," Madeleine warned.

"There you are!" Rebecca's guard had finally found her. She
didn't turn around. He grabbed her by the shoulders and took
her from the wall. She landed heavily on her feet and was about
to strike the guard, when Madeleine ordered him to leave her
be. He looked from one woman to the other, his face a bright

red. "I'll take this matter to Laird Edward." He strode off toward Edward.

"Edward is a chieftain now, Rebecca, you should really go by the rules." Madeleine looked worried.

Rebecca laughed as she climbed back onto her perch. Madeleine shook her head.

"Madeleine you're no fun. I am so full of terror I think I shall faint." She put the back of her hand against her forehead in a dramatic gesture.

Madeleine could not contain her laughter.

"Rebecca, you're what this castle needs . . . a humorous, fresh breeze."

They turned to watch the guard interrupt the sword match.

Rebecca remarked, "The man is a dolt, he couldn't guard a simpleton."

Edward's glare found Rebecca and sent her a threatening expression. She ducked as if to avoid a blow.

THREE

Across the field, Edward seemed to be grinning. Or was that a grimace? Rebecca used her hand to block the sun from her eyes. He gestured toward the stable and the man looked horrified. The guard bowed to him and walked toward the barn.

Rebecca laughed. "He's sent him to clean stalls."

After the guard left, Edward continued his duel. Rebecca watched in rapt attention. She watched his body move, learned his style, and ached to join the duel.

When the men stopped dueling. Edward walked over to the wall and looked up at Rebecca. "If you hadn't been such a naughty lass I'd offer you a duel." He turned to walk up the stairs to the terrace.

Had it been ten years earlier, Rebecca would have jumped on him and wrestled him to the ground. As it was she had to grip the wall to resist the temptation. She watched his back, remembering how he had kissed her long and hard after tying her to the tree that summer . . . long ago. It had awakened all her fifteen-year-old passions. She never forgot that kiss.

As Edward walked up the terrace steps, he thought about Rebecca's pouting lips and remembered how he resisted the temptation to slug her, after having the last briar plucked from his skin. Instead he rendered her defenseless and kissed her. Afterwards, a jump into an icy loch had cooled him down.

He walked onto the terrace.

"My sword arm will go to Hades," Rebecca mourned.

"Edward, I've never seen you treat a guest this way," Madeleine scolded.

"The guest was never Rebecca, dear sister." Edward escorted the ladies to the hall for evening meal.

"The poor girl lost her happy mood. You've ruined her spirit." Madeleine would not let it rest.

"Did you happen to see her guard's spirit? Her spirit could not be ruined—even if Hades froze over. Leave off, Madeleine." He noticed Rebecca's self-satisfied smile.

"Very well. We were discussing the various ways Rebecca bested you all those years ago. What happy memories."

"Madeleine, you better leave off that, too." Rebecca seemed to squirm under his steady gaze.

He smiled, glad that he could cherish those early memories of Rebecca. After a light evening meal, the trio walked each other to their chambers, chatting happily and bidding each a good night. After leaving Madeleine at her door, they reached Rebecca's chamber. Edward lightly kissed her hand and opened the door for her, closing it after she entered.

Rebecca disrobed to her light chemise, climbed the two wooden steps to the bed, and fell into its softness. She could still feel Edward's kiss on her hand. Bringing it to her mouth, she brushed her own lips over where his had been and closed her eyes. She prayed for sleep to take her swiftly.

But instead, she slept fitfully, tossing and turning until a single sunbeam found its way to her eyes. Opening them to a dim room, she rose from the bed and lit a candle. She hated the thoughts that came during this time, when her mind became aware. All her fears tumbled down on her until she could get them under control.

It was impossible to ignore reality. What would her father say? How could she talk to him? She began her daily exercises. Her muscles stretched, thankful for the movement.

Finding a stool, she brought it over to a small tapestry hanging on the wall. She stood on the stool to remove the tapestry from the rod that held it. Accidentally, the rod clanked to the floor. She froze, listening. The guard rustled, but no one came into the room.

The rod weighed about as much as her sword. She began to swing it around, practicing her fencing moves.

"What're you doing?"

Rebecca swung around and saw Edward leaning up against the doorway, his arms crossed over his chest. He had on a blue night robe and his hair lay mussed around his head. He took her breath away. *My God, if I weren't a lady I'd—*

"You better get that look off your face before I forget you're a married woman."

Rebecca raised her chin defiantly. He walked toward her, eyeing her intently. Realizing she was dressed only in a thin nightgown, she held the rod out in front of her.

Edward calmly took it from her hands and laid it down on the floor. "The guards were concerned. Go back to sleep. If you're a good lass, we may visit the maze later this morning."

"I can't sleep." Rebecca's thoughts, far from sleep, sent very pleasant messages to her body. She wanted to wrap herself around Edward and feel his hard body against hers. *I'm losing control.* "But of course, I'll try again."

Rebecca couldn't get into bed fast enough. Her foot slipped on the first step and suddenly Edward was there, holding her. The contact through her gown was brief, as he laid her on the bed. Rebecca scrambled under the covers.

Edward's face turned stormy and his mouth became a thin line. He turned and stalked out of the room; the door slammed behind him.

As she closed her eyes, she wondered and hoped that what angered him was the same as what set her senses afire. Her mind raced over what to do, and what not to do. Finally it collapsed in weariness.

Sometime later, Rebecca awoke to birds singing. Her thoughts were much less cheery. She buried the guilt inside her until it didn't hurt anymore. Remembering Edward's visit, her mind wandered onto dangerous ground. Getting out of bed she splashed her face with cold water from the water bowl.

She sat down on the window sill. The mists still clung to the mountains. A cool breeze brushed against her face, bringing moisture and a sweet mountain scent.

As her eyes turned away, she saw a very fine line in the wall next to the fireplace. Her mind snapped into action. She walked over to the wall and tapped it quietly in different places. Finding a loose brick, she pulled on it and the wall gave way with a loud creak. She stopped its movement and turned to look at her chamber door, hiding her discovery behind her.

No one appeared at the door. Rebecca found the bottle of lavender oil and poured it onto the hinges of the secret door. It opened further without a sound. She could hardly wait to see where it led. Hastily she put on her sandals and lit a candle.

Brushing away cobwebs, she went through a narrow passage and down a stair. She moved cautiously, aware of any living things that might cross her path. Suddenly, she heard the passage door click shut from above.

"Oh, good Lord." Rebecca rushed back up the stair and to the door. In her haste she managed to extinguish her candle. She threw herself against the door. It wouldn't open. She smoothed her hands over the adjoining wall. She couldn't find a latch. As she fumbled in the pitch dark, she pushed down the panic that was trying to surface.

Using her other senses, she swept her hands over the side wall and found her way down the passage. It seemed like an eternity before sunlight appeared and the smell of crisp morning air met her. She sneezed away the dust in her nose and wiped her dirty hands on her chemise. The tunnel brought her to a large cave that opened to the stony shore of a loch. How far from the castle was she?

Rebecca climbed a hill above the cave and saw the castle in the distance. Soon, she would be missed. She would have to hurry. Feeling foolish for even entering the passage in her thin gown, she crept over the crest of the hill. Had she been fully dressed she would not have returned to MacCleary castle.

She carefully skirted the woods, thankful that at least she was wearing her sandals. The chilly air made her teeth chatter and twigs kept getting caught in her unruly hair.

She went through the woods and ran across a clearing. Then she lurked around the castle walls. Arriving at the main gate, she slipped around to the back kitchen door.

"Good lord, lass, what have you been up to?" Gwen's robust aunt looked shaken. Suddenly she grabbed the top of Rebecca's head and ducked her under the kitchen table, throwing her ample skirt over her.

"Good morning, Flossie. Has Gwen been up to Rebecca's chamber this morning?"

Edward's voice shook Rebecca so badly that Flossie had to nudge her with her foot to keep her still.

"Aye, my laird, she'll be down shortly."

"Thank you. I'll wait for my meal until she comes down."

Edward left the room. Flossie lifted her skirt and faced Rebecca. "Get up to your room and back down here—fast." She gripped Rebecca's shoulders, and shook her for emphasis.

"Aye, my lady, thank you." Rebecca whispered, and then flew up the back stairs. Gwen followed behind her. They reached the top of the stair and walked slowly down the hall.

"You'll be the death of me yet." Gwen muttered under her breath. "How did you get into such a state? Another outing?"

"I found a passage, the door shut and I couldn't open it again."

Gwen's eyes widened. Rebecca walked close to Gwen as they slipped into the room before the guards could ask questions. The door closed behind them and they both flew into action. Gwen combed out the twigs in Rebecca's hair as she carefully slipped into a linen shirt and plaid skirt.

Edward watched Rebecca glide into the great hall.

"Good day."

"Ah, good day, Rebecca." Edward rose and pulled out her

chair. He thought he would explode with laughter and worked to control his mirth.

He had heard the passage door creak open and had gone into her room. He had watched her vanish into the passage and shut the door. Then, entering the passage by another door, he followed her progress. He almost crowed when he realized she'd lost her candle flame. But he marveled at her ability to find her way out.

One would never guess what she had gone through to get herself to the table, except for maybe the sparks that played in her eyes and the heightened color in her cheeks. She looked pleased with herself.

Flossie bustled around serving the meal, shooting Rebecca angry looks. She went back into the kitchen.

"I think I'll give the kitchen cat this goat milk, I've no taste for it this morning." Rebecca rose and went to the kitchen.

Edward wondered if she went out of concern for Flossie's feelings. Was her heart that good?

Rebecca came back from the kitchen looking full of remorse. She sat down at the table.

"Has the kitchen cat died?" Edward couldn't resist.

"Died? Oh dear, no. Will I be able to sword fight today?" Rebecca looked up at Edward with wide innocent eyes.

Are women all eternally deceitful?

"No."

"Nay?" Rebecca's frown widened.

"No." Edward got up from the table and pointed his finger at her, "and you may not use that passage again unless your life depends on it." He left a guard in charge of her and walked from the hall.

Rebecca retired to her chamber, sulked in her room all day, and didn't go down for afternoon or evening meals. Eating just a few bites of stew that Gwen brought up, she drank all the wine and asked for more. If she couldn't work off her frustrations with a sword, she would do it with drink.

She sat on the window sill, watching the sun disappear behind the mountains, and cried. She felt so alone. A knock at the door startled her. Trying to wipe her tears away, she went to open the door, thankful that she hadn't yet lit a candle.

"Are you feeling ill?" Edward looked at her in the dim light.

"No, just tired." Rebecca spoke softly, trying to keep the tears from her voice.

Edward moved her gently toward the fireplace and looked at her face. In the firelight, she watched his face soften at the sight of her tear-stained cheeks. Her resolve disappeared with the effects of the wine. She crumpled into his arms. He surrounded her with his warmth, reminding her of that summer long ago and his sweet comfort when her favorite deer hound died.

She could smell wine and wondered if it was from her own breath or his. Calming herself, she moved away from his embrace, looking up into his eyes. Time seemed to stand still as she studied his features and thought of the life he led as chieftain. His responsibilities seemed to be etched on his face in lines he didn't have when she knew him before.

He brought her toward him again and dipped his head closer to her. She could smell the sweet wine on his breath now, as she looked at his lips. Her senses reeled from his closeness. His mouth lowered onto hers. The kiss sent a bolt of pleasure through her body. She tasted the sweetness of his lips and wanted more.

Rebecca's tongue played with his. He pushed the shoulders of her dress down and exposed her breast. His head dipped to kiss her there.

Suddenly her senses came back to her, dousing her passion like ice water. The full force of reality picked the worst possible moment to intrude on her. She brushed Edward away and slipped from his grasp. Yelling into his astonished face, "No! How dare you?"

She backed away from him. His face looked more dangerous than she'd ever seen it before. Fear made her lose control, and she started pounding his chest. He grabbed her hands, and his anger seemed to turn to sadness. He gently held her fists still.

"I murdered my husband, and would do this? What kind of woman am I?" Closing her eyes, she tried to push the pain away.

Hot tears found their way out of her lids. He picked her up and put her on the bed, tucking the covers around her.

Edward sat on the window seat until she slept. How could he lose control of himself? He would bed the woman his clan thought an enemy? Is she more important than his own blood? He needed to prove the Cavenaugh's innocence. If he couldn't, he would be devastated. He'd leave in the morning.

Leaving the chamber, he paused to look at the sleeping Rebecca. His heart ached at the sight of her, and the pain in his chest had nothing to do with her sword. Closing her door he walked down the hall, determined to bring their problems to an end. And he knew just how.

Throughout the night he devised a plan. He informed his men and then settled in for the night. As he lay in his bed he tried to quiet his passions with his mind. Soon enough Rebecca would be his.

As Edward watched morning creep into his chamber he readied himself for the coming confrontations, both with MacKey and with his headstrong daughter.

Edward knocked on Rebecca's chamber door and found her ready for morning meal. They walked down to the great hall. He knew she would have a lot to say about his plans. He would have to insist. Entering the hall, he nodded to his kinsman. Pulling out a chair to seat Rebecca, he sat down next to her. She did not look up or speak, but he noticed her color was up.

As the hall emptied, Edward realized he would have to tell her his plan.

"Rebecca?"

She finally looked up.

"I'll be leaving today to meet your father's army on the road. I'll attempt to be rid of this feud. I hope it won't come to a fight."

Rebecca shot up out of her chair, almost overturning it. "You will do nothing of the sort." Her face drained of color. "They would kill you before you said a word."

"I won't let them kill me and you can't tell me what I will or willna do." Edward took Rebecca by her shoulders and gently pushed her back into her chair. "You will stay in the castle and wait for our return."

"I won't." Rebecca got up with such speed she was able to duck past Edward and run for the door. Running after her, he caught her arm, swung her up against his body and held her there. All his controlled passion from the night before vanished with the closeness of her body. He fought it, becoming angry.

"I realize that you have never had to mind anyone. You've never learned how to follow a command. Your father's coddled you all your life."

Rebecca pulled her arms free and pushed away, slapping Edward on the face. He gripped her again, harder, and took a deep breath in.

"Don't make this more difficult than it has to be."

"Bring me with you. Use me to get my father to talk peacefully." Rebecca's hand caresses his cheek where she had slapped him.

He pushed her hand away. "Don't use yer wiles on me. They won't work. I'm losing what little patience I have left." Edward swept Rebecca off her feet and carried her to the high castle keep. She struggled, nearly causing them to fall down the winding stairs. Once in the chamber, he threw her on the bed and shouted orders to the guards who had followed in their wake.

"Have you no shame?"

"I hate you!" Rebecca screamed and scrambled off the bed.

Edward caught her and threw her back onto the bed, pinning her down with his body. "Don't make me strike you, Rebecca. Quiet—listen to me."

She stopped and looked at Edward with such despair on her face, he wished he could give her what she wanted. Instead, he spoke the words that he'd waited ten long years to speak. "Rebecca . . . I love you. Please understand . . . I must do this."

Suddenly, her body relaxed beneath him. "If you love me, you'll bring me with you. Listen to—" Tears cut off her words.

Edward kissed them away. He rolled off her, sat on the edge

of the bed, and leaned his head on his hands. "What kind of man would I be to put you in that kind of danger?"

"My father wouldn't harm me."

"What if it's not your father we come up against? No, I'll not allow you to go." Edward looked at Rebecca. Standing up, he walked over to the chest and opened it. He pulled out a chastity belt and brought it to her.

"Don't you dare put that thing on me . . . all right, I'll stay."

"Aye, you will stay. And you'll wear this. Put it on." He held it out to her.

"You must be daft." She knocked it from his hand.

"It's for your own protection." He picked it up.

Rebecca backed against the bed frame, shaking her head.

"This is your last chance, *put it on.*" He threw it on the bed.

"Absolutely not." Her look dared him to try.

He lunged at her, struggling with her on the bed. Finally, he gained control by straddling her stomach and facing her feet. After a few rough attempts he managed to pull the belt over her feet, onto her legs, and up under her skirt. She pounded his back. The chastity belt found its mark and *click,* it locked. She scratched him brutally.

"Ow!" Pain seared his back where her nails dug in. Edward's anger flared. His hand slapped her thigh.

"You beast!" Rebecca continued to pound his back with her fists.

"As are you!" Edward yelled back as he pocketed the key and stood to face her. She would not look at him. That felt worse than the fight. *Stubborn woman.*

"You are the most . . ." Edward had to laugh when Rebecca finally turned to look at him, her face the perfect painting of the fury of defeat. "You are the most beautiful woman I have ever looked upon."

Edward leaned onto the bed and kissed her lips. While she still lay speechless, he rose from the bed and went to leave the room, fully expecting Rebecca to attack from behind. When he reached the door he turned to see her looking at him with her mouth wide open. Edward pointed a finger at her. "I *will* have you."

"*Not* if you die tryin'."

"Then I'll not die."

Her humiliation kept her frozen on the bed. Rebecca didn't know whether to be joyous, angry, or sad. Her mind kept hearing Edward's words over and over, "I love you." She suddenly realized that she had no time for these thoughts. Getting out of this hold must be her first concern. She had to reach her father's army before Edward's men did.

As she held onto the bedpost to jump off the bed, it shook in her hand. Slowly and quietly she worked the bedpost off. When she finished she stood beside the door and pleaded, "Guard, please. Help, guard!" Rebecca put up a fuss for quite a while before a frustrated guard stuck his head into the room to see what she needed.

She brought the bedpost down on his head, ready to take on the next guard with a blow to his stomach and then his head. "Sorry, lads, I really must be going." Rebecca ran quietly down the stairs, and very carefully made her way to her chamber.

Once in her chamber, she put on a large cape she'd found in a trunk and opened the passage door. Realizing she had no sword, she quickly made her way to Edward's chamber and took a sheathed sword down from the wall, tied it around her waist with a belt that lay in his trunk. The male scent of Edward still clung to the belt, causing something inside her to come alive with pleasant bursts of sensation.

She checked the hall before she returned to her room. The tiny hairs on the back of her neck bristled when she thought of how angry Edward would be. Angry, but alive. Rebecca grabbed a candle, lit it with the flame from her fireplace, and impatiently made her way down the passage.

Once out of the cave, she climbed back up to the castle and made her way to the stables, her face covered with the hood of her cape. Saddling a large white mare, she rode for the gates as quickly as possible.

Just as she left the castle wall she heard an alert being sounded for her. Nervously, she looked to see how far Edward and his forces had traveled. Not far, but they didn't hear the alert.

Rebecca galloped into the surrounding woods and followed the men at a safe distance. In her haste she realized she had not packed provisions. She always carried some dried meat in her pouch and a water skin, hardly enough for a trip such as this.

Already the chastity belt made her ride uncomfortable. She pushed her discomfort aside, and concentrated on remaining hidden. Then, she reveled in the adventure.

Edward's men finally made camp as the sun began to set behind the mountains. Rebecca felt blisters forming in the most sensitive areas. She found a small stream nearby and washed the soreness away. As she drank some water, her stomach complained from the lack of food. Too tired to wait for an opportunity to take some provisions from the camp, she took a few bites of her dried meat. She curled up in her cape, in the crook of a large tree, with her sword ready.

Rebecca slept lightly through the night and finally rose just before the light of day filtered over the mountains. Walking to the stream, she splashed her face with the ice-cold water and listened as her stomach complained. She'd have to creep into the camp to see if she could take some food.

Gingerly, she made her way into the MacCleary camp, avoiding the guards. Luckily one of the men had fallen asleep before the cook fire. Her heart beat so loudly in her ears, she thought it would wake the whole camp. Rebecca took some bread and dried mutton. Tying it in her shirt, she crept away. She didn't envy the guard when Edward found food missing.

Sitting by the stream, she ate a small amount of the bread and mutton and mounted her horse, waiting to hear the order to march on. In a short time she heard it faintly, already missing the man that sounded the call.

She had certainly never expected to feel the same passion for

Edward after ten long years of heartbreaking feud. He said he loved her, and that he would have her. The thought sent waves of heat through her body. She knew she was being foolish by following. After all, what could a small woman do against two forces of Highland clansmen? She would do plenty. Her determination grew as she rode on.

It was only that determination that sustained her through the long journey. The days wore on as she carefully rationed her food. She went into the camp once more and took more dried mutton, oats, a shield, and a water skin attached to a rope.

Finally, she heard a horn sound. They spotted another army. She went closer to the army and stayed just behind them. As the armies approached each other, she rode swiftly to the side, and put herself in between the two.

Letting her hair fly free, so they would know her, Rebecca arrived just in time to gallop in front of the two front lines holding up her shield.

FOUR

An arrow flew by her as she stopped in the middle of the forces. Rebecca heard her father's booming voice.

"Cease fire!"

Her horse pranced nervously as if sensing the tension in the air. She heard a loud oath as Edward ordered his army to hold, and rode toward Rebecca. His face, pure rage. She turned away to see her father approaching from the other side. Rebecca longed to ride up to her father and throw her arms around him, but she held her ground and waited for both men to reach her.

When Edward threatened to get there first, she rode away from him. As both men arrived, Rebecca smiled; everyone was still alive.

"There'll be no fighting, Father." She bowed to show respect. "I'm here against Laird Edward's wishes." Rebecca bowed toward Edward. His nostrils flared as his horse pranced back and forth. "Laird Edward has come to negotiate peace and an end to this feud."

Rebecca's father laughed, causing Edward to grip his sword from its sheath.

"Daughter, you've gone too far. Step behind me, and let this battle begin."

"No, Father, you must listen."

"Listen to a man who would leave your husband for dead and kidnap you?"

52   *Christine Cameron*

"Father, it was I who struck Ruppert. He was a cruel and evil person."

"I can't save you." Her father's face drained of color. He looked so sad. "Behind me is Ruppert's clan. He's ordered your return. He will have justice." Her father would not look at her.

"Ruppert is alive?" Her heart nearly stopped. *He couldn't be.*

"Aye." Her father charged to the sidelines.

Edward acted quickly and swung his horse away from the force. He whistled loudly, Rebecca's mount followed. Edward motioned for his men to fight. As the battle began he gave the reins to a guard. "Put your sword away, Rebecca. This is no place for you."

The guard sought refuge for them in a nearby glen.

"Let me join the fight!" Rebecca cried.

"Nay, my lady." The guard put her sword back at her side and tied her wrists together in front of her.

A soldier from Ruppert's army plunged through the trees, killing the guard and taking the reins of Rebecca's horse.

When Ruppert's army retreated, uneasiness came over Edward. Why did they stop the fight so quickly? He rode toward the woods looking for Rebecca and found the dead guard. Rage nearly split him in two. He galloped to his forces, and led them after Ruppert's retreating lines.

They rode on, camping a few miles behind Ruppert's army. Edward sat in the dark as his clan rested around him. He knew he needed rest, when was the last time he had slept? Rebecca haunted his mind. Thank God, she wore the chastity belt. He lay down, wrapping himself in his tartan.

Edward tossed and turned, trying to sleep so he would be strong when he faced Ruppert's men. He dreamed . . . *the sun warmed his face. He saw Rebecca in the distance picking flowers and singing a lilting song. Although he walked closer to her, she always seemed to be the same distance away. Edward*

*ran toward her and suddenly an arrow shot through the air,
striking her in the heart.*

Edward woke in a cold sweat. "Nathaniel!"

The man across from him startled.

"I'm going to ride out and scout—see if I can spot Rebecca."

"Don't go in alone, Edward. That would be rash and foolish."

"I'll judge if an opportunity is right, cousin. If I do not return,
take control of the men and go on as planned."

Nathaniel sat up. "Edward, remember, you're of no use to
Rebecca dead."

Edward saddled his horse, mounted, and rode out. He spotted
the campfire, in the distance, and tied his horse to a tree. Using
great care, he crept quietly through the woods. He saw a guard
on the outside of the camp . . . then more guards. Every corner
was covered.

Edward silently climbed a tree to get a better view. His heart
broke as he saw Rebecca in a defeated heap beside the fire. His
warrior blood cried out as he gripped the tree branch, willing
himself to remain quiet. Suddenly he saw Rebecca's head lift.
She sat up and looked around and lay down again.

Damn, why had she left his castle? Edward compared the
size of the Kirkguard force to his own. They seemed to be about
the same. Climbing down from the tree, he returned to his horse
and went back to his own camp. He woke his clan, and they
rode out to surprise the sleeping Kirkguards.

If only Edward's guard had left her untied and ready to fight.
My God, men are so single minded. She had trained all her life
for battle. Why was she always denied it?

Glancing down at the saddle she noticed her sword was still
attached to it. Her hands, tied only at the wrists, longed to seize
it and fight herself free. They didn't know her very well, did
they? Rebecca knew she could easily manage the weapon in
her hands, but she would have to wait until the army did not
surround them.

Traveling on, they kept Rebecca in the middle of their throng.

She tried to hold back the temptation to take up her sword, waiting for the right moment, comforted by the feel of the chastity belt against her skin. At least she would not have to worry about lusty guards. She set her mind on having the strength to wield that sword, using the time at hand to rest her muscles. *I can do this.*

As the sun set over the mountains, Rebecca heard the men make plans to stop for the day. She became alert, and waited for that one moment that could free her. The guards took her to the side as the other men set up camp. Taking a deep breath, she seized the sword in her bound hands, and swung it out toward the nearest guard. She broadsided him, knocking him from his horse.

Rebecca's horse pranced beneath her. She immediately arched the sword around to the other guard, hitting him on the side of his head and knocking him from his horse. Gripping the sword by her side, she set her horse galloping toward the thick woods. Her legs hugging tightly, she struggled to keep her seat.

Rebecca ducked low on the horse's neck, being sure to keep the sword from cutting her leg or the horse. Her wrists ached with the effort. She rode back, retracing their tracks. A noise in the woods alerted her that someone followed. coaxing the already spent horse, she raced on. The trees scratched her arms and clothing as she went.

A guard rode up beside her, took her reins, making her horse stop. The force made her drop her sword. Hauling her roughly onto his horse he brought her back to their camp. Rebecca recognized Ruppert's first knight, Talbot. He smiled at the guard who tossed her at his feet. She prepared herself for the worst.

Talbot pulled her up to face him and stepped back from her. "Rebecca, what a very foolish lass you are." He hit her across the face and she fell before him again. "Oh, look, you've torn your cape and shirt. My goodness, your skin as well." Talbot's sarcastic voice hardly registered in Rebecca's throbbing head.

"With due respect, sir, we are not to harm her."

Talbot took a whip out of his belt. "She tried to escape and was cut by the trees." He laughed as he added more cuts to Rebecca's clothes and back. An empty blackness enveloped her.

When she came to, she heard her father's voice as he cradled her in his arms.

"Rebecca, lass, wake up."

She opened her eyes. "Father, oh, Father. I tried to get home to explain to you. He was so cruel. Father, I failed you, and our clan." Rebecca let all the pain flow from her in hot scalding tears.

"Rebecca, you had no right to harm Ruppert." Her father pushed her away. "He's your husband, you must do as he says. No matter what he does to you."

"Father . . ." Rebecca did not want to believe what her father said.

"I blame myself. I never taught you what to expect. You were such a cheerful and beautiful child. I couldn't bear to break your spirit."

"Why should anyone's spirit be broken? Why should a woman have to be treated that way? Were you cruel to Mother? No, I can answer that. You were gentle and loving."

"Rebecca, not all men are like me."

"Wrong, Father. Not all men are like Ruppert."

"Daughter, there is nothing we can do now. You must honor your vows and pay for your error in judgment."

Rebecca stared at her father in disbelief.

Edward urged his men to be quiet and tried to surround Ruppert's clan's camp. An alert sounded before they were able to completely encompass them. Just as he reached Rebecca, he saw her grabbed up and mounted with a guard. The guard escaped the fight through a very narrow opening. Edward called out to Rebecca.

As he rode after them, an arrow grazed his ear. He brought his sleeve up to stop the bleeding and turned to fight a man pursuing him. He plunged his sword into him and swept another attacker off his mount. Frustrated to have lost ground, he left the rest to his men and trailed Rebecca again.

The hoof of Edward's horse hit a hard object on the ground. Glancing down, he recognized a sword as Rebecca's, the one that had hung in his chamber. With great impatience, he swept his sword down and scooped it up by its handle. His ear pounded with pain. He leaned down gingerly touching his ear to be sure it was not bleeding again.

What had possessed Rebecca to escape his castle? He continued to track her day and night. His horse heaved with the effort, and forced him to go slowly. The trail led to Laird Ruppert's domain. He hoped his army would follow behind him.

Edward remembered his dream from the night before and wondered at its prediction. When he did catch up with Rebecca, he prayed she would not be harmed any further. Surely she would be put to death. He could never live with himself if he allowed that to happen.

Rebecca became alert as the guard coaxed the strong horse quickly on. He leaned low, sheltering her in the saddle; he smelled of a month's grime. Her head pounded and her stomach turned.

Gathering her strength she tried to bring her arm around to unseat the man. All she accomplished was an *oof.* She found herself stomach-down on the saddle, as the Kirkguard slowed the horse. "Sir, please stop. I am going to be sick." The horse came to a stop. Rebecca quickly slid off the saddle and fell to the ground retching. He dismounted and offered her water.

"Sir, you should save yourself and surrender me to Laird Edward. He is sure to be in pursuit and is a very fierce adversary."

"Madame, I am very well aware of Laird Edward's reputation. But I have no intention of betraying my clan, or of being caught by Laird Edward. Do you so quickly forget the vows you made to Laird Ruppert? Another laird would order you

killed instantly for what you have done. Laird Ruppert favors
you with life and you would still betray him?"

"Laird Ruppert is a vile man and lacks any kind of honor."

"You had best stop talking this treason." The guard forced
her to mount and joined her on the horse as they galloped away.

They were headed toward Ruppert's castle. His words echoed
in her head, "Do you so quickly forget the vows you made to
Laird Ruppert?"

Rebecca realized that if Ruppert let her live, she would have
to do as he said, be his wife.

Maybe her honor and her clan's honor could be restored.
Rebecca didn't try to escape again. She recognized the road to
the Kirkguard castle. Every nerve in her body screamed, urged
her to escape. She called out to Edward.

The guard called out, and the gates opened to them. As they
rode through, Rebecca's heart sank. Where is Edward? The
Kirkguard immediately brought her to Ruppert's chamber. Ruppert lay on his bed with a guard beside him. Rebecca tasted the
bile from her stomach rising. It threatened to make her ill again.
She could not believe she had married this horrible man.

"Dear wife, you've returned to me." Rebecca could hear cold
sarcasm in his voice. Ruppert's face turned red, and his large
mouth spat as he spoke his next words. "When I am out of this
sickbed I will kill Laird Edward MacCleary, and I will make
your life a living hell." His stubby finger shook as it pointed
at her.

"As you wish." As the words left her mouth she wanted to
bite her tongue. Was this honor, to betray herself?

"Rebecca, it's a little too late to be contrite. We both know
what lies inside that pretty head of yours. But, we will deal with
it." Ruppert motioned for the guard to come forward. "Take
her to her chamber." He looked again at Rebecca. "In case you
have any ideas of leaving this castle again, it would be good
for you to know that your father is being held in the dungeon—
his life depends on your obedience."

Rebecca left the room with the guard. She refused to be
drowned by her fear. When the guard left her alone in her cham-

ber she breathed in deeply, glad to be alone. Standing in the middle of the room, she caught a glimpse of herself in a mirror. She looked very much as she expected. Destroyed. Her will to live balanced dangerously on the edge. Would it be peaceful . . . in death? The pain in her back throbbed.

No, she wasn't ready to give up. Just some rest . . . Rebecca walked to the bed slowly and lay down. Drifting off, she knew that for now sleep would give her the peace she so desperately needed.

When Edward's clan caught up to him they found a tired and short-tempered chieftain. Nathaniel rode up beside him.

"Edward, stop for the night, before your horse drops dead beneath you."

Edward stopped his horse and looked into Nathan's eyes. His cousin's eyes reflected his own misery. "Thank you for following, Nathan."

"Knowing my chieftain's temper, I would fear for my life if I hadn't."

"No doubt."

Nathan usually succeeded in easing tension. Edward could always count on him to put things into perspective. He directed the men to set up camp. When everyone settled around a fire he conferred with his clan.

A man across from Edward spoke, "We're up against two warring clans. I say we leave them to stew in their own problems."

Another man nodded. "Aye, and I agree, it would be folly to fight this. What would it gain for the Clan MacCleary?"

Edward paced around the men who carefully kept their eyes from looking into his. He stopped and sat down beside Nathan. "You're speaking sense. Do all of you share the same opinion?" Edward glanced at each man in turn as they nodded. "Then I will have to ask for help in my quest. Whoever would support me can join me on this road to rescue Lady Rebecca."

Edward gathered his personal belongings and mounted a rested horse.

"Are ye sure she wants rescuin'?" Duncan drawled.

"Don't make me waste what little strength I have left on your hide." Edward looked at Duncan and hoped he saw the disgust he felt for him. Duncan waved his hand and said no more.

The men gathered around the fire and talked among themselves. Nathaniel removed himself from their group and approached Edward.

"These men will ride with us on one condition. We must all rest before we take this journey any further."

Edward's first reaction was to turn his horse away from the men, and bid them farewell. Then he realized they would not be able to help Rebecca unless they rested. He dismounted and walked over to the group of men. "Thank you for your support, I'll do as you ask."

Rebecca's body and mind did not want to wake. Reality struck her so hard she began to tremble. Ruppert's words echoed in her mind. She remained torn by what was right for her clan, and what her heart told her she must do. Slowly she rose from the bed. The unwashed wounds on her back burned.

Rebecca noticed a large kettle of water, hanging in the unlit fireplace. She removed her clothes, and looked for a clean washcloth but found none. A commotion in the hall drew her attention.

"Let me pass, ye big oaf. The lady must be attended to, no matter what her crime." She heard her lady's maid before she saw her. Sarah entered, her arms full of clean rags and herbs.

Rebecca smiled at her and nearly kissed her feet.

"Word has it Talbot helped yer wounds along, worse than they already were. Well, quit gawkin'. Lay down here, let me see to you."

Words would not come to Rebecca's lips. Her eyes filled with tears, and they streamed down her cheeks.

"Come on now." Sarah hugged Rebecca in her ample arms.

"There's no time for that. Lay you down." Sarah washed her back as she cried into the couch. Rebecca calmed and thought back to her childhood. Sarah had always been there for her. How natural this seemed. Even when they moved to the Kirk-guard castle. Now, she became the strength that Rebecca needed.

"Sarah, you are an angel from God."

Sarah guffawed. "Far from that, lass. I seen what he did to you on your wedding night. I beg your pardon, but I did see. It was I that saved Ruppert's life, but only for your sake. If he died there would be no hope for you."

"Maybe it would be best if I were dead, Sarah."

"Listen to this nonsense. Stop feelin' sorry for yourself. These wounds are not so bad, but for your cape. Ah, these plaids, of the Clan MacCleary yet. Was that who scooped you out of here?"

"Edward MacCleary."

"There's a fine man, and I should have let the Kirkguard die, shouldn't I have?"

Rebecca winced as Sarah finished cleaning her wounds. " 'I don't know, Sarah. I don't know what's right or wrong, honor or dishonor. But at least I did not murder the man."

Sarah shook her head as Rebecca turned to look at her and sat up. She applied the herbs to her back and wrapped it carefully. Then she pulled a clean blouse, drawers, and a skirt of the Kirkguard colors from beneath the clean rags. Rebecca looked at the colors and once again her eyes stung with tears.

Sarah helped her dress, and combed out her hair. "I was glad to see you gone and this head of mess too." She gently joked with Rebecca as she carefully got out the tangles and twigs.

Rebecca felt a sparkle of laughter and reached deeply into herself, bringing it out into the air.

"Ah, that sounds good, Rebecca. All's not lost. I have a feeling of good to be comin' from all this, lass. Never fear, my inklings are always on the mark."

"I'll hold that thought to my heart."

"I best be goin'. I was supposed to leave you to yer own." Sarah gripped her hands once and was gone.

Rebecca did not miss the twinkle in her eye. She sat at the window, her mind a blank. Frustration nearly drowned her, when another lady entered the chamber, all hooded and very large. The stranger approached her so quickly Rebecca stood up in alarm. Suddenly a large hand covered her mouth and she found herself in a warm embrace.

"Greetings, m'lady." Edward removed his hand and replaced it with his lips, kissing her gently. "Let's be gone from this place once more."

"Nay. I won't dishonor my vows and my clan."

"Your vows and your clan be damned." Edward's eyes stared at her own. Not with anger, but with pleading.

"What do I have if my honor and family are gone?"

"You will have a happy life of your own choosing, and a family who will love you dearly."

"Your family is not my own and they feud. It will not be. I'm married to Ruppert."

"Ach, Rebecca, can't we argue about this after we're free of this place?" Edward tugged her arm.

"I can never be free."

"Either you come with me, or I will summon the guard to take my life right here in front of you."

Rebecca lowered her voice to a whisper and gripped his arm. "You are speaking rashly."

"And you're not?" Edward's eyes still pleaded. But now she could detect little sparks of anger too.

"There is my father to consider." Rebecca reached to touch Edward's midsection. "What have we here?"

Edward moved the large cape to reveal the sword she had dropped. He handed it to her.

"I can't leave my father to die. I could never be happy knowing I caused his death. He is being held in the dungeon . . ."

"I know, Rebecca, I found Sarah. She's joined my cause. As we speak she is helping Nathaniel to free your father. Now, come with me."

She began to follow when two guards stormed into the chamber. Immediately, Rebecca and Edward joined together to fight them. Standing nearly back to back they used their swords against the clubs the guards swung at them. Each held their sword with both hands, meeting the spiny weapons with a combined effort.

Rebecca could feel her strength waning and knew she needed more desperate measures.

"Duck!" Edward's voice rang out.

She ducked from the next blow and aimed her sword at the guard's hand, just as Edward ducked and rammed the handle of his sword into the other guard's face. Both guards fell to the floor.

Rebecca and Edward looked into each other's eyes. She heard more people coming. Edward grabbed her free hand and propelled her toward the window. Dropping her hand, he looked at her, his eyebrows raised in question. Rebecca nodded. Sheathing their swords they jumped into a cart loaded with hay. As they landed, the hay swallowed them up and the cart started to move. Rebecca tried to free herself from the choking hay.

"Be still." Edward grabbed her and stopped her movement. "You're both clever and foolish in the same breath." Edward's voice spoke roughly as he held her.

"And you . . ."

"Don't," Edward's brogue got deeper as he whispered, "I still haven't forgiven you for leaving my castle, so don't say another word."

The wagon came to a halt and Rebecca found herself projected roughly toward the end of the wagon.

"Simply tell me what to do and I will do it—you oaf." Rebecca shoved her shoulder against Edward.

"Since when have you ever done what I've told ye?" Edward shoved her back. "Creep down out of the wagon. Peek out first. Is anyone there?"

Rebecca pushed her head out of the hay and saw no one about. Sarah startled her. She reeled back against Edward.

"Oof—how many are about?" Edward whispered in her ear.

"It's just I, you fools." Sarah's voice sounded beyond the hay.

Rebecca crept out with Edward behind her. Leaving the wagon behind they ducked into the morning shadows. Edward grabbed both their hands, leading them toward his clan's camp. They had to walk a long way. Sarah huffed and puffed along without a complaint.

When they finally arrived at the camp, Rebecca found Sarah a place to sit beside a cook fire. Edward put a guard beside them and started to walk away.

"Where is my father—you lied—we've left him to die!"

Edward swung around, "It's to him I go now." and walked away leaving Rebecca with the chill of his words.

"The two of you haven't changed a bit. You'll be free of Ruppert and go down fighting with this one." Sarah's eyebrows quirked in her own funny way.

"What will they do with my father?"

Rebecca heard Edward's voice in the distance. ". . . and get them out of those bloody plaids and into our own." She looked at Sarah and shrugged her shoulders. They both looked up as Edward stomped over to them.

He pointed his finger at Rebecca. "If you leave here, your father dies."

"You—" Rebecca started to yell back at Edward as Sarah smothered her words with her hand.

"Child, you never did know when to hold your tongue."

"How dare he threaten my father."

"Have you lost your memory as well as your sense? Your father is the one they blame for the death of their chieftain, Edward's own father. Ach, 'twas a sad day."

"Then why did you help them?"

"Edward gave me his word, they'll give him a hearing."

"If we leave, that word will be hard to keep, if he kills Father. Edward is a man of his word . . ."

"Rebecca, you'll have to stay." Sarah shook her head. I have that inkling again . . . it's meant to be."

A man brought over two MacCleary tartans and instructed Rebecca and Sarah to put them on, all the time mumbling something about how they needed to be part of the clan to wear them, and about propriety.

"Excuse me, sir, I don't wish to wear these colors any more than you wish me to. What would you have us do, freeze out here on the trail?"

They sat down by the fire. The guard sat down and looked away.

Edward rode up to Nathaniel and Rebecca's father, MacKey, as they escaped from the castle.

"Clever wench that Sarah. She knew where to grab a key, we escaped without notice." Nathaniel glanced over at MacKey.

Edward's feelings of relief came out in a laugh. "She would have to be clever if she survived a life as Rebecca's nanny."

MacKey laughed. "She was the last of many that we tried."

Edward smiled at MacKey, but as they rode back to the camp in silence, his anger at Rebecca's father grew. Edward surprised himself with his own reaction to seeing him again, this older version of the man who was once like a father to him. He remembered how he mourned the loss of him, as well as his own father. They fought side by side many times.

Edward never wanted to believe that the Cavenaugh Clan was responsible, but he could never find proof of their innocence.

"How could you make such a mistake?" Edward finally broke the silence, as they rode up to the camp.

"What mistake do you think I've made?" MacKey glared back at him.

"Selling out your own daughter to that pig."

"My castle was in trouble, we needed the protection of another clan. Your clan was not available."

The MacCleary men closed in around the scene. Rebecca was nowhere in sight.

Edward closed his eyes, seeing red. Opening his eyes, he rode his horse up to MacKey's, and landed him with a punch to his jaw. MacKey fell back off the horse and stumbled to his feet.

"Why don't you just put an end to it, Edward. Kill me, and your revenge will be over."

Edward dismounted, took up his sword, and swung it toward MacKey, stopping just short of cutting him. He looked up at Nathaniel and motioned for a sword. Nathaniel rode over to MacKey and handed a sword down to him.

MacKey defended himself with the same grace and style that Rebecca had. Edward dueled with swift strength, crowding MacKey toward a tree. With one quick move MacKey lunged, shredding part of Edward's tartan and freeing himself from the confining position. Metal on metal sounded through the air. Edward struggled to keep his ground.

His mind kept drifting to Rebecca. He couldn't concentrate. Another parry. He lunged at MacKey. MacKey backed up just in time and immediately swung his sword to meet Edward's with a jarring intensity. He retreated and met MacKey's sword again, losing his balance for a moment.

Recovering, Edward made a full turn, meeting MacKey again, this time with two hands on the sword. He shook his head but his mind would not clear. Edward remembered when he had stormed into MacKey's room and accused him of killing his father. MacKey pretended not to even know it had happened and then rushed out to attend to the chaos that was breaking out in his castle. He never defended himself or denied his guilt.

Finally MacKey forced Edward's sword to the ground and stopped just short of striking a fatal blow.

"A life for a life, Edward. I spare your life and your men do not take mine."

Edward's clansmen crowded in. He motioned them to hold their ground. "Agreed, hut this is not over between us. We will have a hearing and I will watch your every move. God help you if you err." MacKey withdrew his sword and nodded his agreement.

Just at that moment Rebecca broke through the circle and stopped short, staring from one man to the other. "Before me stand the two most stubborn men in our fair Scotland."

Edward walked slowly over to her, his anger still not spent, his frustration so strong he could taste the bitterness of it in his mouth. He grabbed Rebecca and pushed her roughly toward her father.

"What do you think of your daughter now? Don't those colors become her? Wasn't this the way it was supposed ta be? Before you killed my father . . . your faithful friend. Before you married the rose to the hemlock." Edward stared at MacKey, willing him to defend himself.

MacKey reached a hand to Rebecca, frowning at Edward. She took her father's hand and led him away from the crowd. Edward watched her turn, glowering at him. He instructed a guard to take them back to where Sarah waited.

Edward sat alone. He tried to make sense of the man MacKey. What could he do with him? Worse, what could he do about Ruppert? Somehow he would put an end to Rebecca's marriage and this bloody feud. Deep in thought, he jolted back to reality when he heard the sound of horse's hooves thundering towards them.

Edward jumped to his feet shouting, "To your horses!" He grabbed a shield and sword.

"Edward, what shall we do with the prisoners?"

"Give them horses, swords, and shields and let them do what they will." Edward had a moment's concern for Rebecca. Let her fight if that's what she wants so badly. Mounting his horse he set his mind to the fight.

Nathaniel rode up to Rebecca, his arms full of swords and shields. She ran up to him and took the weapons.

"Edward says, 'Do what ye will.' " Nathaniel spoke quickly as he steadied his restless horse.

Rebecca stepped back in surprise. She watched Nathaniel ride off. Sarah found a large hollow in a tree and hid inside holding a sword. MacKey came to Rebecca with two mounts and they took up their swords and shields, joining the Mac-Cleary's defense against Ruppert's men.

FIVE

Men came at Rebecca from all sides trying to unseat her from the horse. Hardly able to think, she swung her sword to meet them with more strength than she knew she possessed. Screams surrounded her, echoing through the air. Everything looked dark and menacing even though the sun shone brightly.

She rode on. Fighting every second for her life, protecting whatever blue and green tartan she could, and fighting the yellow and black. Every now and then her father's red and gray plaids could be seen. The MacCleary force pushed back Ruppert's clan slowly and steadily.

Suddenly a jolt knocked her off her mount. She rolled painfully across the trampled ground, then stood and scrambled under her horse, trying to reach her sword. The ground rumbled beneath her as dust rose up to choke her. Rebecca's head reeled. She tasted her blood. Holding the shield across her back, she left the shelter of the horse and bent down, finally able to reach her sword.

As she wrapped her hand around the hilt she felt someone seize her tartan belt. She was lifted into the air, landed on the back of a horse, and held there. Her shield dropped to the ground as she tried to determine her direction and steady her sword, swinging it at the enemy who still attacked her. She found herself seated backward on the rump of a horse.

"Get your seat, so I can let go." Edward's voice boomed behind her.

Rebecca was too busy fighting to steady herself.

"Rebecca, I'm losing hold . . ."

She tried to wrap her legs around the large horse, but she slipped. Frantically searching for a hold, her feet found Edward's legs. She hooked the top of her feet around his calves, causing her body to lean over the horse's rump. Her free hand gripped the stem of the horse's tail, with her other holding onto her sword for dear life.

The horse kicked up its back legs, causing her chin to hit its rump. Her teeth clanked together. Try as she might, she could not find a way to turn around. Rebecca noticed Ruppert's men thinning out. Finally, a retreat signal could be heard in the distance. Like magic the enemy vanished.

"Whoa . . . whoa . . ." The horse would not respond to Edward's coaxing.

Rebecca felt him lean back into her, and turning her head she saw him pull the reins back. The horse slowed and reared up in protest. Sitting up, she slid down the horse's rump, landing neatly on her feet. She turned to see Edward ride quickly away and gasped when she saw the disturbance.

One of the MacClearys held her father by his throat. She watched as Edward rode up, shouting at the man. He quickly released her father. Rebecca ran toward them, nearly doubled over from the pain that ripped through her legs. Stumbling on, she heard Edward's command.

"I gave him my word. You'll not harm him."

The MacCleary clansman walked angrily away. MacKey found his horse and walked toward Rebecca.

Nathaniel rode up. "Edward, the Cavenaugh saved my life, and those of our clan. He's as good a fighter as ever."

Edward reeled around and looked at Rebecca, his face a stony mask. "The Cavenaugh had best remove his daughter from my sight, before my temper gets the best of her."

Rebecca's thrill from the fight vanished. Edward's anger came as such a blow she remained silent, too stunned to speak. MacKey helped her climb onto his horse and joined her. They rode toward the camp.

Sitting behind her father, she recovered and started berating Edward in her father's ear. "How dare he order—"

"Daughter, you best hold your tongue. I'm trying to keep us alive. Such treason, if heard by a MacCleary, could ruin my efforts."

"Oh, Father, Edward would never kill us. He loves me."

Her father craned his head to see her face. "He *loves* you? His love has not kept him from accusing your family of a deed they did not commit."

Edward looked over at Nathaniel, watching his broad smile turn to a frown. Edward dismounted. He walked, leading his horse. His tense muscles relaxed. Nathaniel followed his lead, as the rest of the men rode back to camp.

"Why the long face, Edward? What a magnificent fight, I never thought she had it in her. She fought as well as we did. And her father, he never even had a second thought."

"Nathaniel, shut your mouth."

They walked in silence. Every once in a while Nathaniel would laugh out loud, apparently at a memory from the battle. Edward ignored his joviality, and thought about how close Rebecca had come to death. He could not imagine what he would have done to the man who harmed her. She acted as if war was played like a sport. How could he show her how deadly it is?

Edward wanted to shake her and scream in her face, but that never worked. As they walked into camp Rebecca ran up to him.

"Get out of my sight." When she hesitated, Edward took a step toward her, stooped down, and put his face directly in front of hers. "Now."

The crushed look on her face only enraged him further. "Any warrior who loses her horse in battle, should not be gloating." Starting to turn from her, he saw her face turn dark and stormy. Edward stepped back and faced her again.

He moved his hand toward her and took hold of her chin. "Listen to me! When I tell you to do something you best do it!" He turned and walked away before Rebecca's anger could land her in more trouble.

Nathaniel followed him away from the camp.

"She doesn't know your after-the-battle moods, Edward. You've never stopped loving Rebecca, have you?"

Edward swung at Nathaniel with his fist. Nathaniel ducked.

"Stop actin' like a spoiled child." Nathaniel swung at Edward and caught him in the chin. Edward punched again and connected with Nathaniel's stomach.

"Oof—fine if that's what ye want." Nathaniel swung his fist into Edward's eye.

"Hell . . ." Edward stormed Nathaniel, uprooting him into a heap on the ground.

"Enough—enough, I'll leave ye be." Nathaniel held up a hand.

Holding his hand over his smarting eye, Edward sat down next to his cousin. "No . . . stay."

"Why? So you can take your ire out on my hide?"

"Sorry . . ." Edward helped Nathaniel up to a sitting position. "She nearly died before my eyes."

Nathaniel nodded. "And she's married to Ruppert . . . sad it is we didn't make it in time to stop the wedding."

"There must be something we can do." Edward took his hand from his eye, wincing.

"And, she's a Cavenaugh." Nathan slouched over, his arms gripping his stomach.

"And, she is the only true love in my life. I'm tired of fighting. I want to live, and to stop taking lives."

"King James wants an end to the feuds, too."

Edward nodded. "First, we must end the feud between our clan and hers. "Nathaniel, I have an idea . . ." He pulled a bottle of whiskey out of his tartan, popped the cork, and took a swig.

"Where'd ye get that?" Nathan chuckled.

"It nearly broke in the battle." Edward gave him a wink and a sly smile, as he handed him the bottle.

* * *

Every bone and muscle in her body protested. Rebecca tried not to show the pain, both from Edward's shunning and from her body. Sarah kept looking at her. She smiled back.

"Ye're such a liar, lass. That smile could freeze a loch in the summertime. We're does it hurt, child? Let Sarah help."

Rebecca let go of her facade; a lone tear rolled down her cheek.

"Here, I'll check your wounds and dress them."

Sarah went to get a bucket of water, leaving Rebecca alone. In the solitude she gave way to the tears that gathered behind her eyelids. Her heart ached too much for anger. After waiting all her life to experience the thrill of the fight, why did she feel so empty?

Sarah returned with water and rags. Rebecca relaxed, lying on her stomach as Sarah gently washed her wounds and smoothed on her salve.

"We'll have to get back home so I can make some more of my healing potions. That lad better be tending my herbs as I told him . . ."

Sarah talked on. The sound of her voice comforted Rebecca although she didn't hear all Sarah said. What could she do? I should go and kill Ruppert myself and be free of this awful marriage . . . or see the Church and have it annulled. Yes, after all she still remained a virgin, and how not with this chastity belt around her?

Her thoughts went to Edward as they always seemed to do of late. How dare he treat her that way? Why would he be so angry after succeeding?

Rebecca's thoughts got interrupted, and her privacy invaded, by a large brute of a man smelling of whiskey and sporting a black eye.

"Laird Edward, Lady Rebecca is not in full attire. Please, leave us be." Sarah spoke sternly.

"Sarah, leave us." Edward stumbled to sit beside Rebecca stroking her hair.

"Edward, leave *us*." Rebecca sat up forgetting her lack of clothes, and batted his hand away.

Sarah quickly covered her naked front. Edward's eyes glistened with a hungry light.

"Sarah, leave here or I shall have ye both." He grinned at her, laughing as she hastily left.

Rebecca's insides turned molten. Thank God for the chastity belt. Edward removed the cover from her breasts. Rebecca could feel the cold night air on them. She moved away, her face growing hot.

"You don't have to be shy with me, Rebecca." Edward's voice was low and thick with emotion.

Her body grew hot just from the sound of his voice. "Edward, you're senseless with drink. Leave this for another time."

"It seems, at times like these, a little whiskey gives me back my senses. No matter, I'll mind my manners." Edward pulled her onto his lap and lowered his mouth onto hers.

His mouth tasted intoxicating. She could not help but taste it. She savored his lips as her body sent signals she could not deny. He stroked her breasts. Rebecca's reason refused to stop him. She didn't feel the emptiness anymore, just a sweet richness inside her. She wanted it all.

Suddenly a sound like a bellowing bull crashed around her ears. Her head snapped up to see her father brandishing a sword and glowering at Edward. Nathan followed close behind. She quickly covered herself.

"This is not part of the deal, Edward. She is another man's wife. Unhand her."

Edward's eyes narrowed. Rebecca moved as Nathaniel and another man lifted Edward from under her. His language could have melted a heavy snowfall. The emptiness returned to her as she watched them drag him away.

"Are you all right, daughter?"

"Yes, Father." Rebecca bit back a bitter retort.

Her father's eyes narrowed as he sat down beside her.

"You're disappointed . . . Rebecca, look at me. Do you love Edward?"

Her father's eyes looked as if they would bulge out of his

head. He gripped her arm. "Put it out of your mind. It can never be." He released her arm roughly.

"And what will be, Father? Would you rather that Ruppert mistreat me for the rest of my life? If I have to go back to him he might as well kill me, for I vow I will not honor him. Ruppert will not help our clan. Perhaps amends can be made between the MacClearys and Cavenaughs."

"You have lofty dreams, my child."

Edward groaned. It had been a long time since he'd been so free with his drink. He cradled his head in his hands.

"So, Chieftain, where do we go from here?" Nathaniel spoke louder then necessary.

Edward looked up to see a self-satisfied expression on his face and gave him a look that only made him laugh. "You remain jovial even when your last breath is about to be drawn?" Edward grinned at his own humor. He picked up a stone and threw it at Nathan, who caught it.

They discussed the different courses of action they could take. Getting back to the MacCleary castle seemed to be the best choice. They would have the Cavenaugh hearing right away. Whatever Ruppert's clan did at least Rebecca would be safe within the castle. No more swordfights for her.

Edward felt lighthearted; Rebecca was safe and in his camp. "Nathan, you did set some guards up at the Cavenaugh fire. Didn't you?"

Nathan grinned at Edward. "Good God, I can't remember." This time he ducked as a rock flew past his head. He walked away laughing.

Edward braced himself for what he had to do next. He walked over to Rebecca's fire. The disapproving glares from the elder members didn't bother him as much as not receiving even a glance from the fair one. Donning his most contrite face he apologized to MacKey for his lack of finesse the night before. He could swear he saw Rebecca put her hand to her mouth to stifle a laugh.

"We'll head back to the MacCleary castle for the hearing. Please ready yourselves for the trip."

Rebecca still hadn't looked up. He paused there a little longer as MacKey nodded his approval, and walked away.

The camp became a hive of activity and finally everyone sat mounted and ready to move on.

Rebecca rode between Edward and her father. She kept glancing at Edward, wishing her father was somewhere else.

"What?" Edward spoke with impatience in his voice.

"Does your head pound today?" Rebecca smiled sweetly.

Edward grinned but did not take her bait. "No, actually I feel quite well. Which reminds me, I am wondering how you managed to keep your seat sitting backwards on a horse, yet lost it riding forward."

He wasn't going to let this rest. She heard her father laugh. Her smile lingered but became more difficult to maintain.

"I do believe that occasionally during a battle even the best men lose their horses. This being my first experience, through no fault of my own, I believe I handled myself quite well. Including keeping my seat riding backward and defending your back." Rebecca paused briefly to catch a breath. "Why Edward, I do believe I saved your life—more than once." Rebecca turned to smile at her father.

Edward guffawed. "In that case, I'm certainly glad I saved your silly arse."

Rebecca laughed in spite of herself.

"Seriously Rebecca, wouldn't you rather forgo the battle and stay home having babies?"

Rebecca aimed her reins at Edward, who moved out of her range.

"All right, all right, I'll stay home and raise the wee ones. I have no taste for war anymore." Edward urged his horse ahead of her.

Rebecca pondered his words. She couldn't stop looking at this incredible man riding ahead of her. Her flesh warmed at the memory of his soft lips on hers. A clan member rode up to Edward at a gallop. Stopping short, he shouted, "They left the dead to rot in the sun, dinna even toss stones on them to keep away the buzzards."

Edward let go an oath and wheeled his horse around. Rebecca saw his face light up as if he had an idea. He looked at her slyly. "Have Nathaniel lead the men on at a slower pace. I'll take some men and see to the bodies."

Rebecca could not believe her ears, he would bury the enemy? Yes, and so would she. It is the most honorable thing to do. She shivered at the thought of the dead bodies. Glancing up she saw Edward watching her thoughtfully.

"You'll come too."

"Aye, of course." Rebecca hid her surprise and followed the men to the field.

The sun beat down on the lifeless bodies. No one spoke as they dug ditches. Rebecca struggled awkwardly, determined to do her part.

As she finally finished one grave, she realized she would have to put the body into the shallow trench. Beads of sweat rolled down her back. Her stomach twisted with discomfort as she looked at the gaping wounds and the stench of death drifted to her nose.

"Was he one of yours?" Rebecca jumped at Edward's voice so close to her.

"Nay!" Rebecca reeled around to face him. *What a vile thought.* "I didn't kill anyone."

"Oh ho! What a warrior. She loses her horse and doesn't kill anyone? Surely you must have." Edward's eyes narrowed.

A buzzard, brave with hunger, swooped down and started to pick at one of the bodies. Rebecca let out a scream and ran toward the bird, waving her arms. It looked up and paid her no heed. She let out a yell and unsheathed her sword, swinging it at the bird. It flew up, dodging a fatal blow, and landed again on the body.

"Edward, make it stop!" Rebecca ran over to Edward. He held her in his arms. She looked up at him still staring at the dead man. His eyes shimmered with unshed tears.

"He was mine." A tear slid down his rugged face, and

splashed onto Rebecca's lips. Her tongue tasted the salty tear and her eyes filled with that same sorrow. "I'm sorry, Rebecca, I shouldn't have made you come. I only thought you should see all sides of this deadly war."

"You're right, and I shouldn't be resting here while the buzzards pick away at these bodies." She pushed away from him. She rolled the body into the grave and began to cover it quietly whispering a prayer, "Heavenly Father, take this soul into your eternal care." Edward paused next to her and then walked away.

Her muscles ached as she lifted the heavy dirt on her shield. She grew frustrated at her slow progress as the men finished most of the job, twice as fast. Rebecca mounted her horse. She looked at Edward and thought to knock him off his horse. Wouldn't he be surprised?

She watched as the other men moved on ahead of them. All reason left her. As Edward mounted she ripped her sword out of its sheath, so quickly he hardly had a chance to blink. She broadsided him before his feet where in the stirrups. He fell hard to the ground, landing on his backside.

Rebecca laughed so hard she could barely spur her horse to escape the fury she saw on Edward's face. Hugging the horse's neck, she charged away.

By the time Edward caught up to her she rode innocently next to his clan members, who had not witnessed the scene. Edward fell behind and whistled softly. Rebecca cursed her mount as it obeyed Edward's call.

"Not so easy to keep on your horse at all times, is it?" She gloated.

"Not with a cunning wench about, to catch you unawares." Edward's voice sounded low and rich reminding her senses how it felt to feel his hands and lips on her.

Rebecca shifted uneasily in her saddle as his dark eyes continued to glare at her.

"If you think you'll get away with that action you're greatly mistaken." Edward grinned mischievously at her.

She wondered at the feelings that his words aroused. He rode up to his men, and they galloped out of sight ahead of them.

Rebecca's heart started to pound in her breast. Her eyes filled with tears, an effective defense. As he returned to her his face held no expression.

"Save it, Rebecca, your tears lack truth. Which could disappoint me into giving you a good thrashing instead of a swim in yonder spring." He pointed toward a rocky area and raised his eyebrows.

Rebecca's eyes dried quickly. He led her to a stony bank and dismounted. Walking over to her horse he offered his hand to help her down.

Edward appeared sincere. She would have to be firm if he tried to seduce her, her bleeding had still not stopped. Was she glad about that? Of course she was. Rebecca looked up at Edward with a frown and opened her mouth to speak.

He quickly placed his forefinger over her lips, stopping her words. "I will leave you to wash in private." Turning away, he held his arm toward her. "Give me your clothes as you undress."

"Edward, don't you trust me?"

"Nay."

Undressing, Rebecca laid each piece of clothing on his arm forcefully. This caused him to laugh merrily. Her irritation grew. As she laid the last piece of clothing on his arm she aimed her foot at his butt and shoved as hard as she could. Edward stumbled forward and she lost her footing, falling backward into the brisk water. She shrieked from the cold.

Edward sat on the bank and laughed until tears streamed down his face, then swiftly removed his clothing.

She swam as fast and as far away as she could. He ran after her on the bank and made a clean dive slicing the water neatly. Rebecca stopped to watch in awe as his splendid body entered the water.Then, remembering her danger, she started to swim away. Too late. Edward popped out of the water next to her. Grabbing her waist he dragged her to shallow water.

He lifted her bottom out of the water and the palm of his hand slapped her sensitive skin. "This is for not staying in the castle." Again. "This is for knocking me from my horse." Edward pushed her back into the water and moved away to see to his own washing.

"Beast!" Rebecca turned away as she rubbed her stinging bottom and finished washing herself. Why did she always set Edward's anger ablaze? Couldn't he take a little jesting? She winked a tear out of her eye.

The water moved behind her. Her body stiffened as she quickly wiped the tears from her cheek.

He embraced her from behind and kissed her neck. "Why do you rile me so?" He rubbed her arms and slowly turned her to face him. Kissing the tears from her eyes, he found her mouth with his own and tenderly kissed her.

Rebecca leaned her head back, stopping the kiss. "How can one man be such a brute one moment, and then so gentle the next?"

He held her and kissed her breasts. She wrapped her legs around his body. "Rebecca, you are everything dear to me." He lowered her and showered her face with kisses.

She could feel his desire against her thigh and felt her skin heat. Once she dreaded the joining of man and woman, now she craved it. Her hand caressed Edward. She watched his face dissolve into pleasure. He lifted her onto the bank. As they kissed, Rebecca's hand surrounded his shaft and she brought him the relief he needed.

Rebecca lay in Edward's arms and let the sun dry and warm her body. She had finally brought pleasure instead of pain to him and it pleased her. Her heart ached with the joy of being in his arms. *Oh, God, this is love.* Rebecca sat up abruptly.

"Oh, this is terrible." At Edward's questioning eyes she answered, "I love you."

"Oh, yes, just terrible. Let me show you how terrible." Edward grabbed her on top of his prone body and kissed her boldly separating her lips with his tongue and tasting her fully. His hands caressed her breasts and then her bottom. Edward's desire grew again. "Damn chastity belt." He sat up keeping her on his lap.

Edward pushed her gently to her feet. She started to dress,

suddenly feeling embarrassed by their nakedness. He chuckled and started dressing himself.

"You do well by a man, considering your virginal state."

Edward's expression questioned her. Rebecca shrugged her shoulders, refusing an answer.

She could not believe her discovery. But hadn't she known it all along? She always loved his company, the games they played. That first kiss.

On her wedding day she had dreamed that Edward would rescue her. She would see that this dream came true, both for Edward and for herself.

As they rode to catch up with the men, Edward wondered what they would do with this love. Ill-fated at best, it was worth all the trouble in the land to see it blossom. To taste each other every day. To live together at MacCleary castle. Would the world let this be? He would see that it did.

They discovered a ruckus as they rode up to the clansmen. He heard MacKey telling the others to let the man speak. Edward grabbed up his clarion and blew it loudly. The scene before them ceased as if frozen in ice.

"Release the man." Edward dismounted and approached his men. They stepped back regarding his ire. "Speak."

"The Cavenaugh castle has been attacked. The lady taken."

Rebecca gasped and flung herself from her horse. "My mother?"

"Aye, Lady Rebecca."

SIX

Edward sat watching MacKey pace before him. Finally, he stood. "And what of Rebecca's safety? Will you deliver her up to that swine, to see your ends met?"

"Don't be an idiot. If once I err, I am not likely to repeat that error."

"And what will ye do when that headstrong daughter of yours slips through your fingers and delivers herself up, to rescue her mother?"

"She wouldn't . . ."

"Aye, and she would. I had to convince her to be rescued when she thought your life in peril. She blames herself for all of this." Edward found his patience growing thin.

"She's not to blame, I am."

"Hah! And have ye tried to tell her that? Has she ever minded you in her life?" Edward could see that he hit a nerve.

"She has!"

"Be that as it may—I'm ready to put aside our differences—my clan is not. The few you see with us are wise, true friends to the Cavenaugh Clan. The others are most likely seizing my castle and title as we speak. I have a need to be swiftly home. What would you do in my position?"

"Go and see your clan safe, Rebecca can come with me. Don't you think I can protect my own daughter? Or that she can protect herself?"

"Of course you can protect her. I would rather keep Rebecca

off your hands and far from Ruppert. You can go. Rebecca stays." Edward nodded to finalize his decision and sat down.

"Aye, and you'll enjoy keeping her off my hands."

Edward feigned innocence.

MacKey sneered. "All right. I thank you for my release. You have my word, I'll deliver myself for trial when my affairs are settled."

Edward felt uneasy as MacKey walked away. He wrestled with the feeling that he should be going along to help and his duty to his clan. He'd been raised always to show loyalty to the Clan Cavenaugh. They had been an extension of his family. How could he ever accuse MacKey of his father's death? MacKey had never been less than honorable to them. Even now, when facing Ruppert's men, he joined to help save the lives of the MacCleary's.

"Have I so erred in your upbringing that you do not remember a woman's station in life, and are incapable of obeying orders?"

MacKey spoke sternly to his daughter as he packed provisions for his journey.

His words rankled at her nearly as much as Edward's decision. "A woman's station, is it?" She moved in front of her father to be sure that he listened to her words. "Father, you raised me as an equal. I have always treasured that."

Her father embraced her. "Dear Rebecca, you are equal and better than most men. But there are still ways that we must all accept. Although you are a chieftain's daughter, you're not a chieftain. Your lot, right now, is one of a prisoner. You need to value the gentleness with which Edward treats you." MacKey spoke into her hair.

"Not so gentle . . ." Rebecca pulled away from his embrace.

"I don't see ropes around your wrists, although there should be." He turned away to finish getting ready for his journey.

"Father, I don't want to argue with you. The fact is, I have to go with you, and I will wreak havoc until I succeed in this."

"Wreak havoc, will you?"

Rebecca turned around at the sound of Edward's voice.

He advanced on her. "As it turns out, you have already wreaked enough havoc to have divided my clan one against the other—so please—wreak a little more." He swept his hands in an effective gesture.

Rebecca's took a step back in surprise. MacKey came between the two.

"Edward? This is so?" MacKey followed Edward as he sat down.

He didn't look angry, just sad. Rebecca followed the men, and sat down between them.

"I've let my judgment destroy my clan, and have placed my sister's life in danger." Edward hung his head. "Even now I counsel with the enemy. The loyal few have joined us here, fleeing from the face of Duncan."

Rebecca finally found her voice. "And these are the men of honor, Edward. They remain loyal to your father's values as well as your own."

"My daughter speaks the truth. You're a man of great integrity and insight. So are the men who join you. I would speak to them."

Rebecca's mind reeled as the men gathered to hear her father speak. Madeleine's life was in danger . . . and her mother's. My God, what could they do? Edward's clan destroyed because he would rescue her? She looked from man to man, panic gripping her heart.

Part of her raced to rescue Madeleine, another other raced to her mother's side, and still another part fought beside Edward to gain back his clan. And Edward would have her do nothing? She could feel her ire as she looked to see Edward watching her. Her heart raced at the tenderness she could see in his expression. He walked over to her and put his hand on her back.

"Don't take this all on your own shoulders, Rebecca. A plan will be devised and we'll make it right."

Rebecca looked into his eyes and saw such an honest passion. She believed his words. He walked away to address the clan.

"People of the Clan MacCleary. I thank you for your loyalty to my cause. I find it impossible to continue the feud with the Cavenaughs. Lord MacKey has defended our clan in the past, and recently. He would speak to you now."

"I have always honored your clan as my own. That your late chieftain should be killed while in my domain has plagued me these many years. I would swear to you, on my honor, I had nothing to do with his death. My mistake was never relating this to you, no matter what your reaction.

"My grief at losing a friend, nay, a brother, on my own soil, clouded my reason. Pride stood in my way—I was sorely insulted that you would even think me capable of this act." This last statement was directed to Edward.

Rebecca watched as Edward's face showed an instant understanding. Rising, he joined MacKey in his reasoning.

"This entire affair reeks of Ruppert Kirkguard. Who's to say that his clan isn't responsible for our chieftain's death? In order to split up our alliance."

"Makes perfect sense to me." Nathaniel spoke his mind from the crowd. The men all seemed to agree with him.

The arrival of the families of the loyal MacCleary men interrupted their meeting. Rebecca helped to gather the wagons in a circle.

At evening everyone settled down to rest and eat. Rebecca's heart ached for her mother's safety. She sat at the fire eating, wishing she could take a few good men to rescue her, but the odds of entering and leaving Ruppert's domain a third time were very unlikely.

"Don't even think about it." Edward loomed over her.

"Insightful? And a mind reader?" Rebecca's light laughter floated up to Edward.

His teasing expression turned serious. "Rebecca, join me in this. Don't try to do it on your own."

"You won't tie me up to a family wagon, refusing me the opportunity to be useful?"

"Nay . . . although if it's useful ye want, I can think of some use for you this night."

Rebecca's face heated as he sat down beside her. Sarah sent him a blistering look. Rebecca took a quick look at her father. He didn't seem to hear.

"Pardon me, Sarah, but 'tis my right. I saved her life, didn't I?" Edward grinned at her, teasing.

"Watch out, Edward," Rebecca warned, "Sarah's ire is only second to your own."

He chuckled and moved to give Sarah a big hug. Rebecca watched her eyes turn merry as she hugged him back. He moved away.

"Rebecca's right, Edward, you *are* a big oaf." She smiled sweetly at him.

"Ah, Sarah I love your old-time brogue." He rolled his R's as loftily as Sarah did.

Edward grabbed Rebecca's hand and turned to Sarah and MacKey. "I shall return her shortly, unscathed. Excuse us please."

They nodded, and exchanged looks. Rebecca didn't have to wonder what they would discuss as they left them.

He tugged her into the woods. "Edward . . . what?"

"This . . ." He lowered his mouth onto hers.

A warm pleasant bolt shot from her lips to her very core. He pressed the length of his body close to hers with one hand on her back and the other on her buttocks. Rebecca returned his kiss ardently, drowning in sweet, sweet bliss.

Suddenly, Edward released her, firmly setting her from him. Looking into her eyes he seemed to reach a conclusion.

Rebecca's fists pounded on Edward's powerful chest. "I will forever hate you, if you don't let me help in all of this. Danger be damned. I will not sit back like some blithering sap of a woman and do nothing."

He held her wrists still, in one hand, and his eyes filled with mirthful light.

"Don't ye dare treat me like a child." Rebecca tried to pull herself free of Edward's grip.

"I'll not treat you like a child as long as you don't act like one . . . I would much rather treat you as a woman."

Rebecca's struggles continued, but she could not break free of his hold.

Edward pushed her shirtsleeve up to her shoulder. He offered his arm, releasing hers. "Roll up my sleeve—do it!"

Rebecca pushed up Edward's sleeve as he had hers. He put his arm next to hers. Even in the dim light, the contrast was obvious. Edward's arm bulged with taut muscles. Hers, although well shaped, looked like a thin spindle in comparison.

"What I lack in strength I have in wit."

"You need more than wit and strength. In battle, you need experience. Do you think young men of my clan, who join in a first or second battle, are found in the front lines with the chief? They must work their way up to the front, if they live that long."

"I can do that."

"No, ye can't. I don't trust even these honorable men with your life."

"At least if I fight, I won't have time to suffer the uncertainty of your life or death while I wait." Rebecca rolled down her sleeve, and turned to walk away.

"Don't walk away from me. We're not finished yet." Edward caught her arm and pulled her up against him, holding her tight. "It seems I will have to find faith in my prayers, or suffer the scorn of the woman I love."

Rebecca looked in Edward's eyes, only to find sincerity and admiration shining there.

"Before you started to pound on me, I was about to tell you that I want you by my side. We'll fight this battle. But I vow, I'll not have much more of this fighting." Edward smoothed her hair with his large hand.

"I beg your pardon, I misjudged your intent." Rebecca stretched her arms around his neck and devoured his lips with her own.

Edward growled playfully, landing Rebecca on her back in the soft pine needles. His body across the length of hers, she wrestled under him. Her lips never left his.

Suddenly his body was heaved off her. He landed on his side, as he drew his sword. Seeing MacKey's furious expression Rebecca rose quickly.

"Father, I have on a chastity belt. It is but harmless fun."

"Fun! You can have fun, when your mother lies in a dungeon?" MacKey looked over at Edward. "And your clan revolts against you."

"Forgive us, Lord MacKey. We can not always control the effect we have on each other." Edward's eyes lowered.

Rebecca watched her father's mouth, as always it forecast his inner feelings.

"You're right, of course, Father. Perhaps we should gather and plan our next move."

"I should say." MacKey huffed away.

Rebecca and Edward followed behind him. She hit his arm, as if to say, look at the trouble you got me into. Edward shrugged his shoulders, raising both his hands.

The men argued back and forth about what their next move should be. Rebecca stood up occasionally and yelled her opinions. Most of the men ill regarded her. But Edward listened to her ideas and most of the time they were agreed on.

The outcome being that the men, who had been on the trail a fortnight, would accompany the families to the Cavenaugh castle. The exceptions being Edward, Nathaniel, and herself. They would make a quiet rescue of Madeleine.

The clansmen who had just joined their cause would head to a meeting place, near the Kirkguard Castle, to await an army of men from the MacCleary clan, and watch for the enemy's weaknesses.

Rebecca finally left the assembly, making her way to the small campfire where Sarah already slept. She startled when she found Edward following her.

"Edward, you frightened me. What do you want?

"That should be quite obvious . . ." Edward began to undo his belts and lay down his plaids.

"What are you doing? Shouldn't you . . ."

"I'll not sleep alone." Edward stretched out, propping his head up.

"What if I should want to sleep alone?" Rebecca asked, crossing her arms.

"I would quickly change your mind . . . may I stay?"

"Aye. Where is the key to this belt?" Rebecca removed her tartan and lay down beside him, draping the plaids over them.

"In a safe place." Edward smiled as he wrapped his arms around her.

Edward watched the clouds drift across the summer moon.

Sleep would not come to him. Thinking about Duncan Mac-Cleary made him furious. He never got along with Duncan, even as a lad. Duncan acted cruelly to those around him. Edward constantly tried to keep him in hand. He was the only clan member who could control Duncan. The rivalry had never ended, never ended, never ended . . .

Edward woke with a start. The sun looked to be bouncing off the earth to rise again. Birds timidly piped their songs. A cool breeze rippling through the trees brought a fresh green scent to his nose. Rebecca's soft body cradled against him creating a sweet ache within him. The only unpleasant feeling lay in the task ahead of them and this gnawed away at his stomach.

Rebecca stirred. Her breath gently caressed his arm. She was not like most women, and thankfully so. He treasured her fire and prayed that her zeal would not be the end of her. Her eyes opened and a smile appeared on her lips. Edward moved her so she lay on top of him, hugging her close. Her hair tickled his neck and stuck in his whiskers.

He heard someone move beside them, and glanced over to see MacKey slumbering. "Get up before your guard dogs awaken." Edward playfully slapped Rebecca's rump.

She giggled and the twinkle in her eye promised retribution. He watched her gather a water jug and small sack, appreciating the way her bottom fit into her breeches. She went into the woods for privacy.

Edward rose and attended to his own needs. When Rebecca emerged from the trees, with her hair neatly braided and a fresh look on her face, the sounds of a camp awakening fell on his ears, the bird's songs no longer heard. There was much to do.

After a quick breakfast, everyone flew into action. MacKey motioned Edward aside. "Edward, a word, please."

"Yes?" Edward followed.

"I feel uneasy that you should approach Duncan without men to back you up."

"If we bring a large force we'll be seen. I know my own outposts. It will be child's play to reach Madeleine without notice."

"I hope your assumptions are correct. Just remember, Duncan won't keep the same posts."

"Aye, and I know his tactics well."

"Aye, well, God speed to you. We meet in eight days." MacKey looked at his daughter fondly. "Rebecca, take care, child. God speed." MacKey hugged her, his face betraying the love he felt.

"God speed, Father."

MacKey released Rebecca and walked to his horse. He mounted and waved, galloping to join the waiting men. Edward glanced at Rebecca and could see the slightest glimmer of tears in her eyes. Walking over, he offered a sympathetic shoulder.

Daring a glance at Edward, Rebecca noticed that his sensual mouth was in an annoyed straight line.

"Am I to know of the plans," she asked, "or remain ignorant as most women are forced to be?"

"Either you change your tone, or you will find yourself tied to a family wagon headed to the Cavenaugh castle." Edward stood close, looking down at her, but didn't touch her. "Holding your emotions in will not make you invincible. It will make you a distracted warrior, ready to fall. I suggest you let out your concerns so that you'll be alert and able when we reach the MacCleary castle."

"Don't lecture me, and remove this damned belt at once." Rebecca held her ground.

"It seems I have yet to teach you manners. I'm not at all sure removing the belt would be wise."Edward's fists clenched at his side.

"I'll not have any more of it. My skills will protect me from unwanted advances." Rebecca stood her ground, even as she watched the storm that approached. "Give me the key—now!" She tried to rip off the leather pouch that hung on Edward's belt.

Edward laughed, pushing her away. "You forget you're no match for me. Who will protect you from *my* advances? And what happened to your gratitude for having the blessed belt?"

"That gratitude vanished with the last pinch and blister I've suffered." Quick as a flash Rebecca's sword was drawn, and rested close to Edward's neck. The thing would come off or . . .

"Put that away."

"Nay. Give me the key."

"Put it away!" Edward moved toward her.

She backed up, reluctant to cut him. She noticed a vein pulsing on the side of his neck. She could remember only one other time, seeing Edward in such a state. Still she persisted, with a little more reason.

"Edward, I don't wish to anger you further. But I really must have the key." She put the sword in its sheath.

Edward looked at her and seemed to be thinking about it. Slowly he reached into his pouch and brought out the key, dangling it in front of her. As she went to grab it, he pulled it out of her reach.

"Just be warned, I'm no longer responsible for what happens to your virtue." Edward plunked the key into her open hand and turned to walk away.

"Thank you."

"You're not welcome," Edward called behind him as he walked off.

Rebecca found a private area and took off the offensive belt, throwing it in a bush with the key still attached. She quickly replaced her clothes, but her hands shook and her victory dimmed in light of Edward's warnings.

Her next meeting with Edward found him in splendid spirits. A wild sense of triumph emanated from his being. Had she been pigeoned? Her misgivings grew stronger, and she quickly returned to where she had left the belt. It was gone.

When she returned, Edward and Nathan waited on their horses looking impatient, and mumbling something about the slowness of women. Rebecca mounted her horse. Snubbing the two, she took off in the lead. She expected to hear a whistle, but heard none and slowed her pace.

Edward rode up beside her, humming a happy tune. The tune brought a flood of memory back to her. As she thought back in time a warm flush crept across her cheeks.

On that summer day, long ago, she had gone on her morning ride when a low melodic voice, singing the same ditty, approached her from behind. Turning, she saw Edward riding his horse and bearing a large basket. Her stomach rumbled at the thought of what the basket held. She smiled and raced ahead to find a beautiful spot where they could eat.

As she expected, Edward followed and brought the basket to her. Removing his tartan, he spread it on the ground. Rebecca, unaccustomed to seeing a man in such sparse attire, stared at the tight breeches he wore.

Edward proceeded to unbutton the top buttons of his shirt and sat down, removing legs of chicken from the basket. "Come on, what are you waiting for? Sit."

Edward's fresh look of innocence further inflamed her passion. She quickly sat and tried to hide her discomfiture. Unsuccessfully. Edward looked at her, and she watched his expression as the dawning appeared with a brilliant smile.

"Aye, and to hell with the chicken. I see you have an appetite for something else entirely." Edward was beside her in an instant, kissing her ardently. It was the sweetest day of her young life. He never asked for more. He just kissed her and made her feel that nothing could be more beautiful.

Edward stopped humming and started to sing the very same ditty about love and beauty, in a lilting style. Rebecca could not help but smile. Did she dare look at him and see the recollection in his eyes? She was no coward. Looking over at Edward, she did indeed see the memory of that day gone by.

He finished the song grinning all the while.

"Ah, Rebecca, what has fate dealt us? To be denied your sweetness all these years has been my painful plight. So when, then, will I taste the fullness of our love?"

Rebecca's thoughts swam amid the flow of his words. Her back felt too warm under the plaids. Her eyes looked into his in wonder that this large rough highlander would have such a way with words. "If your words would make me lose my senses, how much more would your touch? You best keep a distance for the time being." Rebecca spoke as firmly as she could, considering the tumult of emotions she felt.

"Distance is not what I have in mind, fair mistress. You can depend on that."

"Then, sir, I'll have to put you in your place."

"Hah! And this I'd like to see." Edward laughed heartily. But the look on his face, spoke volumes.

Maybe he finally realized the extent of her powers. Rebecca smiled with satisfaction. After all, how could she prove that her marriage to Ruppert lacked consummation if this lusty rogue were to take her? Just the thought turned her lower regions into molten liquid. *Where was that chastity belt?*

Try as she might to extinguish it, the pleasant feeling gnawed away at her resolve. Then a glance at Edward's arrogant face poured cold water on her fires.

"How could you even think of such things when our families are depending on our proper conduct?" She frowned broadly at him.

"The thought of our dilemma would quench anyone's desires, except my own. Our families have kept us apart long enough." As Edward spoke, his frustration appeared evident in the deep and angry tone of his voice. He spurred his horse on, ahead of her and rode in brooding silence.

Rebecca suddenly felt lonely and hollow inside. Her ready temper rose as she quietly slipped from the path they took.

Reason left her to wonder aimlessly, foolishly. Even as she thought it, she cared little about what her action would cause.

Nathaniel followed her off the path. "Lady Rebecca, please join me on the path again. Edward is angered enough by the look of him. You surely know how foolish it is to anger him further."

His gentle manner seemed to calm her. She nodded and followed him back. The sun set toward the earth, creating a brilliance of color over the land. They traveled on to open mountainsides, ever wary of disloyal MacClearys. Rebecca's pounding heart seemed to beat faster as the shadows grew. She saw such determination on Edward's face as they rode along silently.

Nathan excused himself and rode up closer to Edward. Rebecca strained to hear their conversation, but could not. She watched as they argued. Her apprehension became sharper. Riding up closer, the men stopped their words. She watched them both smolder as she rode between the two.

Stopping to eat, each member of the party seemed in turmoil. They struggled with their own thoughts.

"My God, I'm sick of this excuse for food." Edward threw his meat into the fire, sending up sparks. Without a word to the others he readied his horse and rode off.

"He'll be headed for a hunt, and the better off we'll be." Nathan continued to chew the dried meat.

"How do you know?" She studied his knowing expression. "You've been like a brother to him, haven't you?"

"Oh, aye, we're closer than most brothers. He'll not be satisfied until he gets what he wants. But his honor forbids him to take anything you would not give him. The hunt will do him good. Rest while you can." Nathan nodded at her and moved away, to the opposite side of the fire.

"Shouldn't you go with him? What if something happens?"

"Nothing will happen to Edward. He's been hunting since he could walk. He'll be well."

In spite of Nathan's kind words, Rebecca suffered through a restless night and kept waking to see if Edward returned. Exhaustion finally won and in the end she slept deeply and awoke to a heavenly smell and a light kisses.

"Good morning, my love." Edward kissed her cheek and trailed kisses down her neck.

When he stopped, she opened her eyes and smiled at him. He gazed down at her, his cheeks fresh with the brisk morning air made a heart-stopping sight. Rebecca sighed deeply as he helped her to her feet.

"You've been busy this night long. What of your rest?" Rebecca looked at Edward's smiling eyes.

"I won't rest, until you give your favors. Until then, I will have to apply my energies elsewhere." Edward led her to the fire.

"Won't your energies run dry?" Rebecca teased.

"Never."

Edward's gaze cut through her heart.

They found Nathan at the fire, watching three plump pheasants roasting on sticks propped by the fire. They shared a more pleasant meal than the last.

Rebecca's strength returned after eating the delicious breakfast. Relief flooded through her. Edward had regained his senses and returned safely.

She joined the men and mounted her horse, riding behind them in silence, savoring her privacy she fell deeply into thought.

What if she went to King James's court, and was jailed for stabbing Ruppert? How could she have her marriage annulled then? Would he favor her plight, or scorn her treachery? Her stomach reeled and she nearly lost her good meal right there on the trail.

Her mind went to Edward. He deserved his own wife, and not another man's. But then, Madeleine said he had a wife. What had become of her? Did he love her? Her stomach tightened again.

"Are you feeling all right, Rebecca?" Edward looked at her with concern.

"It seems wherever my thoughts go, I'm damned." Rebecca welcomed Edward's company. "If you didn't bring me out of them, I'm afraid I would have been sick here on my horse."

Edward reached over and smoothed her hair. "There's a lot to solve."

SEVEN

The miles went swiftly under a misty rain. Edward hardly noticed. He thought only of his sister as he led them to a narrow path through the thick woods. It traveled up the side of a mountain to a small area of level land against a solid wall of rock.

He dismounted and cleared away heavy undergrowth that hid a cave opening. As Rebecca and Nathan dismounted, he guided his horse through.

"Wait there," Edward called over his shoulder. His horse whinnied with its concern. He added, "Strike up a peat torch, Nathan."

He emerged to find Nathan sitting just within the cave, leaning over a large stick wrapped in dried peat and striking a flint on his sword. A spark caught and the peat blazed. Edward took Rebecca's horse from her and brought it into the cave Nathan followed with his own.

"What are you about, Edward?" Rebecca called after them and followed.

"This cave is a secret of Nathan's and mine. Now it's your secret too." Edward looked back at Rebecca. The torchlight played in her eyes and revealed sparks of delight. She nodded.

"We explored here when we were supposed to be hunting." Nathan chuckled.

"Instead of skirting this mountain we found you can travel straight through it in half the time." Edward hefted the undergrowth over the cave. "It's a safe haven for the horses unless an animal has taken up residence." He drew his sword and took the lead through a dark tunnel.

"Ah, it's cooler and drier in here." Rebecca's voice sounded full of awe. "I've never been in a cave."

"It's quite pleasant. Just watch your step." Edward took supplies from the horses and divided them among the three. He tied the reins onto the saddles and stepped back to see the horses contentedly drinking from the cave's stream.

"Edward, I'll gather some grasses for the beasts." Nathan left the cave.

Edward looked at Rebecca as she stooped by the stream, drinking the cool water and rinsing her face. He walked over to her. As she stood he put his arms around her, leaned into her back, and kissed her neck lightly. She turned in his arms and met his lips with her own.

Then she pushed her hands against his chest." Perhaps we should help Nathaniel gather hay."

"I could think of a much nicer way to pass the time." He held her there.

"Edward." Rebecca's tone could only mean there would be trouble should he decide to disagree with her. They left the cave to gather hay.

His anger rose. Duncan would pay for his insolence. He prayed for the hundredth time that Madeleine was safe. His mind clicked over each of the men he had not seen among his supporters. Troublemakers all. Before he realized it he had hacked down enough grass for them all to carry. Rebecca stared at him.

"I was thinking of Duncan and the others who chose treason."

She nodded her understanding, looking sad.

"The horses will surely not starve, and Duncan's head will surely not remain on his shoulders." Nathaniel laughed at his own wit, as he helped to carry the grass.

The grasses weighed down Edward's arms. They had a heady aroma that reminded him of a highland brew. His mouth watered at the thought. *Ach, for the comforts of home.* Returning to the cave he checked the horses and picked up his supplies. They helped each other tie the supplies onto their backs and continued their journey.

Edward followed the familiar path. He tried to remember how long had it been since he'd traveled these caves. Not since Mary. He shook his head to get rid of the awful memory. This cave served as his refuge when he could not endure the outside world. He crawled into the depths of the earth to be alone and heal his wounds.

After traveling for a long time, Edward stopped them in a cavern. He lit another peat torch even as the other lingered on. Rebecca look around in awe at the large pointed objects that hung from the ceiling of the cave, a few pointed up from the floor.

The slightest rustle or step echoed loudly, along with the sound of dripping water. An occasional drop landed on her arms or head. The air had a strange smell. A stream flowed slowly past and continued down the dark passageway.

"This is so beautiful." Rebecca listened to her voice as it bounced off the walls.

"Aye, we spent many hours exploring. We would have gotten lost had it not been for the stream leading us on." Edward handed Nathan the torch and filled his water skin. "We're almost halfway through at this point. We'll rest for the night."

Thank God. Rebecca's legs ached from walking on the rough surface of the cave. Her stomach growled with hunger. She sat on Edward's tartan after he placed it on the floor.

He handed her a piece of dried meat. "Eat it all. You'll need your strength."

Biting off a piece, she savored its salty flavor. But soon her mouth turned dry and the meat tasteless. She reached for her water and drank.

Nathan sat across from them, placing the torch's handle between stones.

"And now there are more secrets I must divulge." Edward picked up a stick and started to draw in the dirt on the cave floor between them.

A map; Rebecca tried to make sense of it. She started to recognize the halls and rooms of MacCleary castle. He drew the passage she had discovered and a few that she guessed would be there.

"There is the passage from my chamber." Rebecca pointed to the map.

He nodded. "This next passage is known only by myself and Madeleine. You both must swear not to tell a soul." Edward looked at Nathan.

"I swear—I'm surprised you've kept it from me all these years."

"Nothing personal, Nathan. I was sworn to tell no one." He looked at Rebecca.

"You have my word."

"There are two. One from the high castle keep and one from the dungeons."

Rebecca flinched at the mention of the high castle keep and hoped Edward wouldn't ask how she had escaped it.

Suddenly he looked up at her, squinting his eyes. "Or had you found that one?"

Rebecca's shrug was indifferent, making Edward raise his eyebrows.

"They are very well hidden and have not been used in many years. The entrances will take a bit of prying." Edward drew in the two. "The passages empty out on the east side of the castle wall. I remember the boulder that hides the entrance. Finding the door on the inside will be a challenge. We must rest to regain our strength for the morrow."

Edward extinguished the new torch and left the soft glow of the old one.

Nathan moved further down the cave and wrapped himself in his tartan. Rebecca cuddled close to Edward as he covered them both with her tartan. She drifted off into a contented and safe sleep.

Rebecca awoke to a piercing scream, echoing through the chamber only to find it was she. Her skin felt wet with perspiration and her body shook.

"What!" Edward held her still as she struggled against him; Nathan was on his feet with his sword drawn. The old torch still burned, lending an eerie glow to the scene. Rebecca struggled to untangle herself from Edward and the tartans. Once free she didn't feel quite so panicked.

"Good God, was it a nightmare?" Nathan put his sword away mumbling, "At least one of us was able to draw a sword."

"What did you say?" Edward was on his feet and not in good humor. "You try drawing your sword when tangled up with a stricken female."

Nathan mumbled again and turned away.

Rebecca's heart pounded as she tried to get her bearings. Then she remembered the images of her dream. Madeleine screaming in pain—Duncan's evil laughter.

"We must hurry, Madeleine's in danger—I dreamt—it was terrible." Rebecca gathered her tartan and wrapped it around her.

They each did the same, tying on their supplies. Lighting another torch, Edward led them on. Rebecca found herself craving sunlight and fresh air. She coughed and fought the fear that tried to engulf her.

"The air is thin in this part of the cave. Breathe deeply. If you feel faint don't let it overcome you, keep going." Edward reached for her hand and held it, coaxing her on. The newly lit torch dimmed.

Rebecca gulped for breath but forced her body to continue on. Her mind played back her dream until she thought she would collapse with the effort of maintaining her calm. Time seemed to stand still.

Finally, the torch flared up as a gentle breeze met her face. She breathed in the air greedily.

"Stop and rest." Edward stopped and sat down.

She and Nathan did the same. But they didn't rest long, spurred on by Rebecca's fearful dream. In silence they followed the endless stream. When the light of day hit her eyes she shielded them with her hand.

Edward's senses grew more alert with each step toward the Maccleary lands. At the border of his land he called a halt and dismounted. He began to remove his tartan. "Take off your plaids." Walking to the stream he picked up a handful of mud and rubbed it onto his body.

Nathaniel did the same. Edward glanced over at Rebecca as she took off her tartan. He gave Nathan a look of warning.

"Oh, aye, as if I would fool with a lady of yours."

"See that your Scottish eyes don't linger too long."

Nathaniel waved his hand at him. "The thought never crossed my mind." Smiling slyly, his gaze left Edward's and both of them looked at her.

She smoothed on the mud. "Ye best turn both your Scottish heads unless you want a slop of mud in yer eyes." She winked at Edward.

Nathan laughed heartily as both men turned, giving her privacy to spread the mud over her shirt and protruding breasts.

"There's a good reason for a woman to keep to the hearth, instead of trampin' off to war." Edward spoke softly to Nathan.

"Aye, and feed the wee ones."

They both laughed.

The men turned to look at her and were met with fists full of mud pelting their faces.

"I heard that." Rebecca looked ready to flee.

"Edward, sure you're not goin' to let her get away with that action?" Nathan rubbed the mud from his eyes.

"Oh, aye. I am." He wiped at his face with his sleeve.

"Aye?"

"Aye." Edward motioned Nathan to walk back to the horses.

He turned to see Rebecca walking cautiously back to her horse. At the right moment he nodded to Nathan and they leaped at her. Heaving her from both sides, they landed her softly in a mess of mud.

"Pardon, my lady, ye missed a spot." Edward's struggled against his mirth.

"Oh, aye. I think we got it now."

He and Nathan turned to walk toward the horses. When Edward turned back he noticed Rebecca hadn't moved. Stopping, he saw the stubborn tilt of her head and her arms crossed tightly in front of her.

"I forget myself, Nathan. I best help the lady up." He walked back and helped her to stand. Grabbing her close, he smothered her with muddy grit-filled kisses. Stopping just long enough to speak into her ear, "Who, but the fairest could even be lovely under a coat of mud?" He didn't stop until he heard giggles from Rebecca and a grunt of disgust from Nathan.

"Daft as the day you are." Nathan rolled up the MacCleary tartans and tied them with ropes.

Each slung their own over their shoulder and continued on. Edward's thoughts went over all he knew of Duncan's habits and plots. He led them into a wall of trees that seemed to go straight up.

"We'll have to travel the woods instead of the road. Duncan will have it guarded well. Keep your eyes keen for disturbance in the trees. It's likely he'll guard the woods as well." Edward spoke in a whisper and motioned them on.

He watched Rebecca's progress over the mountainous land. She looked as graceful as a deer, her strong legs taking each step with ease. Her muddied shirt and revealing breeches left little to the imagination. Which is why Nathaniel led and Edward brought up the rear . . . and admired it.

Suddenly Nathaniel squatted down. Rebecca and Edward did the same and moved farther into the bushes. Some men walked by them, scanning the area. Edward narrowed his eyes. He knew the men. He clenched his teeth together. *Control yourself.* The words echoed in his head as he realized the betrayal of the kin he had once trusted. His mind swam with the effort.

He glanced at Rebecca in time to see her rage getting the best of her. She almost rose, her hand ready on her sword. Slowly Edward reached a strong hand to stop her. He quietly clapped a hand on her mouth just in case she intended to yell out. Then he steadied her so she wouldn't fall and give them away.

Fire snapped in the depths of her eyes as he continued to quell her. He tried to soothe her with a gentle shake of his head and when that didn't work a warning glance. She continued to struggle. Still he held her and with much effort not a leaf rustled. He turned his glance to a murderous glare and Rebecca finally subsided.

Letting go, he did not take his eyes from her. She sat still. Edward could imagine smoke rising from her ire. Smiling at the thought he nearly laughed. When the men where far away he did laugh. The startled Nathaniel boxed his ear quickly removing his glee.

It was Rebecca's turn to laugh. Her mirth was nearly silent and sent her rolling on the ground holding her sides. Her actions took Nathaniel's eyes off Edward who quickly boxed both of his cousin's ears.

"That one was for what you gave me and the other for the way you looked at my lady."

"It was worth it, my friend, well worth it." Nathaniel smiled.

They all shared a good laugh. Resting against a tree, Edward wiped dirt from his eyes.

Then he became serious. "In case I didn't make our intention clear, dear lady, we are not to let ourselves be known. Not at any time." When she would speak he placed his finger over her mouth. "I'm not here to kill my people, but to save my sister. Do you understand?" He took his finger from her mouth. It looked annoyed.

"How could you stand to look at them?"

"I was having a time of it myself. You do me honor by feeling the same." Edward stood and helped Rebecca to her feet. "We don't have an army and must go unnoticed at all costs. Do you understand?"

"Aye, I do. I'll practice more control in the future."

Traveling on like shadows, Edward didn't see any more men

until they were very close to the castle. He crouched and listened, keeping a wary eye on Rebecca.

"What would you do if Edward came out of the woods?"

"What d'ye mean, what would I do? What d'ye think I'd do?"

"Probably join his cause, you would.

"I might, and so? What would you do?"

"Ach, I don't know. But I don't trust Duncan."

" 'Tis a shame."

"Sure, and 'tis a shame.

Edward motioned for Nathan to make a wide arc around the men as they continued to talk. They stepped lightly and went unnoticed.

The sun sank below the mountains giving them enough cover to reach the boulder that leaned against the castle wall. Edward carried over a large tree branch, instructing Nathan to bring a stone. Nathan placed the stone near the boulder. Edward wedged the branch under the boulder and on top of the stone. He told Rebecca to keep watch. The men had to heave the boulder many times before it broke loose and rolled from the tunnel opening.

They carefully stored the branch in' the opening of the cave. Inside the cave loomed dark and a musty smell rose from its depths.

Rebecca gazed at Edward. "I could stand watch."

"You're not going out of my sight." Edward looked at Nathan. "Nathan, keep watch."

"Aye, I'll watch from just inside. Then I won't be noticed so easily." He looked nervously at the top of the castle wall.

Edward lowered himself into the tunnel. He slipped landing on the bottom with a loud, "Oof!" Getting up he motioned for Rebecca to come down.

She tried to go unassisted and slid clumsily into Edward's arms. He held her there and kissed her ear, then he whispered, "Stubborn wench!"

Rebecca struggled to stand. Edward held her tighter and kissed her mouth gently. Her struggle stopped as she matched his lips with her own.

"Ah! A kiss will see us through this mess."

"Ach! A kiss is what landed us in this mess." Rebecca slid to her feet as Edward released her.

Nathan's voice sounded from above them. "Get on with it, I'm a little large to remain unnoticed for much longer.

Nathan slid into the passage. They were swallowed up by the darkness.

"Hum, does this bring back memories, Rebecca? Would you like to lead? As I remember yer quite good at governing the dark." Edward chuckled gleefully, remembering her adventure in the secret passage.

"Whisht! Get gaun!" Rebecca shoved Edward, sending him on his way, and then grabbed hold of the back of his shirt.

He wondered how he could be in such high spirits even as his castle and clan rejected him. "You're heady wine me leddy." Edward slurred his words to show her the effect. "Hold tight, We'll soon see where they hold Madeleine."

Dust invaded his nose. Finally, Edward came upon the first door. He took his sword and tapped a rhythm on the stone, and then set his ear against it. No answer came. He tapped again.

"Should you be making that noise? We'll be discovered." Rebecca held Edward's arm before he could repeat the rhythm. Then he heard it, ever so lightly. But he heard it. "Shhh." He put his ear to the wall.

"She's a few doors down. She's heard us and answered in code." He led on.

Rebecca clutched his shirt and followed.

"It should be about here." His hands felt along the rough stone wall. There was total absence of light. *No, it's not here, have I passed it?* He felt further down. "Ah, here it is."

Rebecca let go of Edward's shirt and felt the wall along side him.

"Do you feel that crevice? I'll move away, take your sword and start to scrape into it. Take care not to cut yourself . . . or me." Edward heard the steel of her sword as it came clear of its scabbard. He moved aside carefully.

They both worked on the opening. The sound of sword on stone sent unpleasant chills through his senses.

"What an awful clamor. Won't we be heard by a guard?" Rebecca stopped.

Edward stopped and listened. They both heard a rhythm. "That means all is well. Continue. Guards don't stand in the dungeons, only at its entrance. There is not supposed to be any way out."

"I've finished this side, shall I do the bottom?"

"Yes, I'll work on the top. Watch! That was my foot."

"Oh! Are you hurt?"

"No. The door opens into the cave. We can wedge it open. Rebecca, come over on this side. Now wedge your sword right here." He tapped another rhythm on the door and was quickly answered, putting his sword into the door. "Now."

The door wouldn't move. "Stubborn as a woman, it is." Edward grunted with the effort.

A loud grunt from Rebecca and the door squeaked open a very little bit. "Mulish as a man." She commented with a humorous tone.

A loud thump announced the opening of the door. The dim light of the dungeon hit his eyes. Madeleine still leaned against the door, her face in agony. Rebecca sprang to her aid. Madeleine collapsed in her arms.

Edward stared at his sister's pitiful condition. She trembled and her clothes were shredded on her back, red with blood. A loud animal-like sound escaped his throat. Rebecca gently put Madeleine on the ground and clapped a hand on Edward's mouth. He pushed her away angrily.

"Shhh . . . Edward, calm yourself, my love. It will not do your sister any good to get us found out now. Shhh." Rebecca smoothed his brow. "Get a hold, my brave warrior."

When Edward could speak, his voice came out in a hoarse whisper. "I'll kill the one responsible for this." His muscles tensed. Rebecca held his arms tightly. He shrugged her off violently.

Rebecca went to Madeleine. "If you'll not help, I'll get her out of here myself." Her determination pulled Edward out of his rage.

He went over to Madeleine and lifted her. He watched Rebecca reach up and take the flaming torch hanging on the wall. He turned to lead the way.

"Her skin burns." Edward's eyes glistened with moisture in the soft light. "Madeleine, we're leaving this place."

She nodded slightly.

Placing her down, he and Rebecca closed the door firmly.

"Edward, wrap her in a tartan first."

He unrolled his tartan and wrapped Madeleine. Lifting her, he followed Rebecca. He felt a great lump in his throat and his respect for Rebecca grew.

"Can you help her?" Edward feared for his sister's life. He would never forgive himself if she died.

"Aye, Sarah taught me all she knows. I've seen the heat before. There is bark in the woods I can use."

Nathaniel's voice was a welcome noise as they came to the end. "I'm tired of this dreary underground."

The torch had nearly lasted the walk back. The darkness was a welcome blanket as Rebecca emerged from the cave. The castle, having lost its soft tapestry look, became a sinister presence. Edward came out and Nathan handed up Madeleine. He followed close behind.

Putting Madeleine down, Edward whispered, "Help me push the stone back." All three pushed the stone onto the opening. Wiping the dirt from his hands Edward picked Madeleine up once again.

"Let me carry her Edward, and give you a rest." Nathan tried to take Madeleine from his arms.

"No."

Nathan didn't press. Edward set a quick pace toward the woods. Rebecca could feel her strength coming to its limit. Every muscle in her body ached. She started to stumble. Still

Edward continued on. She could see him spending his pain through his action.

"Edward—stop—that stand of trees—let me gather some bark."

He nodded and finally stopped, sitting down with Madeleine cradled in his lap. He talked to her quietly as Rebecca left to gather herbs. Nathaniel helped her pick the various plants as she instructed and tied them together. The fullness of the summer moon helped their progress. She quickly rolled them into her tartan.

When they returned Edward's face expressed concern and fear. Rebecca felt Madeleine's skin. It nearly scalded her hands.

"Where's the stream? Edward, quickly, we must put her in cold water and bring down this heat."

Running, she followed Edward to a pond, the nearest body of water. Rebecca stepped into the water. Edward handed her down. They held her there until her skin cooled.

"We must get to the cave before we can make a fire for your remedies. Travel fast." Wrapping Madeleine once again with his tartan, he took off with great speed.

Rebecca found herself at a run and soon her wet chill turned to trickles of sweat traveled down her back and between her breasts. She gathered all the will she could to keep pace.

Finally they came to the cave entrance. Once inside, Edward tried to light a torch as Nathan put together more torches for the journey through the cave. Rebecca took a deep breath, feeling safe. She removed the tartan from Madeleine and helped her in the stream, bathing her body in the cool water and bringing down the heat once again.

"How much further must we go before we can make a fire?" Rebecca looked up at Edward as a spark hit the peat and finally caught, lighting the passage. For the first time Edward grinned his satisfaction.

"Not too far from here is a chamber with an opening in the ceiling. The smoke can't be seen from the castle." Edward looked at Nathan.

"Aye, and sometimes we did hunt, and only shared the catch

with each other. Speaking of which, I need a good hunt. I'll return with a fresh catch." Nathan watched for Edward's approval and walked away.

Giving the torch to Rebecca, Edward lifted Madeleine from the water and wrapped her again. He led them to a small opening along the passage. Rebecca took a tartan and laid it on a pile of peat in one corner of the chamber.

Edward put Madeleine down on it. Taking some kindling the wood that lay there, he made a fire to warm them. He reached for something on a stone ledge and produced a cook pot. "I'll fill this with water." He walked out of the chamber.

Rebecca turned Madeleine onto her stomach and cut her shirt from her to examine her wounds. A whip had wounded her deeply. The cuts oozed unpleasantly. She still had a small sack of the salve from Sarah and herbs to make more. Reaching into her pouch she smoothed the ointment onto Madeleine's wounds. *But that's not good enough.* She knew she must do something more.

Edward heated the water. She tried to think, her mind a mass of panicked thoughts. He walked over to her as she knelt by Madeleine. Kneeling behind her he gently massaged her shoulders.

"I'm proud of you, Rebecca," his voice, just a whisper.

Her name rolled off his tongue with a musical tone. She relaxed and her body awoke to his touch.

"That's it!" She sprang to her feet and ripped the sleeves off her shirt, throwing them into the water. "Have you got a bowl of some sort?"

Edward still knelt where she left him, a startled look on his face. Then he smiled and rose. Reaching the shelf again he produced a pile of wooden bowls, cups, a water skin, and spoons. She measured a stone to a bowl and threw it into the water.

"Boiled water is very cleansing. Her wounds need deep cleaning. I'll boil the cloth and place it on her wounds. That should help. The stone is to crush herbs. I hope Nathan lands a fatty animal, I'll need the lard for more ointment."

He planted a kiss on Rebecca's forehead and helped her finish the preparations.

EIGHT

By the time Rebecca finished cleaning Madeleine's wounds, Madeleine had opened her eyes just long enough to sip some of the cinquefoil brew. With a sigh she fell back to sleep.

Rebecca took some rags to the stream and soaked them in the cool water. The darkness enveloped her like a blanket. Squeezing the excess moisture from the rags she listened as the echoing cave seemed to speak to her; all will be well. She walked back to Madeleine's side and placed the cool rags on her forehead. Rising, she walked towards the cave's entrance.

Not knowing the time of day, she stepped out of the cave and was met with the radiant morning sun. They had worked through the night.

Edward approached with wood in his arms and a smile on his face. He wore only his breeches, his broad chest bare. "I hope Nathan gets back soon. They'll be noticing Madeleine's disappearance. We need to stay in the cave."

He gave her a look full of intent and brushed against her as he walked past. She followed, watching his body, his muscles bulging and his dark hair waving down his back.

Without turning around Edward spoke. "You better stop looking at me that way. That is, unless you want me to do something about it."

"What way? You flatter yourself." Looking down, she grinned.

She watched Edward take her tartan further down the tunnel.

A warm chill traveled up and down her spine. Pretending not to notice, she busied herself mixing herbs. Her face burned as she leaned over the bowl. Her hair curtained her face.

He came back, took a torch, and left again. Rebecca watched from behind her blond veil.

"All right, Rebecca. I've had enough of this game." Edward reached under her chin and tilted it up, causing her veil of hair to part and her eyes to look into his. She gazed first into his alluring eyes and then at his lips. They were set in a sensuous curve.

Her blood turned to molten liquid that coursed through her body. Inside her head a voice screamed, *Stop! Stop!*

He stepped away and looked at her, admiring her openly.

"Excuse me, I really must bathe." She realized her error too late.

Reaching for the fresh soapwort plant and a torch, she tried to see what Edward did from the corner of her eye. He leaned against the cave wall, arms crossed, looking like a cat watching a mouse.

She grinned and shrugged. "I was fortunate to find these leaves, they lather and clean."

"Do tell." He remained where he was and just stared.

Rebecca's legs wobbled as she walked by. She turned when he followed. Placing her hand on his chest, she gave a gentle shove.

"Mind your manners and stay put." Even to her own ears she didn't sound convincing. Walking toward the stream, she placed the torch upright in a crevice.

Edward took the leaves from her hand. She didn't resist. Turning her around, he lifted her into his arms. He placed her into the stream and knelt beside her, rubbing the leaves over her scantly clothed body.

Rebecca didn't fight the large hands that caressed and cleaned her body. Instead, she savored the feel of them and watched their progress. Her body turned a glowing shade of pink. The heat on the outside was felt in the inside—all reason vanished. She moaned as he slowly peeled the clothes from her. He rinsed them out and hung them on the rocks to dry.

Her heightened awareness commanded her actions. She took the leaves from him and rubbed every part of his body clean. And as he had done for her, peeled his clothes from him.

Pulling her up against his length, she became further inflamed by the slippery feel of their skin. He pulled her closer. His desire strained against her stomach. Gently pulling away she took his hand and led him further back into the cave where the stream made a pool before it babbled on.

She let go of him and plunged under the water. Even the cold water failed to cool the passion that coursed through her. Edward did the same and came up out of the water against her. Lifting her, he carried her out and walked into the alcove where the tartans lay over a soft bed of hay. The torch on the wall burned low casting shadows that seemed to lick the cave walls.

He placed her on the tartan and kissed her lips. His hands wandered along the curves of her body. Her hands smoothed over his broad shoulders and through his hair. He stopped kissing her and leaned back to watch her. Fondling her breasts, he moved his thumbs to caress her taut nipples.

She leaned her head back with the sensation, exposing her neck to him. He kissed it, trailing downward to her breasts. She gasped.

"I've wanted you for so long." His voice sounded throaty and deep.

"Edward, we shouldn't."

"Aye and I would much rather have wedding vows between us before . . . would you marry me?" He kissed her mouth before she could answer. Then he stepped away.

Almost shyly, she nodded her consent.

"I attest that your marriage to Ruppert is over, and indeed never was. And now before the eyes of God we are wed."

She liked the sound of his reasoning. "I do." Her heart suddenly filled with the most overwhelming joy. She thought it would burst out of her chest.

Hugging her, he kissed her fiercely. She returned his kiss

with the same intensity. They kissed for a long time, tasting and testing every new discovery. Rebecca savored the fires he set within her. She wondered if they would leave her a burnt cinder, in the end. Finally, he entered her slowly. She stopped the kiss, crying out from the sharp pain. He held still.

"Don't stop." Rebecca breathed the words as pleasure took over in place of the pain. Her body pulsed, shuddering with each wave of sensation.

Edward moved within her causing the feelings to become more intense. She met each of his plunges with a passionate force of her own. The pleasure grew within her and as she called out his name she could feel a wonderful liquid explosion inside her. She lost control of herself and drowned in the rhythm their bodies set within her. He let out a ragged sigh.

They lay together. Rebecca breathed in the masculine scent of Edward, memorizing forever the essence of him.

Edward kissed Rebecca's shoulder and tasted again her sweetness. The only thing he knew of his future was that he always wanted her by his side. Whatever else happened, he would see that she remained safe and that Ruppert no longer called her "wife." He drifted off to sleep and dreamed of her laughter in the sunshine on a grassy top of the highland mountains.

Opening his eyes, he found her laughing and tickling his nose with a piece of hay. He grabbed her hand and devoured it with kisses. She laughed again and licked the tip of his nose with her tongue.

"If I don't have something to eat soon, I shall eat you." She nibbled his nose.

He rolled on top of her, holding her arms over her head. "Should I show you where to start?" He licked her cheek.

"Ugh, you beast!" Hearing a sound from the other side of the cave, she struggled against him.

Nathaniel cleared his throat. He held bowls of steaming venison. Edward quickly covered Rebecca with his side of the tartan and went to get the food from Nathan.

"I have hunted, skinned, cleaned, cooked this meat, and attended to Madeleine. Now, I will sleep. Kindly remove yourselves so I will have quiet." Nathan spoke sternly but Edward saw the gleam of humor in his eyes.

Rebecca rose already wrapped in the tartan. "Thank you, Nathan, please rest."

Edward watched her face change from pink to red. She proceeded to stub her toe and nearly fell as he reached out to catch her. A string of oaths flew from her lips making both men cringe. Shocked, Edward wanted to shake her for saying such things. He carried her from the alcove and towards the chamber, juggling the bowls as well.

"Rebecca, a lady does not express herself quite that way. Please remember that in the future." He glared at her. "Should you forget, next time I will remind you a lot less gently." He placed her down next to Madeleine. "Now, please attend to my sister."

Rebecca looked at Edward mutinously as she sat down to rub her toe. She opened her mouth to speak.

"You better not speak. Nathan has just reminded me of my duties and I am not in very good spirits. I would much rather bed the day away—but duty calls. We must rescue your mother, and tend to Ruppert." He sat down and started to eat his meal. Her glare didn't change and she didn't move. "Get goin'."

Her teeth worried her bottom lip as if to stop her own words. She turned away abruptly and knelt by Madeleine. Feeling her forehead she sighed her relief.

"The heat is gone. Is that broth on the fire?" She looked up at Edward.

He craned his head to look, nodded, and continued to eat. Watching as she rolled Madeleine over to soothe her wounds again. She worked quickly.

"Bring me a bowl of broth." Rebecca called to him as she finished.

"Get it yourself." He watched her eyes widen as she stood. He ducked as she swung the water skin at him.

Moving in front of him, she put her face close to his. "Get up and feed your sister that broth. Just because we've bedded does not make me your servant." Rebecca stood and cuffed the back of his head.

Edward laughed. "Forgive me, my love. How could I forget my place so easily?" He stood and gave her a mock bow.

Getting a cup of broth he woke his sister and fed it to her, watching Rebecca as she sat down to eat her meal in angry silence.

"It was worth a try." He shrugged at her. She threw a small stone at him, missing. "Watch out, you'll get yourself in trouble again."

She shook her fore finger at him. "Don't you disappoint me, Edward MacCleary. I may love you, but I will not be told what to do and when to do it. I will not wait upon you when you're capable of doing it yourself. Do ye ken?"

"Aye, m'lady." Edward stood, walking over to her he kissed the top of her head. "There are times when I'll have to tell you what to do."

Rebecca nodded. "Now, you'll be tellin' me to take Madeleine to my family's castle while you go off to battle . . . am I right?"

Edward calmly sat down beside her, his thigh touching hers. He chewed his food, thinking. He could feel rather than see Rebecca looking at him. Turning, his gaze met hers.

"Actually, it would take the same amount of time to travel to the meeting place by way of the Cavenaugh castle. Then you wouldn't have to travel on your own, and we can share the burden of Madeleine."

"Oh, and it's a burden I am?" Madeleine opened her eyes and glared at Edward.

"Ach no, dear Sister. That's not what I meant." Edward walked over to her. Touching her brow, he said, "Welcome back."

"How do you feel?" Rebecca joined them and handed Madeleine some venison in a bowl.

"Hungry. Thank you." Madeleine sat up and ate her food slowly.

"I'm sorry, Madeleine. Did Duncan do this to you?" Edward could see the pain in her eyes.

"Aye. He means to kill you, Edward, please be very careful. He's always wanted your position as chief." Madeleine's face went pale.

"Don't worry, I have my very own she-devil to protect me." Edward grinned at Rebecca.

She narrowed her eyes at him.

"I wondered how you were handling each other. It amazes me you're both still standing." Madeleine grinned.

"We've *handled* each other very nicely." Edward winked at Rebecca.

Rebecca looked down blushing prettily.

"It's not a surprise to me." Madeleine laughed. "I've fancied you for my sister."

"Madeleine, Ruppert still lives." Rebecca quickly lost her blush and paled.

Madeleine gasped.

"Now . . . that will soon be remedied. He also holds Rebecca's mother. We'll bring you to Cavenaugh castle for safety. At least part of the MacCleary Clan has joined us. Madeleine, MacKey didn't kill Father. I'm sure of it."

"I never thought he did. Are the MacCleary families safe?" Madeleine's concern showed on her face.

"Aye, they've traveled to Cavenaugh. Now, we must be going. Are you strong enough to walk this cave?" Edward looked at Rebecca for her opinion as well. She looked less than certain.

"I'll give it my best try. After eating, I feel much stronger. They never fed me. I'd only stale water for days."

Edward could feel his anger rising, it gave him the spirit he needed to continue this quest. As Nathan and Madeleine rested, he packed the leftover food and supplies they would need. Rebecca stored the herbs in her bag.

"Don't forget those cleansing leaves." Edward smiled, enjoying the pink blush of her face.

Rebecca followed closely behind Madeleine, watching her. She knew Madeleine would not admit how tired she was. Rebecca's emotions warred—get to her mother quickly—or stop for Madeleine's sake. Edward traveled behind her while Nathan led the way.

Her mind was so busy struggling that she missed a big stone in her path and stubbed the same toe she had before. Sitting down she clamped one hand over her mouth so no one would hear the scalding words she yelled. Holding her toe with the other hand she rocked back and forth.

"That's a little better." Edward looked like he was going to laugh.

Madeleine rushed to her aid, glaring at Edward's mirth.

"Well . . . last time we all heard the words she screamed in pain, and it scalded our ears." Edward shrugged and bent over her toe. "These shoes are not very practical, where's the top? They're just a mass of leather straps."

"They're cool in the summer," Madeleine quipped.

"Bonny shoes." Nathan grinned.

Rebecca laughed and Edward pushed Nathan playfully.

"You're all daft. Now get on your feet, Rebecca. You want to be a warrior and you have a big fuss over a stubbed toe." Edward swiftly hefted her up.

"Mean old ogre," Rebecca teased.

"Ach, Edward." Madeleine clucked her tongue at his rough actions.

As always Rebecca faced him boldly, "I think you should carry—"

"Get on! I think I'll leave you at your castle. Askin' to be carried!"

"Let me finish! I think you should carry *Madeleine*. She won't admit it but I believe she's had enough. She probably doesn't want to be a burden as you so delicately put it."

"Oh." He pushed past Rebecca and told Madeleine to climb onto his back.

"No, Edward, I'll be all right." Madeleine turned away.

"Get up!" Edward sounded like a lion roaring.

Rebecca had to clap her hand onto her mouth again so she wouldn't laugh and attract Edward's attention. She knew Madeleine would comply. She never could stand up to her brother.

Nathaniel was having a merry time grinning ear to ear. When Edward scowled at him, he said quickly, "I'm goin' on, if ye want light you best follow."

"Sorry, Madeleine, but I really think you should rest." Rebecca let out a little titter of laughter.

"Hush yerself, Rebecca, I'll deal with you later."

"Oh, deal with me will you? Then you'll have your share o' dealin'." Rebecca started to sing the ditty that Edward always sang to her. Her sweet voice filled the cave with haunting music. It calmed all the savage feelings and seemed to soothe the moods.

Her song ended and the torch flickered low. They had reached the middle of the cave.

"Breathe deeply, it will pass." Edward instructed Madeleine. He turned to Rebecca. "Would you walk in front of me, please?"

"Aye, sir." Rebecca rewarded his manners with manners of her own. She watched Edward's brows rise, and smiled sweetly at him, hoping he had caught on.

"Really . . . Edward . . . you should put me down . . . it's hard enough . . ."

"No, I'm fine."

Rebecca was surprised that the lack of air didn't affect her as badly as it had before. Soon she could feel a slight breeze. She heard each person take a deep breath.

"What is this place?" Madeleine asked as Edward put her onto her feet. She promptly sat on a large stone.

"It's the secret place your brother and cousin slunk off to

when there was work to be done." Rebecca smiled at her own mischief, winking at Madeleine.

Edward shook his finger at Rebecca. She stuck her tongue out at him.

He looked at Madeleine and shrugged. "The lass never grew up."

"Nor have you by the look of it." Madeleine looked at Rebecca with conspiracy.

"Ach, and now you're joining sides with a Cavenaugh?" Edward grinned.

"Wouldn't it be dull if they had grown up?" Nathan sat beside Madeleine.

"Aye, that it would be." Madeleine laughed.

"We'll rest here for the night." Edward started to unload the various supplies tied around his belts.

Rebecca and the others did the same. Edward handed everyone a piece of the venison. After eating, Nathan chose a spot further down the cave to sleep. Madeleine rested her head on a bag, wrapping her plaid up and around her shoulders.

"Now, I'll deal with you." Edward dragged Rebecca further down the passageway, passing Nathan.

"Oh, please do." Rebecca suddenly became breathless.

"Ah, I intend to." Edward wrapped his arms around her and pretended to devour her neck.

Her heart quickened. He suddenly turned gentle, kissing her lightly wherever his lips could touch. She smoothed her hands through his hair. His kisses went lower. She caressed his back.

He wound her tartan off, ridding her of her shirt and breeches. Then he wrapped the tartan around her to ward off the cold. Rebecca sat hugging the plaid to her and watched as Edward removed his clothing and laid his tartan on the rough ground. She opened her arms and they nestled up closely together. The echoing cave surrounded them with a soft darkness and a symphony of drips and drops.

Edward's lips finally met hers and her body awakened with the desire to be filled. They kissed deeply until every fiber of her being woke to that desire. Then, the tartan forgotten, they entered the world that only true lovers can find.

Edward moved on top of her. She gasped in delight. Rebecca watched the torchlight in his eyes and saw heaven. His face mirrored her feelings. Her pleasure grew, causing her to close her eyes to feel it all.

When she thought she could never feel more, that she had reached her highest peak, it grew even more. Until they both collapsed with one final intense burst. The inner rhythm of fulfillment continued as he held her close, murmuring his love for her.

Morning brought far too much reality for Rebecca. A strange foreboding worried her as they reached the end of the cave. Edward's short temper didn't help. The horses remained content as they had left them. Leading them out of the cave, Rebecca could feel her anxiety grow.

"Edward, I think we're too late. I've a feeling all is not well."

"Then let's get you to the castle, and there you'll stay."

Rebecca looked at Edward as they descended the mountain, leading the horses slowly. Although the air cooled her the sunshine warmed her. "I know you don't want me to join this battle. But I must. My rash behavior has brought this all down on our heads. I will help to set it right."

"You take too much upon yourself. If you had not stabbed Ruppert, I still would have come into your room. Ruppert and I would have dueled and guess who would have won the lady?"

Rebecca stopped in her tracks. Why had she thought Edward had come to her wedding chamber? It had been a raid that was all.

"Lies don't become you, Edward." Could she be the reason the MacCleary clan raided the castle? She continued to walk.

"What lie? I'm only sorry I didn't make it in time to stop the marriage."

"You're saying your clan raided the castle to stop me from marrying Ruppert?"

"Aye." Edward looked at her over his horse.

"Why? Why would you put your clan into that position for me?"

"Because your two clans against us would be our undoing. Because I made a vow to protect you. And knowing you, as well as knowing Ruppert, I realized your spirit wouldn't survive past a week as his wife."

"To whom did you make that vow?"

"To myself."

Rebecca stared right into Edward's eyes daring to believe his words. She quickly turned from his gaze and looked at her feet. The thought, or wish, had entered her mind as she walked the long church aisle. She'd thought her hope of being rescued by Edward only a fanciful dream.

Suddenly, Edward let out a roar that made the small hairs on the back of her neck stand up.

Nathaniel lunged for Edward to prevent him from mounting his horse, catching him from behind. "Rebecca grab his reins. Don't let him go!"

Rebecca followed Nathan's orders. "Why? Edward! Stop!"

He acted like a man gone mad. Then she saw them. Edward's clan—led by Duncan—riding out. They flew the MacCleary and the Kirkguard colors. Duncan had joined the MacClearys with Ruppert's clan. It took all three of them to hold Edward back.

"Cousin, stop this madness or I'll knock ye senseless."

Edward's body relaxed. They all let go only to have Edward dash for his mount and rage down the mountain. Rebecca let out a piercing whistle, and Edward's horse headed back to them.

Madeleine and Nathaniel swung around to stare at Rebecca, their eyes wide. She quickly mounted her horse and met Edward before he reached the others.

"Edward, I'm sorry. I know how you must feel. The same as I did when my father gave me to Ruppert. I begged him not to allow the marriage. He betrayed me in the worst possible way."

Rebecca spoke softly, trying to soothe his raging emotions. She watched his somber face and knew his pain.

Silently they considered each other. A gust of wind sent his hair blowing and her own caressed her face. But that didn't break the spell holding them. His expression remained the same as Nathan and Madeleine caught up to them. Eyes staring blankly, he turned from Rebecca and led them down the mountain.

Edward's mind slowly shed its rage and became numb. *This is too much.* Duncan would always be a thorn in his side, but joining with the Kirkguard Clan against the Cavenaughs after just making amends, could only be pure treachery.

The Cavenaugh clan supported the MacCleary clan during hard times. They considered them a sister clan. When his mother's sister married MacKey's cousin they joined together in many battles. Even after his mother's death they continued to form ties and support each other's clan. Father and MacKey were tight from the start.

Anxious to reach Rebecca's castle, Edward wondered how large an army MacKey could form. He turned toward the others.

"We'll have to quicken our pace if we're to reach the castle before the army heads out. Nathan, are you all right with Madeleine on the horse?"

"We're fine. Set the pace. We're behind you."

"Rebecca?"

"I'm fine." She nodded and gave him a small smile.

Edward turned and spurred his horse to a gallop. His mind raced as fast as his horse ran. Did Rebecca's mother have any hope of survival? What could they do to save her? Leaning closer to his horse's neck, he led them on. He glanced back and could see the tense expression on each person's face.

Dear God. Let her mother live. Let the forces of life and good win.

* * *

The cold air whipped against Rebecca's face. She watched the brilliant colors of the landscape go by in a blur. Her eyes watered with the force of the wind.

She thought about her mother. Please, God let her be safe. She thought about the Kirkguard castle's layout. Her mother would probably be in the high castle keep. No passages led from it. Five guard stations stood along the way to the keep. But she knew where they would bring her should their attack be detected—to the top of the walls. Rebecca quickened her pace gripping her reins tighter.

NINE

Dark clouds rumbled across the sky as the tired travelers approached Cavenaugh castle. Rebecca rode with Edward on his horse, giving Madeleine and Nathan their own mounts. The warmth of their closeness vanished as Rebecca saw her clan members finish digging new graves.

She struggled to dismount, her heart nearly breaking with fearful thoughts. Edward caught her to him and pointed to the figure of her father waving from between the battlements. She waved back as Edward spurred the horse faster. They rode through the yawning castle gates and dismounted.

MacKey walked down the steep steps of the castle wall and hugged his daughter. Rebecca's aunt approached Madeleine and offered her assistance as she led her up to a room.

Walking toward the dining hall, she listened to her father tell Edward about Ruppert's latest attack. His archers shot some of their men from the castle wall before he delivered his message demanding them to deliver Rebecca and Edward to him, or Martha would die.

Her father looked older and very tired. Rebecca remembered the last time she had been home. Home? It seemed like a lifetime ago when she said goodbye to her friends and family, all with heavy hearts. She missed her mother's soothing presence.

As they entered the hall, family and friends greeted her and looked happy and proud to see her. Had her father told them of her perils? She could see no ill feelings.

128   *Christine Cameron*

The ladies of the clan served a meal. MacCleary families mingled together with the Cavenaughs, making the castle an active beehive. The children seemed to have multiplied and mischief abounded everywhere.

"Lady Rebecca, thank you for rescuing Auntie Madeleine." A little blond head peeped over the tabletop.

Rebecca's broad smile sent the wee lass running into her arms. She hugged the child.

"You're welcome, and what is your name?" Rebecca lifted her to her lap.

"Mary." The child's dirty face, endearing.

Another Mary came to her mind. She looked from Edward to the child. They did resemble one another. Looking at Edward again, she asked, "And how old are you, lassie?" Rebecca looked at the child.

"Four, m'lady." Mary held up four grubby fingers.

Just then a woman ran up. "Ach, there you are, Mary, didn't I tell you to stay in the kitchen . . . sorry, m'lady." The woman curtsied. "Come on and see Papa before he must go."

"That's quite all right, she thanked me." Rebecca smiled, relief flooded her at the mention of Papa.

The woman curtsied at Edward as she pulled the child away. Mary waved goodbye enthusiastically.

Rebecca stared at Edward.

"That's Nathaniel's wife and youngest. Is something troubling you?"

"Yes, perhaps something that should have troubled me before I gave in to lust." She felt her face heat up and her infamous anger welled in her breast. Rebecca watched the curious looks of the people around them, and tried to control her temper.

"By the look on your face I think we should pursue this conversation in private." Edward turned away from her.

Rebecca gripped the table, embarrassed by his dismissal. Not wanting to make a scene, she excused herself from the table and walked up to her chamber. The familiar halls helped her feel better. This castle would always be in her blood. She loved everything about it—the smooth wood floors, waxed and clean, and the beautiful family tapestries that were the only form of sewing she would ever take part in.

She stopped to admire her favorite, outside her chamber. Remembering the section she made and the feelings she experienced at the time she wove it. Life seemed so much more simple back then.

She entered her room and took another step back in time. In her mind she could see herself as a small child, playing on the rug. Tears came to her eyes. *Oh, Mother.* She fell onto her bed in exhaustion and drifted to sleep only giving a half-hearted thought to taking off her soiled clothing.

Rebecca didn't know how long she slept, but the next thing she heard was Sarah's beloved voice.

"Ach, lass, how could you lie on this glorious bed with mud-caked clothes?" Sarah gently removed her clothing. "Well look here . . . you've been practicing your herbs. Ach, and you did a fine job on the MacCleary woman."

Rebecca opened her eyes and savored the sight of Sarah. Taking over her own disrobing, she followed Sarah to a tub of steaming water. The sweet smell of roses drifted to her nose.

"Sarah, you really are a magical being." After giving her a quick hug, Rebecca stepped into the tub and sighed as her body savored the warm water.

"Tsk, tsk, there's somethin' different about ye Rebecca Cavenaugh." Sarah shook her head. "I don't have to use too much of my imagination to guess what."

At that moment a knock sounded at the door. Before Sarah could answer it, Edward breezed in.

Sarah shooed him out of the room, her skirts flying. Rebecca laughed at the look on Edward's face, forgetting her anger. Sarah pushed him out the door while she still had the advantage of surprise and pulled the door shut as they left the room.

She could hear them arguing outside the door. Sarah and Edward's voices melted down the hall, and the door slammed in the chamber next to hers.

When Sarah came back her face was red and she huffed

about. "I don't care if the man is a chieftain. I put him in his place. He won't be bothering you tonight."

Rebecca groaned inwardly. If she only had a few days to live she would spend them with Edward by her side, particularly at night. However, she knew a lady's companion would never stop the MacCleary when it came to his woman. Normally she would cringe at the thought of belonging to another person; instead it heated her blood.

"Your wounds are healing. Now get to bed, you need rest more than anything else." Sarah's eye's twinkled. "You send him away when he comes to you."

Rebecca laughed and bid her good night. She put her head on the pillow and drifted to sleep.

Edward stared at the retreating figure of Sarah, cursing her under his breath. He wished she were in his clan so he could take his ire out on her hide. She acted like a mother hen, and how dare she threaten him. Walking further into the chamber a tub of steaming water made his angry thoughts vanish. He quickly undressed and got into the tub.

The warm water smelled of mint leaves, and relaxed his tense body and mind. He began to devise a plan for the rescue of Rebecca's mother. Edward missed Martha's presence. She always soothed her wayward daughter, knowing just what to say to make her peaceful and happy. It amazed him.

Edward's quick mind worked hard and long as he soaked in the now cold water. Finally, he had it. Jumping out of the tub he dried himself and dressed quickly. Then he went to find MacKey. The plan would be risky, but he believed it would work. Asking curious faces where to find MacKey, he finally got an answer and was led to the study. When Edward entered the chamber he found the older man pacing back and forth.

"I've a plan, MacKey. Listen . . ." Edward's excitement dimmed as he smelled a strong brew and saw the drooping body of the Cavenaugh's Chieftain.

"She begged me not to marry Rebecca to that scoundrel. All

I could think of was my own politics. This is all my fault and I shall lose my wife." He drank from a stein.

Edward put his face in front of MacKey's and spoke harshly, "If you say such things, they will be. Is that what you want? There's a way. There always is a way. And we will find it. You'll have to get your senses back if we're to rescue Lady Martha."

"Aye, aye, you're right." MacKey rubbed his bearded chin and ran his fingers through his graying blonde hair.

They sat opposite each other as Edward explained his plan. Drawing maps, they went over every detail possible so the plan would not fail. Nathaniel joined them adding his ideas.

"Father?" Rebecca walked into the chamber, frowning.

Edward sensed that Rebecca's frown meant that she did not feel included. "Ah, Rebecca, I was just about to call you." He winked at MacKey. Rebecca looked doubtful as Edward herded her towards the men.

"I don't think Ruppert will harm Martha until he gets what he wants. We should spend a few days practicing and briefing our clansmen." Edward watched for MacKey's reaction.

"One day—that is all." MacKey's face looked full of pain.

They discussed the plan again, in great detail, and then retired to their chambers for much needed rest.

"Sarah said I should send you away." Rebecca walked in front of Edward and didn't turn as she spoke.

"Shall I tell you what I'd like to do with Sarah?" Edward grabbed her from behind causing her "No" to be a screech. And then putting his lips to her ear he said, "Shall I tell you what I'd like to do with you?"

"No. I will tell you. Hold me all the night long as we sleep peacefully."

Edward groaned and released her. When they entered the chamber he realized he would do as she asked. Her heady rose scent nearly undid his resolve. But her presence was enough to make him happy. As she sighed, he kissed her neck gently and drifted to sleep.

* * *

The next morning MacKey burst into Rebecca's chamber. "And how do you suppose your mother would feel if she knew of your sinful bed?"

"Mother would be happy for me. She would understand that we are indeed married in God's eyes. At least until we can be in the church's eyes." Rebecca willed Edward to remain calm.

Snatching his breeches from the bedpost, he pulled them on under the covers.

"Hah! What a notion!" MacKey glared at Edward.

Edward got out of the bed and lumbered toward him.

"Begging your pardon, Laird MacKey, perhaps we should have a discussion in yer study?" Edward lifted his shirt from where it draped over a chair and pulled it over his head.

"I don't have time for discussions. My wife is in danger even as we speak. If it's my blessing you want, you have it." MacKey slammed out of the room.

"Why, thank you, Laird MacKey." Edward gave a mock bow to the slammed door and turned to Rebecca.

"Get that look off your face, you rogue." She threw a pillow at his head.

He lunged for her and they wrestled, rolling on the bed and nearly falling off the edge.

"Edward, my father will not stand for a delay. We must join him right away." Rebecca always knew just how far to push her father. She hoped some day to learn just how far to push Edward as she stared into his stormy eyes.

"Would you have me with babe?" Rebecca watched the storm turn to hope. "Get out of this bed, Edward MacCleary, before I . . ." Words wouldn't come to her as she watched his handsome body move from hers.

"Before you what?" Edward's hands rested on his hips.

Rebecca shrugged. Her mind was suddenly on her mother and what lay ahead of them. One mistake and . . . no, she wouldn't think of it.

She didn't even realize Edward had walked over to her until he wrapped his arms around her from behind, his comfort surrounding her.

"This will work, Rebecca. I promise." Edward spoke softly into the still morning air.

"That is a steep promise to keep, my love." Rebecca moved to look at his eyes. "Particularly for a man of his word such as you."

Edward gazed down at her but didn't speak. His eyes told her all she needed to know. Then she realized that the plan would work, or they would die.

"Let's join your father before he sends 'the Sarah' to chide us." He gave her an enormously attractive smile as they separated.

She dressed quickly, feeling Edward's gaze following her every move. They walked out of the chamber and down to the eating hall to break their fast.

"Cavenaugh castle is every bit as stunning as MacCleary castle. And where will our babes grow up?"

"You're going to keep that promise, aren't you?" She smiled at the thought. "They'll know both our castles and all that lies between."

Edward nodded his agreement.

After a quick breakfast they joined the forces and told them the plan. Rebecca watched her father and Edward work together. Guards, who did not hear the plan, were set at every exit to the castle. No one would be allowed to leave or enter. All of the clan members were sworn to secrecy. They acted out the plan and repeated it until it remained in everyone's memory. They practiced possible problems that could arise, solving them all. They didn't stop until every movement became precise and fast.

Meals were eaten in between drills, rest taken periodically, and all of the members retired early. The plan would be set into action just before morning broke.

Sarah could not to be found as Rebecca and Edward retired to her chamber. Once in bed they held each other, flesh on flesh. Slowly as the cares of the day slipped from her shoulders, Rebecca could feel a fire kindling inside her.

* * *

Rebecca's skin grew warmer next to his. His own responded in kind. Edward gently kissed her shoulders, her neck, and finally her breasts. Her nipples grew taut and hard as he nibbled on each one. She breathed faster. Kissing the pulse on her neck, his hands explored her lower body.

He drew in a quick breath as she reached for his manhood. In Rebecca's true fashion, her touch was firm and demanding. But he would make her wait . . . just a bit longer. He moved lower, feathering kisses down her stomach and lower still. Rebecca let go of him and gasped.

"Edward!" She wiggled beneath him.

"Mmmm . . . Rebecca." He teased until he felt her hand grip his hair roughly. Laughing quietly he moved up to kiss her mouth deep and hard. He could feel her moan, as she pressed against him.

Slowly and with great deliberation he entered her. His heart seemed to stop as she surrounded him with her silky heat. Savoring the feeling he lay still inside her. Even as she moved he held her hips still.

"Shhh . . . easy. You are as sweet as the honey of the bees." Edward looked into her desire filled eyes and could see there a desperate need. He caressed her temples with his thumbs until the desperation in her eyes turned to trust. Then he slowly moved inside her, hearing her breath match his own and savoring the pleasant feel of her.

He buried his face in her hair and continued slowly until he thought he would lose his senses. Then suddenly Rebecca rolled him over. On top of him, she set a quicker pace. He grabbed her closer to him as they both evaporated into the throes of shear and utter, mindless pleasure. She lay on top of him until her breath became slow and shallow. But his body did not want to leave hers as he drifted off to sleep.

As the birds began to sing, Edward's body awoke. He found himself inside her still, growing harder. She slept peacefully as he began to move. Little sounds escaped her lips. Her eyes remained closed as he brought them both to their world of pleasure. Rebecca's eyes didn't open until he felt her gentle rhythm and heard her sigh.

"What a wondrous dream . . ." She smiled beautifully at him.

He thought he would die of pleasure as his own release came. As fate would have it, Sarah chose that moment to enter the room. Not looking at the couple she tidied and set out newly cleaned clothes.

"I've hanged out your plaids and beat the dust out of 'em. You best rise and face the day."

As quickly as she entered she left. Rebecca dissolved into gales of laughter.

"What's so funny?" Edward failed to see the humor.

"Your—your—your eyes looked like those of an owl . . . wide open." Rebecca demonstrated the width of them with her hands in front of her own eyes and tried to control her laughter.

"Ach, get off 'o me, woman." Edward playfully pushed her over, planted a kiss on her lips, and got up.

Rebecca's body glowed with pleasant feelings. Her determination grew. She went over her part in her mother's rescue and over it again. As they ate a hearty morning meal everyone stayed quiet and thoughtful. Mentally preparing themselves, Rebecca thought, for the two-day journey and what lay at the end of it.

Ruppert paced before the window. According to the messenger they would be arriving soon. The archers on the castle wall would rid the world of Edward MacCleary. If they brought a troop they would all die. The orders were given.

He would finally have the revenge his family had sought for over one hundred years. Both clans that laid ruin to his family in a bloody fight and took most of their lands would be destroyed. He would get the land back along with his bride. Even now his armies prepared for the attack.

Ah, the riders in the distance. How he would enjoy seeing the torment in her eyes. Ruppert grimaced as he ran his hand over his wound.

Quickly he walked the stairs to the top of the castle wall. Martha sat against the wall like a wet rag. Imagine not wanting his attentions. That hadn't mattered when he took her. He laughed out loud at the thought. Grabbing her up he made her stand. When she slumped down he put her tied hands over the battlement, and set her head on the lower section so they would see his prisoner.

A group of five riders approached the castle below Ruppert, four Cavenuaghs and one MacCleary.

"They've brought too many men. Get Lady Rebecca first and let her watch from here the demise of Edward and her father." Ruppert saw that two archers accompanied MacKey and hid behind the battlement that held Martha.

"Show your face Ruppert Kirkguard. I would have my wife—right now!" MacKey yelled up to Ruppert.

Ruppert stood clear of the battlement and observed that Rebecca and Edward were indeed on horseback, their hands tied behind their backs.

"You brought archers? Was it so hard to contain the Mac-Cleary?" Ruppert had to yell to be heard.

"Aye, and my daughter as well. I hope you'll spare her life and see what an asset she would be to your clan."

"Father, how could you betray me again?" Rebecca fought against her bindings.

"Send Rebecca to the castle door." Ruppert demanded.

"My wife first. Let her walk to me and I will send Rebecca's horse."

Ruppert agreed. He no longer needed Martha. He sent her down hoping she could walk on her own.

"As soon as Martha walks free and Rebecca rides toward the door, shoot the MacCleary," Ruppert instructed an archer. To the others he told them to hit the rest of the party, leaving Rebecca untouched.

Ruppert watched as the plan played out in front of him.

* * *

Rebecca heard a sickening wooden thud as an arrow hit Edward in the chest. As she turned he fell from his saddle.

"Edward!" Her scream echoed through the tension filled air. She shrugged off her loose bindings and rode low in the saddle to her mother. Three more thuds met her ears as the arrows hit her father and his archers.

The Cavenaugh archers stayed on their saddle and hit the surprised men on the castle wall. MacKey rode toward Rebecca as she lifted her mother onto the saddle with her. A whistle split the air. Edward mounted his horse and joined the retreating forces. Rebecca's horse responded, and all five rode off at a full gallop. The shields under their clothing had worked.

Edward let out a victorious whoop that Ruppert heard. Fury struck him with a force he could not deny. They'd made a fool of him—this time. When next they fought he would be the victor. He immediately set out with his full army in pursuit. His wound gave him great pain as he vowed swift vengeance.

Rebecca gasped at the sight of blood on Edward's shirt. He didn't seem to notice as he motioned her on. She held her mother, on the saddle. She couldn't hold on for herself.

"Mother, can't you hold on to the mane?"

"Rebecca, I'm sorry. My dear child, I'm sorry." She was sobbing and not in her right mind.

"Shhh. Mama, hold on." Rebecca's could feel a shiver run up her spine, as she understood her mother's ravings. She rode on as if chased by the devil himself.

"Damn him, Damn him to hell." Rebecca sobbed as she pressed on. Let this ride be over, Oh God, let it be over. Her muscles ached as she struggled to keep her mother and herself on the horse. *A true warrior keeps her horse . . . a true warrior keeps her horse . . . a true warrior keeps her horse . . .*

Not aware of how many times she thought the words, she continued to think them. They helped her to concentrate on her task. Her back muscles ached and jumped. Finally she saw Edward's pace slow, and they came to a walk, entering a cool forest. The trees gave her the safety she was seeking. The men led on.

"Stop! You clods! Does anyone think that I am about to drop this precious baggage out of shear exhaustion?" Rebecca's face burned and her pride stung. She hated to ask for help.

Edward turned around and rode to her. He frowned and quickly took Martha from her. MacKey rode over, cursing as he saw the rough shape of his beloved. The archers moved their horses to keep MacKey from turning back to seek immediate retaliation. Instead he took his wife from Edward and they spoke privately as the group rode on.

Rebecca's body had gone numb with the effort her hands shook. Would she be able to handle her sword after using her muscles to hold her mother? Looking up, she saw Edward watching her. Had he seen the doubt in her eyes?

She wanted the fight, didn't she? *Aye.* Then she remembered the bodies on the field and the buzzards. But how could she trust Edward's life to anyone else? How could she wait to see who came home? And who did not?

They skirted the forest. Their clansmen waited just inside the trees to ambush Ruppert's clan.

"Rebecca, I think we both know what you need to do now. Don't we." Edward touched her chin the way he always did when he wanted her eyes looking at his. Her anger flared.

"So—send the archer." Why did she feel like a stubborn child when she said that? Her head bowed in shame.

"There's nothing to be ashamed of. You've done your job perfectly. You don't have to fight now. In fact, I think you would not be good for this fight, with fatigued muscles. Think of how hard it is with all your strength."

"I shall see my mother safely home." Rebecca let the relief flood through her. "But what of you?"

"I will fight as I've never fought before. Just knowing my lady waits for me will bring me home swiftly. I'll rid this world of Ruppert and it will not be the last thing I do." Edward dismounted. "Take off your tartan."

"Why?" Rebecca looked quickly at the other men around them.

"Just do it. You, men, turn the other way." The men complied, none of them wishing Edward's anger to flare.

Rebecca did as she was told, to her own amazement. Edward carried Martha over to her.

"Thank you, Edward, I think I can walk now that I've had water." Martha spoke weakly.

Her voice ripped at Rebecca's heart, bringing tears to her eyes. Edward heaved Martha onto the saddle behind Rebecca. He wrapped the tartan around them and took her belt to hold it. The belt was big enough to hold the two around the waists.

Rebecca could now use her arms to defend them, if need be. She could not stop the flow of her tears. Angrily she tried to sweep them away. Edward mounted and they could hear the rumble of the Kirkguard horses coming their way.

"Damn!" Edward leaned over and tried to kiss away her tears. "Get goin' and go fast. Don't look back or come back! If you do you'll lose my respect from this day forward. Go!" He slapped the rump of her horse, spurring her on.

Rebecca looked back and saw Edward make his way to her father on the front line. *Please God, send them home alive.* She set her mind to the task at hand. Guiding her horse safely through the trees. Her ears strained to hear when the conflict would begin. At least they would have the element of surprise.

She rode on carefully, watching her direction. The road became familiar. She remembered markings along the way. A twisted tree here, and a large boulder there. Slowly her body relaxed. She could feel the rhythm of her mothers breathing against her back.

They rode a long way. Rebecca finally yielded to her body's needs. Opening the belt she took off the tartan and dismounted. She helped her mother down. They hugged, cried, murmured comforting words to each other, and prayed for the men.

She didn't dare set a fire, but mixed some herbs in her

mother's water to ease her pain. They ate dried meat and biscuits. Rebecca found a wonderful berry bush and some wild turnips to eat. They huddled together in eerie silence. She wondered what her mother suffered at Ruppert's hands, and knew it was worse than she would ever say even when she could talk about it.

She thought of Edward and the battle. It would probably be over by now. Had Edward killed Ruppert? Rebecca reached into herself and conjured together all of her intuition. She knew in her heart that Edward lived. A sigh escaped her lips as she looked over at her mother. Yes, her father would be safe too. Somehow she knew.

Something nagged at her good thoughts, but for now she would ignore it. "Mother, I think our men are safe. Can you feel it?"

"Aye, daughter, I can." Her mother's look held many questions.

"Although we should sleep, I've a yarn to spin for you."

Rebecca told her mother the story of her life since her wedding night. Only leaving out the personal parts. But judging from her mother's twinkling eyes, she knew the truth already.

TEN

Each man's face showed surprise as Edward and the army
bounded out of the trees. He searched them to find Ruppert.
The coward didn't even lead the front line. Then he saw him—
the back of him—as he turned to escape their surprise attack.
He is more wretched a man than I ever imagined.

Edward *would* kill him. But the men falling around him made
him realize that he must stay to support his fellows and help
defeat this force. He couldn't chase after the one man he wanted
to fight. Charging on with more power than he knew he possessed, he cared little for the lives he took. Passion drove him.

Suddenly a searing pain penetrated his left arm. *Damn, an
arrow.* A warm and sticky substance slid down his side. His
shirt turned red around the arrow. He drew in a breath, tasting
steel.

He still continued to fight with great deliberation. Not a man
stood that crossed his path. He whipped his sword through the
air only watching for his own men and MacKey's.

The smell of his own blood made him feel light-headed. The
bleeding seemed to have stopped and the arrow did not hinder
him. Soon the troops thinned and the enemy that lived rode
away. The troop looked from Edward to MacKey to see if they
should follow. Edward said aye, MacKey . . . nay.

"We must put an end to Ruppert, and it must be now." Edward winced at his pain. His horse, as restless as himself,
stomped and weaved beneath his reins.

"You're injured. Even if you made it that far, you wouldn't have the might to go through all those men. Ruppert is probably safe in his castle keep as we speak. We'll go back to Cavenaugh and regain our strength." MacKey spoke with authority.

Edward took a quick account of the other men's wounds and reluctantly agreed. The pain in his shoulder demanded his attention. They dismounted. He cut the tip off the arrow and asked MacKey to pull it out. Holding his breath, Edward watched the shaft being pulled from him. Searing pain shot up his arm and his blood flowed again.

Gritting his teeth together so he wouldn't scream from the pain, he used the skills that Rebecca taught him. He pressed the wound to stop the flow and cleaned it with whiskey from a drinking skin. Then he smoothed some salve onto the injury and wrapped a piece of tunic sleeve around it.

Gathering the wounded and dead they traveled back to Cavenaugh castle. Unbearably slow, the two-day journey passed uneventfully.

He always hated this part of war the most. Wives and children with expectant faces, looking for their loved ones . . . some found them alive . . . others dead. His heart ached for the families who lost a husband and a father. Edward always felt responsible. A dark guilt would throw its ugly shadow over his days.

For this reason he rode away from the returning forces and far away from the horses holding the dead. As they crested the hill before the castle, trumpets sounded and people poured out of the castle gates. He looked to see Rebecca astride her horse, searching the crowd anxiously. Edward whistled, sharp and strong. The horse raised its head and lumbered toward him.

He watched as she spurred her mount faster. Her beauty magnified by her haste. As she stopped short beside Edward they embraced, bringing the horses closer together. He felt Rebecca's spine stiffen at the first sorrowful wail. He wanted to cover her ears . . . and his own. He wanted to take her away from the pain.

She struggled free from his embrace.

"Rebecca, don't." Edward watched her eyes grow moist.

"I must." She turned her horse and rode to comfort the mourning family members.

Edward felt like a coward as he walked up to his chamber. On the way he passed Sarah, nursing some of the wounded.

"Laird Edward, you're wounded?" Sarah rushed to his side.

"Aye, but I've learned a few tricks from Rebecca, and took care of it myself." He continued to walk.

"Let me see." Sarah grabbed his arm.

He stopped and rolled up his sleeve. He was learning not to argue with Sarah. She clucked over his wound and pulled him to the fire.

"Sarah . . ." Acting a gentleman, he allowed her to pull him.

Dipping a clean cloth into boiling water, she cooled it slightly in the air, and washed out his wound. She pushed hard on the wound to stop its new flow.

"Ow!" Edward slapped at her.

Sarah laughed and gripped harder.

"Just makin' sure ye've nothin' in there . . . it's fine. Don't slap the Sarah again or I'll put you in your place chieftain or no." She huffed away. Edward watched her amazed that a women of such small stature would bully him.

A giggle from behind let him know that Rebecca had heard every word. He made fast for the stairs and his chamber.

"Rebecca, put some salve on the boorish man's wound, would you?"

"Aye, my Sarah. Come." Rebecca caught up with him, gripping his arm.

"Ach no, not you too. Leave it be, 'tis sore all over again." Edward pulled his arm from her grasp.

"I'll just put a wee bit o' salve on it." Rebecca looked at him. He could see the hurt in her eyes.

"Come to my chamber and see to it." Feeling stormy and sad, he wished only to be alone.

They walked silently up to Edward's chamber. He entered expecting Rebecca to follow but she continued on. Peeking around the doorway, he saw her open her chamber door.

"I'll get the salve." Her voice sounded sad and far away.

Edward took off his battered shirt and threw it on a large trunk at the foot of his bed. A knock sounded at his door. *That driveling woman and her knock-on-the-door manners.* He wrenched the door open and startle Gwen, making her spill some of the water she carried as she stepped back quickly from his wrath.

"Beg your pardon, Laird Edward. I've brought water for your bath."

"Come in." He took the buckets from her. "How's your family doing?"

"Fine, can I get you anything more?" At the shake of Edward's head, she curtsied and left the room.

As he poured water into the kettle Rebecca's voice startled him.

"Edward—"

"Good Lord, woman . . ." The water spilled into the fire nearly putting it out. She must have entered as Gwen departed.

Turning, he found the small bag of salve sailing toward him and bouncing off his chest. Rebecca's nostrils flared and her eyes narrowed.

"See to yourself, you idiot. And don't ye call me 'woman.' " Her hands in fists at her sides, she turned to leave.

Edward caught up with her. "Who're you calling an idiot?" His voice thundered at her back.

Rebecca turned and stood on the tips of her toes facing him squarely, poking his naked chest. "And . . . you are a bad-tempered dolt of a man." Her forefinger poked his chest making each word count.

Edward looked at her dubiously. For a minute the air sparked between them. "Killing men, even enemies, has that effect on me. Seeing families lose members *has* that effect on me. Surly wenches also have that effect on me! The only thing that could possibly make it worse is to continue this ridiculous conversation." Edward hoped she would leave.

Rebecca turned another shade of red and looked like she would strike him. *Oh, please don't, Rebecca. Please, don't.* She swung around, opened the door, and walked out. Slamming the door loudly in his face.

Edward's inflamed temper flared. He opened the door to pursue her, knowing he'd do something ugly and be even more upset with himself. There stood Nathaniel.

"What could ye possibly be fighting about during these times? What could be so important?" Nathaniel pushed Edward back into the chamber, pushing his chest once and then twice. He closed the door. "Cool off, old boy."

Edward looked at Nathaniel and thought how good it would feel to knock him senseless. His arm throbbed and he changed his mind. Instead, he went about fixing his bath again, swearing under his breath.

"We have scouts out to watch Ruppert's moves. Our strength wasn't cut back too much, but we must be careful."

"Did ye see that coward flee the minute we surprised them?" Edward almost choked on his words.

"Aye, I'm glad you kept with us. You're good at those quick decisions." Nathan always knew what to say to soothe his after-the-battle moods. "Did ye tell Rebecca about Ruppert?"

"No . . . no, I haven't." Edward wanted to go to Rebecca now, but not in anger.

"After you've bathed, MacKey wants us to evening meal."

Nathan left quietly.

Using his tartan Edward lifted the hot kettle and poured the water into the bathtub. Steam rose from the water and moistened his face. The warmth felt good. Adjusting the water with some cold, he took off his clothes and stepped into the tub. Closing his eyes, he sighed.

He heard the chamber door open. The slight breeze it made brought the herbal scent of her hair to his nostrils. Edward kept his eyes closed as Rebecca approached, trying to keep the look of victory off his face.

"You haven't won, I'm just concerned about your wound . . . for the good of the clan . . . that is." Rebecca gently rubbed her wondrous cleansing herb over his upper body. She stopped at the wound. He opened his eyes in question.

"Take a deep breath and hold it while I clean your wound." Rebecca's voice was neither gentle nor harsh.

He complied. As he let out his breath, she caught his hands against the tub rims. The sting made him want to slap her. Then he realized why she held him. He watched her eyes turn merry with little dances of victory in them.

In spite of his dark mood a smile grew across his lips. He lost himself in her eyes. His hands took possession of her wrists and he pulled her into the tub with him, tartan and all. Then he kissed her protesting mouth until she answered his playful tongue. Her little giggles tickled his lip as they escaped from her. He laughed deeply as he continued to kiss her.

"You think your kisses will make me forget yer boorish behavior?"

Edward tried to stop her words with his lips. She nipped his lip and he pulled away to look at her, his anger snapping again.

"Listen to me when I talk to you." Rebecca said quietly and simply. Her smile melted his anger.

"I always listen to you, my love." Edward pulled the wet clothes off her, slopping them on the floor. "Ach, your father is waiting for us in the great hall."

He stood in the tub and lifted Rebecca up with him. They pressed together briefly. His finger traced her breast and just as he would step from the tub a brisk knock sounded on the door. The doorknob started to turn.

"Don't enter!" Edward's voice thundered across the room. He stepped out of the tub and helped Rebecca to do the same.

"Laird MacKey is waitin' for you in the hall, and I need Rebecca to help feed the wounded. I can't seem to find her." Sarah's voice sounded angry.

"Go away and I'll see to those problems." Edward yelled to Sarah and then spoke softly to Rebecca. "I'll go fetch some clothes for you." He wrapped a warm blanket around her.

"You don't have to." She walked over to a wardrobe. Opening it, she moved the sparse clothing aside. Then she pushed a small lever breaching her own heavily clothed wardrobe. "Now you know." Her voice sounded low and appealing.

Edward laughed. Rebecca . . . always full of surprises . . . some good, some bad. But he wouldn't have her any other way.

Rebecca dressed quickly. Her hair hung hopelessly limp and wet. Trying to run a comb though it, it only became more difficult the more she tried. A loud knock sounded on the door.

"Are you in there, child?" Sarah yelled from the hall.

"There're no children in here." Rebecca playfully echoed Sarah's old-time brogue, rolling her *r.* She loved the sound and the way it made her tongue feel rich.

Sarah came in holding the sopping wet tartan and her other clothing. She looked ready to burst with ire, and would not even meet Rebecca's eyes.

"Oh, my apologies, I meant to hang those out. I . . ."

"Don't you dare tell me. I don't want to know. In case your wonderin', I wrapped up Edward's wound properly. At least you got him in a better mood." Sarah gave her a sly look and went to hang the tartan out the window. The other clothes she hung around the room.

Rebecca tugged at her hair. "I'm glad for you, my Sarah. I didn't have the proper wrappings or leaves."

"What's that your doin' to your hair? Ach, give me tha'." She snatched the comb out of Rebecca's hand and began working it through her hair from the bottom.

"Sarah, I don't know why you're so upset about Edward and me. You, of all people should know where my heart is. Don't you wish us well?" Rebecca turned to look at Sarah.

"Turn around." Sarah tugged harder at the snares. "You're wed in the eyes of God to Laird Ruppert. You'll just bring trouble on yourself by beddin' another man."

"Edward is not just another man. He was to be my promised."

"It's still not right, you should wait. What will you do? You can't have a marriage annulled if you've had a man." Sarah looked sad as she helped Rebecca into her gown.

"Not to worry. I intend to see this through no matter what. Let's see to the wounded." Rebecca led her out the door.

They walked down to the kitchen and collected trays of steaming food. The smell made Rebecca's stomach growl. Passing through the dinning hall she noticed Edward and her father drinking wine.

Edward started to hum that lilting love song as she passed, grinning at her. Her heart melted, it was all she could do not to drop the tray and go to him. Looking around she noticed the glances she received from the clan members and their bawdy smiles. Rebecca felt her face getting hot and heard Edward's deep laugh.

Gwen, also carrying some trays, caught up to her as she left the hall.

"I had no idea my chieftain sported such a romantic heart." Gwen winked at Rebecca.

"Don't let a little tune fool you, he's still a brute." They laughed together.

"Is it true you joined the men in a battle?" Gwen looked at her with admiration.

Rebecca nodded, not sure whether to encourage her. They left food with some of the women who tended the wounded in a large hall. Sarah and Rebecca went up to her mother's chamber with the last tray.

Martha lay on her pillow, pale and drawn. Her eyes didn't open when they entered the room. Rebecca ran to her bedside and felt her skin. It was warm, but not hot.

"Mother?" Rebecca spoke softly.

Her mother opened her eyes and smiled at her daughter.

"Are you feeling any better?" She smoothed her brow.

"Ach, no." She licked her lips. They appeared cracked and dry.

Rebecca poured water from a ewer into a cup and placed it to her mother's lips. She glanced over at Sarah, who looked concerned.

"Let me see how you're healing, m'lady." Sarah gently examined her and applied more salve. "You're good at the healing arts, Rebecca. Have you remembered all I've taught you?"

"Most of it." Rebecca prepared the tray and sat on the bed, ready to help her mother eat.

"Child, you must be hungry yourself. Why don't you join the others? I'd like to talk to Sarah—alone."

Rebecca tried not to let her see how it bothered her to be called child. Would her mother ever think of her as an adult?

"Very well, Mother." Rebecca kissed her cheek, left the chamber, and walked slowly to the kitchen. The men sat eating when she entered the hall with a plate of food. Edward rose to pull out her chair, bowing slightly and smiling. She sat down, nodding her thanks. Why did her face always heat so? She glared at the curious glances until they looked again to their own concerns.

Edward poured some wine and handed the goblet to her. She lifted it to her lips, smelling the sweet grape scent. As she swallowed the liquid she savored its sweet taste and the way it sent a fiery path down her throat. Her eyes opened in astonishment at the pleasant taste and strength.

"How is the wine, daughter? It comes from our kin who live in France." MacKey savored the taste himself.

"It's wonderful." Rebecca smiled at her father. "You've not yet told me of the battle's outcome. I gather the news is not so good . . . or are we celebrating?" She looked from man to man.

Edward lowered his gaze.

Her father shook his head. "Ruppert retreated, leaving his army to fight his battle." MacKey looked at Edward.

"Do tell!" Rebecca stared in amazement, as Edward remained quiet. "Edward!" She shoved his arm. "Do you see why I insist on joining the fight? Otherwise, how would I know what goes on?"

"I saw Ruppert flee the moment we surprised them." Edward looked sorry.

"You didn't go after him?" Frustration engulfed her and she could feel the heat rising on her face. The cold hands of fear gripped her reason, choking it. Rebecca slammed down the food in her hand and pushed out of her chair, causing it to fall back-wards.

"Rebecca, sit down and finish your meal." Edward's voice was quiet but sounded dangerous. He rose and set her chair up right, his hand on her shoulder forced her to sit as he pushed it in.

Her eyes watered, but she refused to let the tears go down her cheeks. What had she expected? She expected Edward to kill Ruppert so they could live happily ever after. Wasn't that how it was supposed to be? Rebecca finished eating and rose to leave.

Edward joined her, politely saying good-night to the people around them. Rebecca remained mute. Gently he took her arm and led her up the stairway toward her chamber.

"Why didn't you go after him?" She finally let the tears flow. Angered even more by her show of weakness, she yanked her arm out of his grasp.

"I couldna'. Don't you think I wanted to?" Edward took her arm and turned her to face him. He let her go as he brushed her tears away with his fingers.

"You could have!" Rebecca saw the pain in his face, and knew she should stop. But, she couldn't. "You could have if you really wanted to!"

She watched his composure snap and knew she'd gone too far. Before she could flee he gripped both her arms roughly.

"You're a coddled little brat! How dare you doubt my honor just because the outcome doesn't suit you? I did what I had to do, and that was support my fellows." He released her, causing her to stumble backward, and retreated to his chamber, slam-ming the door.

The emptiness returned and filled with anger and shame. Her chamber door loomed in front of her. The thought of entering it alone was unpleasant. Instead, she turned and walked out to the courtyard.

The sun sank behind the mountains, leaving a rosy glow over all but the shadowed places. The air smelled moist, as if it would rain. In the distance a dark cloud loomed. She turned from the cloud and looked toward the red-topped mountains.

A cold breeze made her skin turn to bumps. Rebecca pulled her collar closer to her neck. Reaching up to her hair's binding, she released the folds of it. It bounced around her shoulders and drifted down to her waist, lending some shelter from the cold.

Walking around a big stone fountain, she listened to the softly flowing water. She'd come here many times, as a child, to be soothed by that sound. But it didn't help the restless and impatient feelings that welled within her.

She didn't feel good about the way she spoke to Edward. The unfairness of her words echoed back to her. How foolishly rash to accuse him of making the wrong choice. But the words had fallen, and she couldn't pick them up.

A horse whinnied from the stable. Rebecca walked over to visit her favorite mare, one of her father's horses. She walked past the mare and found a wild-natured stallion. Without much thought she saddled and haltered the animal. Her fingers tingled with anticipation. What a splendid run she would have with this wild one.

She chose a sheathed broadsword from the wall and attached it to the saddle. A Cavenaugh tartan folded over a beam would serve as a cloak. Slowly walking her mount out of the stable she could feel the restless nature of the stallion.

"You and I have much in common." Rebecca smoothed her hand over its shiny black coat. The stallion responded with a whinny.

"Shhh . . . don't give us away." The horse's head bobbed up and down. She laughed quietly.

The small castle gate squealed as she unbolted the lock. She had learned early in life the ease of coming and going through the side gate. Then she used the rough stone wall of the castle to boost herself onto the massive animal. The horse took off as soon as her bottom hit the saddle.

They galloped down the hills and into the open moor. The stallion seemed to know the moor. Rebecca gave him his lead and didn't care where they would go. Why had she never questioned Edward about his late wife? Would it change her feelings for him?

Both horse and rider reveled in their freedom. She rode a long time. Suddenly, a man came riding at her out of the darkness. Swinging his sword he hit her with the flat side of it. She almost fell from her horse. More than surprised, she ripped the broadsword out of its sheath just in time to ward off his next blow. Even though the red light of the sun had disappeared behind the mountains, Rebecca could still see the Kirkguard clan colors.

Her anger sustained her as he kept coming back and striking. His tactics where simple. Her tartan fell from her shoulders. Before she could tire, she had wounded the man and sent him to the ground. She carefully dismounted just as the man got to his feet. He raged at her with his sword and she wounded him again. Evading his deadly blows, she fought with all of her agility.

Inhaling gulps of air, her lungs felt as if they would burst. No longer cold, sweat trickled down her body. She struggled to keep the sword in her slick hands.

Her concentration rested on the man's next move, tasting blood, she realized she had bitten her bottom lip. The sword nearly flew from her hand as she parried. Gripping he sword harder, her muscles stretched to their limit. He missed a parry to her last lunge, and fell to the ground with her sword.

Rebecca collapsed on her knees in sheer exhaustion. She looked at the man in horror. She'd won. *Why do I feel so wretched*? All at once Rebecca realized how much she hated death. She bowed her head into her hands and tried to forget the sound her sword made as it entered the man.

Not able to stand the presence of the dead body, She forced herself to rise. Calling to the stallion, she walked toward it. She tried to mount, but her muscles would not cooperate.

The man's horse grazed a short distance away. She walked over to it slowly and gathered its reins. Mounting it, she led the stallion as she rode back to the castle wall. As she entered the wall she realized that the sky had grown lighter. She'd been gone all night.

She brought the horses toward the stable and could hear a flurry of activity. She entered the barn and all of the activity stopped. The stable boy, her father, and Edward stood there gaping at her.

"Where have you been?" Edward pushed the other two aside and approached her.

"For a ride, an eventful one. Out on the moor lies a Kirkguard spy with a Cavenaugh sword in him. I'm tired." Rebecca calmly turned and walked out of the stable, leaving the horses for them to tend.

Edward was struck silent by her sheer, wild beauty. Neither of the men stopped her. The stableboy took care of the horses. Edward looked at MacKey. They both stood there, speechless.

"What was she doing out on the moor?" Edward looked accusingly at MacKey.

"I don't know. I thought you'd know. Don't you share her bed?" MacKey countered.

"Not last night." Edward turned to go.

"Leave her be, Edward." MacKey's command brooked no argument.

Instead of following her Edward took his sword out to the practice field where others were dueling. Nathaniel welcomed him with a nod and they fenced. It did him good to have his mind on something other than Rebecca. He fought with swift passion and soon Nathan panted hard.

"Stop! I've had enough!" Nathan placed the point of his sword into the ground and leaned on the hilt.

Edward did the same. They laughed at the picture they made as they noticed a crowd of onlookers. The crowd applauded and continued on their business.

Edward and Nathan headed to the dining hall. Sitting down to eat, his body finally relaxed. The men at the table talked to him, making him feel like a chieftain again. He thought of his castle and clan. As the conversation died down, he turned to Nathaniel.

"We need to have a meeting of our clan and make sure we all agree with the plans."

"Yes, we'll gather after evening meal."

"I'll let MacKey know. Have you seen him?" Edward looked around the hall.

A man next to him spoke. "He gathered a dead Kirkguard from the moor, the one that his daughter killed. The whole castle is buzzing with the story."

Edward thanked the man and headed for the kitchen. He found his sister. "How are you feeling, Madeleine? It's good to see you up and about."

"Fine, brother, and what mischief have you been up to?" Madeleine smiled at him.

"I'm not the one who makes mischief."

"I know, I heard the story. And how is it that she got out of your sight?" Madeleine raised her brows at him.

"Never mind. I need a tray to bring up to her, that is if no one has already done that." Edward tried to push his rising temper down. He would not get angry with her. He'd grown tired of the anger. But whether or not he could keep that promise was another thing entirely.

Madeleine helped him fix a tray of food. He carried it up to her chamber, gently knocking on the door. Edward heard giggles on the other side before it opened. A man walked out and calmly bowed, taking his leave. Rebecca's smile turned to a frown when she saw Edward. She still sat on the bed with only a light chemise on.

Edward's mind flashed red—his warning signal. If he wanted the person who angered him to live, he would leave. Instead, with control that surprised even him, he walked over to the bed and placed the tray down.

"Have you eaten, Lady Rebecca?" His voice sounded tight and unnatural. Rebecca looked at him oddly.

"Nay, is every thing all right, Edward?" Concern showed on her face.

"I don't know, you tell me. Was yer visitor very satisfying?" Edward gripped the bedpost as he felt his composure evaporate.

"What is that supposed to mean?" Rebecca hopped off the bed and walked to the window. She turned to hear his answer.

"Just that. Is he as satisfying as I am?" Edward walked toward her.

She turned a bright shade of pink and slapped his face.

He grabbed both her wrists.

"How dare you accuse me of such a thing, have you gone daft? Rowan is a cousin—and a good friend. He was concerned about me when he heard the stories. I can't believe I have to explain that to you. Wasn't I a virgin when you took me?"

Edward shook his head to clear out the red anger that threatened to drown all his reason. He let go of her wrists and started to leave.

"Edward, I love you. I would never betray that love." She gently reached out to him.

He turned around at her gentle touch. She hugged him and rested her head on his chest as he overcame the overwhelming old feelings.

Lowering his head, he kissed her sweet lips. Could he be sure she would always be faithful to him? He continued to kiss her, lifting her in his arms and placing her on the bed.

"Don't ever betray our love, for I would never live through that." He murmured the words against her lips, ashamed of his weakness. Feeling inadequate caused his anger to rise. "Which brings up another issue." Edward moved away from her and took his crop from the belt of his tartan.

"If you strike me with that thing, Edward MacCleary, *you* will be the one betraying our love. And you will never again taste these lips. I vow that to you." Rebecca backed up on the bed, her eyes wide.

Edward looked at the disagreeable object in his hand. Walking to the window, he threw it out. Just as quickly he jumped onto the bed, pinning her beneath him. "How, then, does a man get a strong-willed lady to obey his wishes?"

"He talks to her, listens to her, and hopes she sees his reason." Rebecca kissed the top of his nose. "You're not happy that I left the castle grounds. I need my freedom, Edward. Without it I can't be happy. I will never let anyone take it from me—not Ruppert and not you."

"I understand. I'll have to use less brute force and more wiles on my love. So . . . good day, fair Rebecca." Edward left her on the bed and walked toward the door.

"Where are you going?"

He could see her color heighten. It was working. "To my chamber. Whenever my lady chooses to put her life in danger by leaving the castle grounds, that is where I will reside."

"Oh, Edward, get back here. You're just jealous that I killed the Kirkguard, and you couldn't be the big hero." Rebecca left the bed, walked over to him, and ran her hands up and down his chest.

"No, good day. I'll see you at evening meal." He plucked her hands from his chest and walked to the door. As he opened it, it occurred to him that he might be punishing himself, as well. *It'll be worth it.* Looking back he could tell he'd made an impression by the way her hungry expression turned sour. Closing the door behind him he waited for the coming fury. Within seconds a crash could be heard on the other side of the door. *It was worth it.*

Opening the door Edward added, "There's a meeting of the MacCleary Clan after evening meal. See that you attend and we may well have a pleasant night yet."

ELEVEN

Rebecca took a deep breath while the clans argued back and forth. Finally, they decided to ride to the MacCleary castle. They would help regain Edward's chieftainship, and see that Duncan no longer walked the earth. Taking a little less than half the able men, they'd leave the rest to protect Cavenaugh castle. Rebecca guessed that she would have to put up a fight to be one of the "men" riding out.

She watched Edward talk to the clans. He revealed masterful skills at negotiation. The people could see his genuine feelings for justice and they let him lead. He even bettered her father. Rebecca listened and learned. *Why are there no other women in this room? Don't they care what becomes of their clans?* Ach, how she hated that.

The MacCleary clan would need some Cavenaugh members to support the force heading out. The men began to decide.

Edward's voice interrupted her thoughts. "Rebecca, what would you do? Defend your father's castle, or regain my chieftainship?" His dark eyes seemed to look into her soul.

"Which do you think?" She gave him a shy and completely humble look.

"You would defend my chieftainship?" He looked thoughtful.

"Aye. Can I do you that honor?" She could feel herself walking a fragile bridge. Edward's answer meant everything to her.

"Aye, so be it." He turned from her and began to organize the other men.

That was too easy. Rebecca listened to his instructions for each man. Not caring that she looked like a puppy following Edward around. She watched carefully to see that she wasn't being duped.

He turned to her a few times with curious looks. "Make sure you bring a fresh supply of yer healing and cleansing herbs." Edward winked at her.

"I'll join the fight. I'll not just be a nurse maid." Rebecca looked into his eyes to see if she could find his good faith. It seemed to be there. The men gave her expressions of surprise, humor, and tolerance. She held her head high and vowed to prove her abilities to them all.

As the meeting ended, Edward and Rebecca walked up to their chambers. He paused at his door, looked at Rebecca, and continued on with her. She tried not to grin, failing horribly. Passion started to heat her blood as they entered her chamber.

However, she found herself disappointed when Edward readied himself for bed without even glancing at her. So, she did the same.

He calmly crawled under the covers on one side of the bed. "Good night." He closed his eyes.

"Good night." Getting into bed she contemplated making a fuss. But a sleepy feeling made her decide not to.

The sweet smell of primrose drifted into the window as Edward's eyes opened to the new day. He became aware that Rebecca was not in the chamber. Jumping out of bed, he splashed his face with cold water from a bowl. Hastily, he dressed and headed down to morning meal. She wasn't there either.

He refused to ask anyone if Lady Rebecca had been at the table. Eating, he spoke only to answer questions and to be civil.

Nathan plunked himself down beside Edward, in a humorous mood. "Good day, Chieftain."

"Good day." Edward braced himself, not in the mood for Nathan's teasing.

"Did ye have a good night's rest?"

"Aye." Edward gave Nathan a warning glance.

"Where's Lady Rebecca?" Nathan looked around the hall, a teasing smile on his lips.

Edward didn't answer. Instead, he filled his mouth with bread and kept busy chewing.

"Oh, that's right . . . I did see her this morning, dueling with the men. They had a regular tournament going. She hadn't been bested yet as I could tell."

"And where would tha' be?" Edward's brogue sounded low and pronounced through his mouth full of food. He slammed down the mutton in his hand, finished chewing the bread already in his mouth, and stood.

"The east field."

Nathan's laughter echoed behind him as he left the hall. He would deal with Nathan later. Edward walked toward the castle's eastern exit, impatient with people who would stop him to talk. When he finally emerged he saw a crowd surrounding two men dueling.

"Edward!" MacKey clapped him on the shoulder. "It's so good ta be on the side of the MacCleary's once more." He looked proudly at his daughter, who sat resting across the way. "She's always been an active part of our training, though she never battled until two weeks past. The Cavenaugh men have a lot of respect for her." MacKey looked back at Edward.

"How could you allow your daughter to take part in the men's activities? Surely they protested."

"They didn't protest too loudly. Ach, and how can you deny Rebecca anything once she sets her mind to it? You, of all people, should know that."

"Aye, and the cause being her da never took the time to discipline her." Edward walked away not giving MacKey a chance to respond. He approached the back of the group, trying not to be noticed.

"Who would be the next to challenge our Lady Rebecca?" A man, chosen to moderate, questioned the crowd.

"I would." Edward made his way through the crowd. The men quickly parted as they recognized him.

"A chieftain! He must be stout of heart. For what would his clan think of him should he fail?" The man created a show for the audience.

The crowd cheered.

"M'lady." Sweeping his sword in front of him, Edward bowed.

"M'lord." Rebecca did the same with her own style and grace.

Ach, she's breathtaking when her ire and sport are up. With her hair tied back loosely, and her violet eyes shooting blue sparks, she braced herself before him. Her wrists were wrapped in leather straps and her hands covered with white leather gloves. She looked like a true warrior. Oh, and look at that determination. Here was a chance to teach her a lesson. He waited for her first move. They circled, stalking each other. The crowd grew silent.

She swept her sword at him. He retreated and swung his sword to counter her attack, causing her to retreat. Losing not a second he sent a drill of attacks her way. The crowd gasped at his aggressive attacks as she parried each one with swift strength and skill.

"Mayhaps the men fight a lady, *like* a lady." Edward retreated, easily parrying her blows.

"I think not." Rebecca set about attacking him just as fiercely as he had her. Sparks flew between their swords, creating a metallic smell. The steely sound of their weapons echoed through the air. The audience seemed to be held captive by the show. They watched in awed silence.

Edward saw anger reflected in her eyes, mingled with fear, and a very real need. Well, he had needs too, and he would not let her off easy. Rebecca seemed to lose concentration as he watched her eyes. She nearly lost her sword. A new determination showed as she stared back.

Edward fought for his breath. He saw Rebecca's chest rise and fall just as quickly. Her taut muscles and wild eyes made her look like an avenging Viking. *God, he loved this woman.* Rebecca circled his blade with hers and twisted it from his hand.

The force sent it flying out of his reach. She held her sword point close to his chest. Her shoulders heaved with each breath she took.

Her ravishing smile swallowed him whole, and he saw the spontaneous look of fear in her eyes . . . she cares.

Edward's senses warred as he searched for the right reaction. The crowd waited silently to see what the chieftain would do. Then, he did simply what he felt. As Rebecca removed the sword he knelt next to her, took her free hand, and kissed her palm gently.

"I am most humbly yours." Edward could feel a lump in his throat. His pride, no doubt.

"As I am yours." Her head bowed over their joined hands.

The crowd cheered as Edward rose and the couple bowed arm in arm. They took on other challengers, and the afternoon passed in a festive way. All too soon the crowd thinned, and everyone went to the hall for a large evening meal.

Rebecca carried a heavy tray to her mother's chamber. Every muscle in her body stiff with the day's efforts.

"Good afternoon, Mother." She carried the tray over to the bed, watching her mother closely.

"Rebecca! I'm terribly lonely. Will you join me?" Her mother's smile looked fresh and promising.

"Aye, of course." She sat comfortably on the bed with the tray between them.

"Tell me what scandals you've been creating today." Her mother smiled knowingly.

"I won a duel with Edward." Rebecca beamed.

"Oh dear, how did he handle that?"

"With the highest gallantry I've ever witnessed. He charmed the occasion, and lost not an ounce of pride in the process. He truly is a study." Rebecca could feel the glow on her face. Her mother's smile made her blush even more.

"God bless you both. I'm so pleased that you've finally met your match." Martha laughed.

"Ach, surely Edward has met his match in me." Rebecca joined her laughter.

"I hope your dealings with each other are more civilized now, than when you were younger."

"Ah . . . nearly so." Rebecca grinned as her mother's head shook back and forth.

"And now you will go to fight with the men." Her mother looked sad.

Rebecca knew that she was no stranger to death. "Don't worry, Mother. I'm careful, and I have a brave seasoned warrior watching over me. Ready to scoop me up should I lose my horse." She playfully reminded her of her first real battle and how Edward swept her from certain death, landing her onto the back end of his horse.

"This time do get on the horse facing the right way." They laughed together, trying to make light of a serious situation.

After enjoying each other's company for a while longer, a knock sounded at the door. Rebecca rose and opened the door to a well-dressed Edward. His glossy black hair waved around his shoulders. A white linen shirt stretched across his broad chest and tucked into his breeches. A thick belt crossed over his shirt and around his waist, holding his sword. Tall leather boots with MacCleary hose finished the picture to perfection.

"I came to see how the Lady Martha fares."

Rebecca led him into the room.

"Edward! Come in and let me properly thank you for so bravely rescuing me. I've been busy since then, and I want you to see what I've been up to."

"Mother?" Rebecca wondered what she was talking about.

Martha rang a bell summoning her lady's maid. Motioning her close, Martha whispered to her.

"Are all the Cavenaugh women so full of mischief?" Edward looked amused.

"Where do you think I got it from?" Rebecca winked at her mother.

"Are you feeling better?" Edward changed the subject.

"Aye, thank you. I'm looking forward to getting out of this bed. But Sarah forbids it, just yet."

"Aye, Sarah can be quite forbidding."

Their conversation stopped when the maid announced the blacksmith. A group of men carrying peculiar-looking metal and leather vests stepped into the chamber.

Martha looked at Edward. "I noticed that the wood armor didn't quite do the trick. You bled during my rescue, was it very severe?"

"Nay, m'lady, just a nick that bled a lot at first. But recently an arrow did more damage. Luckily, not to my sword arm." Edward looked at the armor. "Have you designed this?"

Martha beamed. "Aye, right down to the arm guards. The blacksmith tried to make it strong and yet not so heavy. See what you think."

Edward took a thick leather suit from one of the men. He lifted it over his head, looking very impressed. "That is much lighter than any I've ever worn. Splendid job, Lady Martha."

"Try the arm guards, they strap around." Martha rose from the bed, her large robe swimming around her. She reached up and attached one guard and then the other.

When she finished, Edward moved his arms around. "It leaves the arms free moving. Lady Martha, you're truly a woman of action." Edward smiled and looked at Rebecca. "I must tell you that I am letting your daughter join us—I hope you understand."

"Just knowing my daughter gives me all the understanding I need. Rebecca, close your mouth, and try on yours."

A man moved forward with a smaller version. It fit perfectly and although slightly heavier than clothes, it was relatively light. "Mother, you always surprise me in the most unexpected ways." She hugged her and kissed her cheeks.

"Now all you must do for me is rid the world of the evil called Ruppert." Martha's eyes lost some of their light as she mentioned the name.

"Aye, and I will," Edward vowed.

"She was talking to me." Rebecca watched Edward's face turn stormy.

"You both just keep each other safe. Ruppert's demise will come at the proper time, by the right person." Martha suddenly looked very tired. She swooned.

Edward caught her and carried her to the bed. "I'll see that the men are outfitted with the armor." Edward held her hand and bowed over it.

Rebecca hugged and kissed her mother tearfully saying her farewells. They would leave early the next morning. Her heart heavy, they walked to her chamber.

Suddenly, Edward scooped her into his arms. A group of ladies in the hallway tittered at the show and whispered among themselves.

"Put me down, you're making a spectacle." Rebecca pushed against Edward as she noticed some men walking past. Men she had dueled today. "Put me down!"

"I'll teach you to best me in a duel." Edward's chuckle held the promise of arduous retribution.

Rebecca's body responded immediately, although her head wished it wouldn't. Edward kicked the chamber door open and kicked it shut. She heard the men laughing outside the door.

"You can get to your own chamber. If you think I'll stand for you soiling my repu—" Rebecca's words were cut off by Edward's soft lips, pressing away her protests. She stopped trying to talk and he parted from her lips to give her the most passionate look she had ever received.

"I commend you. Your dueling has improved, and so has the MacCleary men's opinion of you. Clever, clever, lass." His lips fell on her smile, causing her heart to beat faster. He stood her before the fire.

"And you haven't diminished in their sight?" Rebecca leaned back to study his eyes.

"It would take far more than that to ruin my reputation. Most of my men have had a taste of my ire and have no wish to bring it upon themselves. As for your men . . . word travels fast."

Edward smiled. He had such a charming debonair quality to him. Rebecca's heart ached with love for him.

"You're truly the most pleasant sight these eyes have ever beheld." Rebecca caressed his body, feeling the heat rise in him. Then she began to remove her clothes. She stood naked before his impassioned eyes. She tried to remove his clothing.

Instead, Edward pulled her closer to his fully clothed body, devouring her mouth again with his own. She melted against him. His rough clothes were driving her wild for his soft flesh.

"Edward . . ." *Please, remove your clothes.*

"What, my love?" Edward's hands caressed every inch of her skin.

"Please . . ." *Take off your clothes!*

"Please, what?" His voice sounded thick with passion.

"Take . . ." His kiss stopped her words again, as she struggled against him. Her struggle only made her discomfiture worse.

"Go ahead . . . take them off." Edward moved so she could open his belt. Her fingers fumbled in her haste. "Slow down . . ." Edward held her hands still until she moved slower.

Rebecca groaned her frustration. He continued to smooth his hands over every part of her body, her face, and through her hair. She slowly removed his clothes. Finally, they fell away to the floor.

Now it was Rebecca's turn to caress his body. Edward took a sharp breath in, as she nearly touched his most sensitive part.

"Two can play at this game." Her soft laugh turned to a screech as he swiftly impaled her with his desire, and carried her to the bed.

Edward climbed the steps to the lofty bed and they fell onto the soft down quilt. Rebecca had the feeling of being on a soft cloud, floating in a clear blue sky. Edward moved slowly on top of her, cradling her head in his hands as he watched her. She met his gaze. Staring eye-to-eye, they gave each other the greatest gift of all.

As Rebecca stared into the passionate depths of Edward's gaze, she forgot all else and surrendered to his sweet love.

* * *

Edward caressed Rebecca's arm with light circles, as they lay together. Her skin felt so soft under his touch. A knock at the door interrupted his peace.

Edward growled an oath. "Who is it?" He pulled on his shirt and breeches.

"It's Sarah, I'm coming in." Sarah's voice echoed his tone of voice. She entered the chamber. Straightening and muttering. Muttering and straightening. Picking up the clothes from the floor, she moved back toward the door.

Edward looked at Rebecca. She motioned for him to leave. He shook his head, no. She motioned stronger, pointing her finger to his chamber. He mouthed the words, "I'm coming back," and left the room.

Edward walked into his chamber and removed his clothes. A fragrance, reminiscent of his last bath, drifted to his nose. He strode to the tub, removing his clothing on the way, and gingerly placed his body into the warm water. He relaxed. Closing his eyes, he went over the duel with Rebecca in his head, planning a counter-move for the next time.

Another knock sounded at the door. Edward wondered if anyone in this castle ever left you alone. He suffered from fewer interruptions at his own castle. Rising from the tub, he threw on a black robe and went to open the door. MacKey stood in the hall looking lost. He walked in absentmindedly and paced before the fireplace. Edward knew something must be weighing heavily on his mind. He shut the door.

"What is it? Laird MacKey?" Edward waited patiently as MacKey paced some more.

"The bastard raped her . . . my Martha . . . he raped her." MacKey paled and looked like he wanted to say more, but no words came.

"My God. She told you that?" Edward gripped MacKey's arm and let it go.

"Aye. Edward, I'm going to kill that man. I don't care what it costs me. I am going to kill him. We'll go to Kirkguard castle first and put an end to that monstrosity. Martha said he kept talking about how our clans destroyed his family a hundred years ago and that justice would finally be done."

"I remember hearing stories about the Kirkguard lands stretching past both our holdings," Edward thought out loud. "That gives him reason to separate our clans to weaken us. He's the one who killed my father. He's mine." Edward stared into MacKey's eyes.

"We do this together, Edward. Then we'll be sure not to fail. Hurry and get your castle in order. We'll deal with Ruppert when you get back. Take care of Rebecca. If Ruppert comes while you're gone I'll handle him. God speed, Edward."

"God keep you and yours . . . until I return then." He bowed his respect.

MacKey left the room. Edward suddenly felt very tired. He climbed through the hidden door in the wardrobe closet, and knocked on the back of the door in Rebecca's room.

"Come in." Rebecca laughed as Edward emerged with a skirt sweeping across his head. He brushed it away impatiently and looked around.

"Did your father come in to say goodbye?" Edward moved to the bed and crawled in beside her.

"Aye." Rebecca cuddled close to him.

"Sleep . . . we leave at dark."

The chill in the air woke Rebecca. She opened her eyes and looked at the window. In the darkness she noticed that Edward was not in bed. *He better not leave without me.* She muttered an oath and jumped out of bed.

"Excuse me? What was that you said?" Edward stood beside the fireplace in the shadows, his arms crossed.

"Ah . . . nothing, I thought you'd left without me. Pardon me."

"Rebecca . . . don't you trust me?" Edward almost looked hurt.

"Nay." Rebecca's teased. She shivered.

Edward laughed. Walking over, he swooped her up and brought her to the fire.

She dressed with her mind on all that she needed to bring. She heard a suspicious sound and turned to see Edward holding a chastity belt.

"Oh no—get away from me." Rebecca quickly found her sword and pointed it at Edward. "I'm serious, I will not wear that thing." Rebecca lunged at him. Grabbing the belt, she threw it into the fire.

"Rebecca!" Edward grabbed the sword out of her hand and fished around in the fire. He tried to remove the belt but failed. Putting down the sword, he faced her. His face glowing with rage and his hands in fists at his sides.

"Settle down. I don't need that damn belt. I can take care of myself."

"Don't tell me to settle down. Were you taking care of yourself when Ruppert's men had ye tied at their campfire?"

"Nay, Edward, I *couldn't* take care of myself, because *your* guard tied my hands and refused to let me fight! Those were *your* orders. One of your unwise decisions, and it almost cost me my life." Rebecca faced him, feeling her face flush with the heat of her anger.

Edward seemed to be finding it hard to look at her eyes. He spun away from her with a sound of annoyance, walked to the window, and looked out. "Good God! It's a surprise attack."

"Don't change the subject—*what*?"

"Those maggots are crawling all over the castle. Quick, go wake your father and tell everyone along the way. Quietly— we'll give *them* a surprise or two." Edward picked up Rebecca's armor and shoved it at her on his way out. "Put it on." He grabbed his own, shrugging it on. Then, taking his sword he ran out of the room.

Rebecca dressed in only a shirt and breeches, slipped on the armor and pulled on her boots. Already out of breath she picked up her sword and ran to her father's chamber. Members of both families emerged as she knocked on the doors along the way.

"Surprise attack . . . surprise attack . . ." Rebecca whispered to the people as she passed.

Her father and mother still slept as she entered their chamber. She saw a shadow at the window. Rebecca kept quiet and swung at the man as he entered through the window. A Kirkguard.

"Father!" She saw the man fall, his arm badly severed . . . *Talbot*! "We're being attacked."

MacKey pulled on his armor and swept up his sword. Martha set out to help gather the women and children to safety. Rebecca ran to other rooms, alerting everyone. As she passed a chamber balcony some Kirkguard men climbed over its rail. She fought them with a few MacCleary men backing her up. Two enemies were struck down and the rest escaped down their ropes.

The swift and silent alerting of the castle inhabitants made the MacCleary and Cavenaugh clans victorious. They had few injuries and no deaths.

Rebecca's head swam as she helped to clean the blood off the castle floors. Tears came to her eyes. Enemy or not, killing is a cruel and horrible thing.

Then she saw Talbot's body. He would sneak into their castle and kill her father while he slept? Her eyes dried. She was glad the world would be free of this man.

The men carried the bodies out to be brought to the Kirkguard castle, as a warning. She shivered as she realized that they would give Ruppert even more reason to seek vengeance.

Rebecca walked through the courtyard. The morning sun began to burn off the mountain fog, promising a clear day. She made her way to the great hall and sat next to Edward. Some guards brought in five men wearing MacCleary colors. The guards pushed them toward Edward as he stood to receive them.

"Laird Edward, they regret their decision to follow Ruppert and wish pardon to join with their chieftain again."

Edward's eyes narrowed and his muscles grew taut. One by one he stripped the men of their colors. "You'll not wear the MacCleary colors again. Throw them in the dungeon, there's been enough killing for one day." He looked directly at each man. "It's your lucky day. You can rot in the dungeon, instead of dying, at least for now."

Rebecca watched as his gaze came to hers. She saw the hurt there. But his expression turned from hurt to pride as he joined her once more at the table.

"Rebecca. You're amazing to me. I'm sorry I didn't let you fight the day you were captured. Please forgive my foolishness." Taking her hand, he kissed her palm.

TWELVE

Rebecca huddled in her tartan, attempting to ward off the cold morning air. The gloomy clouds in the sky matched her mood. They'd already ridden a long way from Cavenaugh castle. Leaving home did not seem so difficult with Edward at her side.

He rode beside her now, quiet and thoughtful. Suddenly, he perked up and motioned for the army to ride into the trees.

As she peered from the cover of the dense leaves, Rebecca noticed the colors of the Stuart Clan. "It's the royal clan," she whispered to Edward.

He nodded and motioned for the army to stay. "Come with me, Rebecca. King James doesn't know just how dangerous you are, so a man and a woman will look less threatening." Edward grinned at her as they rode from the trees.

Rebecca returned his look with derision. A voice at the head of the King's party called a halt. Edward and Rebecca approached the leader.

"Well, well, Laird Edward MacCleary. Greetings to you, and your lovely lady."

"King James," Edward bowed in his saddle, "Greetings to you. This is Lady Rebecca of Cavenaugh."

Rebecca also bowed. *Edward knows King James?* "It's an honor to meet you, Your Majesty."

"The honor is mine." The King of Scotland's horse edged closer to Rebecca's as he took her hand and kissed it. Then, looking at Edward, he frowned. "I've much to take up with you, Laird Edward. It seems you've not been seeking the peace—as we've discussed—although, a Cavenaugh riding with a Mac-Cleary is surely a good sign."

"Aye, our clans have made the peace. However others are less for the common effort." Edward bowed respectfully, once more.

"We've a fresh catch of venison, would you join us for an early midday meal?" King James smiled at Rebecca.

"Aye, with pleasure, Your Majesty." Edward scrutinized him while he wasn't watching.

When the king turned to speak with Edward, Rebecca studied them both. What a picture they made, two noble men, to be sure. King James wore his Stuart plaids proudly and a growth of beard only added to his royal demeanor. His build matched Edward's and his face was nearly as appealing. A grin tugged at her mouth.

Edward looked at Rebecca with warning in his eyes. As they rode away he whispered, "Behave yourself."

"I know how to behave myself with royalty." She tossed her braid to her back and turned from him.

He didn't look reassured as they rode back to their clans. She watched him give the men directions, and they fell in behind the royal forces.

"He's not much older than we are." Rebecca was still surprised that the King would know Edward, and yes, impressed.

"We hunted together at Traquair House in Ettrick Forest. We had much in common. Our fathers died within a few years of each other. Sharing our grief, we became friends. We also discussed ideas and dreams for our fair Scotland."

"You got along well, then?" Rebecca didn't hide her awe.

"Quite well, actually." Edward seemed to be gloating, just a little.

Rebecca fell silent, absorbing this. Riding a short way, the Royal clan selected a field to set up camp. They set to making fires and were given the fresh meat to cook. Edward and Rebecca ate with King James. The two friends talked.

"Sorry to hear about the deaths of Mary and the child. How terrible for you." King James ate the meat hungrily.

Edward's eyes got so large that Rebecca thought they would pop out of his head. "The child wasn't mine. The lady was hardly missed except by some other men of my clan."

"Aye, and I thought the lass was a bit free with herself."

King James looked at Rebecca; she refused to show her reaction. *Mary was unfaithful.* She began to understand Edward more. It's no wonder he reacted the way he did to her cousin. Their gazes met and Edward's dared her to speak.

"So . . . what brings Rebecca of Cavenaugh to your side?" King James turned at her.

"In truth, we were always meant to be together. However, we keep running into problems. First, my father's death and the clan's feud, and now Rebecca's marriage to Ruppert Kirkguard." Edward inched closer to her and put his arm around her protectively.

The contact warmed her heart and made her feel more secure with the daunting presence King James presented.

"The story has come to me. We would hear your version." Edward started to tell the story.

Rebecca interrupted. "Perhaps I should tell it . . . if I could?" Rebecca looked at Edward for his approval.

"Aye, that would be best." He nodded to King James.

"Tell it all, Rebecca, don't leave anything out. It may very well save your life." King James looked at her with such intensity that she felt as if she were on trial, and rightly so.

Rebecca told him everything. She watched Edward's reaction and felt him stiffen next to her as she told of the events before he entered her marriage chamber. The others around the fire looked away with discomfiture as she finished the story.

Edward continued with Duncan's betrayal of him, and explained the reason for their direction, this day.

"Well, Laird Edward. As it goes, we happen to be in need of

a place to restore ourselves after being on the road for many days. We'll help you get your castle in order, and you can give us some of your Scottish hospitality."

"Splendid idea. Lady Rebecca, would you get me some of your wonderful herbs? My arm is beginning to ache." Edward looked at her innocently.

Rebecca looked at Edward with suspicion, but did as he asked.

"I must tell you about Lady Rebecca's . . . zeal. She's always been interested in swordplay. Because of her sword training from childhood and into womanhood, she is fighting along with my men. At first it was not much to my liking. However, she can be very stubborn . . . when I finally did let her fight she earned my respect."

King James laughed heartily. "Lady Rebecca's celebrity precedes your explanation. She is an extraordinary woman. One who, knowing you as I do, suits you well."

"Aye, she does . . . very well."

When Rebecca returned, Edward shrugged his shirt from his shoulder. Unwrapping the bandage she looked at the wound closely. Preparing for the cleansing, she put water in a clay pot and placed it on the edge of the fire.

"Lady Rebecca, you're a woman of many talents." King James smiled at her.

"Thank you, Your Majesty. And you are a man of remarkable insight and plans for our fair land—as wild as it may be." She smiled back.

"Aye, and wild it is, m'lady." He grinned at Edward.

Just then Rebecca splashed his wound with water and cleansing herbs, knowing it would sting terribly. Edward took a deep breath in. She watched his knuckles turn white as he gripped his tartan, but knew he would not strike out in their present company. Rebecca gave him an impish smile that only his eyes could see. His features relaxed as she washed out the herb with warm water, and applied the salve.

After a good meal the armies assembled and rode on to MacCleary castle.

* * *

Rebecca spread her tartan on the ground next to their small fire. Sitting down, she watched Edward as he prepared to rest. The day's travel had brought them far. She'd spent most of the ride listening to Edward and King James talk. Now and then she joined the conversation.

Edward turned to her watchful gaze. "What?" His hands rested on his hips.

"What d'ye mean?" Rebecca wondered at his ire.

"Why're you looking at me with those big doe eyes?"

Edward's tone demanded an answer.

Rebecca spoke softly, hoping that Edward wouldn't actually hear her. "I didn't know Mary was unfaithful." But no such luck was with her. For one look at Edward told her that a storm brewed.

"That is none of your concern." Edward spoke in a fierce whisper, pointed at her, and narrowed his eyes.

"Ach, I do so *love* the sound of your brogue when you're angered." Rebecca stressed her own as she spoke. When he said nothing, her ire started to rise.

"Of course it's my concern. I wonder how Mary remained alive for that long—being unfaithful to you."

"You're on very dangerous ground, Rebecca Cavenaugh, and if you continue to speak of Mary, I will take you out into the woods and thrash you, our *love* be damned."

"Our love be *damned*?" Rebecca nearly screamed the words and moved away from Edward as she spoke. "Why don't you just do it out in front of His Royal Highness—to whom you're so eager to impress with your good manners?" She opened her mouth to say more as he caught her, clamped his hand over her mouth, and dragged her back to their fire.

"There's only one way to stop that beautiful mouth of yours." Edward gracefully forced her down onto the tartan, lying on top of her. He lowered his mouth onto hers without regard to her struggle and effectively stopped the words she tried to speak.

Rebecca struggled even more. Aware of the force of his

mouth bruising her lips and also aware of her own traitorous body responding to his kiss. She stopped her struggle and let him kiss her. His kiss grew gentle. When his lips left hers and he lifted his head to look at her, she aimed a slap at his face. The slap never made its target. Edward caught her wrist.

"Be glad that I stopped you. My patience is at an end. I'll tell you about Mary when I am ready to, and not before." The hand gripping her wrist tightened. "Agreed?"

"Agreed." Rebecca's body relaxed as he let go of her.

"Good night." Pulling his tartan over them, Edward rolled off her, his back forming a wall between them.

He sets a fire within me and then turns away? Rebecca had other plans. She moved her hands over his back, rubbing his muscles as Sarah had taught her to do for ailing backs.

"Mmmm, Rebecca, go to sleep. It's late—mmm—we need our strength."

She continued to rub his back, moving lower to his buttocks. The hard muscles under her hands further inflamed her passion. She pushed him onto his stomach and worked her way down each leg, her back causing the tartan to form a cozy tent above them. His sigh made her hopeful.

She rubbed between his legs to see if she was having the desired effect. Edward moved around on her so fast that she found herself underneath him in an instant, the quickening of his passion very apparent.

"Does that answer your question?" He kissed her, his hands exploring every part of her. With amazing skill, Edward made her clothes leave her body even as he caressed it. Edward's own clothes joined hers in a heap on the ground beside them.

"But Edward, what of our strength?" Rebecca's laugh came from deep within her. Her body thrilled to his touch.

She explored his body as he did hers, keeping apart from him as long as she could stand it. Then the coupling came swiftly and full of the fury that only their wild and passionate natures could bring. Moving together, he lifted her to the heights of ecstasy and together they plunged to the deepest depths of sleep.

Here's a special offer for
Romance Readers!
Get
4 FREE
Zebra
Splendor
Historical
Romance
Novels!
A
$19.96 value
absolutely
Free!
© ENNIS
Take a trip back in time and experience
the passion, adventure and excitement of a Splendor
Romance...delivered right to your doorstep!

Take advantage of this offer to enjoy Zebra's newest line of historical romance novels....Splendor Romances (formerly Lovegrams Historical Romances)- Take our introductory shipment of 4 romance novels -Absolutely Free! (a $19.96 value)

Now you'll be able to savor today's best romance novels without even leaving your home with our convenient and inexpensive home subscription service. Here's what you get for joining:

- 4 BRAND NEW bestselling Splendor Romances delivered to your doorstep every month
- 20% off every title (or almost $4.00 off) with your home subscription
- FREE home delivery
- A FREE monthly newsletter, *Zebra/Pinnacle Romance News* filled with author interviews, member benefits, book previews and more!
- No risks or obligations...you're free to cancel whenever you wish...no questions asked

To get started with your own home subscription, simply complete and return the card provided. You'll receive your FREE introductory shipment of 4 Splendor Romances and then you'll begin to receive monthly shipments of new Zebra Splendor titles. Each shipment will be yours to examine for 10 days and then if you decide to keep the books, you'll pay the preferred home subscriber's price of just $4.00 per title. That's $16 for all 4 books with FREE home delivery! And if you want us to stop sending books, just say the word...it's that simple.

4 Free BOOKS are waiting for you!
Just mail in the certificate below!

If the certificate is missing below, write to: Splendor Romances, Zebra Home Subscription Service, Inc., P.O. Box 5214, Clifton, New Jersey 07015-5214

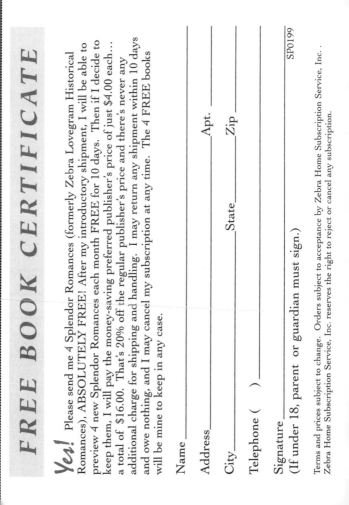

FREE BOOK CERTIFICATE

Yes! Please send me 4 Splendor Romances (formerly Zebra Lovegram Historical Romances), ABSOLUTELY FREE! After my introductory shipment, I will be able to preview 4 new Splendor Romances each month FREE for 10 days. Then if I decide to keep them, I will pay the money-saving preferred publisher's price of just $4.00 each... a total of $16.00. That's 20% off the regular publisher's price and there's never any additional charge for shipping and handling. I may return any shipment within 10 days and owe nothing, and I may cancel my subscription at any time. The 4 FREE books will be mine to keep in any case.

Name _____

Address _____ Apt. _____

City _____ State _____ Zip _____

Telephone ( ) _____

Signature _____ SP0199
(If under 18, parent or guardian must sign.)

Terms and prices subject to change. Orders subject to acceptance by Zebra Home Subscription Service, Inc. . Zebra Home Subscription Service, Inc. reserves the right to reject or cancel any subscription.

Awakened by the cold, Rebecca huddled closer to Edward. His arms surrounded her and his warm breath fell on the top of her head. The fire must have just burned out. She could smell the smoky essence of it as it lingering in the air. Then came the dreaded words.

"Time ta get up." Edward pushed her away and reached for their clothes. Throwing hers on her head, he laughed. "Get up. We have the royal army at our service."

Rebecca spoke through the clothes, "I told you we needed our strength." She rolled over, wrapping herself tighter in the tartan.

Edward, dressed in everything but his tartan and belts, pulled the tartan from her with a hard tug. Her clothes fell from her head and she hissed her protest as the cold morning air struck her nude body. Frantically she pulled her tartan around her. "Suppose King James comes looking for us?"

"Would serve you right, you should be dressed by now." Edward turned to put on his belts.

Rebecca mouthed his words silently behind his back as she quickly pulled on her clothing. As he turned, she smiled sweetly back. He picked up the belt that she used to hold her tartan on.

She could feel her smile fade as she remembered where she got the belt—Edward's chamber. She wrapped the tartan around her, and reached a hand out for the belt.

"Where did you get this belt?" Edward held it out of her reach.

"I borrowed it, and this sword, from a most generous and loving man." She hoped he recognized them as his own.

"Generous and loving? Is he also the most attractive man you know?" Edward smiled, putting her at ease as he handed her the belt.

"By far, there's no one else as comely." The sincerity of her statement melted even her own heart. She could feel it melting to her toes.

It seemed to be having the same effect on Edward. He gently wrapped the belt around her waist, up around her shoulder and around her waist again. He fastened it and took her in his arms, kissing her with a sweetness that made her senses swirl.

"And a sweeter lady he will never find." With one more quick kiss, he took her by the hand and rushed them to King James's fire.

A wonderful breakfast of fresh salmon and berries awaited them there. Rebecca savored the delicate taste of the fresh fish. She could not remember the last time anything had tasted so delicious. The day promised to be a good one. The sky already cleared of the mists and sparkled, pure blue. With the Royal Army behind them, they should have an easy time getting Edward's castle in order.

The men discussed how they would approach MacCleary castle. King James made suggestions but left the decision to Edward. He agreed with riding up and demanding entrance. If denied they would attack and penetrate. Once inside they would restore his chieftainship. Having no wish to kill his traitorous kin, he decided to banish the traitors.

King James worried about the bad humor floating about the highlands, but Edward would have it no other way. Rebecca admired the confidence he held in his decision.

Riding the front line beside King James and Rebecca, Edward considered his clan. He couldn't imagine so many of them turning from him to follow Duncan. He knew a few that might have but so many?

Edward breathed in the scent of the pine trees around them. This was the last stand of woods and they would skirt the mountain. He would never take such a force through the cave, even though it would be faster.

An overwhelming feeling of impatience twisted in his stomach. An impatience to be rid of Ruppert, Duncan, and war. An impatience to settle into a life with Rebecca. Although he knew that it would not be peaceful, he could feel glad that it certainly wouldn't be dull. For a life with Rebecca, he would be patient and make no mistakes with her life or his own.

Having her fight beside him was a mixture of good and bad. He knew where she was and could protect her. But would his protection be enough for them both? Yes, he would see that would be. His resolve made him more alert and gave him more endurance.

He glanced at Rebecca, she wrapped her tartan up around her head in a hooded fashion. He watched her knuckles whiten as she gripped her reins tightly. He could tell that she too grew restless.

Her head turned slowly. Inside her hood he saw a storm brewing and a frown frozen on her face. "Right under our noses the Kirkguard Clan twisted our lives against each other . . . all these years. Where would we have been if they hadn't done this?"

Edward watched Rebecca's anger crumple to sadness as tears streamed down her face. It's a good thing that she didn't know the truth of what Ruppert did to her mother.

"It's a waste of precious energy to ask that question. There's not a thing we can do to change the past. Dry your tears." Edward didn't let her see the compassion in his heart—instead he spoke sternly.

She looked at him as if he had just slapped her and turned her head away, drying her eyes on her tartan. That's how he treated his apprentices, while training. Apprentices who later failed to show up with the loyal men of the Clan MacCleary.

"You won't be worth a damn fighting with bad will and tears flowing all around you. Look at me when I'm talking to you."

Rebecca looked at him, the storm back on her face, but she didn't speak.

"Forget about the past. Use your wonderful stubborn nature to gain the future for us and our families." Edward smiled, and the returning smile from Rebecca had its usual devastating effect on him. He longed to hold her in his arms, and let her cry away her fears.

"You're right. I just have to let the past go. If only I knew about your past, then I could let it go all the easier."

The impudent look on Rebecca's face endeared her even more to him. She took advantage of every situation to gain what she wanted. Her mind was sharp she wouldn't put their lives in peril any more than he would. Edward looked away remaining silent.

Although he knew her hooded face still turned toward him, he didn't look at her as he explained. "Mary was a roll in the hay. She was fun, and of good lineage. I thought I had caused her to be with child and we married. It turned out that she had quite an appetite for a lot of different men in her bed. Then she told me the babe was not mine." Edward looked over at Rebecca. Her lips were a narrow strip, her eyes much the same.

"What did she look like?" Her words came as rough as gravel but carefully devoid of emotion.

"Rebecca, why . . ."

"I asked you a question. What did she look like?" Her face paled, her words tightened.

Edward sighed. "She had solid black hair, much like mine, but longer. A small build and a fair face."

Rebecca swung her head away from him and hid once again in the folds of her tartan.

"Of course . . . not nearly as fair as yours." Edward thought he might have heard a snort coming from the hood. He laughed, causing her hooded face to look at him again.

Her eyes looked like they wanted to pierce his soul.

He could feel his patience growing thin. "Do you enjoy torturing yourself with these petty things that should be left alone—and then grow angry at me? You're the one who asked the questions."

"Edward, these are not petty things. I remained true to our love regardless of the feud. For ten years!"

Now it was his turn to snort. "Oh, aye, and marrying Ruppert is what you call remaining true?"

"I had no choice!" Rebecca flung back at him. Their conversation grew loud, causing King James to look over with concern.

"When have you *ever* not had a choice? You could have run away. God knows you know how to do that. You could have come to me for help." Edward couldn't stand to look at her face as he spoke what his heart had asked so many times.

"I had no one to run to. Your clan wanted me dead. I couldn't run to you." Rebecca's face looked a little less certain. "Here we are arguing about the past. Didn't you just say we should forget it?"

"You're the one stirring it up."

"She died in childbirth?"

"Aye, I never touched her for being unfaithful, I didn't care . . . because I held no real love for her. But—her behavior dishonored me. Her death is painful for me to remember because of the rumors my people spoke. Many believed that I killed her. And I mourned the babe because of its innocence."

Rebecca had the decency to look ashamed. "I'm sorry to have brought up such painful memories."

"Ach, I guess you have a right to know. Now we can let it rest." Edward reached over and squeezed her hands on the reins. "Relax while you can."

She nodded, pushing the tartan from her head. The day was warming under the summer sun. The cloudless sky gave no relief from its glaring light. Land spread before them, snow capped mountains on all sides, grassy hills rising and falling under the horse's hooves.

Moisture hung in the air, the sweet smell of the grasses drifted to Edward's nose. His stomach growled with hunger. Reaching into his pouch he took out some dried meat.

Edward chewed the hard meat, taking drinks from his water between bites. He handed a piece to Rebecca. She shook her head. Still chewing his own he nudged her arm with the hand that held the meat. Reluctantly, she took it from his hand.

The sun sank lower and lower, toward the mountains.

"King James, may I suggest we either reach the castle before nightfall, or stop far enough away to rest for the night and reach the castle on the morrow?" Edward firmly hoped that the king would choose the first choice.

"We should pick up the pace."

"Good choice, Your Majesty." Edward grinned at his friend's understanding. The horses were set to a fast gallop over the hills. The people of the castle would hear them coming by evening meal.

Edward watched Rebecca's easy control of her mount. She and the horse seemed to move as one. Her hair lost its binding and flew behind her. Becoming uncomfortable in his saddle, he decided to think about something else.

What *had* become of his young apprentice? Edward tried to make his spirit a fighting one to no avail. He continued to be gutless. Even though he was young, he lacked the courage of other boys his age.

Soon, the horses breathed hard, their mouths foamed. King James motioned for them to slow. The castle could be seen in the distance. It looked forlorn and dark, even in the cloudless twilight. Edward's heart went out to his lost clan members, the hurt hardening him against what must be done. He glanced at Rebecca. *Is she crying again?*

"You might as well turn around and return to your castle." Edward's cold words sent a chill through the warm air. The look on Rebecca's face told him that his words affected her, as he wanted them to. She wildly wiped her eyes, mumbling oath upon oath to her own driveling emotions.

Edward laughed with good nature. She didn't smile, but neither did she strike out in anger.

"Your castle looks so lost . . . so dark and sad." Rebecca's gaze would not leave the image in the distance.

"I was thinking much the same."

Rebecca turned to look at Edward. Her eyes glistened with the moisture of the tears. In an attempt to shrug off her sadness she said, "What an exhilarating ride." Her spontaneous laughter sparkled through the air, causing more people to smile than just Edward.

Her laughter seemed to leave a feeling of impending good and success. *God, he loved this woman.* They got closer to the castle, as the sun got closer to the mountains. A trumpet sounded and people flooded the castle wall.

"King James, we are honored. Please enter." The caller from the wall wore MacCleary colors, but didn't look familiar to Edward.

"Rebecca, do you recognize that man?" Edward spoke softly to her.

"Aye, one of Ruppert's top men." Rebecca's voice seemed panicked.

Edward reached for his archer's bow.

"HOLD." King James's voice brooked no argument.

Edward winced, his rage just barely held in check.

They slowly entered the castle, each man tense and ready. Edward noticed a boy weaving his way through the men.

"Master, don't go any farther, it's a trap." Edward's young apprentice looked pale and scared as he walked beside him.

"Well, well . . . be glad I am mounted, or I would tear you to pieces." Edward aimed a half-hearted kick at the boy. He ducked from it.

"You don't understand. Our clan is being held here, against their will. Well, most of us. I'm serving as a spy, and so seem loyal to the Kirkguard Clan." The boy spoke in hushed tones and his gaze darted around.

He'd never lied to Edward before.

"What do they plan?" Edward gave him a serious look.

"They're surrounding the MacClearys in the courtyard. Leaving them without weapons. They will wait for you to gain entrance and attack from all sides. Above are archers, hiding behind the battlements. I've managed to supply some weapons to the MacClearys."

"Get yourself away from here. Your job is done—well done." Edward turned to reveal the plan to the men before they gained entrance.

Archers were assigned to each battlement. King James ordered them to hit the enemy archers before they could even release an arrow. The lines moved in on horseback looking innocent enough. They tried to surround Edward's captive clansmen. Greetings were murmured.

Edward's control nearly left him when he smelled the stench of dirt and filth in his castle's courtyard. The sight however, appeared worse than the smell.

When the last of their men entered, the enemy raged into

action. The royal archers did well to quell the enemy's bowmen. However, many arrows made it past them and skimmed through the air. They bounced off shields and armor, striking flesh here and there. Edward found many of them aimed his way. They bounced from his armor and shield, but all missed the mark.

Then the Kirkguards emerged from the outlying walkways with their weapons in hand. The combination of Stuart, Mac-Cleary, and Cavenaugh joined as one to fight and kill the Kirk-guard Clan that dared to take Edward's castle. Whenever Edward had a chance to glance at Rebecca he saw her fighting with a fury that only she could possess.

THIRTEEN

The fight raged on regardless of straining muscles and wounds, until the last Kirkguard fell. A sudden hush came over the courtyard. Edward rode his horse about wildly, checking all the corners to see that no one escaped. A man rode up to Edward.

"Laird Edward, Lady Rebecca left the castle wall in pursuit of an escaped Kirkguard."

Edward's oaths silenced the men around him as he reeled his horse quickly through the gate and stormed out of the castle. His mount carried him swiftly, and he whistled loudly just as she and her horse penetrated the woods.

He watched as Rebecca fought the horse to no avail. She rode up to Edward, shouting oaths at the animal.

"You miserable, traitorous, no-good horsemeat . . ."

Edward struggled not to laugh as she approached. Her ire turned from the horse to him.

"You let him get away." She sounded as if he'd broken her heart. Then she yelled in his face, "He'll flee and tell Ruppert . . ." Her horse bumped against his.

"Rebecca!" Edward gripped her shoulders and lifted her like a feather onto his saddle. He whispered in her ear, "Then, so be it." He punctuated his words with kisses.

Rebecca tried to slap him away and to dismount. "I almost had him. Edward!"

Edward's kisses turned to a growl. "Hush—sit still."

She stilled and sat rigid in front of him. He didn't have to see her face to know her nostrils flared. He urged the horses toward the castle. Once in the castle wall, they dismounted and set the horses out to graze. Without speaking, he led her into the great hall.

The tired men gathered there. Edward cringed with guilt as he saw the MacCleary men, half starved. The hall was littered with spoiled food and bones. He couldn't stand it.

He let out a yell that could freeze the blood of even the bravest warrior. Rebecca moved farther away from him, looking confused. Her eyes seemed to say that she wanted to comfort him. But he didn't want comforting, not even from Rebecca. He took up his bow and arrows and stalked out of the room.

"Where will he go?" King James spoke behind Rebecca.

"He'll hunt. We'll have a feast in the morn." Rebecca looked at King James. "The castle never looked like this while Edward ruled."

"I know. I'll join him with some men." King James bowed to take his leave.

"Thank you, Sire." She curtsied to him.

Rebecca looked around. Suddenly, her tired body turned to a lively mass of activity. She found the cleanest room to be a sitting room, far from the kitchen. Ordering fires to be set in the fireplaces, she instructed the men to bring the wounded there. If anyone questioned her, one look would usually quell him. If not, her loyal fighting companions did the rest.

Soon, all of the MacCleary women nursed the wounded. The men began to clear the courtyard of its Kirkguard stench and rubble. Left on her own, Rebecca walked into the dining hall and began to clear out the debris. Lighting a fire, she set to burning most of the rubble. Her stomach reeled at each new discovery.

A young man began to help her. She recognized the spy.

"Thank you, for your helpful information."

"You're most welcome, m'lady. You shouldn't be doing this work."

"I must do what must be done." Rebecca wiped her brow.

"I'm thinking more of what Laird Edward would think." The boy smiled sheepishly.

"You let me worry about that. Is he a good master to you?"

"Aye, though I never measured up to his satisfaction." He looked ashamed.

"You have now, lad." Rebecca smiled at him, as he swept a little more proudly.

She recognized one of Edward's elderly stewards as he went around lighting lanterns. She thanked him, having hardly noticed the dimming light. How she wished Sarah were here. She felt so alone. Rebecca emptied lilac oil into buckets of water. She threw bucket after bucket of the water onto the floor of the dining hall. Sweeping it toward the kitchen, she used the excess water to push the filth out the back kitchen door. She kept hearing a thump, thump. "What could that be?" Looking for the source of the noise she opened a storage cabinet and found Flossie tied and gagged.

"Oh, Flossie." Rebecca struggled to untie her. "I wondered why I hadn't seen you at my castle." She took the gag out of her mouth, and hurried to get her some water. Helping her drink, she watched the dear lady's face begin to relax. She led her to her room.

"My thanks, Rebecca. I'm glad you're home."

The sound of the word home sent a warm pleasant feeling through her. "You're welcome. Rest, and the morning will bring us happier times." Rebecca quietly left Flossie's chamber, closing the door behind her.

As she entered the kitchen a soft scent of lilac replaced the stench, and the fireplace no longer belched black smoke. She put a new log on the flames and hung a kettle of water over it. Finding a wet cloth she wiped the tables and chairs.

Searching her pouches, she found her favorite chicory herb. Putting the herb into a cup she poured some warm water over it.

With a sigh, Rebecca sat at the table and sipped her drink. Laying her head on her arm, she rested.

* * *

A sweet smell met Edward as he entered the hall. It reminded him of Rebecca. He smiled as the hall sparkled back at him. No doubt this was her doing.

He left the carcasses of the ducks, his hunting prizes, on a dining hall table. Rushing up the stairs, he noticed the hallway still lay in disarray. He stopped at Rebecca's chamber wondering if he should knock. Instead, he flung the door open to an empty room.

"Rebecca?" He walked out. Checking his own room, he found that empty too. Edward's blood pumped through his body, leaving a tingling as it traveled. *If anything happened to her.*

"Rebecca?" He made his way down to the dining hall. He entered the kitchen and found her, a tired heap, asleep with her head on the table and a cup spilled next to her. His heart nearly burst with relief, and pride.

Edward lifted her into his arms. She made a small noise and her arms curled around his neck. A smile played on her mouth, but her eyes remained closed. Flossie came out of her chamber with linen bedclothes.

"Ah, Laird Edward, I was just goin' to put these on the lass's bed." She bustled in front of him.

"Are you well?" Edward noticed her figure stood a little less robustly as he followed her.

"As well as can be. Your Lady rescued me from my bonds just before I would expire. I've had a good rest now. Did you bring us a good hunt?"

"Aye, Flossie, will you fix it for us?" He grinned at the answer he knew she would give.

"Oh, aye. Aye, we could all use the food. Those pigs never hunted and left our kitchen coffers empty, even hit the wine cellar." She walked into Rebecca's chamber.

Flossie ripped the old linen off the bed and replaced it as Edward held Rebecca.

"I'll get to the catch right away." Flossie bustled out of the room.

Edward nodded his thanks and looked down at Rebecca. She

watched him, and the grin on her face told him what was in her heart.

"My wild mountain man has returned." She breathed an exaggerated sigh.

Edward lowered his head to kiss her. Their lips met as he moved to set her onto the bed.

"Many thanks for ridding the castle of the stench." Edward stood, thinking that he would leave her to rest.

"Not so fast, Edward MacCleary." Rebecca grabbed his arms and pulled with all her might. He didn't budge.

"Good lord, woman, can't a man rest?" Edward grinned at her, knowing he would not deny her.

"Rest here m'lord. I'll not bother you." The twinkle in her eye told him otherwise.

"Ach, you still have your plaids and belts on. Is that any way for a lady to dress?" Edward bounced onto the bed beside her.

"No . . . you best take them off." Rebecca reached for his belt buckle as he undid hers.

He could feel his body coming alive and straining in his tight breeches. Rebecca's face took on a pink hue and her eyes brimmed with desire. Her lips, just slightly parted, seemed to beg him to kiss her. Abandoning the undressing, Edward grabbed her and cradled her head in his hands. He gave her lips what they asked for.

She moved under him, further inflaming his desire. Her hands found the top of his breeches and he moved his body so she could pull them off. She curved her fingers around his desire.

"Ah, Rebecca." Edward moved from her, unwrapping her from her clothing like a gift.

Her skin glowed in the firelight.

"Did you have a good hunt?"

"Not nearly as good as this one." He dipped his head and kissed each pink peak. Lifting his head he watched her again, his fingers circled her nipples. She closed her eyes, and leaned back against the bed, raising her lower body to his.

Edward slowly entered her. Written on her face was the pleasure of their joining. As her eyes opened he filled his arms with her. He rolled them over across the bed, ending up on top of her again. Then he moved gently within her, enjoying the moist silky feel.

"Never let me forget how fortunate I am to have a woman so full of life, so strong, so very bonny." Edward rolled them back across the bed again.

Rebecca laughed. "Aye, and I'll never forget how very honored I am to be loved by the chieftain of this fair castle." Rebecca knew just what he wanted to hear.

It felt good to have his castle back, to be home.

"But castle or no, I would still be wildly in love with this brute of a man." Rebecca moved under him creating glorious sensations.

Edward slowed their movements causing them both to cry out in the throes of passion. He denied her any fast movement. He melted into her. Their bodies, unable to stand a higher pleasure, reached the summit together. He could feel the waves ripple through her body like the swells of a pond after a leaf falls.

"I love you, Lady Rebecca of Cavenaugh." Edward rained kisses on her moist face, as their bodies still echoed their desire.

"I love you, Laird Edward MacCleary." Lying still, Edward watched Rebecca fall asleep in his arms, and closed his eyes.

Rebecca chatted happily as she and Edward walked down to midday meal. His clan must have risen early and cleaned the rest of the castle. Wonderful smells wafted up from the kitchen. Hungry MacCleary clan members crowded into the hall for the feast. King James sat at the opposite end of the main table.

"Good day, Your Majesty." Edward bowed his head.

Rebecca curtsied.

"Good day, Laird Edward. Lady Rebecca, you look stunning in a dress." The king grinned with mischief.

"My thanks, Your Majesty." Rebecca returned his grin. It did feel good to be free of a scratchy tartan.

As they walked to their table they nodded and wished people well. Everyone began to enjoy the meal. Edward caught up with all that happened while he was gone. His apprentice ate proudly beside him. Rebecca smiled at the boy and turned to see Edward looking at her.

"We should have some wine. Come with me to pick out some bottles." He took hold of Rebecca's hand and led her to a narrow stairway in the corner of the kitchen. Lighting a torch in the fireplace, he said, "Follow me." He walked down the stairs and she followed. The oath he spoke caused her to turn and walk back up the stairs. His hand grabbed her skirt.

"Rebecca, get back down here. I won't take my anger out on you. Those pigs nearly emptied my cellar. Ah, here are a few good bottles. Take this, and this." Edward handed her two bottles and carried a small wooden crate under his arm.

The air smelled dank. The cold bottles gave her a chill when they touched her skin. As she walked up the stairs in front of Edward, he grabbed her rump and laughed.

"You best watch yourself or I'll drop these bottles on your head." Rebecca joined his laughter.

The crowd grew merry as the wine flowed into their glasses. Joviality filled the air and toasts were made to their chieftain and his lady. Rebecca had never felt so happy.

After the meal, Edward took her to the gardens. They walked for a while without speaking. He stopped at a rosebush and picked a flower. Breaking off the thorns, he handed it to her. She raised it to her nose, breathing in its sweet scent.

"I wish I could hand life to you like that, without the thorns." Edward kissed the top of her head.

Rebecca's blood sang in her head. She nearly cried as the sweetness of his words sank into her senses.

"In a way, you are. I'm just helping to clear away the thorns." Rebecca hugged his arm as they continued to walk, and continued to hold the sweet smelling rose.

"Even the hedges are getting overgrown. I never realized just how hard my clan works every day to keep things as they should be." Edward reached up and broke a branch from the hedge.

"That's because you're working just as hard."

"Such kind words, m'lady." Edward held the branch picking off leaves as they walked.

Rebecca's eyes opened wide as she recognized the guard that came toward them. Before he delivered his message he sent her a most scathing look.

"Laird Edward, the Stuart clan found a Kirkguard spy lurking in the upper keep." He looked again at Rebecca. *He remembered.* Her throat dried. Rebecca smiled apologetically, but his look promised retribution.

Edward looked from Rebecca to the guard and laughed, he seemed to remember who he had left to guard her all those days ago.

"I believe you must owe this gentleman an apology." Edward demanded.

"Of course. I *am* so sorry, sir. Please forgive my rash behavior." Rebecca colored beneath the man's scrutiny. He didn't look satisfied.

"Just what did you do to the man?" Edward still held the branch, now leafless.

Rebecca eyed it nervously. "I . . . well . . . hit him on the head." She knew she'd pay for this one day.

"With what?" Edward's mouth twitched.

Was he trying not to laugh? "With . . . the bedpost. I hope you recovered all right, sir." Rebecca saw Edward's face turn red with anger? Or humor?

"Knocked you out did she? Don't feel bad, man, she's done worse to others. Would you like a swat at her with this?" Edward held the branch out to the guard.

"No . . . thank you, sir. Uh, King James would like to talk to you." The guard smiled widely.

"I'll go to him. Are ye sure? Last chance, you might wish you had . . . some day." They both laughed as Edward and Rebecca followed him.

Rebecca's face burned, and she swatted Edward's arm. His eyes widened and he released her from his arm and playfully swished the branch at her. She darted from it, biting her tongue so that the oaths on it would not be said.

Edward laughed, threw the branch away, and hugged her roughly to his side. He looked down at her smiling. Rebecca could not help but smile.

"Suppose he'd said aye?" She narrowed her eyes at him.

"T'would serve you right. Besides, he wouldn't have dared." Edward winked.

Rebecca stuck her tongue out at him. He pulled her around to face him and kissed her. She opened her mouth to his tongue and it played with hers sending luscious messages through her body.

He stopped kissing her and said, "That—is what you do with your tongue." Edward frowned when he saw King James waiting for him on the terrace. He sighed deeply.

Edward bowed and Rebecca curtsied as they joined King James.

"The Kirkguard has been thrown into your dungeon. I thought that we should send him back with the bodies of the dead Kirkguards, riding behind him in a wagon." King James looked to Edward for his approval.

"Aye, that seems a good idea. I would talk to him first. Excuse me, please." Bowing, Edward left their company.

"There's a lovely glow to your cheeks, Rebecca. Perhaps now would be a good time for me to get a taste of your dueling. Would you mind?" King James stood and offered her his hand.

"Not at all, Sire. It would be my pleasure. We could make the game sweeter by entering the maze at different ends and meeting in the center." Rebecca's sporting blood started to churn within her.

"Splendid idea. Swords?"

"They're in the middle." Rebecca led King James to the maze. His bodyguards followed, looking dubious.

Shortly after, they met in the core of the maze. Rebecca felt strange dueling with the King of Scotland. Especially with his bodyguards watching.

He moved on her first. Their swords swished through the air. His unique style gave her a few ideas of her own. She used her favorite move and surrounded his sword. But he countered, almost ridding her of her own blade.

"A move like that only works once. I heard the story of your duel with Edward. I expected that." King James breathed heavily as he spoke.

"Then I shall need a new move . . . like so?" Rebecca's breathless voice cheered as the king's sword flew through the air. She grew fearful as she noticed his frown and heard the guards gasp.

"You've found my greatest weakness. It nearly cost me my life—more than once." King James seemed to be more upset with himself then with her. He walked over and picked up the sword. "Try that again."

Rebecca moved her sword the same as before. King James's sword flew through the air again.

"Damn! Again." A look of great intent crossed his face.

They practiced the move over and over until the king no longer lost his sword.

"Rebecca, I am most grateful. The men who train with me see my displeasure and make it too easy . . . so I never learned to counter that move. Thank you." King James kissed her hand.

"You're most welcome. To be perfectly honest, I wasn't sure which to do myself." Rebecca removed her hand from his and went to put away her sword, becoming nervous with the intense look the king gave her. A lot of time had passed and she wondered what Edward would think of their absence. She had no wish to remind him of his late wife.

"You speak with such sincerity." He moved closer speaking in hushed tones.

Feeling uncomfortable Rebecca replied, "Let me put your sword away. We should get back." It wasn't that King James was not an attractive man. But she knew where her heart was, and there it would stay.

He gripped the arm that reached for his sword, and pulled her to him. Rebecca gritted her teeth and planned what she would do should he not listen to her words.

"I don't care if you are the King of Scotland, unhand me now or I'll do you bodily harm." She spoke low and with menace so as not to be misunderstood.

King James looked into her eyes as if to measure her sincerity. He released her, and put his sword away.

"And you would rather be a chieftain's lady, than a queen?" His voice seemed lighter than was warranted.

"Aye, without question. My heart is with Laird Edward." Rebecca looked at his eyes to gage her comeuppance for spurning a man of his station.

"I beg your pardon, m'lady. I have only been testing your sincerity. I've decided to pardon you for the crime of stabbing your husband. It's not in my power to annul the marriage, but I will speak to the church." King James put the sword away and reached for Rebecca's arm.

"I'm relieved." Rebecca laughed her relief and they walked out of the maze.

Looking out a castle window, Edward found himself, once again, catching Rebecca at mischief. Her hair mussed, she walked out of the maze arm in arm with King James. Colorful oaths sprang from his lips. His heart ached with a familiar pain, familiar, but far worse. He tasted bile in his mouth.

Irrational thinking clouded his reason. Snatching up his sword he made his way out of the castle and onto a grassy knoll. He labored away his anger with his sword, working it through the air and practicing all the moves he had ever learned. His arms ached with the effort, but he continued.

Rebecca looked up at the castle windows nervously. Testing her is well and good, but what of Edward? Thankfully, he was no where to be seen.

"Excuse me, King James." Rebecca stepped from his grasp and bowed.

"Certainly, I thank you again, you have given me a life saving skill."

"Good day." Rebecca curtsied and left hastily.

She walked into the kitchen and took a slab of bread on her way through.

"Flossie, have you seen Edward?" She tossed over her shoulder.

"Nay, m'lady."

Her day dwindled and there was so much she wanted to do. Walking past Edward's chamber she paused and knocked. No answer. Continuing to her own chamber she searched the wardrobe for her riding clothes.

She only found a split skirt. No . . . men's pants were really more comfortable. The ones she always wore did not seem to be there. She would have to speak to the seamstress and have some fitted to her before they rode out again.

She just had to have a good ride. Rebecca found herself in Edward's chamber, staring into his wardrobe. Grabbing a pair of worn breeches, she tried them on. Edward's waist was small for a man with such broad shoulders and height. The breeches fit. Although they were large in some areas they would do. Taking them, she walked back to her chamber.

Where is Edward? She hoped to get him into the woods today, and maybe take a swim, then maybe . . . Rebecca laughed at her own thoughts. Shutting the door, she found a large shirt to wear over the breeches. She tied the waist strings and also the leg bottoms. Remembering her last outing she took her sword, and made her way to the stable. Rebecca searched the castle and could not find Edward.

Growing impatient, she decided to go by herself. Reaching the stable she looked at the horses within. Wishing her favorite mount to rest for the next journey, she chose a beautiful black gelding she had not ridden yet. He looked tame enough. Rebecca slipped on a halter and saddled the large horse. Slowly she walked to the castle gates. No one could say she was sneaking out. She greeted everyone along the way and even asked after Edward.

Once outside the castle gate Rebecca mounted the horse. The gelding reared up. Her long practice in riding was the only thing that saved her from a bad fall. Calming words and strokes did the trick. The horse and rider were soon on their way.

The wind whistled in her ears. The fresh smell of the air set her mind on more carefree times. Then she saw him, wielding his sword fiercely through the air. What a vision he made with pure male strength and his body in perfect proportion. The sight had its usual effect on her. She rode toward him, reaching him quickly on the spirited horse.

"There you are, I've been looking for you." Rebecca tried to control the horse and keep a safe distance from his sword. Instead of stopping, as she thought he would, she saw a grimace on his face as he continued to swing the blade.

"Get away from me."

Rebecca noticed that his wound had begun to bleed under the pressure of his movements.

"Edward! Stop, your arm is bleeding again. Let me tend to it." Rebecca dismounted.

"Get back to the castle, and leave me be." Edward's face looked like pure rage.

She wondered what could be wrong. "Your arm!" Rebecca stepped back as Edward stopped the sword and advanced on her. His mouth clamped shut and his hand in a fist.

"Why are you out here?" He stopped in front of her.

"I came out for a ride. I looked for you to join me . . . Edward, what's wrong?" Fear crept into her when his anger didn't fade.

His eyes narrowed, he turned around, and walked toward the castle.

"Edward!" Rebecca mounted the horse and watched Edward's back as she rode away. He never looked back. She raged. A nagging fear at the back of her mind tried to surface, her anger would not let her listen to it.

Instead she rode out blindly her anger spurring her on. She didn't care where she went. The nagging fear surfaced like a stench from a boggy moor. He had seen her leaving the maze with King James and imagined the worst. *How dare he think that she would betray him*. Now it was Rebecca who didn't know what to do with her rage.

Yes, she did know what to do. Riding back to the castle she gathered items from the kitchen. She would leave, clear her mind, and decide whether to return to Edward's or her own castle. She went to her chamber and took her MacCleary tartan—after all she had fought for them—and a few other pieces of clothing.

Rebecca's heart quickened with her newfound freedom. Her life was in her own hands. She would ride the gelding. It seemed too untamed to be trained to answer to Edward's whistle. Taking all the back stairways and halls she slipped from the castle without being seen.

FOURTEEN

The weather had turned cold and the sun dim by the time Rebecca reached the cave. She fashioned a peat torch on a stick. Pulling a flintstone out of her pouch, she struck it against her sword. Little sparks leapt onto the dried peat, causing it to smolder into flames.

Bringing the horse with her, she entered the dark cave. The torch held out in front of her did little to quell the shivering of her body. The hairs on the back of her neck rose. She wasn't used to being in the cave alone.

The horse gave no sign of fear as she led it to the stream that ran through the cave. She tethered the reins to a large stone. Finding an abandoned peat torch, she lit it and left both torches wedged between rocks on the cavern wall.

Walking out of the cave, Rebecca gathered as much dried peat as she could find and brought it back inside. Carefully, she took a torch and made her way to the same chamber they had lit a fire in—last time—last time seemed a long time ago. She put it from her mind the best she could and hoped Edward felt half as bad as she did.

The empty ache inside her wouldn't stop, but she refused to cry. *In time it will go away.* She laid peat on the wood already in the fire pit, and lit it with the torch. The heat on her face felt good.

Picking up a stone, she threw it as hard as she could toward the part of the cave where she first discovered how real love felt.

Edward slammed around the castle. As he entered the kitchen, Flossie looked up.

"I found some supplies gone from the kitchen. Are you riding out?" She seemed to be standing taller, just daring him to get his ire up at her.

"No . . . what's gone?" Edward tore off a piece of fresh baked bread from the table and put it in his mouth. His heart ached as he thought of Rebecca's hurt face. How could she not know what was wrong with him?

"Edward, are you listenin'?" Flossie's hands rested on her hips.

"What?"

"I said, A loaf of bread, flour, herbs, dried mutton, and some vegetables." Flossie looked confused.

"Where *is* Rebecca?"

"Why, I saw her leave the kitchen as I entered, saying she needed rest and would retire early. She had a bottle of wine in her hand, as I remember. She did seem in a rush."

Edward nodded and made his way up the back stairs. She probably planned on spending the night drinking with King James, who also could not be found.

Feeling the heat rising again in his blood, he stormed into Rebecca's chamber. Empty. Looking around Edward noticed her sword was gone, as were her—*his* MacCleary tartan and belts. *So—they ran off together.* Edward's emotions turned cold. He needed to get away from this place . . . the memories.

King James stood in the open doorway, looking at him. "Edward, you're an easy man to track. I just listen for some slamming around and there you are. Are you ailing?"

"How dare you come to me as if nothing is amiss! Did you wish to shame me further with your confession?" Edward's senses told him not to anger a king. To hell with that, see if

King James could take his lady and not feel the sting. He reached for his sword and walked toward him.

Awareness dawned on the king's face. "Edward!" He stepped back, putting his hands up and shaking is head. "If this is about Rebecca, you're greatly mistaken. She merely fenced with me and helped me to work out a great flaw of mine.

"I admit to walking out of the maze with her feeling friendly . . . my word, we shamed you not." King James's teeth clenched together and his eyes narrowed. He took out his sword and started the attack toward Edward. His face pure rage, he fought with stinging blows.

Taken aback, Edward said, "What say ye?" He breathed heavily, fending off the king's angry blows.

"In truth, dear friend. I tested her with a marriage proposal, as we once discussed we would do for one another. I also pardoned her crime." The flat of King James's blade hit Edward's hip.

He'd forgotten that agreement. Edward stepped back to stop the duel. "What did she answer, yea or nay?"

The king wouldn't stop. Edward didn't return the blow, but he continued to defend himself.

"She said nay, ye big oaf." King James grimaced and smiled. " 'Twas a sting to my pride. Turning down a handsome man such as I—and being queen! Imagine, all for a sot of a man like you." He laughed and put his sword point down on the stone floor with a clank.

"Nay, oh my God. I thought . . ." Edward's sword hit the floor and he paced. "I beg your pardon, Your Majesty." He had to smile as King James continued to laugh.

Thankfully, none of the king's bodyguards were present or Edward would have had to pay more dearly. King James's face softened and he forgave Edward with a shrug. Edward explained his concern for Rebecca and King James agreed to watch over the castle so he could ride off to find her.

Edward walked to the stables. As he saddled his horse he thought about his friend's advice to be easy with Rebecca. King James knew him better than he realized. His ire was already rising at the thought of her taking off on her own. What could she have been thinking? Had she guessed? Mounting the horse he galloped toward the cave.

Rebecca sucked on the wine bottle until it was empty. Throwing it at the wall of the cave, she listened to the crash it made with great satisfaction. The action helped her get rid of her anger.

Lying down, she tried to sleep. Instead, her mind played over each intimate moment she had shared with Edward. Why must she torture herself? She stood and wrapped the tartan around her shoulders, took a torch, and walked to the chamber in the cavern in which she'd lost her innocence.

Staring at the empty place, she likened it to her heart. A sudden sound from the cave entrance made her jump. Just as suddenly, she realized that her sword lay in the other chamber. Her stomach clenched tightly and her hands shook as she put the torch down.

In the darkness she made her way toward her sword. Her legs wobbled as she tried to walk through the dark cave without stumbling. A large man stood by the fire, his face hidden in a black cape and masked with a scarf.

Backing up, she realized she could not escape—but she had to try. The man caught her from behind as she tried to reach her horse. He dragged her to the fire's edge, forcing her onto the ground and holding her arms down at her sides.

"Let me go!" Rebecca kicked at the man, his knees came down on her legs to stop them. She struggled, her curses filling the air. The intruder lifted the scarf from his mouth and lowered his lips onto hers. She was about to bite his lip when the familiar scent and taste of the man struck her like a blow. She pushed away. "EDWARD!"

Laughing, he let her go and pulled the disguise away from his face. Rebecca saw red. She slapped his face as hard as she could. He stopped laughing as she railed at him with colorful words.

"Shhh, Rebecca. Enough!" He took her by the shoulders and shook her.

She stared up at his face, her hand print still apparent on his cheek.

"I'll amend to you, I let my past get in the way of my good judgment . . ." Edward rubbed his cheek, looking annoyed.

"You scared the life out of me. You made me cry for hours. You think I'm like Mary!" She slapped his other cheek.

Edward looked surprised and sat back on his heels. His eyes pleading. "Please, Rebecca, try to understand—you're my life." He looked to be bracing himself for another slap. He pointed a warning finger at her.

Rebecca laughed, a little out of control. She stood and wove her way to the other side of the cavern. "Of course I understand. But did you have to come up on me like that?" She turned to him.

"I wanted to teach you a lesson, since you saw fit to take off on your own—again."

"Hah! And who got the lesson?"

Edward got to his feet and walked over to her. Looking at the broken bottle pieces on the floor, he said, "You're drunk."

"No."

"Don't lie to me, Rebecca Cavenaugh, you're drunk." He picked her up, "Don't worry, I'll take care of you." He smiled wickedly.

"Take advantage of me, you mean." She wiggled to get out of his grasp.

"Oh . . . don't worry, you won't mind." He sat her on a smooth stone. Picking up the tartan, he put some hay down and placed the tartan on the soft bed it made. He lifted her again and showered light kisses on her neck as he lowered her onto the tartan. He looked over at the broken bottle again. "I'm glad I didn't arrive earlier."

Rebecca's mind swirled around her. She smiled at the sensations Edward awoke in her. The emptiness was gone.

He rose and started to remove his clothing, all the while staring at her with a smoldering intensity. She could feel her passion rising as if he were touching her where his eyes gazed. Her breathing got faster. She watched his magnificent body as it slowly appeared from beneath his clothing.

The cavern filled with his wonderful male scent, it mingled with her own. She started to feel a little dizzy, the effects of the wine diminishing. Edward reached into his pouch and brought out a fresh skin of wine. With a smile, he pulled out the cork with his teeth.

He handed her the wineskin, and as she drank he started to undo her shirt buttons. She continued to drink.

"All right, that's enough." He reached for the wine. Taking it from her, he drank from it for a long time.

Rebecca laughed and grabbed him in a very private area, causing the wineskin to leave his mouth. Wine spilled onto his body. She looked at where it landed on his skin and knew what she must do.

"Rebecca . . . Ah . . ." Edward's eyes closed as she kissed and licked the wine from him.

A sound down the cave stopped her movement. They both sat up, listening. They heard whistling in the distance.

"Ach . . . that would be Nathaniel with news of Cavenaugh castle."

Rebecca screeched as she fumbled to button her shirt. Her wine-laden mind wouldn't let her move fast enough. Colorful oaths escaped her lips. Edward, already dressed, tried to help her as the whistling got nearer.

"Hold still. Here . . ." Edward's laughter didn't help Rebecca's struggle as the buttons went into the wrong holes. "I'll go meet him—finish dressing." He kissed her cheek and taking a torch, walked down the cave passage.

"Edward! What a surprise." Nathaniel clapped him on the back.

"Aye . . . a surprise." Edward tried to smile.

"What're you doin' here?" Nathaniel tried to walk past him.

Edward blocked the way. "It's a long story, I'll tell you later. Rebecca is . . ." Edward waved his hand toward the cavern.

"Ah ha, that's what you're doin'." Nathan grinned. "Sorry, old boy."

"She should be dressed by now."

They found Rebecca sprawled out on the tartan, fast asleep.

"She had a little too much wine." Edward motioned for him to sit.

"Oh, ho!" Nathan ducked from Edward's fist and changed the subject. "We survived another attack, but lost a few good men. Rebecca's cousin, and his father." Nathan kept his voice low.

Feeling grief for Rebecca, Edward's shoulders drooped. She would feel responsible. "How weak are the forces now?"

"It doesn't look good, Edward. I came to get more men . . . I only hope we make it back before the castle is lost. The MacCleary families wanted to return. I wouldn't let them without an army to see they arrived safely. The Kirkguard Clan would cut them down. I tell you they have no principles."

"Aye, I know. I'll wake Rebecca, we should leave for the MacCleary castle right away." Edward moved toward the sleeping Rebecca.

"Can Rebecca travel in her condition?"

"She'll have to. Did you hear about our illustrious guests?" Edward knelt by Rebecca, gazing down at her peaceful face. He hated to wake her and hand her thorns . . . instead of a sweet rose.

"No, who?"

"King James, and his royal army."

"Hah! Tell me another!"

"I tell you true! They helped us rid the castle of the Kirkguards. He even pardoned Rebecca." Edward watched Rebecca as she stirred, a frown playing on her lips.

"Wake up, love." Edward smoothed her hair from her face. She opened her eyes. "Can't you leave me be . . . for a bit?"

"No, we must leave." Edward made his voice sound stern—but his heart ached for her.

Rebecca's eyes opened wider. "What happened?" Sitting up she gripped his arms. "Tell me!"

"I'll tell her, Edward, 'twas my message to carry."

Rebecca's face turned white. She released Edward's arm and rose. Nathan stood to face her. Edward moved away from the two, turning his back to them. He heard the words from Nathan and the sob from Rebecca.

"I have brought grief upon my family. My father and mother . . . ?"

Edward turned to see tears streaming down her face.

"They're well. But Rebecca, unless you're the one who led the Kirkguard Clan on this raid, you can hardly say you've brought this about." Nathan watched Edward as he walked over to her.

"This is all a consequence of that fateful wedding night." Rebecca paced back and forth.

Stopping her, Edward leaned down and spoke close to her face.

"This all stems from my father's death. The Kirkguard Clan is to blame, not you."

Rebecca collapsed toward him. He wrapped his arms around her and thought about what usually followed her tears . . . rage.

As if she knew his thoughts, Rebecca pushed away from him and gathered her belongings. Shaking the tartan clean she wrapped it around her and strapped it on.

"I'll leave for the Cavenaugh castle. My family needs me." Turning to Edward, her eyes wild, she continued, "Don't even think about stopping me."

"Rebecca, take a deep breath, and think about this. We need to go back to MacCleary castle and gather the armies. Don't lose your edge with grief, or be careless with your life. It's not your own to be careless with. I hold it as dear as you do. Come back with us. Then we'll head out together."

"You take a deep breath yourself. It *is* my life and I will do what I must." Rebecca turned from him and walked toward her horse.

He heard a sharp intake of breath from Nathaniel, who

seemed to be the only one taking good advice. Edward followed her, his blood nearly curdling with the heat of his building ire. Still, he remained calm.

Rebecca turned to look at him as she reached her horse. "If you have any understanding of me at all, you'll not stop me. And if you do, I'll rethink how worthy of my love you are." She mounted her horse.

He raised his hand to catch her, stopped, and thought about her words. "Leave, m'lady and I would not want such a rash woman being responsible for my family—or my heart." He turned from her, not believing his own words. Not believing he didn't just haul her off the horse.

Nathan seemed to feel the same. He stood with his mouth gaping. Edward turned to see Rebecca weighing his words. Time seemed to stand still as they looked into each other's eyes in the dim torchlight.

The rising color in her face told him of her anger as she turned the horse toward the cave opening. She ducked so she would not hit her head as she wheeled out of the cave.

"Headed in the wrong direction, isn't she?" Nathan's voice sounded full of humor.

"I'm finished with women. I'll not give a damn. Let her get killed. I'll not give in to her whims." Edward kicked out the peat fire and led his horse from the cave.

Nathan followed behind him. As Edward emerged, he looked around to see if Rebecca was still in sight. He didn't see her. Mounting his horse with a loud curse, he turned in the direction of Cavenaugh castle.

"I'll have to teach her to be reasonable," he vowed to Nathan. "Go on without me. I'll return to the castle—with Rebecca." He followed her horse's hoof prints in the dim light.

His attention to the ground ended abruptly when he looked up to see Rebecca barreling toward him. She turned her horse carelessly into the woods to prevent a collision. He watched helplessly as she flew off her horse, crashing to the ground.

"Rebecca!" He stopped his horse, jumped off, and ran over

to her. She yelped in pain. A prickly bush had broken her fall. Her horse stood beside her, looking sheepish.

"Ah, justice is served." Edward tried not to laugh with the relief that she had not suffered a mortal injury. "Isn't this the same wee lass that tricked me into the brambles, so long ago?"

The words springing from her mouth assaulted his ears.

Swiftly, he responded to her scoffing. He grabbed her up out of the bramble and threw her over her horse's saddle, her briar-filled rump in the air. With great relish, he proceeded to pull each thorn from her. Although she remained silent, he carefully guarded his jewels from her feet as they kicked.

"Good you had on this thick tartan."

When he finished, Rebecca slid herself from the saddle to face him. "This is what I get for returning to do your bidding?"

"Noh, this is what you get for sinning against me in the past." Edward's laughter sang out into the woods.

Rebecca turned to mount her horse. Catching her up against him, he turned her to face him. He stopped laughing long enough to plant a kiss on her stiff angry lips. She made a sound of annoyance, twisted from his grip, and mounted her horse.

He watched her proud form with great admiration. Mounting his horse he followed her toward the MacCleary castle. They traveled quickly through the woods and into the open hills.

Riding up beside her, he said, "I'm glad you changed your mind, Rebecca."

She looked over at him. "I'm glad I did too. I'm sure I would have suffered your wrath if I hadn't." Rebecca wiggled in the saddle. "Damn brambles. Weren't you getting a bit careless running your horse through the woods, gazing at the ground?"

"Aye, I was, and I promised myself I wouldn't be. You bring out the very worst in me, my love . . . the worst, and the best."

Suddenly Rebecca seemed worlds away. Her eyes grew moist, glistening with unshed tears. Edward left her with her thoughts as they rode on.

* * *

The pain of the brambles dimmed to the pain in Rebecca's heart. Rowan. Rowan, who cared little for battle and killing. Rowan, who lived for the time he could spend painting—putting to canvas all his feelings and skill. She could feel her heart lurch inside her chest, as if it shifted at the loss of him. He told her to run away before the wedding. He told her to run to Edward.

Rebecca's mind floated over fond memories of her cousin. They gave her pleasant thoughts that, for the time, helped her to push away her grief. Rowan's father, too, had been an important part of her life. He doted on how she embraced life, and taught her many of her sword fighting skills. The lump in her throat worked its way to her eyes as hot tears ran down her cheeks.

She glanced over at Edward and quickly wiped her tears away, but new tears kept coming.

"Go ahead and cry, Rebecca. You have more than enough cause. Should we stop?" Edward's face looked soft with concern, and his eyes glistened with a wet brightness.

Rebecca shook her head. She would not stop until Ruppert and his clan could feel the wrath of her sword. With the castle in view Rebecca prodded her horse to a fast gallop. The cold air soothed her hot, tearful face. The wind dried her tears.

She looked over at Edward galloping beside her. Were those tears streaming from his eyes? Her love grew stronger at the sight of this great Highland laird, tearful for her. They would survive. And they would survive together.

Nathan met them at the gates of the castle. "The army will be ready to move in an hour. The women have put together a meal that will send us on the road with full bellies. I suggest you eat. We don't know when our next meal will be."

The dining hall, loud and teeming with people, seemed strange for this time of day. Every MacCleary woman served steaming food to the masses of men. She excused herself to help.

Edward stopped her. "Your duties will come soon enough. Sit and eat."

"I'll just check on Flossie, she'll be running . . ."

"Sit down, Rebecca." Edward's soft whisper spoke volumes. She sat down realizing just how spent she was from the gallop home. Home? Yes, that feeling was right. Edward's castle felt like home to her.

"Wouldn't it be nice to leave the MacCleary castle in your hands?" Edward looked at Rebecca as he chewed.

"Not on your life. Don't start this old fight again, Edward. You've seen that I'm capable of surviving a battle." Rebecca felt her heart quicken. "You should stay at the castle if you're concerned about it."

"You know that's not what I want." Edward's face colored.

"You also know what I want. This is my battle. I would never forgive you if you did anything to keep me from it." Rebecca turned to her food, hoping her words would make an impression. She could feel Edward's brooding, as he remained silent beside her. Not daring to look at him, She gazed straight ahead.

"How can I get used to your ways when the ways I learned as a lad say that women just don't do this? Not gentlewomen. Don't you know that if anything happened to you I would not be able to live with the guilt." Whispered fiercely, his words sounded like a hissing snake. Appropriately so, for it made her feel betrayed.

"I thought you believed in me, Edward. I thought you understood my feelings. Have you just been indulging my whims? I assure you, this is no whim." Rebecca's voice hissed back matching his own.

Edward's mouth clamped shut.

"My Laird, a word with you please?" A royal guard approached them. Edward nodded and led the guard to a deserted room.

Rebecca quickly left the table.

Edward watched the guard pace nervously in front of him.

"If you'll remember, I delivered a message to your father the day before he died. I wasn't supposed to, but I stayed just inside the castle that night. Weary, I slept beside the main gate."

"I woke to hear a woman's voice. From the shadows I saw the back of her as she let a man in and led him through the courtyard. I didn't think much of it, at the time. After I returned to my home, I heard of your father's murder." The guard looked ready to flee.

"Why didn't you tell anyone?" Edward weighed his words carefully.

"I was too far away by the time I heard what happened. I feared being taken to task for not following orders."

"Did you recognize the woman?"

"Not until tonight, which is the reason I mention this at all. The woman, sir, was Lady Rebecca."

Edward staggered backward as if the words assaulted him. "You must be mistaken."

"No, 'twas her, I swear. I must be going, my laird. My apologies for not telling you sooner." The guard bowed and left the room quickly.

Edward's mind crowded with confused thoughts. But one thought continued to rise above the rest bringing him comfort. Rebecca could not be the woman who let the murderer in. There had to be some explanation. He would find her and it would be solved.

Walking to the dining hall, Edward noticed the guard leaving the castle. His thoughts warred. He wanted to talk to the man more. He wanted to question Rebecca. Torn between the two, he decided to go to Rebecca. She was gone.

Edward checked the kitchen and ran up the steps from the kitchen, two at a time. *She's gone!* Immediately he sent up an alarm. Men scattered, combing the castle, the stables, the passage, and the gates. No Rebecca.

Edward's heart turned to a piece of cold steel. His thoughts tempered it into a sword with their heat and hammered away such a worthless feeling as love. He packed the rest of his gear and went to the stables.

Nathaniel came into the stable as Edward tied the last of his pack onto his horse.

"Why did Rebecca take off again?" Nathaniel looked into Edward's eyes, and seemed to shudder.

"How the hell do I know?" Edward stamped away leading his horse outside.

"You do know, now tell me!" Nathan yelled back at him.

"Edward, I haven't seen that look in your eyes since yer father died. Tell me!" Nathan blocked his path.

Edward nearly spat the words at his cousin's face. "It seems a witness has finally appeared. He told me that it was Rebecca he saw letting a man into the castle that fateful night." Edward winced at his own words.

"And you believed him?" Nathan matched his ire.

"No, I didn't. He only saw the back of her. I went to find Rebecca, to ask her. I found her gone. She must have recognized the guard, and ran." Edward wiped the sticky sweat from his forehead. A tremendous feeling of loss weighed on his shoulders. The same feeling he'd lived with for ten long years. The same . . . but *much* worse. The incessant pounding of his heart sounded in his ears again—still tempering the sword.

"Edward, think about this. You know Rebecca, can you honestly think her the cause of your father's death?" Nathan held both his shoulders, and looked like he wanted to shake him.

Edward jerked away from his grip. "I know how deceptive and cunning women are. *That* is what I know."

"You can't judge Rebecca by Mary's standards."

"I can, and I will." Edward walked out into the still air. The light scent of rain filled his nose. *Good, rain was what he needed.*

"All right, Edward. Just do one thing for me and for your clan. Don't tell anyone about this. Don't start the feud again. I think King James would agree."

"Aye. I'll deal with it on my own." Edward yearned for a strong drink. He walked away from Nathan, not missing the sad shaking of his head.

FIFTEEN

Uncertainty gnawed at Rebecca's stomach. Had she done the right thing? Edward might have tried to stop her. She couldn't take the chance. She wouldn't be left behind to worry about her loved ones. She had to do her part.

The hills yawned before her, wide open and vulnerable. The distant light of the morning sun threatened to disappear under looming black clouds. The woods to her left looked far more inviting. She urged her horse toward the cool stillness of the peaceful forest. The shadows of the trees swallowed her.

Again, uncertainty urged her to return to the castle, and go with the army. "Nay. I will not." She said a prayer for all to be well.

Finding a narrow path in the woods she kicked her legs to prod the black horse on. Her heart ached, already missing Edward. His words echoed back to her, "Leave, m'lady and I would not want such a rash woman being responsible for my family—or my heart."

She groaned out loud. Understand her or not, he could do as he pleased. Why was she so worried about it? It wasn't as if she couldn't live without him. Of course not. Of course not . . .

The thunder of horse's hooves interrupted her thoughts. She stopped her horse and peered through the foliage. From her vantage point she watched the Kirkguard colors blur past her. Her blood ran cold and she snapped to attention. Swinging her horse around she kicked its flanks. How could she reach the castle before the army? She raced through the trees, trying to keep pace with the Kirkguards.

With one last crack of a branch her horse leapt free of the woods. Her eyes narrowed to judge the direction of the enemy. Black clouds chose that moment to hide the rising sun. She shivered. Her skin crawled at the thought of Ruppert. Glancing down at the ground, she slowed to find the fresh hoof prints her horse had made. They marked her direct route from the MacCleary castle.

Relief flooded her senses. She could do it. The Kirkguards rode a little too far to the west on an indirect path toward the castle. If she took a more direct route, she could make it there before the enemy. But, would they see her? She would have to try.

Spurring the horse faster, Rebecca left the woods. She glanced at an enormous black cloud and could smell the rain just before the cloudburst sent down a stormy torrent. The deluge pelted her eyes, blinding her. She urged the horse on. Trusting her mount's homing instincts, she loosened the reins and hugged the horse's neck.

"Come on—you can do it—easy." She spoke soothing words close to the animal's ear.

Closing her eyes against the sharp sting of the rain, she listened to the hooves hitting the ground. The slick ground caused the horse to slip. She gripped tighter to hold herself onto the saddle. "Easy, boy, easy." She didn't have to urge the animal to run.

Although the deafening sound of the rain continued, it no longer pelted her. Opening her eyes she realized that she'd made it to the shelter of the castle wall. Edward walked from the shadows with two guards, his face dark and foreboding. She faced his rage.

Water streamed down her body from her wet hair and tartan as she tried to catch her breath to speak. "The Kirkguards!" Another breath—, "They're coming."

"Take her." Edward's words cut her to the depth of her soul. The men hauled her from the horse.

"Edward? What . . ." Rebecca used the rest of her strength to try to free herself from the men. They held her arms with bruising strength.

"Take her to the dungeon." Edward turned from her and walked away.

"Edward!" As if in a dream, Rebecca heard her voice screaming his name, over and over again. It echoed through the courtyard.

Edward closed his heart to the sound of Rebecca's screams. He strode away to instruct his waiting army.

Nathaniel approached Edward matching his pace. "You must be daft from lack of sleep. Can't ye see that Rebecca came to warn us? Nearly killing herself to get here. And you still believe her deceitful?" Nathan pushed Edward. "Get her out of that dungeon—now!" He pushed him again.

Edward turned to Nathan's red face. "No, there's no time to discuss it. Get the men ready!" When Nathan didn't move Edward swung his fist toward him.

Nathan ducked from the blow, and continued, "Get her out, now man, or I'll do it meself." Spittle flew from his mouth.

Edward had never seen him this angry. "You get her out and I'll banish you for treason." His blood rushed in his ears as madly as the rain rushed to the ground. "She'll be safer in there." Edward swung away but turned back to warn Nathan. "If you let her out and she dies, I'll kill you. Cousin or no."

Nathan followed behind him. "Maybe there's a grain of sense in that."

Edward led the way to the stables. Most of the men, already mounted, waited for their chieftain. They stormed out to surprise the Kirkguard army.

The MacCleary clan hid beside the walls. His clan easily surrounded and defeated the enemy. The royal army took care of any Kirkguards that managed to make it to the castle.

* * *

Dim light flickered from a torch outside her cell. Rebecca struggled with every stone that appeared loose, trying to find a way to open the passage. None would move. She finally collapsed in tears. Her sodden body shivered on the icy stone floor. Her sobs echoed back to her.

"Child . . . lass . . . here, take these dry clothes." Flossie peered at her through the dim light. Her arm reached through the bars, holding out the clothing.

Rebecca jumped up and ran over to Flossie, she gripped her arm. "Flossie! Let me out!"

Flossie pulled away from her, dropping the clothes onto the floor. "Nay." She walked away.

Rebecca stopped the harsh words before they left her lips. She shouldn't have asked. Flossie would never disobey Edward. Taking off her wet clothes, she listened to them as they sloshed to the floor. She put on the dry shirt and tartan skirt. Groping through her wet tartan, she removed her herbal bag and tied it inside the skirt. The MacCleary colors seemed to taunt her. She huddled into a corner of the dungeon.

The warmth of the dry clothing lulled her to sleep. A deep sleep. She dreamed about her childhood.

Running carefree and happy through her favorite meadow. She nibbled on sweet berries and picked wildflowers. A young Rowan walked toward her.

"When are you ever going to learn? Rebecca, listen to me. I know of what I speak."

She threw the flowers at his face and ran away.

Laughing at her flippant ways, he caught her arm and held her, becoming serious. "Think about it. I told you to leave before the wedding could take place. I told you to go to Edward. Wasn't I right?"

Confused, she struggled to continue her carefree play. It wasn't like Rowan to hold her so roughly. His face darkened.

"You must be careful of your love, now. He could destroy you. His eyes are clouded by false feelings. Look for someone who has your image. She will hold the answer."

Rowan's body seemed to float off into thin air.

"Rowan, come back. What do you mean? What answer? Rowan!" Rebecca woke screaming out Rowan's name. Her heart pounding, she ran to the bars. She yelled for Flossie. She yelled for Edward. She remembered the battle.

Her face heated. She would lose her mind thinking of Edward fighting without her. He would pay for doing this to her. Throwing her in the dungeon like a—her heart froze at the thought of his cold stare. Pulling stones again, she finally found the trigger and pushed forcefully against the wall with her body. A loud creaking announced the opening of the passage door. Taking the torch from the wall, she entered the passage and closed the door.

Walking through the darkness, she tried to get her bearings. She followed the passage, all the while thinking of a way to upturn the stone over the opening. A patch of daylight signaled the end of the passage. The stone had already been rolled away. She put the torch down, stamping out its flame.

Climbing the passage wall, she could smell the damp earth. She tried to grip the side of the tunnel, slipping and shouting oaths until she emerged from the passage. Brushing the dirt from her hands, she stood, and looked up to see Edward leaning against the stone wall of the castle. His battle-streaked face wore a look of satisfaction.

She approached him like a spitting cat, her nails out and more than ready to rake at his smugness.

"Easy, lass. Don't you want to hear about the battle?"

His chuckle took away all her self-control. She jumped at him, scratching, hitting and kicking wherever she could reach.

Edward managed to hold her just far enough away, although a few strikes did hit. "Rebecca—calm down—you don't want the royal army to see you behaving this way. Ow! Stop it! Or I will have to give you a very sore hinderland." Edward laughed at his own humor. With a swift move he lifted her up over his shoulder. "If you do my back any damage, I will make good my threat." The humor was gone from his voice.

Rebecca found her voice but resisted filling his ears with every vile word she knew. Clearly, his anger did not need more fuel. He held her at a disadvantage. "Edward, put me down, please. I'll walk calmly beside you and then you can explain your recent behavior to me. And make amends for throwing me in that miserable hole."

"You really think you've gotten away with it. You have no idea that I know your dark secret. Do you?" He placed her on her feet roughly.

Stumbling, she struggled to keep her footing. Once standing she swung away and walked toward the castle gate.

"You best keep your promise and walk beside me." His voice held such menace it did not even sound like his own.

Rebecca stopped and turned to looked up at Edward as he came toward her. "What evil thing has bitten you? And what do you mean by my dark secret? I've no secrets from you." She searched her mind and could not find one that would matter.

They walked into the castle and up the steps to their chambers. Rebecca tensed at the thought of being alone with him.

"You're sure you have no secrets, say about ten years old?"

"I'm sure."

He opened the door of his chamber. Rebecca tried to continue down the hall. His arm snatched her by the waist and pulled her inside his chamber.

Rebecca tried to scream out for help. His hand clasped her mouth, silencing her cries. He picked her up and threw her onto the bed. Every muscle ached and her teeth chattered with a chill she'd caught from the cold dungeon floor. All humor left her.

"What you did to me is unforgivable. I warned you not to get in the way of my will."

Edward did not react. His cold stare chilled her as he strode from the chamber.

Rebecca scrambled off the bed and went toward the door. A woman entered with buckets of water.

"Laird Edward forbids your leavin'. Please rest while I fix your bath."

Rebecca nodded and sat heavily on a chair.

"I don't know how you do it. Battling like a man." Clucking, she shook her head. "There, Lady Rebecca, let me help."

Already feeling uncomfortable about being in Edward's chamber, Rebecca certainly did not want help. But her tired and confused mind would not decline the woman's offer. She didn't fight the gentle hands that rid her of her clothing and helped her into the warm tub of water. The bath soothed her.

The woman washed her hair, and dried it. Occasionally, she put more of the heated water into the tub. After a long while, Rebecca sighed and signaled that she was ready to get out. She stepped into the soft robe the woman held up for her.

"Many thanks."

"Aye, m'lady." The woman walked quietly from the room.

Rebecca walked to the bed, feeling sleep take over even before she lay down.

When Edward entered his room a bottle of wine later he was struck by the beautiful and peaceful Rebecca asleep in his bed. His loins woke from the folds of steel that kept them cold. Shaking his head, he tried to clear away the tired, unreal feeling that engulfed him.

Nathan was right. How could he think she was guilty? But he didn't have proof of her innocence. Yet in his heart he knew she could not be responsible. Wasn't her sweet face proof enough? Lying down beside her, he lost all thought and drifted off to peaceful sleep of his own.

Rebecca reached for the covers, her body shivered. What time of day could it be? Still half asleep, her mind traced over the day before. A small sound escaped her as she remembered Edward's actions. Her eyes opened with a start. She glanced across the bed to find the object of her frustration.

Every muscle tensed. Slowly, steadily she worked her way across the bed . . . away from Edward. Watching him, all the while. She made it to the side of the bed, he moaned and his large arm swung toward her. Rebecca ducked. His eyes remained closed, but his large hand made contact with her thigh, and held it tightly.

"You're not goin' anywhere." Blurred with a thick brogue, his tone told her that even now his ire was up.

No matter. "Let go of me, you insufferable ox." Rebecca tried to pry his hand from her leg.

"You're already in deep water, m'lady, don't push me further." His eyes opened just a slit, within which they held a dangerous glare.

"I know why I'm upset with you, but as yet, I don't know why you're so upset with me." Silence. "If it is for my leaving—twice—I wish to make amends. I won't leave again. I let my emotions get the best of me." Rebecca's leg burned under his touch. The heat spread through her body. *Just let this fight be over.* She reached over to caress Edward's arm. His other hand reached out to hold her arm.

"Don't touch me." His expression sliced through her heart. He released her arm.

Rebecca put her hand to her chest. Her face heated, but she refused to bow her head and admit defeat. Closing her eyes against his stare, she could actually see her blood coursing through her eyelids.

"If you display the temper you're brewing, I will not be responsible for what happens to you—go and get dressed." His hand pushed down on her leg and let go of it.

Rebecca shook with a barely controlled rage. She got off the bed, facing Edward.

"Don't forget what you just told me. You will not leave again." Edward stretched his arms out, bringing both of his hands behind his head. As he dallied, she noticed his gaze never left her.

Rebecca quickly wrapped herself in the clothes Flossie had left for her and walked from the room. With a sigh of relief she entered her own chamber. Her body wouldn't stop shaking. What had she done? Was he tired of her already?

Maybe Edward wanted a taste of his late wife . . . she could do that, flit around the other men. She would see just how sick of her he was. Rebecca's anger faded as she pictured the mischief she could create. The door to Edward's room slammed so hard it rattled her chamber door. Suddenly, that kind of mischief seemed childish and unwise.

If he couldn't tell her the reason she angered him so, she would have to find out from someone else. Flossie? Nathaniel? When would they leave for Cavenaugh castle? What of her family? Her ire rose again with the unanswered questions. She stormed out of her chamber. Her door slammed even louder than Edward's had. A guard standing outside her door raised his eyebrows.

Rebecca quickly walked down to the garden maze, not even caring if the guard followed. She walked out of the castle. Something had to be seriously wrong. She couldn't find Nathaniel.

She walked over to the bushes that formed the maze. Her memory served her well. Without error she arrived at the center of the maze. Unsheathing her sword, she attacked the bushes around her with a savage fury. Taking out her anger on the innocent shrubs.

Her anguished scream rent the air as she speared the ground with her sword. Falling to her knees, her hands covered her face as she sobbed. Her angry mind longed to hurt Edward as deeply as he had hurt her. She doubted that she could. He didn't care about her. It was over . . .

"Get up!" The harsh voice shook her.

She looked up, startled to find Edward towering over her.

"I said—get up! You call yourself a warrior? You look like a blubbering woman to me." Edward paced back and forth, his hands raking through his hair. "We're ready to ride out. I suggest you dress and prepare, immediately."

Rebecca stood as tall and proud as she could. Rage sounded in her ears like the roar of the great ocean. Sheathing the sword with steady hands, she stared back at Edward matching his intense glare.

"I'll be ready." Her voice strong and certain, as her heart wilted within her breast.

* * *

Edward fought the lump that formed in his throat as he witnessed Rebecca's pain. His eyes stung, even now, at the thought
of her anguished performance.

He had judged her wrong once. Could he love her even if
she was responsible for his father's death? Did she really have
no idea? Edward's need for Rebecca battled with his doubts of
her innocence.

Rebecca didn't know whether to be tired or wide awake.
Sleeping now and then for a couple of hours and traveling at
night only served to waste her energy. All because of her jum-
bled emotions. From now on she would make sure her mind
led her and nothing else.

Her body jarred with each step the horse took, still sore from
her chill. She rode on her favorite white steed as they journeyed
toward her castle. Edward did not speak to her. No one spoke
to her. Whatever tormented his mind remained a mystery.

She tried to get alone with Nathaniel over and over again.
Edward always stood in her way. Rebecca's heart threatened to
break yet again. Instead, she sealed it up in a block of ice to
survive the hurt.

Another raid started. Thunderous screams sounded in her ears
as the enemy poured out of a narrow path in the mountains,
shields and swords swung into action.

Rebecca fought with deadly accuracy, her frozen heart giving
her the skill to survive another day. Her attention riveted on no
one but herself. The blood of many mingled together, splashing
her face. She closed her mouth to the salty taste of it. Her stomach reeled.

The attack ended in a short time, with no casualties to either
Edward's or Rebecca's clan members. They stopped to tend the
wounded. She pushed her emotions aside and settled next to a
fire. Pouring water from her water skin, she splashed her hands
and face. She took bread from her pouch and chewed it slowly,
sipping her water between bites. Cavenaugh castle lay just over

the next rise. Normally, so willing to tend the wounded she did not move to help. She hadn't seen Edward since the battle.

"Lady Rebecca, would you help my brother? His wound is deep. I fear for his life." The MacCleary man knelt on one knee beside her.

Frowning, Rebecca nodded her head and followed the man. She quickly prepared a treatment for his brother's wound. Rebecca could feel her body coming alive. Being needed made her feel better. She worked without stopping. Cleaning and stitching wounds, she boiled torn shirts to wrap the wounds. She worked until the wounded had been tended.

All the while she fought her thoughts—where is Edward? Is he hurt? Was she really too proud to inquire? She sat down at the fire again and looked up as Nathaniel sat down beside her. She stiffened and could feel the blood draining from her face.

"Are you ill?" Nathan spoke quietly. He looked around.

"Are you goin' to tell me if your bullheaded chieftain is alive or dead? And if he does live, what makes his heart so cold?"

"He lives, and I would say the deceit of a woman has turned his heart cold." Nathan glared at Rebecca. "I had to steal away from him just to get to your side. We must talk . . ."

"Nathan, a word, please." Edward's voice made them jump. He looked pleased with himself.

"He's having a word with me. Leave us be." Rebecca spoke smoothly with courage borne of her frozen heart.

Nathan glanced from one to the other. An expression akin to horror appeared on his face. He groaned. Shaking his head, he rose to his feet. "I'll not talk to either one of ya. I won't be caught in the middle of this." He walked away.

Edward followed after him. A moment later she heard their voices raised in anger. Crawling from her sitting position, she stole closer.

They walked into an area of thick woods, away from the other men. She followed, staying close to the ground and listening.

"Edward, she doesn't have any idea why you're so angry with her. Doesn't that alone prove her innocence? Have you talked to her to see if there is even cause to suspect her? Have you asked her if she let anyone into the castle that night?"

"The man swore 'twas her. I don't want word to get out—that was your idea, if you remember—so I haven't spoken about it."

"So you treat her as if she's guilty?" Nathan paced around Edward.

"Nay—I'm just keeping my distance." Edward's hands raked through his hair.

"Do you really think she's guilty?" Nathan's voice held a tone of pleading.

"I don't know. But I do know, if you question me further I'll make the rest of your trip much more painful." Edward advanced on Nathan, his hands in fists at his side.

The men walked away and continued to talk. How could he still think her responsible for his father's murder? After all they'd been through. Her first thought was to flee. But she wasn't guilty. She would stay to prove that . . . for now.

She could feel Edward's glare boring into her before she turned around to face him. She gave him a lofty look.

"Where have you been?" Edward strode toward her, getting far too close for her comfort.

"That's not your concern." Rebecca breathed in his masculine scent. Her emotions came very close to the surface.

"I asked you a question." Edward's hands rested on his hips and his head ducked down to her smaller stature. He faced her eye to eye.

"Pardon me, m'lord, I went into the woods to piss."

Rebecca's voice dripped with scorn as she smiled sweetly.

Edward's eyes narrowed, his jaw tightened embellishing its square shape.

Satisfied, she swept away from him and sat down by the fire. He followed, sitting beside her and looking very tired. Taking out some dried venison, he chewed it slowly. Rebecca wanted to knock some sense into his thick head. But what she really wanted was not even remotely possible at the moment.

* * *

Edward hated the doubts he held toward Rebecca. Why couldn't he just forget what the messenger had told him? How did he even know if the man could be trusted? But until he knew the truth, he would not give anymore of his heart to her.

The closeness of her body at this moment nearly undid his resolve. He longed to hold her and smooth away the worried lines that scored her face. Her fighting earlier held a concentration he never thought she would have. Maybe his cold behavior did benefit her, for now. The chilling glare she sent his way made it clear how much pain he caused her. Would she be able to love him again?

Standing abruptly, Edward barked directions to set the army riding again. His orders went quickly into effect. Edward turned his head to adjust his horse's saddle. Rebecca mounted her horse. His body heated at the sight of her tight fitting breeches. They did nothing to hide her shapely backside.

"Where's your tartan?" Edward mounted, and rode closer to her.

"It's far too warm to ride with it on. I took it off . . . it's here." Rebecca pointed to a roll on her saddle.

"Put it on." He shouldn't have had to give the order a second time.

"Put your eyes back in your head and lead on Chieftain. I'll not wear the tartan." Rebecca rode away.

A whistle split the air. The horse turned back. Edward seized her rein. Bringing her horse close, he snatched the tartan roll off her saddle. Looking into her wild eyes, he dared her to disobey his order again as he shoved the roll into her hands. "Wrap it 'round, and I better not see it off again."

Without waiting to see if she complied, he rode toward the head of the forces. After a short time he whistled and Rebecca's horse dutifully trotted to his side. He had a hard time not laughing when he saw the rage flashing in her eyes, her tartan wrapped around her tempting curves.

Edward watched the light in Rebecca's eyes soften when Cavenaugh castle came into view. She spurred her steed faster.

Edward's whistle slowed her horse and it fell into step with his own.

"Patience, my love."

Her eyes flashed with an angry light and she moved her horse from his reach. "Now it's 'my love'?" The angry light turned cold.

Edward could feel her pain. No matter the questions he held, Rebecca would always have a hold on his heart. "Let's put this game aside, for now. You have a grievous situation to face. You've been a help to me. I would help you now."

Edward lifted her from her horse and set her in front of him in the saddle, leaving her horse to trail behind. The warmth of her body filled him with the yearning he had been pushing away. Maybe he was tired, but he wanted nothing more than to be alone with her.

"The game of which you speak, is only in your own mind. I would have peace between us, and much more." Rebecca shrugged her shoulders.

Sighing deeply, she nestled her back up against Edward's chest much like a child cuddled on a parent's lap. Edward's sharp intake of breath made her smile. The guards on the castle wall signaled their arrival with a blast of a horn. Her father rode out to greet them. They went quietly into the castle.

Giving their horses to the stable boys they walked to the great hall and greeted Rebecca's mother. She didn't look well.

"Mother, you look so tired. Can I take you to your chamber?"

"Aye, my dear. Let's leave the men to talk."

They excused themselves. Rebecca noticed the hungry look on Edward's face as he nodded to her. Let him hunger for her. She would not give in . . . but as she thought it, her own body denied the very idea.

"Has Edward been keeping you happy?"

Rebecca laughed. "I can't begin to tell you. Since I've seen you last his words have been both like poetry and Hades itself." She never minced words with her mother.

Martha laughed. "I've always known you'd give a man a real go of it."

"Me? What about Edward? Do you know he locked me in his dungeon? Mother, stop laughing, it really wasn't funny at all." Rebecca smiled in spite of herself.

They reached her mother's chamber and went inside. Surprised at the disarray she saw there, Rebecca commented on it. "Mother, are you feeling all right? I've never seen your rooms in such a state."

"I've been fine. Just a little out of sorts since my run-in with Ruppert. I've discovered life is too dear to spend it cleaning and straightening. I've been enjoying the outdoors more." She did have some extra color in her face.

"I feel so responsible . . . I wasn't even here to stop him. I will be this time. Mother, Ruppert didn't . . . I mean, did he harm you?" Rebecca saw the color drain from her mother's face. "Nay—Mother!" She gripped her arms gently and looked into her eyes. The pain in her mother's eyes made the answer plain. An oath escaped from her lips. She walked to the window. "I'm so sorry."

"It's not your fault, Rebecca. I've been through many things in my lifetime. I can handle this . . . in fact, I feel much better now." Martha hugged her from behind, and kissed the side of her head. "Go and wash up for evening meal. I'll see you then."

A soft knock sounded on the door as Rebecca walked toward it. She opened the door to Edward.

He walked past Rebecca to her mother's side. "How are you, Lady Martha?"

Rebecca quietly left the room, her feelings hurt once again. It seemed her emotions had gotten trod upon a lot lately. She walked to her chamber.

Opening her door, the sight of Sarah made her thankful. Helping her into a warm bath. Sarah's gentle words soothed her.

SIXTEEN

Familiar scents of stewed meats and baked breads met Rebecca as she walked into the dining hall. Sweeping across the room, she greeted her family members with either embraces or nods. She glanced around now and then to see where Edward might be.

Also recognizing the MacCleary families, she greeted them. But . . . no Edward. Finding her seat, Rebecca smiled at her mother. Did her mother look strained? What had happened when Edward spoke to her?

Rebecca whispered next to her mother's ear. "Mother, what did Edward say to you?"

Her mother winced at Rebecca. "He spoke very properly and coldly. Something's bothering him. What have ye done, Rebecca?" Her mother's look held very little patience.

"Me? Why should the blame always come to me?" Rebecca could feel her face grow hot under her mother's inspection. In hushed tones Rebecca tried to explain. "A messenger approached Edward at his castle. Evidently, the messenger told him I was to blame for his father's murder. Why would he believe a stranger? He never even asked me about it." Rebecca looked around nervously to see if anyone had heard.

"He thinks you're guilty?" Her mother's color heightened.

"He doesn't know." Feeling very sad at the thought, Rebecca frowned.

"Edward MacCleary is an idiot." With a thump, Martha put her linen napkin on the table and stood up.

"Mother, he doesn't know that I heard them speaking of it."

Her father walked over. "Martha? Is something wrong?" MacKey put a hand on his wife's arm.

Dismissing his comment, she sat down again. Turning to her daughter she spoke heatedly. "You listened in on a private conversation?"

"Aye, Mother, can we discuss this later? I really don't think it wise . . ." Rebecca's gaze darted from her mother to her father.

Martha turned to her husband as he sat down beside her. "I'm fine, just a misunderstanding."

Rebecca thought it could not possibly get any worse. But then she sensed another person, and looked up into Edward's glittering eyes. The food she would swallow stuck in her throat. She reached for a drink of wine to wash it down.

"Ah, there you are. Edward, come and sit." MacKey stood, and offered him the chair next to Rebecca. He sat next to Edward at the head of the table, leaving his daughter and wife to talk.

Martha nodded at Edward and looked at Rebecca. Rebecca could feel a nervous tickle of laughter threatening. The corners of her mouth twitched, trying to form a smile and release her humor. Edward's leg brushed against her as he sat down. She nodded politely to him. He returned her nod and faced her father.

Martha's wide smile almost undid Rebecca's control. She made a stern face at her mother, opening her eyes wide.

"So, Rebecca dear, tell me what you plan to do now." Martha's voice bubbled with humor.

"Mayhaps I should seek refuge in a convent." Rebecca lost control of her laughter and it bubbled from her, making a musical sound.

Martha laughed along with her. "That nunnery would never survive your passionate nature. Although they would probably learn from your honest and pure soul." Martha spoke her last words loudly, causing the people around them to look up.

Edward and MacKey stopped talking and turned to the ladies. Rebecca braved a glance at Edward. His eyes held an alarming wealth of warmth as their gazes met.

"Martha?" MacKey looked concerned.

Martha smiled warmly. "Just women talking, dear. Don't mind us." Turning to Rebecca, she whispered, "It looks as if Edward would rather believe you innocent."

Rebecca smiled knowingly and turned to her food. While she and her mother talked she tried to listen to what the men said. MacKey thanked Edward for bringing his forces to help defend his castle and talked of their clan's peace. Edward spoke very little.

Rebecca could feel her body sag with fatigue as the warm meat and barley broth filled her stomach. Her eyelids grew heavy. She sat back from the table.

Martha's eyes looked moist as she brushed the wayward curls from Rebecca's face. "You look tired, daughter. You should rest while you can . . . you're home now, at least for a while."

Rebecca nodded. The sound of the word "home" made her sad. It reminded her of how, just a short while ago, she called another castle home. As she stood, her father and Edward also stood.

"If you'll excuse me . . ." Rebecca started to walk away.

Edward reached for her hand, his eyes questioning her.

"May I walk you to your chamber?" Edward looked uncertain.

"No, I can go on my own." Rebecca denied her body what it craved. She would follow her mind. It tended to be less painful.

"Very well." Releasing her hand, he sat back down beside MacKey.

As Rebecca walked to her chamber her body and mind warred. Would it harm her to be with Edward while she could? He would soon take himself out of her life, wouldn't he? What if she carried his child?

In her mind she counted the days that had passed since her

last bleeding. Relief flooded her, as she realized that she was not due for another five days. Disrobing, she looked down at her belly. A sad feeling descended over her relief. Maybe following her mind would be less painful, but listening to her emotions was infinitely more pleasing.

Putting a robe over her nude body, she walked toward the hidden door in her wardrobe. She hoped that Edward had returned to his room also. Pulling aside the clothes, the sight of Edward crawling through the secret door sent her reeling backward.

Without a word, she backed away from his foreboding look. When her back hit the wall his expression changed. He smiled . . . getting closer. As he reached her, he started to caress the top of her arms. The warmth returning to his eyes.

"With what scent do you bewitch me?" Edward held her under her chin, his thumb tracing her lips.

"The highland rose, m'lord." Rebecca savored the feelings that grew within her. She wanted to cry out to him *I've always been true to you and your clan*. But she didn't want to break the spell.

Reaching toward Edward, she put her hands on his chest. He brought her up against his body and cradled her head in his hands, kissing her gently. Rebecca wrapped her arms around him. Pressing her body close, she could feel his arousal. His deep moan vibrated with pleasure against her lips.

Letting go of her head, he lifted her up. Only then did his lips leave hers as he looked hungrily into her eyes. She loved the way the candlelight danced in his dark eyes. *Here is the man I love.*

As he carried her toward the bed, his smile told her just what he intended to do. Placing her there, he smoothed the robe off her body with caresses. She thought someone must have given her a drugged wine. Her body and mind focused on him. With one shrug he let his robe fall to the floor. Rebecca's breath caught in a sigh as she gazed at his body.

Reality no longer existed. She let him lead her into the wonderful world where only their love dwelled. Her hands touched his body, lingering on the soft private places. A wild light played in his eyes. She held his throbbing member in her hands.

Edward traced her body with his hands, his gaze lingering on every part of her. Rebecca's world pulsed around her. Her body heated. She watched her skin turn rosy under his hands. Waves of pleasure flowed through her until she thought she would scream.

Finally, he joined her on the bed. Moving on top of her he pulled her hands over her head, matching his large hands to her small ones and pressing them into the bed. His knee nudged her legs apart and very slowly he entered her.

She closed her eyes as pleasure rippled through her. As he moved inside her, she answered his passion with her own. Fusing her body with his, they created wonderful sensations moving wildly apart and together. She didn't slow until she felt his fluid releases overflowing with her own release.

Floating gently to earth, he remained with her. He didn't leave, as she feared he would. Soon she could hear his deep shallow breathing.

Propping her head up and resting her chin on her hands, she watched Edward's peaceful face. This man held her very heart and soul in his hands. Hands that could be cruel. Hands that could bring her more pleasure than she ever knew possible. She loved and feared this man. Although to him she would never admit that fear.

Softly she whispered the words she could not speak to him. "I'm innocent. I never caused your father harm. How could I . . . I loved him too." Tears filled her eyes, blurring her vision. But she didn't miss the way Edward's eyes opened. She backed away. He put his hand on her shoulder to stop her.

"I know . . . Rebecca, I know. Go to sleep." He hugged her closely to him.

"Then who did you let into the castle that night?"

Harsh daylight fell on Rebecca's eyelids as she closed her eyes to Edward's angry words.

"I just need to know what happened. If it was an accident, I'll understand." He shrugged into a clean linen shirt.

"I'll tell you one last time. I never let anyone into the castle that night." She pulled on her skirt a little too roughly.

"You prefer Cavenaugh colors?" Edward's eye glistened with anger as he looked at her plaids.

"I would say Cavenaugh colors are more appropriate. Since the MacCleary chief is so quick to blame me for his problems." Turning from his angry gaze, she picked up a brush and tried to run it through her unruly hair. She tugged away at the knots, only making them worse.

"Perhaps Kirkguard plaids would be more appropriate."

Edward's deep laugh mocked her.

Throwing the brush down, she swung around to face him.

"The messenger I spoke with saw a woman open the gate to a man that night. He said he recognized you." He finished pulling on his knee stockings and shoes. Standing, he walked over to pick up the brush and strode back to her. His glare burned through her brazen stare.

Rebecca did not trust what he would do next. The light in his eyes softened. He laughed, whirled her around, and started to smooth the tangles out of her hair.

"Many men in history have been undone by the wiles of their women." He tugged a little too hard.

"More women have been undone by their men—and even killed." Rebecca tried to step away.

He held her hair so she couldn't and continued to brush. Whenever she tried to move away his hand gripped a thick piece of her hair to keep her there. "Hold still—I'm almost through. Done." He turned her around and picked up the silky locks of her hair, letting them glide through his fingers. "Beautiful."

Rebecca pushed his hand away, trying not to let him see how he set her senses reeling. "The messenger could not have seen me at the gate. I never left my room that night." Sitting on a trunk, she laced her shoes. "And . . . I don't happen to have any fresh clothes in the MacCleary colors."

"You never open the castle gates after dark?" Edward stood above her, with his arms crossed over his chest.

"Not to let anyone in." Rebecca grew hot under his gaze.

"What for? No—wait—I can guess. You went romping about in the night, even under your parent's nose. Did you ever leave the gate open after you left?" Edward knelt down to look into her eyes.

"Aye—but not on that night! Why do you continue to question me?" She stood, nearly knocking him backwards.

He stood, staring at her. He looked ready to pounce. "You get my ire up a dozen times a day, Rebecca." He wrapped his tartan around himself and put on his belt.

A knock sounded at the door. She went toward it, happy for the intrusion. "Nathaniel, how good to see you!"

"Aye, same here. Is Edward about?" Nathan looked past her to Edward. "We're having a meeting in the upper hall. You're needed right away. And you, Lady Rebecca."

They walked up to the hall, listening as Nathan told them the problem. "The MacCleary clan wishes to leave for home. However, we can't spare an army to guide them safely. Also there's the question of waiting for an attack or attacking." Nathan looked at Edward and grinned.

"What are you grinnin' about?" Edward's voice sounded annoyed.

"Just happy to see you and the lady getting along again." Nathan also grinned at Rebecca.

"Don't be so sure." In spite of his own comment Edward grinned back.

She laughed. Nathan's such a romantic. How could his wife let him go off so much? "How's your wife, Nathan? And the children?"

"Quite well. The wee one asks about you, often. You caught her fancy."

"I'll have to visit them."

As they walked into the meeting room, her father gave her a scathing look. She walked over to him.

"Good morning, Father." Standing on tiptoe Rebecca kissed his rough cheek. Her charm always worked well.

"I missed you at morning meal." Was that accusation in his eyes?

"Please excuse my absence, I caught up on some much needed sleep." Rebecca sat on the right side of her father, daring him to object. If she sat there she held authority.

"Aye, naturally. Rebecca, sit on the other side." He rose and pulled the chair to his left out for her. And motioned for Edward to sit where she had been.

Rebecca feigned innocence, but her emotions boiled within her.

Edward thought the meeting would never end. The answers seemed so obvious to him. Why did it take so long to get the clans to agree? His eyes looked past MacKey, straying to Rebecca. She twisted a piece of her hair around her finger, looking wearied. Her gaze met his with smoldering intensity.

Finally, the clan decided on the safest course, to stay at the castle and wait for the Kirkguard clan to make a move.

As the meeting broke up, it seemed like every man in the room wanted to speak with Edward. He watched Rebecca's back as she left the room. Knowing he could not catch up with her, he sent a message to her.

"M'lady, Laird Edward wishes you to stay on the castle grounds. He'll escort you off grounds, later on."

"Thank you for the message." Rebecca already wore her riding clothes, and walked her horse to the side gate. The boy lingered, staring at her.

"You'll tell him I told you?"

"Of course. I guess I'll have to wait . . ." Rebecca smiled as the boy left. ". . . or maybe not." She continued on her way. Taking a key out of her pouch, she opened the lock.

"Didn't you get my message?"

Rebecca jumped at the sound of Edward's voice, dropping her key. He stood just outside the gate. He wore black breeches reaching just below his knees. The pants met MacCleary colored stockings. New leather boots adorned his feet. A pure white linen shirt with large sleeves clung to his broad shoulders.

A vein pulsed at the base of her neck and her heart quickened. She could not remember ever seeing him in anything other than his tartan. He looked very striking.

Edward's gaze never left her as he waited for her reply.

Rebecca smiled. "Aye . . . interesting outfit. You look dashing."

"Don't change the subject. Why don't you ever follow my directions?" He walked toward her.

A man came around the castle wall with a horse. "Your horse, Laird Edward. Lady Rebecca, good to see you home." The man nodded at her.

"Thank you, it's good to be back." She nodded back to the man and bent down to pick up the dropped key. The man walked away.

Rebecca stood and reached for Edward's collar, tugging it and smoothing the fabric of his shirt with her fingers. "I think that it would be my mother who gave you these clothes."

"You're a witch who casts spells on mortal men." He took her hand away from his shirt, and held it. "Answer my question, Lady Rebecca. Why don't you follow my directions?"

"Because, Laird Edward, my spirit is such that it must be free. No one can tell me what to do without causing it harm." Rebecca used her other hand to caress his cheek. "You wouldn't want to harm my spirit, would you?"

"I might. If it meant you'd live to an old age."

The evil gleam in his eye made her believe that he might.

Swiftly he held both her hands in one of his. "I've another question for you. Do you have the key to the main gate there in your pouch?" With his other hand he emptied her pouch onto the ground. Only small bundles of herbs fell from it.

It was a good thing Edward held both her hands. She wished she could strike him. "Evidently not, I never had one."

Releasing her hands, he knelt down to pick up the contents. She also knelt and slapped his hands away from her belongings, picking them up for herself. His soft laughter made her clench her teeth tightly together.

"Good, you're learning to control that quick tongue of yours." Still kneeling, Edward rocked back on his heels, watching her.

Rebecca finished tying her pouch onto her belt, and with both hands she shoved him backward. Wasting no time, she jumped onto her horse and left him in her dust. Her laughter rang out. She looked back to see him recover and leap onto his horse, pursuing her. Laughing into the wind, she headed for her favorite glen.

A cool wind made her hair fly wildly about her. The gentle scent of heather made her breathe more deeply. She loved the feelings that awakened in her. These were the times she felt most alive. Her mount, one of her own, seemed to revel in the run as much as she did. Just see if this gallant horse would answer to Edward's illustrious whistle.

She turned her head to see him gaining on her. She'd have to slow for the trees ahead. Changing direction, she skirted the woods that arched to the left, giving her more distance between them. She lost sight of Edward. Bringing her horse to an abrupt halt, she slid off, wrapped the reins on the saddle, and left the animal to graze.

She ran for the woods and her childhood tree house. Nimbly climbing the rotting rope, she crawled onto the small platform. Standing, she bumped her head on its ceiling. The roof caved in on her, sending a flood of pine needles and leaves all around her. Some landed in her startled, open mouth. As she sputtered and spit them out, she heard gales of laughter from below.

Edward doubled over in merriment. His hands rested above his knees to keep him standing. He could not speak. Rebecca brushed the needles off her clothes and bent down to scoop up a large armful of the stuff. She turned toward Edward, who chose that moment to look up again.

She smiled as the things of nature slid from her hands and covered him. Without wasting time she went to the other side of the platform to her escape rope. She'd always needed one. Just as she was about to climb down she realized how dangerous it would be for Edward to climb the rotten—

"Aghhh . . ." A loud thump sounded below . . . and silence.

"Edward!" Rebecca scrambled down what was left of the rope. Jumping the rest of the way, she saw Edward lying very still on the ground. "Edward . . . Edward?" Kneeling down, she touched his neck and checked his head for injuries. He seemed fine . . . Rebecca lowered her ear onto his chest. Did his heart still beat?

Quicker than a flash, Edward had her. His deep laugh blended with her startled shrieks. She struggled to get away as they rolled around the soft pine needles. Soon, she found herself laughing instead of shrieking. Playfully, they wrestled. Finally, Edward's much larger body lay on top of her. She couldn't move.

"Ow—there's a rock under my back." She tried to lift her back from the painful object.

"Good, ye deserve it." Edward reached under her and removed the rock, throwing it aside.

Quietly she breathed, "I—I thought you were hurt." She looked into Edward's eyes. It wasn't just his eyes that appealed to her. His face rosy from their play, and his dark hair curling over his forehead, made her body warm to his.

"Ah . . . ye do care." He kissed her cheeks hungrily and pretended to devour her neck. Then, kissing her lips, he rolled off her and cradled her head on his arm.

They lay there, not talking. Just staring up at the beauty of the pines from their vantage point on the forest floor. Rebecca enjoyed the fresh smell of the trees, and the warmth of Edward's body. The peacefulness of the forest would have lulled them to sleep, if not for the cool air around them.

She sat up, looking at him. "Did you bring your sword?"

"Of course. Would you like a duel?" Edward sat up. "And you have yours?"

"Aye, always." She sat beside him.

"Good." Lifting her chin, Edward lightly touched her lips with his own. Standing, he helped her to her feet.

After retrieving their horses and swords, Rebecca brought Edward to a clearing in the small glen. It used to be her place to go when life at the castle grew oppressive.

"You came here often, didn't you?" Edward slowly drew his sword from its sheath.

"Aye, I fought many a dragon and black knight in this clearing. And them with my first small blade." Rebecca matched his motions, drawing her sword.

"And, you always won?" Edward moved his sword through the air in a graceful arch.

Rebecca mirrored his arch, standing ready. "Not always. Sometimes I never quite dispelled the dragon, and its putrid breath hung around. I can still smell it, and it's been ten long years since I first tried to slay it."

Edward's eyebrows rose. "Guilt can have an awful stench should ye not confess it." Edward lunged toward Rebecca, the steel of his sword glaring in the sunlight.

Holding her sword in both hands, she swung her blade out deflecting his lunge to her right. Striking to her left, the blades connected again. Her muscles awoke to the challenge. Power, once held in reserve, coursed through her body. She lunged forward, gaining ground.

"Guilt, is not the name of this dragon. It never was and never will be." She turned her anger into more strength. Releasing one hand she met his sword.

Edward gave her a wary look.

"You still think . . ." Rebecca's sword missed a parry, nearly causing Edward's blade to cut her arm.

Seeing the danger, he quickly drew back. "You better not speak of it now—take this advice, or I'll duel no more." Edward sent her the same attack.

This time she didn't miss the parry.

"Let me show you why I fear for you in battle." Holding his sword with two hands he hit her blade with his own.

Rebecca tightened her grip, but instead of meeting his sword forcefully, she gave hers some slack. The force of his sword jarred her to her toes. With great effort she let her body yield and quickly stiffened again so she wouldn't fall. She kept hold of her sword, only losing a little ground.

"Let me show you why you shouldn't fear." She countered his attack strongly. "Don't you . . . think my teachers taught me . . . how to deal with my lack of brute force? In fact . . . I think your father . . . taught me that move . . . it makes sense, really." Rebecca gasped to regain the air that her words had cost her.

Edward's sword stopped. A sour look appeared on his face. "He did dote on you . . . it makes me wonder . . ."

"Aye, it makes me wonder why you continue this untoward interrogation." Turning to walk away, she immediately knew she shouldn't have turned her back on Edward. A whoosh sounded behind her as she turned swiftly, her blade stopped the flat of his blade on its way to her backside.

Edward blinked, looking surprised. "Very good." He gave her a mock bow.

Pressing her lips together, she narrowed her eyes at him. She turned again, walking toward their horses. Edward walked up behind her as she mounted her horse and gave her rump a playful slap. She hid her grin under the veil of her hair as she leaned over to get her stirrups.

Edward mounted his horse and they rode back toward the castle at a slow pace. Suddenly, a loud commotion sounded from the castle. Their eyes met. With a startled cry she spurred her mount toward the sound.

"Rebecca, wait!" Edward raced behind her. "Stop, you're not thinking. Think, woman!" His horse bumped into hers as he hauled her onto his saddle. He reined his mount to a halt.

Her shoulders hurt as he continued to hold her, wrapping his arms around them.

"Lady! Whoa!" She called to her horse. It stopped and came back to her. "What would you do, warn them? Let me go!"

"This is one battle that neither of us will fight." His whisper fell on her ear fiercely. "Steady, Rebecca."

"Nooooo." She struggled back and forth nearly toppling them both to the ground. Helpless frustration threatened to drown her.

"Aye. We wouldna' have a chance." He guided them beneath some trees. "Look. Look at the size of that army. If they saw us, they would have what they want . . . no, Rebecca, unless you want to see me struck dead and live the rest of your life in misery."

She could feel her body go limp. What he said made sense. But to watch? "This is too much to endure." With more disappointment and self-loathing than she ever before endured, her reason left her.

Edward released her, slipping her down the side of the horse. He dismounted beside her. She spun toward him landing a hard punch to his jaw. He staggered back, enraged. The pure fury on his face brought a flood of reason back to her. She recoiled from his open hand.

"Edward! Stop, please." Her whispered words stopped his palm before it connected with her face. She covered her mouth with her shaking hand.

He turned from her, hands on his hips and bowed his head. She walked to her horse. Gripping the saddle front and back, she rested her forehead against the animal. Hot tears burned a trail down her cheeks.

"I can't endure this. I promised my mother I would be there this time. Our families . . . what can we do?" Rebecca turned toward Edward, hating the way her tears continued even as she tried to stop them. He didn't move but still gazed at the ground.

For many long moments they stood there. Finally, Edward's shoulders rose as he took a deep breath and turned to her. "We wait until they are all inside the walls and then follow, attacking from behind." His voice sounded cold and unfeeling.

But in the depths of his eyes she could read the same torment that she knew. Walking over to him she offered comfort.

"Get on your horse, and be ready to move." He shoved past her and mounted his horse.

SEVENTEEN

Rebecca mounted her horse. Her mind snapped into action. Of course—the passage would bring them into the castle without being seen. "Edward! Follow me! A passage—hurry."

"Go! I'll follow."

She guided her horse into the woods and past the tree house. Counting the trees as she rode, she dismounted at the thirteenth and tethered her horse to that tree. He quickly followed her lead. Then, counting five paces, she knelt down and cleared away the pine needles to reveal a wooden trap door.

Edward helped her to raise it. "We have no belts. We'll have to carry our swords . . ."

The door fell to the ground on the other side, landing with a *whump*.

"My father always left a few extra plaids and belts at the end of the passage. It also empties into the weapons room where we can find a shield or two." Rebecca smiled, feeling victorious. Edward MacCleary would wear her clan's colors.

"There's no peat for a torch." Edward walked back to his horse and untied his sheathed sword from his saddle.

Rebecca did the same with hers. "I never brought a torch as a child, so I know the passage well." She handed him her sheathed sword. Walking over to the passage entrance, she climbed down the rope. The coolness of the underground chamber surrounded her.

Edward handed the swords to her and climbed down. The

damp smell of earth made her nervous. She tried to remember the last time she'd entered the cave. Her pulse quickened as the memory came.

"I just had a thought. This tunnel wouldn't be how a certain lass eluded a raging chieftain's son, after she stole his clothes as he bathed in yonder spring?" Edward found her in the dark and pressed his hands softly around her neck.

"Not now, Edward, we've a siege to attend." She smiled in the darkness at the memory. Rebecca pushed his sword at him. Finding his other hand in the dark, she led him on.

"Aye, that must have been how . . . let's hope the spring hasn't found its way into this passage." Edward's words came like a prophecy.

The sloshing sound of water and a chill that went through her boots, let her know that what Edward feared had come to pass. But the ground still felt solid. Rebecca let go of him and ran her hand over the walls. "Seems you're right, although the wall still feels sound. I think we can continue." She shivered with the cold, reaching to hold Edward's hand again.

"All right, lead on." Edward squeezed her fingers.

The water got deeper. The muscles of her legs strained to walk against its current. Frigid water, having risen as high as her waist turned her body numb as she forged on. The sound of the rushing flood roared in her ears.

"How much further?" Edward yelled above the noise.

"Not too far. We should be on higher ground soon." She pushed against the force and around a curve in the tunnel. The current lessened and the water lowered. Rebecca groaned as she spotted light up ahead. "I hope the tunnel is passable." As they approached the daylight, relief flooded through her. She could see that the tunnel continued on.

A build-up of soil blocked part of the passage. He lifted her over the mound, his hand resting on her wet rump a little too long. His deep breath made her wish they could escape into their private world and forget about the real one.

Edward handed her his sword and climbed over. Giving it

back, Rebecca breathed deeply in surprise when he grabbed her up against him. He rubbed her chilled arms.

"Ah, wouldn't I like to warm you up." Then he released her with a sigh. "Lead on."

Their closeness sent a fiery heat through her. "Ah, but ye just did." Rebecca laughed, taking his hand again, she found the way to a stone stairway. On the top of the stair light seeped in from the walls. They were above ground. The chamber held piles of extra tartans and weapons that were put there for times such as these. "And it will warm my soul to see you in my family colors."

"Humph," Edward teased, looking at the plaids as if they were bugs. "I just need the belts."

"Come on. . . ." Rebecca handed him a tartan and started to wrap another around herself. Holding it on with one hand she reached for a belt. Too big, she handed it to Edward and found a smaller one for herself. She watched, wondering why it would matter to her if he didn't don her colors. He put the Cavenaugh tartan around his body.

"I like that." She grinned widely.

Wrapping the belt around his waist, around one shoulder and then around his waist again, Edward laughed. "It's not the first time I've worn these colors. I used to fight in your clan, remember?"

"Aye, and I turned green with envy over it." Attaching her scabbard to the belt, she remembered the first time her father refused to let her do as she wished. She wanted to fight that battle, to use the skills she'd learned. "Precisely why I stole your clothes."

As he pushed the panel, it slowly opened to a sitting room. No one was about. The brightness of the light made her squint. She took a shield from the wall.

Edward did the same and turned to her. "And I allow you to put your life at risk."

Rebecca stood on her toes and put her face close to Edward's. "You allow me? It is not because you allow me to. I fight because I want to. No one is responsible for telling me not to. Understand that, Edward!" She turned from him.

"Rebecca." His voice sounded understanding. Walking up behind her he gently kissed the back of her head. "Be careful, my love."

She smiled, feeling sheepish. "I will. You be careful too."

"Aye. Let's go."

Rebecca followed Edward toward the sound of swords clanking and men yelling. She heard a fray in a family chamber. *Oh my God, the families.* They both turned and ran toward the sounds.

A door stood open. Inside two Kirkguard soldiers terrorized a MacCleary family. A Kirkguard held two wide-eyed children forcing them to watch as a soldier handled their mother. He wrestled her to the ground, ripping her clothes. Edward rushed in and lifted the Kirkguard off the woman by his hair and knocked him out with one swift blow from his shield.

The other Kirkguard shoved the children, sending them scampering behind some thick curtains. He lifted his sword as if to slice through the curtains as he turned to face Edward. Rebecca's cry stopped him just in time. As he turned toward her, her blade sliced the back of his neck and he fell. Blood everywhere.

She turned to see Nathan's wife sobbing in Edward's arms. Turning back, she ran to the curtains and found the frightened, children. Little Mary stood and hugged her leg tightly.

The older boy stayed still, staring at the bloody body on the floor. His mouth hung open and the color slowly drained from his face. Rebecca quickly lifted Mary and ran for the older child. Covering his view of the dying man with her body, she herded him toward his mother.

"Take them to the passage." Edward gently pushed Nathan's wife from his arms and rushed away.

Rebecca handed Mary to her mother and led them away. Edward followed with more MacCleary families and Sarah.

They all moved into the secret opening. Edward left before

Rebecca could see them all safe inside. She hugged Madeleine, trying to remain patient. Rebecca's need to follow Edward consumed her. "All will be well. Keep as quiet as you can. If you hear someone at the door, flee down the passage. There's water in part of the passage—watch the children."

"Rebecca be careful." Sarah crossed herself and hugged Rebecca to her.

"I will. Sarah—let go. Don't fear. Only hope." Rebecca quickly left the chamber. She closed the panel firmly and looked for any evidence of their hiding place. Smoothing the carpet, she gripped her sword tighter and left the room.

The hall spread before her, a gory mess. Clansmen, from all sides, fallen. Her heart in her throat, Rebecca saw she could not help any of them. What of the Cavenaugh families? They would know the other passages and make their escape. Just to be sure, she checked her family's chambers.

The fighting sounded further away. Hopefully, the Kirkguard clan would withdraw their men in defeat. After finding her family's chambers empty, she ducked behind a column on the balcony that looked down over the main hall.

The scene unfolding before her eyes made her gasp. Edward fought Ruppert with a passion born of pure hatred. Behind Edward a Kirkguard man stalked, his blade raised. Rebecca held her sword in front of her and ran the length of the stairs, her gaze unwavering.

Her footsteps echoed in her head. Each step jarred her body. She tried to run as fast as she could without losing her footing. If she cried out, Ruppert would slay him. If she didn't, the Kirkguard would.

Her teeth tightly clenched, she got nearly close enough to attack the Kirkguard. Suddenly a burly man tried to trip her. He laughed at her. Glancing back she saw Nathaniel take down the Kirkguard behind Edward. Relief flooded her senses.

She swung back. Her ire aimed at this man who dared to laugh at her. She attacked him with all her might. The look on his stunned face gave her back any confidence he might have taken from her. He stepped back and readied his attack. But before he could swing his sword he lost his footing, stumbled over a fallen kinsman, and impaled himself on a protruding blade.

The sight and sound of it made Rebecca feel sick in the pit of her stomach. She looked to where Edward and Ruppert fought, but only found a wounded Nathaniel, lying in a small puddle of blood. Running to Nathan's side, she saw that the wound would not be fatal.

Someone seized her from behind. She nearly lost her sword. But instead she brought it around hard into the man who would accost her. He slumped to the floor. A spiral of cold unfeeling emotion roiled around her.

Rebecca retrieved her sword and fought off another man. Her shoulders ached with the effort, but she could not cease her battle. An arrow finished the man for her. Her shield saved her from a fatal blow as she swung her sword toward the next attacker. Another arrow found its mark. The archers above certainly watched her course.

A horn sounded the sharp notes of retreat. The Kirkguard clan melted into the shadows. A ghostly silence fell over the castle. MacKey called to Rebecca, his leg glistening with his own blood. Taking off his belt, she wrapped it around his leg to stop the flow.

She shouted orders to her clansmen, and they began moving the injured MacCleary and Cavenaugh men to their beds. Seeing her father safely to his chamber, she left him in Sarah's capable hands. All the while her mind frantically wondered where Edward was. Questions. Everyone asked her questions.

"But where is Edward?" No one answered her. Her frustration grew as she got the women and children out of hiding. She set them to work on the wounded.

Sarah and Rebecca slaved over the half dead men for hours. Her tortured mind never getting an answer to her question. "Where is Edward?"

When clan members would try to assist her, she screamed at them, "For God's sake, find Laird Edward." Soon her mother stood by her side trying to comfort her. No one had seen the chieftain.

Finally, the crisis died down and Sarah insisted that Rebecca go to the dining hall to eat. Rebecca's emotions warred. Sarah and Martha practically had to force her bodily to the eating hall. Then she spotted a man whom she had asked to find Edward and report back to her. He sat there, eating. She pushed both women from her and attacked the man.

A voice that sounded like heaven itself called her from behind. "Rebecca!" Edward's hand gripped her by the belt and heaved her from the man, placing her beside him.

Her eyes filled with the wonderful sight of Edward. She watched as he glared at the man, who rose to face him.

"Did you disobey an order from Lady Rebecca?"

"My laird, she asked me to find you. I could not. It isn't her place to order about a clansman."

Rebecca wanted to strike the man. But instead she watched Edward's reaction. His face went taut with anger.

"It is her place. You'll remember that." With a swift move Edward punched the man—knocking him out cold.

Rebecca's stomach fluttered pleasantly. She stared at Edward, not caring that her mouth hung open. Then she remembered her hours of fear. "Where have ye been all this time? Didn't you even think to look for me? I've been half out of my mind . . ."

Her words trailed away as she realized the hall had grown quiet and all present witnessed this woman who would rail at a chieftain. The rage on Edward's face calmed her tone. "I beg yer pardon, m'lord. I feared for your life."

Edward's anger softened at the sight of her discomfiture. The emotions that churned inside him, after a battle, made it impossible for him to be civil—normally. But this wisp of a woman possessed the ability to set on fire, enrage, *and* calm the animal within him.

"M'lady, I must also beg your pardon. I came to your side as quickly as I could. I've been in pursuit of Ruppert, who has fled from my sword yet again. It seems I will never rid the world of him." Lifting her hand to his lips, he gently kissed her palm. He led her to the table and waited until she sat down.

Edward turned to see Rebecca and her mother as they embraced briefly. Her mother gazed at him over Rebecca's shoulder. Her thankful expression spoke volumes as she smiled at him. He returned her smile, thinking that they shared the same relief. Both he and Rebecca survived another battle, unharmed. Edward breathed a prayer of thanks. Rebecca turned to look at him.

Her gaze took in the length of him, he knew she looked for wounds. Her hand went up to the shoulder that had been wounded. "Your wounded arm, did it hinder you?"

"Not so much."

"You're lucky the arrow entered where it did."

"And your luck, as well, seems to be holding." Edward sipped the soup from his trencher.

"Luck? You told the archers to watch me, didn't you?"

Rebecca's violet blue eyes looked straight into his.

"What of your father? I don't see him at the table." His concern grew as he looked around. "And Nathaniel?" He stood suddenly panicked.

"Wounded, Edward, they're just wounded." Rebecca rose from her chair.

"Why didn't you tell me?" Edward's voice roared, silencing the hall again. He watched Rebecca's face grow angry. *My lady, don't disregard my temper now.*

"I'll take you to them." Rebecca turned and walked toward the living quarters.

Edward followed her closely, impressed with her controlled temper. But she couldn't control the color that flooded her face.

"Nathaniel took a knife after he saved your back. Nothing serious. MacKey suffered a leg wound, he bled strongly, but not too long. Twenty are dead and in the chapel for viewing. Various other clansmen are wounded and have been treated." She walked briskly and with purpose.

Arriving first at Nathaniel's chamber, she knocked on the door. Lorelei opened it.

"Lady Rebecca, Laird Edward, come in." Her smile warmed Edward's heart. Nathan had married a sweet lass. "Thanks to you both for saving me and the children. And to you, Rebecca, for seeing to Nathaniel's wound."

"No thanks are needed, Lorelei. Any thanks should go to you and your family, for all you've done for this clan." Edward kissed her hand and smiled holding it a little longer than necessary.

"Hey, MacCleary. Get ye gone from my lass." Nathan's voice, a mixture of ire and humor, bellowed from the massive bed. "Before I regret saving your life."

Looking at Rebecca, Edward noticed the twist of her lips and guessed that she'd turned the slightest bit green at his attention to Lorelei. "Good God, we're in for a rough time of it. Your wife needs all the tender love possible with a bedridden mongrel like you. If I remember, you turn nasty when you're ailing." Edward walked toward the bed.

"And you're the cause of my wound. What became of those eyes behind your head you've always boasted of?" Nathan smiled and laughed. "Oh." He held his side. "And that wench of yours is no better. Stuck me with a needle five times, she did."

Edward laughed. "Is that all? Should ha' been ten! Just where is this wound?" He turned from Rebecca to Nathan.

Rebecca lowered Nathan's blanket proudly revealing her handiwork. She stopped just above his private area. The stitches looked small and neat. "It hasn't bled again?" Feeling his brow, she turned to Lorelei.

"It hasn't." Lorelei looked bleak.

Rebecca walked to the water ewer and washed her hands. Taking salve out of her pouch, she put some on her fingers and gently rubbed it around the stitches. "You should wash the area and apply more salve at night and in the morning. Like this."

Lorelei watched Rebecca.

"Hands like an angel she has." Nathan sighed with exaggerated pleasure.

"Don't haggle with me after a fight, Nathan." Edward got a hold on his warring emotions, feeling a bit green himself. "But truly, I do thank you."

"You're welcome, friend." Nathan turned serious. "How many did we lose?"

"Twenty." Edward grimaced. "We better be off to see the wounded and then the dead." How he longed for a good hunt, preferably one with Ruppert at the end of his sword.

"Stay put—Nathaniel MacCleary. Don't ye dare leave this bed until Sarah or I say yea. And if you give your lady a hard time I'll take her under my wing and teach her my ways." Rebecca smiled tantalizingly. "Maybe I'll do that anyway."

Edward's loins grew warm at the shear beauty of her. He heard Nathan laugh, groan, and heartily promise to treat Lorelei as a queen.

As they left the chamber Edward reached for Rebecca's rump and received a sharp look.

"What? Your ire is gone, and now I have to deal with your lust?" Rebecca sniffed and walked faster.

Edward watched her walk ahead. He really did get a tumble of strong emotions after a battle. He caught up to her and took her hand in his own. "You must be exhausted. Why don't ye rest? I'll visit the wounded." He stopped walking and held her hand.

"Nay, I have to check the wounds once more to be sure of no bad effects." She looked like the world rested on her shoulders as she knocked to enter her father's chamber. Martha opened the door looking worried.

"He's got the heat, Rebecca, he's not making any sense." Tears filled her eyes.

Rebecca rushed past her mother. Her father thrashed around the bed, tangled in the blanket. Edward followed her and helped hold him still. "Mother, is there water heating?"

"Aye. Do ye need rags?" Martha snapped into action.

"Aye, put some more wood on the fire. The water must boil.

Can we bind his arms?" Rebecca looked at Edward. The pain in her eyes pierced his soul.

He nodded and used ropes from the curtains to tie MacKey's wrists to the bedposts. Sarah burst into the room and then to Rebecca's side. Edward kissed Rebecca lightly on the cheek and left the women to do their healing magic. He took Martha's hand and squeezed it. She nodded her understanding. Letting go he started to leave.

"I'll see to the others and let you know if anyone needs more care."

Rebecca nodded and tried to smile.

He opened the door and walked out of the chamber.

Edward knocked quietly on the chieftain's door. He could feel the strength draining from his body and more painfully from his soul. Rebecca opened the door slowly. Her eyes circled in black, looked dull. He walked into the room, putting his arm around her. They moved to her father's bed. Martha slept on the couch. MacKey looked pale and still tossed restlessly.

"We've done all we can. Now we wait." She looked at a chair next to the couch, but would not leave her father's side.

Edward tried to lead her to the chair. She refused.

"Let me watch him for a while. You sleep." He tried again.

"No!" She pulled away from his grasp and stood stubbornly by her father.

"What good can you do if you faint with lack of sleep? What if someone else should need you? What if the Kirkguards return?" Edward watched her expression turn sour.

"If the Kirkguards return, I'll do my best to kill them all." The stubborn tilt of her head showed him that he would not win.

He pulled a small couch over to the side of the bed. Then gently removed Rebecca's belt and tartan. With strong insistence he sat with her on the couch, covering her with the tartan. Rebecca started to resist, but he shook his head. She made a face and looked at her father once more.

With a sigh Edward removed his belts and leaned his sword beside them. He rested with her on the couch.

A loud knock startled Rebecca out of a sound sleep. Without being let in, Sarah opened the door and rushed to her side.

"Sorry, Lass, I've been busy the night through and half the day with the wounded—we lost two more. I'm glad that you stayed with your father." Sarah leaned over MacKey to examine Rebecca's work.

Rebecca looked at Edward as he stood. His face, full of sleep, did not look happy. "My father has come out of the fever."

"Good. We'll need to discuss our next move. I'm sure the army has retreated to the Kirkguard castle. Maybe we should move on that and attack the castle." Edward started to pace the chamber.

"Get you a belly full of food first. Have you been keepin' your wound clean?" Sarah advanced on Edward.

"Aye, but it could use a good cleanin' by now I'm sure." Edward backed away from Sarah.

"Let me see it."

Rebecca walked over to see his arm, feeling guilty that she hadn't seen to it last night.

"Here than, don't make such a fuss." Edward brushed their hands aside and unbuttoned his shirt, shrugging it off his shoulder.

"Edward! When did it start to swell?" Rebecca stared with dread at the red swell on his upper arm.

"I don't know. Just over night, I would guess." Edward put his hand to his brow. "That could be the reason for this ache in my head . . ."

"Ach, no . . ." Rebecca snapped into action. "Get ta bed, Edward, now! I'll not have ye ailin' when you're needed to lead our clans." She propelled him toward the chamber door.

Sarah finished wrapping MacKey's leg. Martha came into the chamber with a tray of food. She looked at Edward's arm and frowned.

"We're taking care of it. It's not serious . . . yet." Rebecca hugged her mother. "Father is fine, food is just what he needs."

Edward and Rebecca left the chamber. She could feel her guilt quickly turning to a temper.

"How could you let your arm get infected? Did you run out of ointment?" As they walked Rebecca moved faster to keep up with his stride. She reached up to feel his brow. It felt hot. "Ach, both the chieftains ail, and Nathan too. I guess I'll be the one to lead our men." She tried not to smile at her jesting, knowing full well the reaction she would receive.

"That's enough of that talk, lass. You get that idea out of your head." Edward opened the door to his chamber.

"Don't you think I could?" Rebecca walked into the room before him and moved directly to the fire. She scooped hot water into an empty cup and sprinkled herbs into it. Setting it down next to the fire, she called for Gwen to fetch more water.

"You probably could . . . but I wouldn't let you." Edward grimaced and held up his hand. "Wait, I can see I've not said the right thing. Rebecca, my love . . ."

"Don't try to charm your way out of that one. I'll lead the men, if need be."

"The need will not be." Edward sipped the tea she handed him and made a bitter expression.

Gwen knocked and entered the chamber with buckets of water. Rebecca took one from her and they both poured them into the tub. She thanked Gwen and took a tartan to lift the hot water into the bath. Steam floated up to her. The warmth of it moistened her face. She poured some soothing oils into the water.

"Get in the bath and I'll bring you a meal." She walked to the door stopping to turn toward Edward, seeing if he followed her instructions.

Edward stood there looking puzzled. "Why is it, my lady, that I must take orders from you . . . yet *you* will not do as *I* ask?"

Rebecca turned once again toward the door waving an impatient hand in his direction. Her body ached for a bath, and her stomach growled, feeling hollow. Gwen passed her carrying two more buckets.

"These are for your bath."

"Thank you, Gwen. I'll be right back." She continued down the hall and to the back stairs. Descending, she walked into the kitchen. "Mavis? Is that you?" Rebecca could not believe her eyes. "Where have you been these long years? We thought you were dead."

Two children clung to her skirts. They all looked tired and dirty. She ran up to Mavis and they embraced.

"I . . . I went off with a man and married. He died a fortnight ago. I had nowhere to live . . ." Her eyes glittered with tears.

"Of course, you're welcome here. Oh, Mavis did you know about . . . your father and brother?" Rebecca's eyes filled with tears as Mavis nodded her head.

Mavis's body stood stiff and she moved away quickly. "I came for food to take to my mother. I'm rather tired." Mavis's eyes would not look into Rebecca's.

"All right, Mavis, we'll talk later. I'm glad you're home." She looked changed, probably had a hard time of it. Rebecca gathered a beaker of wine, two goblets, a loaf of bread and a chunk of cheese.

Deep in thought, she walked back to Edward's chamber. Mavis had disappeared the night Edward's father was murdered. Something bothered Rebecca about what Mavis had told her. She ran off with a man on that night? She'd have to question her more fully. Deciding to just be glad that Mavis still lived, her thoughts turned quickly to Edward as she entered his chamber.

She put the tray down and walked over to his bath, automatically feeling the water to see if it needed warming. Edward reached his hand out and grasped her wrist. He couldn't be feeling too bad. "And do you intend to pull me into the water once more, fully clothed?"

"You're hardly clothed, and walking around the castle as such?" He sounded like her mother.

"Ach, I hardly noticed." Rebecca's cheeks grew hot as she

tried to remember who had seen her. "The halls are strangely empty, I just saw Gwen, and . . ."

Edward released her wrist and stood. "I have no time to wade in this bath. There're bodies to bury and families to see. Your father can't perform his duties, I must."

"You'll do no such thing. Please, Edward. I'll do my father's duties. You must rest and lose this infection. Please listen." Rebecca grabbed a blanket from the bed and handed it to Edward. "Don't touch the wound. Let it dry on its own."

"Your demands never end."

" 'Tis for your own good." Rebecca could see the love shining in his eyes and knew his words held no malice. She smiled and moved toward the door.

"Where're you goin'?"

"To take a quick scrub. I'll be back in a wink to share a meal with you." Rebecca left the chamber and entered her own. Gwen waited there.

"Lady Rebecca, can I help you?" Gwen took the clothes she discarded and hung them in the wardrobe.

"Oh, Gwen, thank you so much. You wouldn't believe how much there is to do." Rebecca looked up at her as she stared with awe.

"What? Oh, Gwen, shouldn't you be helping with your brother?" Gwen shook her head. "I am so grateful to you and Laird Edward for saving my family. My mother told me how you saved the children. I am honored to assist you. My mother would have it no other way."

"Thank you, Gwen. Has it been hard being away from home?"

"Aye, a little. But the feeling here is much like my own home. We've been very comfortable, and welcome."

"I'm glad. Would you help me do my hair, ach, what a mess." Rebecca stood and took the blanket that Gwen handed her.

In minutes, Gwen's nimble fingers on the brush made Rebecca's hair shine. Rebecca quickly put on a dress of black wool. How she hated the scratchy clothing. But she needed to attend the burial of the deceased clan members.

"Thank you, Gwen. See to your brother and if all is well would you help Sarah?"

"Aye, I'll do that."

They left the room together, parting outside the door. Rebecca walked the short distance to Edward's chamber and knocked on the door. No answer. "Edward?" Opening the door she peered into the deserted bedchamber. "Edward!" Rushing from the room she nearly collided with Sarah. "Edward has gone without eating and bed rest." Her voice shook with anger.

"It wasn't so bad . . . did he bathe?" Sarah looked as if she would like to be three places at once.

"Aye, Sarah, Gwen can help you. You'll find her with Nathan. I'll find Edward."

Sarah put a hand on her arm, stopping her. "Remember your manners, lass. You're not a girl any longer. You're a chieftain's daughter, full grown, and doing the chieftain's duties. Whatever disagreements you have with Edward, must remain behind your chamber doors."

Rebecca sighed and nodded. What Sarah said held truth that she would rather not hear. Trying to remain calm, she walked out to the stables and found her mount ready.

"Laird Edward said you would be needing a mount." The boy blushed.

"Aye, thank you." Rebecca smiled at his boyish grin. Mounting the horse with the cumbrous dress further frustrated her efforts of the day. "Ach, I've forgotten my sword. Are there any in the barn?"

"Nay, can I fetch it for you?"

"No, I'm tardy already, I best be on my way." Without any more thought she rode out of the castle gate toward the sad occasion.

EIGHTEEN

Galloping on the horse, she gained some strength from the wild beauty that surrounded her. The rich shades of green that lined the mountainside and hills dotted with bright yellow and blue wild flowers. The fresh smell of the air and its coolness made her cheeks feel rosy.

As Rebecca approached the crowded burial area, she slowed and quietly slipped from her horse. Tying the reins to a tree, she looked to see Edward across the crowd. As she made her way to his side, the force of her ire heated her body. And the wool made her itch.

Rebecca stood, fuming and not daring to move. One word from Edward and she knew her manners would fly to the wind. She tried to breathe in deeply and concentrate on the rector's words. *Whatever you do, don't look up at him.*

Not able to follow her own advice, she looked up at Edward. His face looked rigid with emotion. Finally he glanced her way. His expression served to remind her of Sarah's words.

As men lowered the bodies into the ground, the rector named each one. All the temper melted from her as their names filled her ears. Tears welled up in her eyes and tumbled unhindered down her cheeks. Edward put his arm around her waist just as her legs buckled beneath her. Suddenly Edward's body went rigid.

His fierce whisper sounded next to her ear, *"Where* is your sword?" He gripped her tighter around the waist. "As we speak the corrupt Kirkguards are readying themselves in the trees, south of us." No sooner did the words leave his lips and the charge began. Edward pushed her into the nearest grave. "Grab the sword!"

God forgive me! Rebecca grabbed the sword from the arms of the dead man. Edward helped her out of the grave and the fight began.

"Just drink it—and drink it all." Rebecca handed the bitter drink to the complaining chieftain. "Don't be such a wee one."

"I'm feeling better." Edward pushed her hand away refusing the drink. Sitting in the chair he brooded.

"I'll just get Sarah, then."

Rebecca placed the cup down on her way out, hearing Edward's grumpy reply as she closed the door.

"Go ahead—you think I can't handle Sarah?"

Something thumped against the door.

Rebecca raised her eyebrows and could feel laughter filling her chest. She couldn't resist opening the door to see what Edward had thrown. The chunk of cheese lay on the stone floor by the door. "Picking up my bad habits?" She laughed.

A metal chalice sailed toward her as she quickly shut the door. The cup clanked against it and bounced loudly onto the floor.

At that moment Rebecca's mother walked up to her. "I probably shouldn't ask what that noise is about."

"I think, mother, that was one of your prized wedding chalices. Would you please threaten that stubborn man into taking his fever brew?" Rebecca smiled at her mother.

Martha laughed. "Listen and learn."

Rebecca stayed outside the door as her mother opened it and did not close it.

"Edward MacCleary? You've dented my favorite wedding chalice! And the cheese is nearly ruined. Do you think it's easy to feed all these mouths? And you would feed the mice?"

Rebecca brought her hand to her mouth and held it tightly.

Her mother's courage surprised her. She would like to see Edward's face.

"Lady Martha! I didn't know . . ." Edward's voice faltered. Silence.

"What is this cup? It smells like fever brew. Drink it. Don't you know that without you our clans will not survive? They need your leadership, Edward. My daughter tells me you're a great leader. Oh, yes, brags about it."

Mother! Rebecca's hand left her mouth and went to her side, forming a fist.

His masculine voice answered, "Oh, aye? That is the vilest concoction I have ever tasted. Did a certain daughter put you up to this?"

Rebecca could hear a shuffling in the room and got ready to run. Suddenly the door swung open revealing Edward. A small scream escaped her lips as she ran to her chamber. Slamming the door, she collapsed on her bed in laughter.

Sobering at the feel of the black wool against her skin, she shrugged out of the dress. It formed a heap on the floor and she silently vowed never to wear it again. Plaids fared much better in a battle.

The Kirkguard clan must be getting weak. They turned tail and ran as soon as they realized that the Cavenaugh and MacCleary clans were ready for them. No blood was shed. Afterwards she made amends openly and returned the sword to the warrior's grave as his family wished. Edward railed her all the way back to the castle for not having her sword.

Slipping into her chemise, Rebecca thought about all she must do before the midday meal. First, she would see to her father and get instruction from him about her duties. Then, if time remained, she would see if Nathaniel behaved himself.

She chose a dress of her own design. After being kissed by Edward that summer long ago, she had been inspired to create an elaborate combination of the MacCleary and Cavenaugh plaids. The upper body of the dress sported the MacCleary colors, laced up in the middle to a plunging V-neck. The short puffy sleeves were made of Cavenaugh colors along with the top half of the sweeping skirt and MacCleary plaid on the bottom half.

A talented seamstress matched the plaids with artistic skill. They actually complemented each other. At first it was a kind of joke for Edward to enjoy. He never saw it. During the feud it was a treasured reminder of her heartbreak. Now, it held an all-together different meaning. It would be very appropriate for these times. Rebecca savored the soft feel of the flannel.

Walking to her dresser she dabbed rose water on her neck and chest. The scent filled her with sweet anticipation. Leaving her chamber, she wondered what Edward would think of it.

She knocked on her father's chamber door. Edward opened it. She bristled, walking past him and to her father's side. She asked how he felt, feeling his brow. He just nodded and dismissed Edward to talk in private with her. Rebecca's throat tightened. She swallowed.

Edward bowed slightly his eyes seem to glitter with appreciation as he left the room. The door closed. Rebecca opened her mouth to speak, but her father put up his hand to silence her.

"That dress will turn a head or two. Before you get your ire up, listen. I have asked Edward to lead the clan while I'm in this bed—"

"Father—" Rebecca's face burned as her heart sank to her toes.

"Don't interrupt me! You're a woman, Rebecca. Edward is a man—"

"Don't insult my intelligence—"

Before she could finish her father's voice shouted. "I told you not to interrupt me—you don't have the skill that it takes to lead a clan. You lack the brawn and the maturity." MacKey crossed his arms over his chest.

Rebecca knew from experience that once his arms crossed, the argument was over. "Father, the men respect me, and Edward is no more mature than I."

MacKey laughed. She turned her back to her father, not wanting him to see just how much his laughter hurt.

"Rebecca, love, ye know how proud I am of you. The men may respect you, but asking them to take orders from a woman would be asking too much. We need as much unity as possible in our clans. Edward is what unites them, aye, and you, dear child. That is why I gave Edward direct orders not to make any decisions without your approval . . . and though I suspect he didn't like that, he never once had the gall to interrupt me. And certainly not twice."

Rebecca turned around to face her father, his eyebrows raised. "I beg your pardon, Father."

"But then, he's not my beloved coddled daughter." Her father's smile melted her heart, as it always had.

She smiled back, suspecting her smile looked a little sly, as his words; without your approval, rang sweetly in her ears.

"Don't take advantage of the power I've given you. I think that sometimes you forget Edward is much bigger than you are. I expect you to deal delicately and fairly. Should I hear differently I will take away that order."

"So be it. Did Sarah tend to your wound today?"

"Aye, its been seen to."

"Then I'll get on with my visits." Rebecca kissed her father lightly on the cheek. "Get better before Edward and I kill each other." Rebecca winked at her father and left the room, his musical laughter following after her.

She made her way to Nathan and Lorelei's chamber, watching the way people reacted to her dress. Some of the faces turned sour, but most smiled and bowed to her.

Knocking at the chamber door she heard Lorelei's sweet voice calling for her to enter. She looked tired and not at all happy.

Rebecca walked with her to his side. His face looked like stone. Although his eyes glittered, no other emotion showed. Rebecca touched his brow and could feel no heat. His mouth looked clamped shut. He would not speak.

"Have you cleaned his wound recently?" Rebecca looked at Lorelei's frightened face.

"He wouldn't let me. He's been an ogre." Lorelei's voice shook.

"Then I'll have to do it, and don't think I'll be as gentle as Lorelei." Rebecca removed the cloth surrounding his wound carefully despite her words. "Seems I'll have to teach Lorelei my ways, take a little sweetness away and give her some spine." She winked at Lorelei. "Don't feel too badly, Nathan. I would've taken her under my wing even if you behaved nicely."

Nathan bellowed in pain as Rebecca poured a cleansing tincture over his wound. "I'll get you, Rebecca Cavenaugh. You wait until I'm out of this damned bed—and you'll stay away from my wife."

"Tsk, tsk, is that any way to show your thanks. Healing your wound as I am. Maybe I'll have to ask Edward to teach you some manners. No . . . I'll let Lorelei have the honor of that task." Wrapping the wound, she turned to Lorelei. "Come to the great hall with me, we'll eat and talk." Rebecca put her arm around Lorelei and asked her oldest boy to see to the children. Waving to Nathan they walked out of the chamber.

"Rebecca! Lorelei!" Nathan's bellow could be heard down the hall.

Rebecca noticed how Lorelei trembled and stopped walking, at the sound of his cries. "Don't ye dare go to him." She gripped Lorelei's arm. "You're just as important as that bellowing mule. Don't ever think you're not . . ." They walked to the great hall to sup.

The meal had been announced and still Rebecca did not enter the hall. Edward washed his hands and drew his dirk from his belt. As he cut his bread, he looked up to see Rebecca and Lorelei. What an exquisite dress.

Edward rose and pulled out a chair for Lorelei. "Lorelei, how's Nathan?"

"Well enough." Lorelei sat down.

"He's been a bear has he?" He gave Lorelei an understanding smile as she nodded. Pulling out the chair next to his for Rebecca, he kissed her lightly on the cheek as she sat. "Rebecca Cavenaugh, you're full of surprises." He smiled down at her.

His hand caressed the soft material of the skirt, his eyes savored the soft mounds rising from the low-cut neckline, and his nose breathed in her sweet scent.

"Do you like my creation?" Rebecca's smile was winsome.

"I do. Maybe we should finish this meal in my chamber." Edward looked like he would rise.

"Nay! That would not be appropriate at all." Her gaze darted to the other people.

"They could only imagine." Taking her hand under the table he brought it to rest on the evidence of his passion. Holding her hand there he watched as the color of her face nearly matched the rhododendrons that adorned the table.

Edward followed her gaze as it fell on a visiting clergyman. He quickly released her hand. She pinched him soundly on his thigh before moving her hand to her own lap. Then she quickly washed her hands in her wash bowl.

Ow. Edward narrowed his eyes and tried to make his feelings known with the look he gave her. She didn't flinch and even looked victorious. Her father must have told her the condition he gave Edward. So when did he ever not ask her opinion . . . he knew better than to ask that question out loud.

"Did the talk with your father go well?" Edward watched the look of victory die on her face. He preened.

"As well as it could." Her eyes narrowed. But then he noticed that she brushed away her anger. Composing herself, she began her meal.

"Very good, Rebecca." Edward lifted his goblet of wine toward her in a salute.

"We'll see who of us is more mature." Rebecca chewed a little harder.

"Is that what he said? You're not mature enough?" A short laugh escaped his lips.

The look on Rebecca's face could only be interpreted as a wish to bite off her own tongue. He laughed loudly.

"No . . . aye . . . I don't want to talk about it." Her eyes became glassy and she wouldn't look at him.

Edward patted her leg. He tried to listen to the conversation she held with Lorelei.

"You see, Lorelei, through the ages women have made many mistakes. But the worst mistake is to let a man . . ." Rebecca whispered the last few words and then turned to Edward. "This is a private conversation." She turned back to Lorelei. "Women don't realize the power they wield over men . . . look at Cleopatra . . ."

"Ach, Lorelei, I hope you're not listening to this drivel. Cleopatra was evil." Edward gave Rebecca a stern look.

"Do you mind?" Rebecca returned his look.

"Finish your meal, Rebecca, and stop filling Lorelei's head with foolish notions." Edward turned back to his food.

"The way to handle a man is to let him think he has the upper hand. Then take things into your own hands, when it really matters, that is."

Edward glanced over and saw Rebecca pat Lorelei's arm.

"We'll talk more later. For now if Nathan is anything less than a gentleman to you, just refuse to help him."

Lorelei seemed to finally find her voice. "Oh, I couldn't."

"That's where you're wrong. Just try it once. Nathan can't do anything to you in his state of health. I don't think he would ever hurt you, he doesn't seem that way."

"I suppose if he acts as badly as he has been . . . I could try it." Lorelei actually looked hopeful.

Poor old Nathan. Edward suddenly liked the idea of Nathan having to put up with a woman behaving as Rebecca did. "But, Lorelei, always make sure ye get a bit of this . . ." He kissed Rebecca full on the mouth as she struggled. ". . . and that." Edward stood and swooped Rebecca out of her chair. Very calmly he carried her out of the great hall.

Rebecca's color rose beautifully. She whispered under her breath, "My father will be very upset with you—" Then she smiled the most glorious smile at someone behind him.

Edward looked in the direction of her gaze. A clergyman stood there, looking rather upset. Edward let Rebecca slip from his arms to her feet.

"Dear sir, is this not Lady Rebecca, the wife of Ruppert Kirkguard?" The clergyman spoke calmly.

"Yes, but only by a very unfortunate error. She was to be mine. Do you know what goes on between the Kirkguard clan and the Cavenaughs?" Edward could feel his color heighten as the stout man walked closer.

"Please excuse us, Lady Rebecca. Would you go back to the dining hall?" The man walked over to Edward with confidence and guided him to a private room, like a sheep.

Edward thought seriously about drawing his sword and teaching this man a lesson. However, he did have a healthy fear of God. Instead, he found himself on the receiving end of a lesson.

Rebecca knew she must be blushing horribly and did not really want to enter the dining hall again. A nervous laugh played in her throat at the thought of Edward being lectured by the clergyman. But she could see the wisdom of her returning to the hall so she walked back to her chair. Her laugh finally escaped when she saw the look of concern on Lorelei's face.

"Seems my reputation won't be soiled too much this night." She winked at Lorelei and they both laughed. Rebecca finished her wine. "I'll walk back to Nathan with you and check him once more."

Lorelei nodded, she seemed to be deep in thought. "But suppose while I'm not helping Nathan, he falls or . . ."

"Lorelei, don't make excuses. You can still watch. Just refuse to listen to anything other than polite words. Would you let even your eldest son talk to you as Nathan has?"

"No, certainly not."

"Then why should you take it from Nathan? You shouldn't. He'll respect you for it."

As Lorelei and Rebecca entered the rooms they were met with a commotion of voices, full of accusations. All of them seemed to be saying, "How dare you leave us alone."

"Whist!" Lorelei's loud voice silenced the cries. "I have been to dinner with Lady Rebecca and enjoyed myself thoroughly.

You are all more than capable of taking care of yourselves once in a while. Son, have you gotten your father's dinner?"

"Nay." Her son looked stunned.

"Then you best get a-goin' before all the best meat is gone. Go!"

He scrambled out of the room.

Rebecca beamed proudly.

Nathan's glare threatened to singe her hair. "Just you wait Rebecca Cavenaugh. When I'm out of this bed I'll teach you both a lesson."

Lorelei stood taller. "Don't you threaten us Nathaniel Mac-Cleary. You're not the only one who can use given and sir names. You'll show some manners or you'll be stewing in your own juices. Literally." Lorelei walked toward the bed.

"Speaking of which," Nathan whispered, "If you don't help me soon . . . please Lorelei, I'm in pain."

Rebecca laughed. "I'm leaving, Lorelei. I think you can manage. I did hear some manners." Rebecca left the chamber feeling victorious.

She saw Edward walking down the hall and tiptoed up behind him.

"You'll have to sneak a little softer than that if you want any advantage." Edward didn't turn as he spoke.

Rebecca reached up to hit the side of his head with her palm, just as he turned. She withdrew her hand, pretending to scratch her head. Edward's eyebrows rose, she hadn't fooled him.

"How did you fare? Did you have your own private sermon?" She watched his face carefully and could feel her stomach tighten. "What happened?"

"I'm not to touch you until the marriage can be taken care of by the church." He frowned.

"No one will know of it. After all we already have—"

"Nay, Rebecca, I gave my word."

"Why!" Rebecca looked around to see if anyone heard her scream. "Why did you promise?"

"I had to. Right now I think it's for the best. We need to keep our minds on the battle and winning. It's for the best." Edward looked like the stubborn highlander that he was.

"Ach, right! And so instead our minds and hearts will be tortured for want of each other. That's a good way to keep our minds on the battle?" Rebecca wanted to stomp her feet.

"Rebecca . . . it won't be long now. Use your passion to help us defeat the Kirkguards." Edward's voice sounded husky. His hand reached out to caress her cheek.

She breathed in his musky scent and could not stand the verdict. A slap echoed through the hall as she hit his hand away. "Don't touch me." Feeling like a spoiled child, she stomped past him to her chamber. Hot tears burning her cheeks.

"That's it, my love, keep the passion burning. When we can be together at last, it will be all the more sweet." Edward grinned at her as she turned toward him once more.

"And will it be sweet when one of us does not return from the battle?" Rebecca almost ran when she caught sight of the fury on Edward's face. He strode toward her. But instead she could only stand there, frozen in place. Before she could move his hand landed a stinging slap to her wet cheek.

He gripped her shoulders and shook her. "Take those words back—don't you ever say such a thing—don't you even think it."

Rebecca watched the raw emotions on his face. She didn't answer. He stopped shaking her.

"Take it back—now!"

"I can't take it back, it's what we must face." Rebecca tried to free herself and turn away.

Edward held her tighter. "The first way to fail is to think it. Now wipe that thought out of your head. Tell me we'll not fail. We'll live to see our children's children. Say it." He shook her once.

A small crowd of people gathered, watching.

"Say it." Edward's voice turned from a roar to a quiet pleading.

The fever had not left him, her shoulders ached with the pressure of his hands and their heat scorched her. Feeling foolish, she realized the truth of his concern. "We'll not fail. We'll live to see our children's children." Rebecca heard a murmur from the crowd.

"Say it again." Edward shook her again and would not release her.

"We'll not fail. We'll live to see our children's children." She pushed against him to be released, her muscles tense, fear in the pit of her stomach. *Why don't these people go away?*

Edward turned toward the people. "Leave us." This time he hugged her tightly against him and she felt his whisper on her hair. "Again!"

The people walked away.

"We'll not fail. We'll live to see our children's children." As she spoke the words her muscles relaxed against him.

Edward let her go. "Whenever you doubt that as the truth, you say it until you believe it. Promise me."

"I promise." She let her tears flow and with that flow all the poisonous thoughts left her. She looked at him with pleading.

He held her, gently kissing her hair, her eyes, and the trail of her tears. Then he set her away from him and walked toward his chamber.

Rebecca entered her chamber, as if in a dream. She walked to her dresser and poured water from a ewer into a large bowl. Setting the ewer beside the bowl, she smoothed her hands through the cool water. Leaning over, she splashed the water onto her hot face.

A light knock sounded at the door. Rebecca dried her face with a blanket and walked to open the door. Sarah walked in.

"Sarah, how do you always know when you're needed?"

"It's hard not to know when you stand in the hallway making such a display." In spite of her words, Sarah's face showed her understanding.

"Please, go to Edward. He still has a fever."

Sarah nodded. Without a word she headed to Edward's chamber. Rebecca lay down on her bed, closing her eyes.

She didn't know how long she rested when the sound of Edward's yell, and a crash, caused her eyes to open in alarm. Heart pounding, she ran to his chamber with her sword drawn.

"You see, Sarah, I told you. I have my own she-devil to protect me." Edward chuckled and winced as Sarah drained his infected wound.

Rebecca thought she must look a sight and meekly lowered her sword. She went to Sarah's side to help with the procedure. "Why didn't you call me?"

"You slept peacefully, for once, I didn't want to disturb that. I've handled worse." Sarah smiled at Edward. 'Twasn't so bad, see?"

"I'd rather not." Edward closed his eyes and moaned. "Sarah you're makin' my arm nearly worthless for battle. We should be headed out now, while they still assemble their forces."

"Nay, I'm savin' your life and your arm, dear as they are." Sarah continued to dress the wound.

Edward gave Sarah the most charming smile. Rebecca could feel her blood running hot within her. Perhaps she had the fever now. Absently she cleaned up the herbs and bowls that Edward caused to spill onto the floor. Her mind going over the words he had spoken. She could assemble the men and lead them to Ruppert. She could rid the world of a few Kirkguards. Edward needed to rest.

How could she spirit away an entire army without Edward knowing? Just as the thought entered her mind her hand picked up a small bag of valerian root, ground to a powder. Could she dare? A strong dose of this root in wine would surely keep him asleep. Before her senses could rebel against such a treacherous act, she slipped the contents of the bag into his wine goblet.

Rebecca's senses begged her not to give the wine to Edward. Her stubborn nature handed the goblet to him.

"This should make the pain less." Edward looked at her as he raised the glass to his lips. "What . . . Rebecca, what are you thinking?" He didn't drink.

"Nothing, I'm tired." She tried to look innocent as Sarah and Edward stared at her.

"We should take action quickly, but it may be what they

expect. We'll have a meeting later on, get some rest and I'll summon you when it's time." He finally took a sip of his wine.

Rebecca could not bear to see him drink the mixture she'd given him. She turned away nodding, and quickly left the room.

How could I do such a thing? She started to walk down the hall, her mind circling dangerously over what Edward would do to her when he found out. She paced the hallway. Maybe it wasn't too late to stop him. Running back to his chamber she burst in.

Sarah looked red in the face her hands rested on her hips. Edward lay on his pillow, eyes closed. Too late.

"Sarah, is he all right?"

Sarah nodded and walked toward Rebecca. "Did you put that valerian root in the wine, Rebecca?" Her eyes sparkled with the brightness of unshed tears.

Rebecca looked nervously at Edward's still form. "Sarah, he needs rest. I'm afraid I'll lose him if he tries to fight now."

"He's a strong man . . . he can fight. You might lose him for what ye just did." Disappointment blazed in Sarah's expression. She turned from her.

"Did I put in too much root?"

"Nay. How do you think he'll feel when he wakes to find you gone with the army? Get from my sight. I'll not look on you now."

"Sarah . . ." Rebecca fought the lump that rose in her throat. She ran from the room. It was done. She would continue.

Sarah thumped Edward's leg with her fist. "Laird, what was that about? You want her to think you drank the wine?"

"Aye! And don't start makin' excuses for her, Sarah. She tried to put me to sleep—and do you know why?" Edward could feel his reason leaving him as he rose from the bed. "Ach, wasn't it nice of her to check and be sure she didn't kill me? She's gone too far this time."

"Laird Edward, she's worried about your health, and so am I. Suppose the fever gets worse and you're in the midst of battle.

She had a point—it could get you killed. What would be worse dead or asleep?"

"Worse! Let Rebecca lead the men, and I'll give you worse!"

"Oh, aye." Sarah lowered her eyes.

NINETEEN

Before her brashness could leave her she went to her father's chamber and knocked lightly on the door.

She walked into the chamber and let her father know that Edward wouldn't be able to lead the fight. Forcing her eyes to meet his, she wondered at the unpleasant taste in her mouth as she asked to lead the clans.

"Will Edward be well?"

"Aye, after a while." Rebecca lowered her eyes. "He wanted to call a meeting."

"Call the meeting. Get the men together. I do not wish the Kirkguard Clan to darken our castle gates again. And if Edward is not able to rise by that time, you will lead them." Her father closed his eyes.

"I'll call the meeting, Father." Quickly leaving the room, before he could change his mind, she heard her mother voicing her objection.

Rebecca found a guard with a clarion. As the horn sounded, she made her way to the meeting room. Group after group of men came in to fill the chairs surrounding the large table. The room quieted all of the men looked at Rebecca. Her stomach muscles clenched tightly, it seemed her sensibilities always let her know when she was about to blunder.

"I am sorry to inform you that Laird Edward is not in good health and will not lead us in this fight." Rebecca paused to clear her throat of the untruth. "My father has given me consent to lead you."

The men in the room murmured to each other.

Rebecca spoke louder. "Let us first agree to set out to attack the Kirkguard castle. Say aye if you support this action."

The room quieted. All the men seemed to be looking past her. She turned.

Edward and her father loomed in the doorway. "It seems I've got my health back. Please be seated, Lady Rebecca. Let us discuss our actions more fully."

He and her father walked slowly to the head of the table, where she stood. A warm wave swelled through her body and she began to shake. Edward caught her as she swooned and lightly kissed her cheek. *This must be how Judas felt.* He helped her into a chair. Her father sat next to her. Rebecca looked at her lap. She knew her cheeks must be stained red from her guilt.

"As you can see I'm recovered enough to lead this fight. My thanks to you, Rebecca, for acting while I could not."

Looking up, Rebecca did not miss the steel daggers in the depths of his eyes. Her heart ached and tightened in her chest.

Tears burned in her eyes, blocking her vision. She fought to contain them and put on a brave front, listening respectfully to Edward. At least he had not humiliated her.

His words droned on, but her mind could not digest them. He seemed to be arguing with the men, trying to convince them to stay and protect the castle.

She couldn't look at her father. Her shame gripped her until she could barely breathe. A thunderous aye brought her out of her thoughts. As the men left the room Rebecca stayed in her chair, looking at her hands folded in her lap. She glanced at her father as he rose.

"Walk me back to my chamber, daughter." His voice sounded rough. She knew the pain in his eyes went deeper than his mortal wound.

"Aye, Father." She put her shoulder under his and her arm around his waist for support, glad to be spared Edward's wrath at least for a time.

"My disappointment in you cuts me deeply. Do you see why I did not put my trust in your leadership?"

Rebecca nodded.

"You let your emotions rule your head. You don't think of the harm you'll do. I should have you put into the keep and be done with you. But, I think that would be kind compared to what Edward may have in store for you."

The hot tears finally flowed from her eyes. Her heart broke into millions of little sharp pieces. Rebecca and her father entered his chamber. Her mother would not look at her.

"I'm sorry, Father. I was badly mistaken. I thought what I did was for the best, for Edward—and as you say—I let my emotions lead me in the wrong direction. I'm sorry." Rebecca slowly left the room but didn't miss the quiet words her mother spoke.

"God speed, Rebecca."

"It seems I've put my trust and life in the hands of someone who is undeserving of both." Edward's words cut through her like a cold blade.

"I made an error." Rebecca fenced his words. Keeping a healthy distance between them. "I know it won't help to make amends, but—I was wrong."

"And maybe you were wrong about other things. Maybe that *was* you the messenger saw with the man who undoubtedly killed my father." He advanced on her.

"Nay, I never made that error." She moved farther away.

"How am I to believe your words when your actions undo me? Didn't you think I would smell the herb in my wine?"

"I didn't think . . . I just acted."

"What will it be next? Hemlock?"

Rebecca gasped. "How could you think I would kill you?" Her stomach churned as the broken pieces of her heart stabbed her. He would never love her again. But the tears would not come. "Please believe that I acted only for your good."

"Get ready for the raid, Rebecca." A loud slam announced his departure from her chamber.

Rebecca got control of her thoughts and rose. As she prepared herself a flood of emotion made her nearly rend the dress from her body. But her hand stopped before she could destroy another thing of beauty.

Unbuttoning each tiny button nearly undid her resolve. Was she really that badly in need of growing up? She could fight a man's fight, but did she lack honor? The confused thoughts tumbled over and over in her mind. How foolish is it to go off into battle with a fever?

Sarah walked in unannounced. "I brought extra herbs for you to take. Ointments, fresh roots. Can you think of anything else?"

"That should do." Rebecca put up a solid wall of stone between herself and Sarah. Because if she let her emotions show, even a little, she did not think she could ever recover herself. She walked purposefully away from Sarah's always-open arms.

"Fine then, Rebecca, be well. You'll see this through, I have nay doubt. Brighter days are ahead." Sarah left the room.

Pulling on her breeches she thought over what would be needed in her pouch. She put on a saffron linen shirt with loose sleeves, her clan hose and black leather boots. Finally, she reached for her tartan. Picking up the Cavenaugh plaid she sighed as she caught a glimpse of the MacCleary colors folded beneath it. Her arm paused, what colors should she wear? Cavenaugh.

Just to be sure she carefully rolled the MacCleary tartan and wrapped it in an extra belt. Well, she thought, she might need a blanket. Rebecca couldn't remain upset with herself for very long. She would survive whatever happened, with or without her heart.

She finished filling her pouch. Taking Edward's ointment in her hand, she made her way to the kitchen coffer to gather her food for the trip. When she arrived at the kitchen she met Edward as he filled his bag with supplies.

"Here is your ointment. I suggest you pack it and use it often." Rebecca poked the small bag into the crook of his arm.

Edward turned toward her and steadied the ointment. "Did Sarah prepare it, or you? If you did, I'd rather get my own."

"Sarah did." Rebecca swallowed back the words that would flow from her lips. Not for Edward's sake, but for the children and others who crowded the kitchen.

He seemed to look into her soul. His dark eyes looked empty and so lonely . . . almost lost. Rebecca's eyes filled with tears as he turned to pack his food. Her aunt came to her rescue.

"Rebecca, here lass, take this food." Mavis' mother smiled at her with a quivering lip.

"Isn't that wonderful, Mavis being back?" Rebecca smiled.

"Aye . . ." Her aunt looked as if she would like to say something more.

"Is everything all right?"

"Aye, we're fine. You take care of yourself." She hugged her.

"I will." Rebecca took her bag of food and left the kitchen. She welcomed the cool air that met her face as she left the crowded castle. Making her way to the stables, she hoped they would not be overly busy with people.

It seemed she made it to the stable before most of the men. A few saddled their horses. Rebecca found her white mare and remembered how she had ridden into the middle of the two clans proclaiming peace. It seemed so long ago. Those ever-present tears came flooding down her cheeks. She ducked between the hay mounds and sat down heavily.

A few loud sobs escaped her before she could control her latest tumult of emotions. Suddenly a huge slobbering tongue licked her wet cheek. Her eyes flew open to sleek black fur.

"Galahad? Galahad! Oh my, how did you get out of the pens? All the people in my life have caused me to forget my faithful hound. How could I?" Rebecca patted and hugged the writhing mass of dog. Her Galahad. The men had laughed at her when she first trained him for battle. Later on they began to train their own dogs.

Galahad learned fast and was very useful. When she rode her

horse, she taught the dog to retrieve weapons. Then she would pretend to fall from her mount and set it running, Galahad would chase the horse and return, leading it by its reins. Even the men joined her games and they found that the dog could remember whose horse belonged to whom, always leading each horse to the correct person.

"Sit! Galahad, down." Would he remember? "Let's give it a try. You'll join us, we'll put some of that learning to use."

A shadow darkened the stall. "That hound is not coming with you. Do you think this is a holiday?" Edward went to grab the large dog's collar.

Rebecca jumped to her feet to stop the dog's inevitable reaction. "Stay! Leave the dog to me."

Galahad growled deeply in his throat.

"On second thought, you may need the protection." Edward calmly led his steed away.

"All right, boy, here's your chance. I hope you remember everything I taught you." Quickly she haltered and saddled her horse.

She watched Edward speak to some men across the yard. His glare never left her. Carefully she placed her horse's rein into the dog's mouth. He immediately sat and stayed. "Good boy!"

She went back to the kitchen and packed a bag of scraps for Galahad. She also got another water skin. Running up the back stairs to her chamber, she rummaged through an old chest and found the small leather saddlebag she had made for her dog. It fit like a vest and served as armor. Breathing in the familiar scents, she looked around her chamber one last time, and walked out.

She should say goodbye to her mother and father, but that would be too hard. Her already raw emotions told her to leave quickly.

The sight that greeted her as she crossed the yard almost put the laughter back into her. Edward tried to get the reins from Galahad without success. The dog growled and even managed a bark through clenched teeth when Edward got too close.She whistled and her dog quickly brought the horse to her.

Edward put his hand on his hips and actually smiled. "Useful hound."

"Aye." Rebecca pretended not to care, but his smile sent a healing to her heart. She quickly fit the harness onto Galahad, whispering endearments. "Good Gally, good boy."

"Are you ready?"

"Aye." Rebecca mounted her horse, the dog sat beside her, ready. "Good boy."

"What?" Edward looked puzzled as he mounted his horse.

"The dog. I said, 'good boy' to the dog." Rebecca laughed. Her heart healed some more.

Edward rode to the head of the army. Rebecca followed beside him. He slowed his pace to ride beside her.

"What else can the dog do?"

"He knows how to retrieve horses, swords, and other weapons. He's had lots of practice learning how to run beside horses, and not get trampled. Galahad will attack anyone who gains advantage over me."

"And get himself killed, most likely." Edward looked down at the dog.

"He's very smart and very fast."

They reached the head of the line and Edward raised a horn to his lips to signal the men. Two short blasts move out. The force moved toward the castle gate, with Edward and Rebecca in the lead.

"Let's get some things understood. You'll ride by my side and not leave it. You'll not say nay to any order I give you, or you will suffer what any man would for disobeying a chieftain. Do you understand?" The frowning Edward narrowed his eyes as he glared down at her.

"Understood." Rebecca struggled to keep her composure.

"And . . . Ruppert is mine," he pointed his finger at her, "you stay away from him. *I* will give him his due." As soon as the words left his mouth, he kicked his mount and rode through the castle gate.

She snapped into action following behind. Galahad galloped happily beside her, his tongue lulling out the side of his mouth.

Rebecca heard her name being called from the gate. She stopped to see who called her.

"Mavis?" Rebecca and her mount slipped to the side of the men and back to the gate where Mavis stood.

"Rebecca, don't ride out. Stop the clan. I know that Ruppert's army is waiting in the pass for you . . . a surprise attack. Tell them not to go!" She ran back into the castle, clearly in a panic.

"Wait! Mavis, how do you know?" But Rebecca's voice did not reach her.

Edward already looked for her. She galloped to catch up, her thoughts whirling in her head. She took one last look at Mavis' back. Her hair is the same color as mine. Was it Mavis the guard had seen? How could she know what the Kirkguards planned . . . unless . . .

"Already you aren't following my orders?" Edward swung his horse around hers watching how Galahad moved from being trampled. His dark gaze fell on Rebecca.

"Edward, I know who the guard saw that night."

"Spare me your lies." He rode on ahead of her.

"Listen to me! Mavis just told me—"

Edward continued on—too far away to hear her words. Rebecca could not believe he would ride away from her as she spoke such important news. She saw red. Breathing in deep gulps of air she rode to catch up to him. *Calm down.* She approached as he gave some men instructions.

"Edward, I must talk to you, in private . . . please." She swallowed her pride.

"Not now." He dismissed her without even looking her way.

"Now! Edward." She halted her horse in the middle of the throng of men. The men eyed her with concern. Her face burned with the fire of her anger.

He stopped and turned to see what kept her. "Get goin' Rebecca!"

She crossed her arms and sat unmoving on the horse, her hound sat dutifully beside her as the men streamed past her. She watched as Edward moved to one side to let the men continue. Riveting her with a deadly stare. Rebecca still sat in the same place, even as the last man went by.

Edward rode up to her with an evil glint in his eyes.

Galahad jumped up at his horse, teeth flashing. Edward's horse stepped away.

"Galahad! Stay!"

The dog sat, a growling smile on his face.

Edward rode his horse around the other side of her and grabbed her by the scruff of the neck. "What is the meaning of this?"

Galahad barked wildly until Rebecca hushed him again.

He would have done better to hold her arms. Rebecca could feel her rage becoming complete. With steel will she controlled her impulse to strike him. Instead she clenched her hands into fists. "I am trying to tell you something important."

Edward released her roughly. She almost fell from her mount. "And I am trying to tell you we have no time for disagreements and petty—"

That did it. Before Edward could wink an eye, and with the sound of metal on metal, she unsheathed her sword and held it to his throat. "Ye'll listen to me Edward MacCleary, and listen now."

"You must not value your life—speak."

Her horse shifted and she took the blade away, afraid she would actually cut him. "My cousin Mavis must have been the woman the guard saw and thought was me. She disappeared that same night. We thought she was dead."

"Rebecca, this is hardly the time to be beggin' innocence."

"Just listen to me, you bull-headed highlander."

Edward launched himself at her knocking them both into a heap in the heather. Galahad bit and growled, trying to get at Edward and protect Rebecca. The fall knocked the breath right out of her. As Rebecca struggled to regain her breath, the dog's teeth nearly contacted with Edward's injured arm.

"Galahad, stay! Edward! Have ye gone mad?" Her body ached as she tried to sit up.

Edward looked into her eyes. His eyes danced with a familiar hunger that she could feel deep within her as soon as their bodies made contact. "Tell me, then." His voice sounded thick with emotion.

"Mavis just spoke to me and told me that the Kirkguard army is waiting in the pass for us—we must stop the men."

"Damn!"

They both scrambled to their feet to see the army nearly at the pass. Edward leaped to his horse and galloped toward them. Rebecca found Galahad with her sword hilt in his mouth. Taking it quickly, she mounted and spurred her horse on after Edward. She watched as he took out his clarion and blew a long tone, and another, announcing the attack signal.

Her world seemed to go in slow motion as the massive army wheeled around to see the chieftain waving the horn in the air and pointing to the pass. As if as one the clansmen reeled back to the mountain pass and drew their weapons.

The Kirkguard clan, hearing the alert, began to flee.

"They must not have enough men, they needed the surprise advantage again." Edward ordered the men to give chase.

They traveled single file through the pass. Some of the Kirkguards remained hidden and attacked. Some clansmen fell. Edward and Rebecca rode at the end of the chase. The rage on his face told her that, should the retreat horn sound she would be smart to get as far away from him as she could. Maybe she should go back now. She had to find out what Mavis was guilty of before the clan got to her.

Just as Rebecca started to turn a flash of Kirkguard colors caught her eye in a tree above Edward. Before a sound could leave her throat, the man jumped onto Edward's horse, unseating him and just barely missing Edward's neck with his sword. Her scream caused Galahad to jump at her as if to say, "Don't forget me!"

"Go! Get the horse!" Rebecca followed the dog as he ran toward Edward's mount. The Kirkguard turned to charge Edward, blade flashing. Edward stood ready, holding his sword in both hands. Suddenly a black flash jumped up on the surprised Kirkguard, knocking him from the saddle. Edward shook his head as if he couldn't believe Galahad's battle sense. The other man got to his feet, sword ready.

The men, equally matched, battled on foot. Rebecca charged to one side, causing the Kirkguard to lose concentration and fall to the ground under Edward's swift sword.

Relief flooded Rebecca and she laughed. "Lost your mount did ye, Chieftain?"

She turned her horse to see Edward standing rigidly, sword in hand, staring at the hound who sat calmly holding his mount's reins. She watched in amazement as he went to the dog and offered a quickly produced piece of meat from his pouch. He spoke words of affection as Galahad's tail wagged and he chewed up the meat. "Good boy!" Edward mounted quickly and rode toward Rebecca. "One word from you and I promise you won't sit for a week!"

His quick smile, as he whisked by her, mended her aching heart a wee bit more. Suddenly, her urge for the fight surged stronger. Mavis would have to wait.

They charged after their clans. The green mountains whipped by on both sides of her in a blur. A damp smell in the air made her look to the skies. Angry clouds rolled over the mountain south of them. The sound of thunder mingled with the thunderous sound of the horse's hooves. The further they traveled from her castle the more uneasy her thoughts became.

"Edward!" She tried to yell above the noise.

He looked back briefly and continued on. Then he sounded a loud blast from the horn. Retreat. The blast sounded from other horns and slowly the force turned. Rebecca and Edward were once more in the lead.

She rode quietly behind him, and watched her hound fall into step with Edward's horse. *Traitor.* Still, she was glad for the many feats she'd taught Galahad. It amazed her that he remembered how to retrieve horses.

Edward slowed his horse to ride beside her. Galahad, apparently remembering himself, fell into step next to her. She looked boldly at Edward, who stared back at her, a frown creasing his brow.

"How did that animal know to knock the Kirkguard off my horse?" His expression seemed to tell her not to mince words.

"That used to be his favorite trick. We performed it quite a bit. Galahad has a superb memory. Even when we all set out on different mounts—he'd remember them. We never could fool him."

"Amazing." Edward stared straight ahead his face looking blank.

The cold wall between them began to grate on her emotions. She decided to have some fun. Whistling at Galahad, she galloped ahead. They went through a range of tricks they used to perform. She threw a bag down and the hound returned it to her while they both continued to gallop. She slid her sword down onto the ground, stopped, and waited for the dog to bring it to her outstretched hand, which he did just as the army caught up to her.

The men applauded her efforts. She smiled her appreciation. Reaching into her pouch she produced a few morsels and threw them to Galahad. He caught each one, slobbering them down. Her horse fell into step with Edward's mount.

"Are you going to forgive me then?" She reacted to her own words with a molten flow of emotions running through her.

Edward looked over at her frowning. "I don't want to speak of it now."

"Well I do!" Rebecca could feel heat creeping up her neck and to her face.

"Then I suggest you speak it to the wind and far from my ears." Edward urged his mount ahead of her.

Her emotions rolled in her stomach and she thought she would vomit. The sick feeling took her by surprise and caused her to ride slower. She watched the powerful form that Edward made as he rode. His body moved with the horse as one. He looked so natural on his mount.

Rebecca continued to watch him ride, lost in the beauty of his whole being. He couldn't turn her love away. Damn, he'd promised the clergyman. She took her gaze away from Edward and looked at the trees in the distance. Maybe that's why he kept up this guise. Her mind fell to thinking of a tumble they'd had. Her body tingled to her toes.

Suddenly, a flash of metal caught her eye. Before she could draw her sword her body flew backward, the dull side of a sword pushed against her neck. She drew her dagger, but stilled her actions as she turned to see Edward's angry face next to hers.

"Dreaming on the trail will land you in a deep earthy hole. Don't let me catch you at it again." He took the sword away and released her. "At least you kept your horse."

Her legs ached with the effort. She rubbed her neck and watched her good feelings melt to the dirt. Her shame sparked her ire. Just as she would swipe her knife at him, she noticed the other men watching. This time she knew she had to make the right choice.

Swallowing a great lump of pride, she found her voice. "You're right of course." But as her nature would have it she added quietly, "Perhaps if you kept your lady satisfied she would not be dreamin' of it." The words only reached Edward's ears.

His eyes narrowed. "I suggest you learn to face life's events with a bit more maturity and self control." He spoke privately in return.

Rebecca glared into his eyes and he glared right back.

Control. All right, she would show him control. She made her heart freeze into a piece of ice. Ripping her gaze from his, she rode on.

The castle loomed ahead, looking dark and lonely. The clouds cut short the gloaming and darkness covered the land. A heavy rain began to fall. Edward quickened the army's pace. She shivered as the freezing rain pelted her face, and startled as a large streak of lightning lit the sky. As the thunder sounded, the ground beneath them rumbled.

Every nerve in Rebecca's body sagged beneath the pouring rain. Her legs held fast to the bounding horse. She glanced beside her barely able to see Galahad running. Holding her reins in one hand she brought her tartan up around her head.

They reached the castle and dismounted next to the barn, the stable hands took the horses. A man came to take Galahad.

"Leave him be." Rebecca's rough voice stopped him. The valuable animal would lounge in front of her fire for the work he'd done this day. Without a glance for anyone, she walked the dog up to her chamber.

Drying herself by the warm fire, she peeled each sodden piece of clothing off her body. A knock on the door sent her running for a robe, which she wrapped around her naked body. Tying her sash as she walked to the door, she opened it to Sarah. Rebecca tried not to look disappointed as she walked in.

"Try not to look so happy ta see me." Sarah grinned at her.

"Have ye seen Edward—checked his arm?" She lowered her eyes, remembering Sarah's shunning of her after her misguided deed. Rebecca walked to the fireside and took off Galahad's harness.

With a loud yawn, the dog settled next to the fire.

"I tried. Are you wounded?" Sarah walked closer to her, reaching out for her hand.

"No. Have you seen Mavis? Ach, what a mess. Did you ever notice how Mavis looks like me from behind?" Rebecca faced Sarah.

"Aye, I saw them take her to the dungeon. Her hair is the same shade and texture as yours. I think you know what she's guilty of. Do ye not?" Sarah looked sad.

"Aye. But why would she do it?" Rebecca sat down on a footstool by the fire as Sarah combed through her hair.

"She fell in love with a Kirkguard spy. Those are his children she brought with her. Ruppert killed him for no good reason. Mavis fled back here."

Rebecca turned to gape at her.

"She came to me after she warned you."

"She may as well have killed herself." Rebecca could feel a rage building. Betray her family for love of an enemy? "I have to see her."

"Rebecca, I must warn you. I tried to see to Laird Edward's arm and he nearly threw me out bodily. I'll try again now, but

I'll not speak to him." Sarah finished combing and moved toward the door.

"I'll come with you." Rebecca quickly took off her robe and put on her chemise. She lifted a sleeveless surcoat over her head. The warmth of the dry clothing made her feel good, as did the idea of seeing Edward. She was a helpless case, either he would love her or—

Edward burst into the room, swept past Sarah and advanced on Rebecca. She forced her body not to run away from the rage that showed on his face, her hands made fists at her sides. Beads of perspiration stood out on his face.

"Edward, are you all right?" Rebecca took a step back as Galahad growled quietly.

"Nay. I am not all right. Get that animal out of your room!" He pointed to Galahad who rose to lick the finger Edward pointed at him.

Rebecca laughed. Her laughter stopped as Edward swung at the dog, missing as Galahad scrambled away. Taking a deep breath she sought for the control that she lacked so badly. "Sarah, would you take the dog to the kitchen for me?" Her voice sounded a lot calmer than she felt.

"And leave you alone with this dragon?" Sarah didn't flinch when Edward sent her a scathing look.

"Aye. Please go." Rebecca took Galahad by the collar and guided him to Sarah.

Sarah left with the dog.

Edward bellowed at her, "Have ye not done enough, and now this?" He grabbed her shoulders and shook her.

Rebecca could feel the heat of his fevered hand through her chemise sleeves. "What? What is it I've done?" She yelled back.

Edward dragged her to the door and opened it. He shoved her along into his chamber. Slamming the door behind them.

Rebecca punched at his chest, tired of being manhandled. "I've done nothin'!" She stomped on his foot with her heel. When he released her to hop around in pain, she ran for the door.

He got there first. "Not so fast, wench."

"I don't understand. What do you think I've done?"

He pointed to a cup that sat on the table by his bed. When she lifted the cup, a strong smell hit her nose. Poison.

Pure unthinking emotion took over her actions. Livid with rage, she could deal no more with his doubts. She lifted the cup to her lips. She would drink it and the pain in her chest would end—along with her life. In an instant the cup was struck from her hand and it flew across the room. Its deadly contents scattered on the floor.

"What would ye do!" Edward dropped the crop and seized her shoulders again.

She tried to remove his hands. Tears of rage fell hotly down her cheeks. She would have given up. "I am tired of being pushed around and blamed for crimes I do not commit."

TWENTY

Edward thought his head would burst. He lifted his hands to his face and turned from Rebecca. "Who poisoned it then?" Lowering his hands, he turned again to glare at her.

"I don't know!" She glared back at him.

Edward tried to get hold of his warring emotions. *Of course she wouldn't poison me.*

"It's time for you to trust me, Edward." Rebecca's hand reached to feel his brow. "You're burning with fever! We need to get you into some cool water."

"No. I'll not sit in cold water." Blackness enveloped him.

Rebecca tried to catch Edward and found her body wedged between the wall and the huge highlander. Unable to hold up his weight she slid to the floor with Edward on top of her. "Ach, you great big stubborn oaf of a man!" He lay in her arms breathing slowly. She heard a titter from the doorway.

"Rebecca, lass, what did you do? Knock him out?" Sarah laughed heartily.

"Sarah! Help me." Rebecca tried to get out from under him, but couldn't.

"Pah! You don't suppose I can lift him?" Sarah added her efforts and Rebecca slid clear.

"Let's get some men. Here, I brought water, pour it in the tub. I'll get help." Sarah left the chamber.

Rebecca poured the water into the tub.

Sarah looked concerned when she returned with two guards. She instructed them to pick Edward up and place him in the tub. They looked at each other and shook their heads.

"He's burnin' with fever. Stop this cowardice, and pick the chieftain up!" Rebecca pounded one of the large man's arms, pushing him toward Edward.

She guided them as they lifted Edward, carrying him over to the tub. They lowered him into it. When they let him go, his head slid under the water.

"Get him up!" Rebecca's order to the guards was not necessary.

Almost immediately, Edward's head came out of the water, His eyes flew open and he gasped for air. Little veins of blood stood out in the whites of his eyes. The men nearly tripped over each other as they left the room.

A long string of oaths filled the air. Sarah shook some soap wart leaves at him. "Any more o' that and I'll gladly wash your mouth with these."

"Sarah, really . . ." Rebecca thought Edward would leave the tub and throttle them both.

Sarah winked at Rebecca. Edward looked at the two women with glazed eyes and shut them. They put wet towels on his brow and Sarah washed his wound.

"The wound is back to a good color. He's over the worst. The fever should go now that the infection is gone. See, it doesn't ooze." Sarah prodded Edward to stand and step from the tub.

Rebecca helped her to remove his clothes. She glanced at Sarah with a grin. Sarah swatted at her, but smiled.

When she came close to her, Rebecca whispered in her ear. "Come on, Sarah, isn't his body magnificent?"

"Do you gawk over all the men's bodies you treat?" Sarah spoke out loud.

"Certainly not." Rebecca gave her a look that she hoped would show her the extent of her treacherous words. They squatted to retrieve the wet clothing.

While they stooped, Edward pushed both women onto their butts and took care of his own needs. Wrapping himself in a blanket, he glared at the two women. "Are ye done with me?"

Rebecca held her mirth in with a hand until Sarah burst into laughter. They ran for the door, and as it closed, Rebecca heard the roar of male laughter behind it.

"Ach, we didn't give him the tea." Sarah looked much more sober.

"You go and give it to him. He thinks I'm trying to poison him." Rebecca moved away from the door.

Rebecca made her way to the kitchen and scooped some hot stew into a trencher. The sweet spicy smell of it reminded her of her own hunger. She took another trencher and put stew into it.

"M'lady, can I get something for you?" A kitchen boy spoke from the door.

Startled by his voice, Rebecca nearly dropped the trencher. "Aye, a tray please. I'll also need a sealed bottle of wine, and some cheese and bread. Are there some goblets about?"

"I'll see to it all, m'lady. Sit down and try some pastry." The young man went to work gathering all she needed.

Rebecca sank her teeth into a sweet cake and thought she would faint from the sheer pleasure of it. She savored the cake to the last crumb. The boy, Rebecca realized, was Mavis's brother. He put the tray on the table.

"I can take it up, if you like." He smiled at her shyly.

"No . . . yes, would you? Take these to Laird Edward's room and I'll take my own." Rebecca watched the boy's reaction to her words.

His smile turned to a frown and he coughed. "Is Laird Edward ailing? I'm Mavis's brother . . ."

"I know you are, Laird Edward does not." Rebecca thought of the poison and could feel her ire rising. "By the way, who was the last to bring him some wine?"

"Mavis. She brought it up before the men arrived." He paled. "What did she do?"

Rebecca picked up her food and stood to walk from the room.

"She poisoned it. On second thought, I'll bring the food to him and I'll see that your family is reassigned duties."

She put her food back on the full tray and picked it up. The poor boy turned a lighter shade of white and his mouth stood open. Rebecca, too angry to be fair, gave him a new order. "You will come with me, and tell Laird Edward who served his wine last. Perhaps he can decide the fate of your family. Follow me."

Mavis's brother followed her, looking like a man about to lose his life. He opened the chamber door for her and let her enter before him. He looked as if he would flee.

"Laird Edward, this boy has something to tell you." Rebecca placed the tray on a small table beside the fire. Edward still sat in the chair, frowning. She gathered her food and made for the door.

The boy walked before him, bowing slightly. "Laird Edward, Lady Rebecca asked me who brought you the last goblet of wine. I answered her truthfully. 'Twas Mavis, my sister. I didn't know she would do such a heinous thing or I'd never have sent her."

"And how much did Lady Rebecca pay you to tell me that story?"

Rebecca stopped just as she reached the door. She spun around to see Edward stand.

"Nay, sir, it's the truth. I wouldn't take such a bribe."

Edward paused and turned back to Rebecca. "Take him down to his sister and see that he gives her one hundred lashes with that crop." He pointed to the crop that lay on the floor. Then he turned to eat his food, dismissing them.

Rebecca swallowed the words that welled up in her throat. Who does he think he is? Ordering her around like a steward. He should be amending his false accusation to her. She should have left before he could give the next order.

"Leave your food here and you can eat when you report back. I want to know my order was carried out." He spat out his words as if they were poison on his lips.

The kitchen boy took the food from her hands and quickly

brought it back to Edward. He grabbed the crop, pushed her out the door, and closed it before her opinion could be heard.

The meeting with Mavis upset her so badly, she knew the food would not stay in her stomach. She walked slowly back to Edward's chamber. He'd become a monster.

Pausing at his door, she decided not to enter. Let him come to her if he wanted a report. She walked to her chamber and quietly opened the door with every nerve taut and her ears straining for even the slightest sound. Her stomach growled its objection as she slipped into her room and closed the door without a sound.

With a sigh, she lay on her bed and all her worries melted away as sleep overtook her.

Ruppert bellowed as he heard of all the his clan had made at Cavenaugh castle. He smiled when he heard that Mavis would poison Laird Edward. Soon Rebecca would be his and this time he would make sure she was—truly his.

Ruppert gathered up all his forces and set out for Cavenaugh castle. His wound, healing nicely, ached slightly and was becoming an ugly scar. A constant reminder of Rebecca. He felt strong and able again. If Edward were not poisoned, Ruppert would enjoy piercing his very soul.

Edward paced the length of his chamber. As usual Rebecca did not return as he asked. He should go to her and . . . and he knew what he really wanted to do to her. But the clergyman was right. He shouldn't cause her to go against the church, although he already had. His mind circled over each thought. Could he trust Rebecca? Why had her cousin betrayed him?

The same thoughts interrupted his sleep, over and over. Finally, he could feel his body sinking to a deep restful sleep.

* * *

Rebecca sat upright in bed. Her heart pounded. Sweat streamed down her face, or was it tears? She remembered her dream. Edward watched as Ruppert raped her. She got out of her bed in a panic. Pushing the heavy curtain aside she leaned her head out the window. Fresh cool air hit her face. She breathed in deeply. *We'll not fail. We'll live to see our children's children.*

Sitting on the windowsill, she could feel a pain in her chest as her heart struggled to survive Edward's effect on her last night. Maybe he did despise her now and would give Ruppert what he wanted. No . . . she couldn't believe that. Edward was ailing.

Well, enough of this. Reminding herself of the duties that awaited her she walked to her wardrobe The morning was still young. She would eat and bring food up to the wounded She removed the chemise she slept in, and put on a fresh one. She let her hair free of its ribbon and combed out the ever present knots.

Rebecca put on her mixed plaid flannel dress and pulled on her hose and shoes. As she walked out of her chamber she looked at Edward's door with a worried frown.

Looking around at the empty hall, she slowly opened the door and looked into the darkness. He slept. She tiptoed into the chamber, over to the bed, and leaned over him. The male scent of Edward wafted to her nostrils and caused a familiar stirring in her body. His face did not look peaceful. Even in his sleep it looked etched with worry. Rebecca carefully and gently felt his brow. Cool, it felt cool to her touch. *Thank God.*

His deep slow breathing continued as she withdrew her hand from his brow and left his chamber. One less worry. Sleep would be the best thing for him. Rebecca saw Sarah walking down the hall, looking at her with suspicion.

"Nay, I just checked on him. He's sleeping and the fever is gone. We should leave him sleep until he wakes on his own."

"Aye, your Father wishes to see you. I'm afraid you'll have

more Scottish temper to put up with." Sarah looked as though she pitied her.

"How's his leg?"

"I've just seen to it. It's healing nicely and he can use it. Nothing was damaged for good."

"Good. Sarah, please let every living being in this castle know not to disturb Laird Edward." Sarah nodded and went on her way. Rebecca walked slowly to her parent's chamber and knocked on the door. When her father's steward answered the door she swooped in merrily, all smiles, and bid them a great morning.

Sour looks met her but she still went to her father's side and kissed his cheek.

Her mother spoke up. "Charm will get you nowhere this day."

"Father . . . your still upset with me?" Rebecca sat beside him not letting his demeanor disturb her.

"I want to know everything you know about Mavis. Both ten years ago and today." Her father grabbed her arm painfully.

"Now I've earned your mistrust as well!" She could feel her color rise.

"Don't get angered with me, lass, or I'll do what I should have done when you were a child. Answer me." He released her arm roughly.

"I knew nothing of Mavis's affairs ten years ago. Now I've learned that she fell in love with a Kirkguard and betrayed us all, and continues to betray us. She nearly poisoned Edward last night before she was thrown in the dungeon. She also brought back two children sired by the Kirkguard." Rebecca looked at her father's sad face.

"I'm sorry, lass. You've been through a lot, I shouldn't take my ire out on you." He patted the bed next to him.

Hot moisture filled her eyes and she sat down. She longed to be a small child again and escape into the loving arms of her father. He sat up and embraced her. She cried into his shoulder.

"Edward has been a beast." Rebecca sniffed and grimaced as she looked up into her father's eyes.

"I would expect no less of him after your deed. Did he think you put the poison in his wine?"

Rebecca nodded her head.

"Serves ye right." He laughed. "I trust that has been cleared up."

"Aye. He's sleeping and everyone has been ordered to leave him be. The fever is gone." Rebecca smiled.

"Well, chances are the Kirkguard Clan will attack again. We may as well get ready for that event. I'll walk around a bit and see that the castle battlement and archers are ready. You will see to the other men and pass the word?"

"Aye."

"Get a small force to ride out and scout the lands around the castle. You need not go with them."

"I'll do that. No, I wouldn't go with the men unless Edward also came." Rebecca could taste her bitter words.

"You can't change what you are, daughter." Her mother came over to her offering comfort.

"I know." Rebecca wished her parents well and went to inform the men of the coming battle. She found Galahad and he walked beside her as she traversed the halls to informed each man. Carefully choosing men to form the small group that would scout the land. The men respected her orders and began preparing right away.

Rebecca longed to mount her horse and ride the wind. For Once she admitted that times were far too perilous. She settled for a romp with Galahad in the gardens behind the castle.

The roses bloomed around the herbal gardens she and Sarah tended so carefully. The scent of lavender mingled with the light smell of fuchsia. It made her think of the grand gardens at MacCleary castle. Would she ever see them again? She picked a rose and when the thorn pricked her finger she remembered Edward's sweet words, "I wish I could hand life to you like that, without the thorns."

Galahad crouched at her feet, his hindquarters up in the air and a stick beneath his front paws. His tail wagged. Prying the stick away from him, she threw it across the garden and watched the dog bound after it.

Sadness came over her as she thought of the fun she'd had with Edward. Then she laughed as she remembered Edward's face when she dumped the leaves over him. Had that just been two days ago?

Galahad lumbered up to her with the stick and bounded away as she tried to grab it. She ran after the dog laughing and yelling. It helped. Soon the large animal grew tired of the game and lay down next to a stone bench. Rebecca took the opportunity to sit down. Maybe Rowan would duel with her. Rowan—Rowan is dead and his sister a villain.

Tears seemed ever ready to spring to her eyes. They blurred her view and spilled down her cheeks. She let them, totally surrendering to the hot flow, not even lifting a hand to wipe them away.

A clarion called the castle inhabitants to mid meal. Rebecca stood and walked to the fountain. Catching some water in her hands she washed away the tears and headed for the great hall.

Putting Galahad in the kitchen, she walked into the hall. Her father and mother sat at the table engaged in conversation. Edward's chair remained empty as she sat in her own. Nathan and his family came into the hall. She smiled up at them.

They sat down on the other side of the table. Nathan looked uncomfortable.

"Should you be up and about yet, Nathaniel?" Rebecca gave him a sincere look.

"It was get up or starve. Actually, I'm healing quickly and needed the activity. And how do you fare, Lady Rebecca?" His smile looked a little fixed.

"Not so bad—" Rebecca stopped talking as she saw Edward enter the room.

Nathan turned to see what had stopped her words and laughed. Rising, he loped across the room and greeted Edward. They spoke for a while and came to sit down. Edward nodded to the various people at the table before he sat beside Rebecca. She could feel her heart melt into her stomach warming her lower regions. A laugh from Nathan made her look his way with a warning glance. His expression told her that she would get the comeuppance he'd promised her.

"You don't need to finish telling me how you've been. I think I know. Do you want to know how I've been?" Nathan fairly crowed his enjoyment.

"You look fine. It's Lorelei I'm worried about." Rebecca looked at Lorelei who seemed to sit up taller and had a special sparkle in her eye.

"Not to worry, I think you put the spice back into our marriage, you did. My thanks." He reached across the table and patted her hand.

"That's wonderful Nathan." Rebecca managed a smile.

"Now all we need is to deal with that stubborn chieftain of yours." Nathan looked at Edward.

He did not look amused. "Perhaps, dear cousin, we should ask if you're ready for the battle field. If you can bed your woman, I guess you would be."

Rebecca watched the happy expressions turn to sadness. Lorelei looked ready to cry, the sparkle gone from her eyes. Rebecca clenched her teeth together and thought she would gladly stamp on Edward's foot and punch his sore arm. She spoke her mind instead.

"Can we dispense with a discussion of a battle while we sup. Most likely we should rest the idea." Rebecca looked at Edward's angry face.

"I won't *rest* the idea, as you so sweetly put it, until Ruppert lies dead in the ground." Edward tore some meat off a chicken leg with his teeth. "And don't tell me what I should discuss."

Rebecca could feel her face beaming red as she looked over at her parents for support. They ate their food and would not look at her. The meal passed quietly with no one bothering to talk. Rebecca seethed inside but composed herself on the outside.

Edward cleared his throat. "Rebecca, come out to the garden with me for a duel. We've also an issue to discuss." He stood and pulled on her arm forcing her to stand.

MacKey also stood. "Laird Edward, I hope you will use utmost care when dueling with my daughter."

"Oh, aye, Laird MacKey." Edward bowed his respect and led Rebecca away.

Little comfort that. Rebecca whistled for Galahad, who galloped out of the kitchen happily.

"Leave the dog."

"He enjoys the fresh—"

"I said, leave the dog." Edward gripped her tighter.

"Galahad Stay!" Rebecca wished she could say, attack. The thought brought a giggle that lodged in her throat. Instead of being terrified by this bad tempered man, she felt invigorated. She needed a good duel. She would teach him some manners. Anger never made a warrior fight well.

"Now, tell me why you failed to report back to me last night. Did the boy carry out my order?" Edward looped his arm around her and walked closely beside her.

"He carried it out, and I had no stomach for food afterwards. I went to my chamber and slept." Rebecca looked into his dark eyes fearlessly.

"I told you to report back to me. You didn't have to eat. Don't disobey me again, Rebecca, or you'll get worse than I'm about to give you." He stopped at her chamber door. "Get your sword."

Rebecca happily opened her door and shut it in his face. The door opened immediately with a swish of air and Edward walked in. He shut the door.

"So . . . you want to play it this way?" He advanced on her.

"I don't want to play it any way, Edward. You're behavin' with bad manners and a vile temper. I suggest you get control of yourself. I need to get on a pair of breeches and shirt. It would hardly be fair for me to fight in my gown. Please leave." She stood with her hands on her hips, waiting.

Instead he strutted into her room and sat down to watch her.

"Fine." If he wanted a show, she would give him one and test his Scottish honor. Either she'd anger him further, or he'd not be able to keep his promise to the clergyman.

Taking her time, she stripped her clothes off one by one. Stretching this way and that. Leaning down, she took her time finding a clean pair of breeches in her chest of clothes. She could hear Edward shifting position in the chair. Her unadorned derriere in the air, she tried to decide which pants to put on.

A sigh of exasperation sounded from the chair. "Get dressed—now!" Edward leapt up and pulled a pair of breeches out of the trunk and threw them at her.

Rebecca nearly laughed at his discomfiture. It had been worth the pain to see how she could fire his hunger. "I asked you to leave."

"Don't toy with me, Rebecca, you'll not talk me out of this. I'll teach you this lesson and you'll never forget it."

She remained calm and did not let her anger rise. "Fine, then, go right ahead and teach me." She tied the string on her breeches and grabbed her sword, a pleasant smile on her lips.

Her pleasant attitude seemed to make Edward's anger blaze higher. They walked to the garden and to a private clearing within a stand of apple trees.

They faced each other, swords drawn. His first move came swiftly. Rebecca parried his attacks, one after the other, until she thought her arms would snap. But she never blinked.

She watched his every move intently, looking for that one moment he would let his guard down. There. Edward turned around and in the split second he faced away from her, she landed a blow with the flat of her sword on his buttocks. Her sword was ready when he came around. The glint in his eye promised her she would not be so lucky again.

"That is for being so rude to the people we supped with." Rebecca struggled to keep her strength and attention.

He lunged and Rebecca parried, coming behind him and giving him another blow as before. He almost blocked it. She couldn't help but smile at her success.

"And that is for treating me so horribly."

She turned quickly and nearly got a blow herself, just barely blocking it—her sword flew from her hand. Her heart leapt into her throat as she ran for the sword. Just before his would connect with her bottom, she dove for the ground and tumbled forward. She landed on her feet, in front of her sword. Picking it up she parried his next few attacks.

Now Edward smiled. "You are good. I see now your advantages against my strength." He kept at her.

Rebecca parried again, her quick movements and grace landed her another hit to his backside. This time she couldn't speak. The air tore at her throat her chest ached for each breath. *Concentrate.* Getting a second wind, she attacked and made him lose ground.

Her arms slowed, her muscles nearly refused to move. She didn't know how much longer she could hold the sword up. Over and over she tried to envelop his blade with hers and make it leave his hand. It didn't work. Finally her efforts sent her own sword flying through the air.

She fell to her knees, gasping for breath, her head bowed in defeat. Edward held his blade above her as if he would strike.

"Get up! Get your sword." He lowered his blade as she stood and took her own.

They resumed the duel.

"Edward, I'm tired." Her voice croaked with the effort to speak.

"Keep goin' " His hard eyes pierced her heart.

They dueled until tears filled her eyes and she barely stood. Edward's attacks grew slower, but just as strong. Forcing her to defend herself. She lost her sword again.

"Pick it up!" Edward shouted at her.

She picked up her sword with the point resting on the ground and dragged it over to him. He made her practice the move over and over again. Her tears dried and anger took over until she couldn't feel her pain. Her mind seemed to make her body go without her conscious thought. Every time she made an error or missed a parry, he made her do it again, until she didn't miss.

She tried to speak, to beg Edward to stop. She couldn't. Finally, she mustered all the strength she had left and fell to the ground as she watched Edward's sword sail through the air.

Edward walked to get his sword. Rebecca reacted quickly

and grabbed his leg causing him to fall. Hopping on top of him, she held her dagger to his throat.

"No more." Her voice rasped out the words.

He removed her dagger from his neck and pushed her from him. "The lesson is over." Walking to his sword he left her there, without looking back.

Too spent to cry, she lay on the ground wishing it would swallow her. Closing her eyes, she found that even her sense of smell had left her.

After a while, she opened her eyes. The sun set behind the mountains and her body shivered with a chill. She stood slowly, every muscle screaming. Then she saw Edward sitting beneath a tree. He rose and walked over to her.

Rebecca glanced at his sword with dread. She couldn't meet his eyes.

"If you insist on being one of the men, then you'll train like a man. What you just lived through is an exercise that every warrior must pass before going into battle. You did well. You lasted longer than I would have imagined." He reached for her hand and tucked it under his arm gently supporting her.

Rebecca's weak knees nearly buckled with the impact of his touch.

"Tomorrow we'll do it again." He smiled at her.

"Nay."

"Aye."

Rebecca looked at his face and thought she'd like to hit it . . . or maybe just kiss it. Aye, she'd like to kiss every inch of that hard unyielding face until he yielded completely to her. And she did.

"Rebecca . . . stop it. No, I told the clergyman. Rebecca!"

TWENTY-ONE

Steam surrounded Rebecca like an ocean mist. The warm water, steeping with chamomile and lavender herbs soothed her aching body. She woke up this morning so stiff she could barely fill her bath. What had Edward been thinking? She probably couldn't even pick up a sword, much less fight. Even the muscles she used to breathe hurt.

Sarah entered the room without knocking, as they had agreed, so Rebecca would not be startled by a knock that might be Edward's. Sarah had come to rub down every muscle in her body. It always helped. When Rebecca first began the rigors of training at a very young age, Sarah had done the same.

Rebecca lay stomach down on a blanket spread before the fireplace. Sarah began to rub Rebecca's shoulders and worked down the sore muscles of her arm.

"Ahhh. Sarah, have I told you lately what an angel you are to me?" Rebecca savored the feeling as her muscles loosened.

"Not lately." Sarah laughed and worked on one spot with vigor.

"Ouch!"

"There's a knot the size of an egg there. Let me work it out or it'll give you problems."

Rebecca took a deep breath and dispelled the air slowly to lessen the pain. A knock sounded on the chamber door. Rebecca yelled, "Go away, we're busy!" Lifting her head she watched the door swing open.

Edward stormed into the room. "Who's busy with you?" His mouth a thin line.

"Why, Sarah, I think his face is stuck in that position. I haven't seen it any other way for days. Is there an herbal remedy for that?" Rebecca lay her head down to stifle her laugh.

"With a wench like you around it's no wonder." Edward's words seemed to hold a glimmer of humor.

"Get goin' out of here." Sarah continued the massage.

"I've seen her all in all before." She heard Edward's footsteps getting closer. "Why are you doing that?"

"Soothing her muscles because of their being too harshly used." Sarah snapped the words at Edward. "What could've caused that, I wonder?"

"Training that will save the stubborn lass's life."

Rebecca heard Edward's sharp intake of breath as Sarah rubbed toward her naked bottom.

Rebecca's body, already warm from her administrations, heated further at the thought of Edward's gaze on her.

"Ah . . . Rebecca, when you're through, there's a meeting on the practice field to estimate what force of men we still have. After the meeting we have business in the gardens again." Edward's footsteps sounded across the floor and the door closed quietly.

"Stubborn man." Sarah rubbed harder.

Rebecca lifted her head and turned to look at Sarah, only to see her knowing smile.

"I'm done, stand and see how you feel." Sarah stood, rubbing her own arms.

Rebecca got up and could feel the difference right away. Although she still felt sore, her muscles were not as stiff. Hugging Sarah, she quickly dressed in her shirt, breeches and plaids.

Sarah paused at the door looking concerned.

"Don't worry, I can handle Edward." Rebecca smiled.

"Aye, you probably can!" Sarah laughed as she opened the door and walked out of the chamber. Rebecca could faintly hear Edward's deep voice speaking to Sarah in the hall.

* * *

A fresh chill in the air met Rebecca as she walked out to the practice field. The first cold spell that signaled fall would soon be here. An even cooler breeze ruffled the stray curls of her hair. She had plaited it tightly, so it would not hinder her duel, and wrapped it on the back of her head.

The towering mountains around them still looked green with summer, although the highest snowy peak looked a little whiter than it had the days before. Rebecca took a deep breath, grateful for the cold air. She would need that when she battled with Edward again.

All the men who could still walk attended the meeting. Edward asked Sarah and Rebecca to judge who would be ready for battle according to their wounds. It didn't look good. Their numbers had dwindled and if they were to ride out they would need more able men. The risk would be too great.

"Damn," MacKey vowed under his breath. "We need to stay in the castle and defend it. Leaving will put the castle and our able men in peril. What do you say we gain our strength and hope the Kirkguard clan leave us alone for a few days?"

"We could put off their attack if we lead them to believe that we're on our way to attack them." Edward looked thoughtful.

"How would we do that?" Rebecca questioned him, afraid of what he would suggest. Mavis. Why did she still care for the woman?

"Mavis." Edward gave Rebecca a warning look.

"How can we trust her?" MacKey looked from Rebecca to Edward.

A man from Edward's clan stood. "We hold her children and if she betrays us, the children die."

"Nay!" Rebecca looked at Edward for his support.

"Nay, the children will not be killed. If she doesn't return she'll be banished, never to see her children again." Edward looked to Rebecca . . . for approval?

"That sounds fair to me." Rebecca agreed, titillated that he looked to her instead of her father.

"Good plan, Edward, will you tell her? I fear what I would do if I had to face her." MacKey winced.

"Aye."

MacKey put the plan before their clans and all agreed. The mildly wounded would organize themselves as archers, along the castle walls and balconies. The others planned their strategies and practiced their skills.

After all was planned, Edward approached Rebecca. "Ready?" He walked toward the gardens.

"What difference would it make if I trained with the men? I always have. They never did a drill like the one you gave me yesterday." Her stomach tightened as she inched away in the other direction, wishing she could flee.

"They kept it from you then." Edward moved swiftly to her side and took her hand in his own. Firmly, he pulled her along with him. "Don't try to get out of it. You'll be a seasoned warrior before I'm through with you. I'll not worry about you when we face our biggest battle."

As his hand touched hers, a trail of pleasant feelings flowed through her. "Ach, couldn't we just be seasoned lovers?"

Edward stopped and pulled her arm, swinging her up against his chest. Her body tingled and warmed to his. He moved his hands up her back and to her head. Gripping her hair, he pulled her head back. Her lips became a perfect target for his scalding kiss. He stopped the kiss before she even had a chance to answer it.

Then, just as quickly, he grasped her hand again and pulled her on. She ran her tongue over her moist lips, tasting his kiss once more. Her body and mind rebelled. She tried, without success, to return to their previous position.

Her anger grew more with each step they took. She was nearly blinded by it when they reached the garden clearing. She used it to give her strength. He drew his sword with one metallic sweep. She drew hers with another. And the duel began.

Rebecca tried to step back from her body, to watch the different stages it would go through. She learned what moves to use when she tired and when to parry with less force, to pace herself. Her mind stayed sharp and she made few mistakes.

The red haze took over about the time she missed a parry.

"Stop. You keep making the same mistake."

"I do not! I never missed that parry before."

"Near misses . . . so that when you're tired you finally do miss it."

"I won't miss it again."

"Let me show you how—"

"No—I won't miss it again."

"Fine."

She missed the parry again. He brought the flat of his blade against her thigh with a stinging blow. Rebecca gritted her teeth and tried again. She missed. Her thigh suffered another slap from his blade.

She missed the parry yet again, but this time deflected his sword before it hit her thigh. "All right—show me!"

"Say please."

There it came again. She backed away and deflected his blade. "Please!"

"Go like this . . ." Edward showed her which way to swing the sword around.

She practiced the move by herself, over and over. Strange how she hardly noticed her tired state now.

"Bring it up higher." Edward showed her with his sword.

She imitated his move. Her sword sliced the air a few times and his sword joined in again. Enjoying the lesson, she could feel her body respond with vigor. Ah . . . what you think during a fight makes a difference in your strength. She smiled at her discovery, and rid Edward of his sword.

"Well . . . there you go." Edward walked to his sword and picked it up.

"There I go?"

"Aye, there's your secret weapon. Just one beautiful smile from you and any man would lose his sword." Edward's grin looked sheepish.

"Nay. Just you." Rebecca laughed as he renewed his attack.

"I do believe you're enjoying this. Why do you savor war and killing so?" He slowed his sword.

"I don't savor killing." She began to feel her body reaching its limit and matched his slowing pace.

"No, I guess you don't. It's just the forbidden fruit of it that you savor." He laughed, his gaze heating with that certain look.

"And the power. Are we done?" Rebecca parried, using her newly learned move.

Edward lowered his sword and sat down. "Aye. Now sit here and tell me what you've learned today." Edward patted the soft grass beside him.

It didn't take her a second to drop her sword and herself down onto the sun-warmed grass. The sweet smell of it filled her tired senses. As her breathing began to slow she watched the sun's reflection play on the steel of her sword. Edward sat beside her and moved to recline on his side. He plucked a long blade of grass and chewed it, his eyes squinting at her.

His dark hair glittered in the bright sunlight. She longed to run her fingers through it. His clothes still fresh and holding his scent and his musky essence was altogether pleasant.

"I'm waiting . . . unless you want to resume our duel?"

"I learned that if you think about being tired during a duel you will be. But keeping your mind on your purpose will give you strength to continue."

"Good. It's all where your mind is. Don't ever limit yourself. Think of yourself without limit and when you need the strength it'll be there."

The soft tone of his voice circled her senses, caressing her soul. She watched how his lips moved as he talked. Then she sent her gaze to rest on his large arms, firm and strong, to the open buttons on his shirt and the curls of dark hair beneath it. To his . . .

"Are you enjoying yourself?" Edward reached over and touched her stray curls, his fingers trailing down her cheek.

"Oh . . . aye." She reached up to caress his arm.

"Rebecca . . ." Edward gently took her into his arms.

She lay against him in the sunshine. His feathery kisses fell on the top of her head, down her nose, and finally onto her mouth. She opened her lips to take in his kiss. It tasted sweet. A shock of sensation ran from her lips to her toes, and everywhere in between.

"Edward . . . couldn't we talk to the clergyman?"

"No." Edward stood up, lifting her with him.

The moment over, Rebecca poked her bottom lip out. His arm still held her around the waist. She quickly tucked her lip in and put on a brave front as they walked toward the castle.

"I'm off to see Mavis." Edward let go of her and walked away.

"I'll go with you." Rebecca followed.

He stopped and turned to her. "All right."

"Don't argue with me. I have to . . . what did you say?"

"I said, all right." Edward's deep laugh devoured her senses. She walked closer to him, nestling her arm around his waist. His arm went around her shoulders and she leaned her head against him as they walked.

"She fell in love with a Kirkguard."

"I know."

"She destroyed our lives by letting them get to your father." Rebecca looked up at him to gauge his feelings.

"How do you know?" His face looked stormy.

"You'll see." She leaned her head onto his chest again.

Just before they entered the dungeon Rebecca spoke. "Let me go in alone. Give me a few minutes with her. Then come in."

Edward nodded, looking wary. She walked down the stair to the dungeon, lifting the key off its peg on her way. Working it into the lock, she opened the door. Mavis sat in a dark corner.

Rebecca walked to her and spoke softly. "Mavis, I need you to stand and face away from the door."

Mavis did not move and seemed not to care. Slowly, she stood and did as she was told. Rebecca fixed her hair like her own and hid in a small cloister outside the cell. She watched Edward approach from the shadows.

"Rebecca! Where's Mavis?" He roughly swung Mavis around, looking surprised he let her go quickly.

Rebecca stepped out of her hiding place.

"She . . . you . . . ach, Rebecca. I must make amends." Edward swallowed, looking ashamed.

Rebecca thought she knew how he felt, swallowing his pride. "There's nothing to amend." She shrugged.

"Oh, aye, there is." He turned toward Mavis, appearing ready to vent his ire on her.

"Edward, if you wish to make amends, then tell the woman her mission and don't let your anger damage the spy." Rebecca stared into his eyes, which were tearing with what must be the effort to keep his control.

Edward moved close to Mavis, speaking in dangerous tones. "Do you know how you've ruined other people's happiness? Killed their loved ones?"

Mavis cowered away from him but did not look away. He advanced on her.

"Edward." Rebecca spoke his name quietly. "It's done, in the past. Leave it, please . . . for me?"

"Do you know what you've done?" He continued to interrogate her. His voice held a harshness Rebecca had never heard from him before.

"Aye, I've thought of nothing else . . . he made me . . . he threatened to kill my family if I did not do as he asked."

"Who?"

"Ruppert. And he threatened to kill my husband. He did kill my husband. I know that shouldn't have mattered. I never should've betrayed my clan."

"Now you will attempt to make up for your horrible error."

Rebecca entered the chamber Madeleine always stayed in when she visited as a child. The room had long exposure to the sun and was decorated in bright-colored tapestry. Memories flooded back to Rebecca as she glanced at Madeleine lying in bed. Her face looked pale. She had always been sickly.

"Rebecca . . . I've been doing a lot of thinking. When I'm better I want you to show me how to wield a sword. How to protect myself. I can't bear to be helpless and weak any longer."

"It would be my honor." Rebecca smiled at her.

"Edward won't approve—"

"Don't you dare let Edward tell you what to do. He's a lamb, once you get to understand what's here." Rebecca thumped her chest with her hand.

Madeleine looked uncertain.

"Come on, we'll start right now. It'll likely be good for your health, too." Rebecca jumped up and found a comb on Madeleine's dressing table.

"When I'm better—"

"Ach, Madeleine, you're better enough. Get out of the covers and sit up." Rebecca swept the covers from her and nudged her.

"Rebecca!" She finally sat up crossing her legs in front of her, a broad smile on her face.

"What!" Rebecca laughed as she jumped onto the bed and sat behind her, untying her long black hair. "Beautiful, beautiful hair. Why do you bind it so?"

" 'Tis proper."

"Bah! Proper is for the daft. Look how long . . . scoot up so I can comb it from the bottom."

Rebecca gently worked the knots out of Madeleine's hair, all the while telling her of the battles and lives of the people around them. Madeleine nearly fell from the bed in laughter when she told her about Lorelei and Nathaniel.

"You see, if Lorelei can manage Nathan, you can surely stand up to Edward. You're his sister, I'm sure he's much gentler with you."

"Aye. I've always been frail. But I think he loses patience with that frailty."

"Aye . . . he would. We'll find you a lovely dress."

Madeleine, only five years older than Rebecca, looked old enough to be her mother. Her arms were like spindles, so thin and fragile. Rebecca noticed an untouched tray of food beside the bed and decided to mix her an herbal tea to stimulate her appetite. Leaving the bed, she opened her pouch and brought out some herbs and made the brew. She brought it to Madeleine.

"It will improve your appetite. You need some more meat on your bones else you won't be able to pick up even the smallest sword."

"Maybe that was just a silly thought . . . what was I thinking? You've too much to do already."

"It's not silly, Madeleine, we'll do this together. I want to help. To be truthful with you, I need something to put my mind to . . . besides Edward. The boor promised the clergy that he would not ruin my chances at heaven any further, before our union could be blessed by the church."

Madeleine laughed and turned to look at Rebecca.

"It's not a bit funny, Madeleine. It's terrible." Rebecca tried not to get into a temper thinking about it. She could feel her bottom lip poking out again.

Madeleine playfully thumped Rebecca's lip with her finger. Rebecca laughed and grabbed a pillow from the bed, flipping it onto Madeleine's head. She screamed and gripped the pillow, swinging it back at Rebecca's face. They wrestled for possession of the pillow. A loud ripping sound split the air and feathers flew everywhere.

Rebecca stopped and watched Madeleine freeze in horror. Taking that advantage, she flopped the torn pillow at Madeleine, sending a myriad of feathers into the air. They each threw feathers, laughed, and tried to spit the feathers from their mouths.

Finally, they collapsed on the bed. Rebecca's side hurt from laughing. As the feathers settled, both women turned to see Edward looming over them, a stern look on his face.

"Well, now I'm certain that your brother's face is stuck in that position."

Rebecca renewed her laughter and was surprised when Madeleine joined her. She looked at Madeleine with conspiracy, gathering fists full of feathers. "Let's feather him to death, maybe that would help."

Madeleine's expression pleaded with Rebecca as she shook her head, even as she gathered feathers in her hands.

"Don't you dare." Edward backed up.

"Now!"

Before he could flee, the women showered him with feathers. His deep laugh spurred them on and soon all three fought on the bed, feathers everywhere.

A loud scream from the doorway halted their movement. This time when the feathers cleared, Martha stood there looking as if in a dream. Her fierce gaze darted from one to the other.

"Lady Martha . . ." Edward looked at Rebecca as if he would strangle her.

"A word, Rebecca." She walked out.

"I can't believe you two got me into this . . . mess . . ." Edward batted at the feathers that stuck on his face.

"Quit squawkin' like a chicken. You were having fun too." Rebecca brushed the feathers from her clothes.

"Ach, I feel like a child that's just been caught in mischief." Madeleine held her hand to her mouth so Martha would not hear her laughter.

Rebecca walked toward the door and turned to see feathers floating in her wake.

"Hope you get a hiding." Edward's laughter rang out.

"I'm not a child." Rebecca threw back at him.

"No?" Edward rose from the bed, brushing away still more feathers.

Rebecca walked out of the chamber and saw her mother's back. Were her shoulders shaking? "Mother? What's wrong?"

Her mother turned with tears flowing down her cheeks, but her mouth showed the tears to be of sentiment. "For a moment I saw you all as children again . . . it touched my heart. You all grew up so fast, and with the feud starting . . ." A few sad tears escaped her eyes.

Edward came into the hall and put an arm around Martha. "Ach, Rebecca, you've made your mamma cry." His charm stopped the flow of her tears.

"And surprised I am to see a chieftain in such games!" Martha's eyes glittered with humor.

"You know Rebecca started it." Edward smiled back at her. "I'll be on my way."

"You'll not be on your way unless you want me to regale this story around the castle. Help the ladies clean up, Laird Edward." Martha winked at Rebecca.

"But of course, Lady Martha." Edward walked stiffly into the room.

Rebecca got out some brooms and they all worked to gather the feathers. Madeleine promised to sew the pillow back together. Edward vowed not to visit his sister tomorrow.

When they finished Edward looked at Rebecca strangely and picked some feathers from her hair. She did the same for him, waiting to hear what he had to say. But instead of speaking he kissed her lightly on the lips and walked away.

Rebecca watched the people sitting in the main hall as she and Madeleine entered. Heads turned and whispers started as they glimpsed the new Madeleine, evening meal was all but forgotten.

Rebecca looked proudly at her friend. She looked stunning in one of Rebecca's favorite gowns. The scarlet brocade matched Madeleine's color so well. A white surcoat over it quieted the red color, making it more modest for an unmarried woman.

They sat down at the table, washing their hands in the bowl before them. Edward's chair remained empty. Rebecca tried to push away her dismay. She'd wanted him to witness his sister's grand entrance.

"Father. Where's Edward?" Rebecca felt uneasy.

"He could not make the meal. He had some business with his clan."

Rebecca's unease grew when she noticed that the hall didn't look as crowded. The MacCleary families were not present. Are they at a meeting? Why was she not invited?

"Rebecca, eat your meal and retire early. *That* is an order. And there will not be any more discussion on the matter."

Rebecca willed herself not to speak. Her father was not telling her something. "Why, Father?"

"Because I need to know I can count on you to follow orders."

"All right." Rebecca did expect her father to come to that. But, oh how she needed a good gallop. The meal passed pleasantly. Madeleine drew quite a few Cavenaugh men to her side and talked happily to them all.

After the meal, they both walked to their chambers. Her heart swelled to see Madeleine's happiness.

"I feel like I was just born. I've never really lived, have I?" She looked at Rebecca.

Rebecca shook her head.

"Well, I'll have to make up for the time lost."

They laughed together. Rebecca looked to see if a guard followed them. None did, but she would retire and regain her father's trust.

"What do you know of Malcolm? Is he an honorable man?" Madeleine's face turned a pretty shade of pink.

"Aye. He used to be a close friend to my cousin, Rowan. I don't believe he's been spoken for. Why, Madeleine, are you taken with him?"

"I feel all fluttery when he's near. No one ever made me feel that way. I met him a fortnight ago and spoke with him again, tonight." Madeleine looked scared.

All Rebecca could do was smile.

"Ach, stop that."

They laughed as they reached Madeleine's chamber and hugged.

"Thank you."

"You're welcome. Sleep well." Rebecca walked toward her chamber, pausing at Edward's door. She knocked . . . no answer. Quietly she opened the door. His room seemed oddly deserted. He must be training with his men.

Closing the door, she walked to her own chamber. Once inside she slipped out of her clothing. Her full stomach and tired muscles made her crave sleep. Maybe she should talk to the clergy. But what would she say? My dear sir, have you any idea how plagued we've been? How can we fight a battle? Where is Edward? At least they could lie down together . . .

The next morning Rebecca checked Edward's chamber again. Empty. As she walked back out into the hallway she nearly bumped right into her father. "Father! Tell me, now! Where is Edward?" Rebecca didn't try to quell her fury.

"I'll tell you where Edward is when you show me some manners." Her father yelled back at her. "Get to your chamber."

"Father, I'm not a child. Don't insult me by ordering me to my room." She held her tone strongly controlled.

"I said, get to your chamber. Now!" He walked toward her far too much anger showing on his face.

Rebecca reeled around and ran to her chamber. What is going on? Had she suddenly lost all respect? No, I will not stay in my chamber. Then it hit her. Edward is gone! Back to his castle, with the MacCleary families? An anguished cry escaped her lips.

She entered her chamber and quickly found breeches and a loose shirt. Her mind in a whirl, she couldn't think. Pulling on the clothing and belting on her sword, she snatched up Galahad's harness and went out to find the dog. After a whistle, he came trotting toward her. Funny how dogs actually smile when they're happy.

"Hey! You kept yourself free of the pens, I see. Good boy!" Rebecca knelt and rustled the dog's fur. She gently put on the harness, and they walked to the stable.

"Rebecca, do I need to put you in stocks?" Her father's angry face loomed over her.

"Nay, Father. I'm just goin' for a run with Gally."

"And I'd believe that if I were a horse's arse."

"You'll have to believe it! Isn't it bad enough that you and Edward deceived me?" Rebecca glared back at her father.

"We couldn't tell you or you'd have gone. I need you here."

"Then why didn't you just order me?" Rebecca let the hurt

show on her face. "I'll not go where I'm not wanted. And now I'll have a gallop to work out this damn ire."

MacKey looked as if he would slap her. His hand came up just as a voice caught their attention from behind.

"Laird MacKey? A word, please." The infamous clergyman stood there.

Rebecca shot him a scathing glare that raised his eyebrows as if surprised that she did not appreciate his interruption. Then realization entered his expression and he smiled with understanding. Could he possibly know what she was going through?

"I beg your pardon, sir. I'd let her go." The holy man's voice held authority.

"Go then, daughter. But we are not finished with this."

Rebecca left them and found her horse saddled and ready.

"I saw you coming m'lady." Admiration shone in the stable-boy's eyes.

"Many thanks."

Rebecca mounted. She and Galahad walked slowly to the gate. "Ready, Gally? Get ready, boy." She sparked his anticipation. His tail wagged wildly.

Once free of the castle gate they ran wild to the wind. The deep smell of the green mountains assailed her senses. The crisp air heightened the colors around her. The wind whistled in her ears.

TWENTY-TWO

Galahad shot over the hills like a steady arrow. Rebecca slowed her horse and watched as the dog continued his run of freedom. *All living things need their freedom.*

She thought about Edward and wondered how far they'd gotten. The broken pieces of her heart stabbed at her emotions. Why had he left without saying goodbye? She would have understood if she couldn't go. Did he really think she'd give him trouble? A voice pecked at the back of her thoughts, "You have before."

She dismounted by the line of woods and left the horse to graze. Walking in the cool green forest of trees always brought back memories. But today memories only served as an irritation. Why did Edward's absence bother her so? An empty, lonely feeling assailed her senses. Although she suspected as much, she now had to admit to herself that Edward held a very vital part of her happiness in his hands. That knowledge did nothing for her peace of mind.

A patch of fresh chamomile caught her attention and she bent to dig it up. The garden could use a fresh stock of the herb. With a gentle probing of her fingers the roots came free of the earth. She breathed in the scent of it. Taking an extra pouch from her belt, she put the roots in with the flowers and leaves hanging free of the bag.

She gathered some borage and adder's tongue. Usually, a find like this would set her heart racing. Now her heart raced, but not with happiness. When did she lose control? When did she start depending on Edward for her happiness? The brisk forest air could not cool her rising temper.

She would be happy with or without Edward. It should be as simple as that. Then why did her heart not sing? Why did this strange emptiness take her soul?

The sound of horse's hooves disturbed her thoughts. Ducking in the trees, she saw a horseman riding toward the castle. He wore no colors. She tied her bag back onto her belt and ran toward her horse. The sword at her side gave her comfort.

Rebecca followed the tree line and kept the man in sight. He rode to the gate and was permitted to enter. She rode up quickly behind him.

The rider spoke to the keeper of the gate. "I've a message for Laird Edward MacCleary. Is he here?"

"He's ridden out with his clan." The gatekeeper looked at the man wearily.

"In which direction did the army ride?"

Rebecca spotted a tartan folded away in the strangers pack. Just a corner of it showed but it could not be mistaken, Kirk-guard plaids. From behind the newcomer's back, Rebecca glared at the guard, daring him to speak. She spoke first. "They've ridden toward the Kirkguard castle."

The rider turned to her. "Through the woods or glen?"

"Through the woods."

The Kirkguard looked at the guard, who nodded his agree-ment.

"Would you leave the message with me?" Rebecca held out her hand for the parchment the man held.

"Nay, I must deliver it to Laird Edward in person, of course."

"Ah, would you have some refreshment before heading out?"

"Thank you, but I must be on." The messenger turned and left the castle gate.

Rebecca waited. Ignoring the gatekeeper's warnings, she fol-lowed after the man just before he left her sight. Galahad ran to follow beside her. Keeping just below the rise of each hill, she could follow without being seen.

When he entered the woods to the south she could see smoke from a fire. A camp. She would have to be careful. Her heart fluttered, with every nerve in her body alert. She spoke quietly to Galahad saying, "Shush." The dog squatted down cautiously. Rebecca smiled. He remembered his training.

When the camp could be seen within the trees she dismounted, tied the horse to a tree, and crept through the woods. Galahad followed quietly beside her. Every rustle drew her attention. The wind began to blow around the trees effectively covering up the sounds of their footsteps. She signaled Galahad to stop and then listened.

"She spoke the truth. The army is heading for Kirkguard. You sure you'll not be questioned when you return?"

"Quite sure. I'll not be missed if I return now." Mavis moved toward her horse.

"Nay, you'll need to stay the night."

"But I must leave now."

The men snickered.

Rebecca shivered at the thought of what they would do.

"Please." Mavis ran toward her horse.

Rebecca watched as the men took her and tied her to a tree. They bound her hands behind it. She watched as Mavis bowed her head in defeat. Why didn't she fight? Didn't she care if her children had a mother? Why had she made so many bad choices?

As summer darkness fell, the various clansmen went to sleep, leaving three men awake at the fire. They passed around a bottle and laughed loudly. Rebecca waited, planning what she would do. She couldn't let the men know she rescued Mavis or her clan's scheme would be put asunder. Then the men wouldn't return to the Kirkguard castle with news of an attack.

Rebecca checked her herbal bag and found a small bottle of tincture. At least she had learned from her mistakes, and would never again try to put someone out with plain valerian root powder. This tincture contained valerian, hops, and cowslip. Hopefully, the men would be too imbibed in the spirits to notice the taste.

Rebecca gave a command that set Galahad running through the woods barking. When the men ran to see what the noise was about, she poured the entire herbal combination into their bottle, shook it up a bit, and quickly untied Mavis' ropes.

"Stay put until you see that the men sleep. I'll wait for you due west of the woods. Be sure they sleep." Rebecca hissed the words at her, wondering why she bothered. The children gave her reason enough.

Galahad barked and ran far from the men. They gave up the chase and returned to the fire to sit and drink, arguing about what to do. When Rebecca was sure that they would continue to drink, she withdrew to where her horse waited.

She shivered with the cold. Untying a MacCleary tartan from her saddle, she wrapped it around herself and waited. The tartan warmed her, just as the man who owned it had. Her blood heated at the thought of Edward. Both ire and passion stormed her senses.

Still, she remained alert to the sounds around her. As time passed she tried to name them all. An owl hooted in the tree above her, and little creatures scampered and squeaked below. She likened herself to the mice, unaware of the birds of prey and when they would strike.

A flash of movement in the trees caused her to draw her sword. Mavis appeared, raising her hands in fear when she saw the sword.

"Get on the horse—fast!" Rebecca put away her sword, and helped Mavis up as she tried to mount. Then, swinging herself up behind her, she kicked the horse's flanks. They took off toward the castle at a gallop.

Galahad caught up with them and ran alongside the horse. Rebecca watched the dog and laughed at the untiring delight he had for adventure. He loved it as much as she did.

Before they reached the castle a group of men rode toward them. The moon lit the face of her angry, worried father.

"With all respect, Father, we must make for the castle before undue attention is drawn to us. Quickly." Rebecca hoped the cool air would soothe his ire, before she faced him. Really, she'd not done anything wrong . . . it all went right.

"And so you see no harm is done and we are assured the false message will make its way to Kirkguard castle."

Rebecca's father finally stopped pacing in front of her. He looked at her, his eyes wide. "You astound me! How could you put yerself in peril for a person such as Mavis?" MacKey's face reddened.

"Tell me something, Father. If it had been Edward who performed this task would you be railing at him now? Or would you be patting his back in a proud fashion?" Rebecca crossed her arms in front of her. "Would you leave a woman of our clan to be used by the lusty Kirkguard men, no matter what her crime?"

MacKey's mouth dropped open as if he would speak, but no words were forthcoming. He paced some more. "That's beside the point. Maybe, that *is* what she deserves."

"No one deserves to be treated so horribly. I carried out an admirable feat. It's insufferable that you don't appreciate my efforts." Rebecca stormed from the room, afraid of what she might say next.

She walked to her chamber, too tired to even feel angry. Shedding only the sword, tartan and belts, she crawled under the covers on her bed. Taking a few deep breaths, she finally relaxed. A feeling of comfort engulfed her. Her father might not be proud of her, but she knew she had done the right thing. She could feel proud of herself.

Rebecca entered the chamber to see Sarah bent over MacKey's wound, as she cleaned the area with herbal water.

"Prove a point for me, Father. Don't tell Edward that I rescued Mavis. See if he's not pleased."

"All right, daughter, we'll see." The grin on her father's face did little to quell her uneasiness.

"And when will he return?" Rebecca's heart fluttered out of control at the thought.

"By the week's end. Are you worried your caper will anger Edward?" MacKey smiled broadly at his daughter.

"So what if it does?" Rebecca shrugged her shoulders.

She saw the glint in his eyes, and quickly changed the subject before her father could tease her already inflamed emotions. Leaning over Sarah's shoulder she asked, "How is it healing?"

"Just fine, 'tis mendin' strongly. The ride he took did no harm." Sarah turned to frown at Rebecca.

Rebecca pursed her lips and reached into her bag, producing fresh adder's tongue. She handed it to Sarah.

"Good, that will help." Sarah applied the herb to the wound and wrapped it.

"Father? Is there any exercise the men didn't give me when I trained?" Rebecca looked deeply into her father's eyes.

"Aye, according to my orders, the duels of endurance."

"Don't you think I need them now?" Rebecca quickly produced a parchment, ink and quill pen. "Please annul those orders." She placed the parchment in front of him, dipped the quill into the ink, and held it out for him.

"Aye, *now* you do. I never dreamed you'd be in the battles." He laughed quietly and wrote the order to include her in all the practices.

"All my thanks, Father." She waved the parchment through the air to help it dry. Hugging him, she turned and strode to the door.

"Why Sarah, I don't think I've ever felt so used. My daughter gets what she wants and then has no more use for her old da."

Rebecca turned toward them. "Nonsense, Father, there is just so much to do . . ."

"Go, daughter, wreak your havoc." MacKey waved his hand, dismissing her.

She rolled up the document and tucked it into her pouch. "I won't feel guilty, Father, so don't try that. Just you mend quickly." Throwing him a kiss she walked out of the chamber.

Walking through the castle, Rebecca thought about what her

father said. Yes, Edward would be angry, but not for long. As she left the castle the fresh air hit her face and she thrilled to the thought of a good workout with her sword.

"Lady Rebecca!" The dog keeper ran up to her leading a young hound. The animal wiggled with elation.

"Here's a pup Galahad sired. I thought you might put him to use." The young man explained what the dog could do so far.

She complimented him and promised to have the men work with the dogs. Rebecca walked away, looking for the man in charge of the dueling. She found him and handed him the order.

They immediately rated her skills. Many surprised looks exchanged from man to man. Rebecca noticed them all. She stood up to the men, test after test, and rated higher in their standings than any would have thought.

The men who ranked under her balked at the thought of a woman bringing them to their limit with a sword. Rebecca seethed inwardly, but would not let it show. She set out to test the man directly below her skills. The man's eyes grew wider and wider with each swish of her sword. She nearly lost her sword with laughter.

Rebecca surprised herself with the ease of bringing the man to his limit. Concerned for the man, she tried to show him what he could do better. Slow this way, swing that way. She could tell he only half listened.

"Not listening to my advice may well cost you your life." She showed him once more the way she had learned.

This time he heeded her and practiced each stroke.

Then it was her turn. A strikingly handsome MacCleary took her to train. Second cousin to Edward. His skill matched Edward's in most respects. He did have a few moves she didn't know. She practiced them with tireless concentration.

His resemblance to Edward put an ache in her heart. Rebecca let her body go through the stages of force and weariness. When the training ended he took her hand and bowed over it.

"Well done, Lady Rebecca. My cousin is a lucky man."

Bowing, he left her to rest.

She nodded her thanks. Rebecca breathed heavily and could

feel rivers of sweat streaming down her body. Madeleine came out on the field, holding a small broadsword. She looked uncertain. Although small, the sword weighed down her arm.

"Madeleine, are you ready?" Rebecca smiled, feeling pride in Edward's sister.

"Aye, can we begin?" Madeleine looked at the sword with distaste.

"Don't think of it as a weapon. Think of the sword as an extension of yourself. Watch me. It's like a dance, make it graceful and free." Rebecca wielded her sword in flowing arcs around her, her weariness forgotten. She showed Madeleine swift defensive moves put together to make an extraordinary dance.

Breathing in the moist morning air, Rebecca smelled the sweet primrose. With the dampness, the plants around her seemed to be waking with fresh scents. Out of habit her mind identified each essence and its use.

She drew another deep breath and looked to the tops of the mountains laced in early morning mists. The castle grounds seemed eerie and quiet. A quiet that told of how the birds still nestled asleep.

Rebecca had kept busy. She showed the men the benefits of using dogs on the battlefield, trained hard, and helped to start Madeleine defending herself. All of these activities gave her satisfaction. But she couldn't shake the feeling of incompleteness.

Edward's absence for the past week affected her more than she wanted to admit. Her knees wobbled every time she thought about seeing him again. Maybe he wouldn't come back . . . didn't care to be with her. Didn't love her. She could be nothing but trouble . . . at times. More trouble than she was worth?

Rebecca walked to the fountain. Leaning over, she scooped the cold water into her hands and splashed it onto her face. A figure walked across the courtyard toward her. Gradually, she could see it was Madeleine.

Their routine of early morning meetings proved to be wonderful for both of them, in body and in soul. Although Madeleine complained of sore muscles, she kept working and showed a natural flare for swordplay.

Rebecca smiled at Madeleine and nodded to her. They began their dance. Moving together, their swords swished through the still air. They both seemed in good form this morning.

As they finished, Rebecca looked across the courtyard. A man walked from the mists. She froze, not able to move a muscle. Edward walked to her—an utterly alluring look on his face as he approached.

He gazed at her until he stood in front of them and turned to Madeleine. "That's very good, dear sister. And I have Rebecca to thank, I'm sure. You're not thinking of entering the battle, are you?"

"And what if I should?" Madeleine stood as tall as she could, facing her brother.

"You shan't." Edward turned to Rebecca and stepped closer. "You're very quiet this morning." He lifted her hand and kissed her palm, then covered her lips with his own before she could speak.

His kiss promised her heaven. She put her arms around his broad shoulders and lifted herself, wrapping her legs around his waist. His arms moved to support her, gripping her bottom.

"Mmmm. That's better." Edward continued to kiss her, as her world swirled around. Tearing his mouth from her, he swore a quiet oath. "Let me go and I'll smite that clergyman, then we can be on with this."

He put her down and drew his sword, walking toward the church.

"Edward!" Her body already missed his.

He turned. "What?" A smile played on his face.

"You can't do that!"

"The hell I can't." His laughter echoed through the courtyard as he sheathed his sword and ran to her. Scooping her up, he swung her around. " 'Twould solve our problem."

" 'Twouldn't. That is the height of the stubborn Scotsman.

You would rather kill the man than break your word to him!"
She laughed.

Edward put his arm around her, guiding her to the kitchens.
"I've a raging hunger, Rebecca Cavenaugh."

She remembered her ire and stopped to face him. "I'll not
give you a crumb." She pushed his arm from her. "You never
even said farewell! You slunk away like a dog and I knew not
where you went!"

"Ah, m'lady, ye know I couldn't tell you."

"You could have!"

"Could I have? And you wouldn't have slunk away with me?"

"You didn't want me?"

"I always want you! But . . . we can't always have what we
want." Edward took her hand and held it to his cheek. "Your
scent is like heaven itself. I think I'll lose myself with you."

"Ach, come and have some food. It's swooning from hunger
you are." Rebecca held his hand and pulled him along.

"Aye, hunger . . ." He took her hand, swinging her up against
him, and kissed her again.

They walked into the kitchen, arm in arm. Everyone present
smiled to see them and welcomed Edward back. Sitting at a
table, they ate warmed oats with milk and honey.

"Is King James still at MacCleary castle?"

"Nay, but he left an army to safeguard it. He's headed this
way to seek the peace among our clans." Edward looked at her
sadly. "I amend, it plagued me the entire trip . . . my not bidding
you farewell. Or was it the lack of you that plagued me?"

Rebecca smiled. "I suppose I'll forgive you."

"Good. And what mischief have you been into?"

"No mischief. Only good." Rebecca smiled as she remembered her rescue of Mavis.

"Only good mischief, by the look on your face. What did
you do?" Edward's eyes met hers with fierceness. "Spill it."

"There's naught to spill."

"Liar."

"Get on with you. We should see my father."

They stood and walked up to MacKey's rooms. Martha greeted them at the chamber door.

"Welcome back Edward, did the MacCleary clan get home safely?" She led them into the chamber.

"Aye, Lady Martha, and how is your husband?"

MacKey stood before the fire. "I'm in fighting order now. Thanks to good treatment. We should be hearing from our scouts soon." He offered them seats around the fire. "Mavis did as you asked and was nearly killed. A Cavenaugh rode out and rescued her, just before the Kirkguard men would misuse her. We've let her go to her family, but she's forbidden to leave the castle."

"Good. But how could she be rescued and not have alerted the Kirkguard Clan of our deception?"

"Quite carefully. It seems the Cavenaugh watched the camp, created a diversion, drugged the drinks, and untied Mavis. When the men slept, Mavis escaped. They were not the wiser."

Edward swung around on his chair to face Rebecca. "You did *that?*" His voice sounded tight. He stood and paced in front of the fire, his face a combination of fury and caring. "You could have—"

"I could not have." She stood to confront him. "I used utmost care and didn't do anything foolish. How would you know it was I?" Rebecca faced him boldly. She glanced at her parent's stunned expressions and back at Edward.

"Ach, how not! For Mavis?" His fury seemed to dwindle in the presence of MacKey and Martha.

"For any man or woman who serves us and would be mistreated or killed." She sat back down in defeat. "Wouldn't you have done the same?"

"Aye, but not with such a creative plan." Edward's eyes seemed to smile at her. "What was the diversion?"

"Galahad."

Edward's laughter seemed to put everyone in the room at ease again.

A knock sounded at the chamber door. Martha opened it to see a clansman. He rushed past her and approached MacKey.

"Chieftain, the Kirkguard clan approaches. They are only an hour behind me. My apology for not getting back sooner. We lost the other men in the scouting party. I just barely escaped."

Rebecca and Edward helped her father alert the clan. The castle became a fury of activity. Men suited up for a battle. Archers set themselves up on the castle battlements. The iron portcullis lowered to protect the main gate. The wounded and families gathered in the innermost chambers, with Madeleine and younger men to protect them.

Back in her chamber, Edward helped Rebecca into her thick leather armor. She, in turn, helped him. They didn't speak. Rebecca could feel a peace between them, an accepting of what was to come. Savoring every inch of Edward with her eyes, she memorized his facial expression, his dark perceptive eyes, and his sturdy build.

She carefully tied his armor over the most tender areas. They knelt together, each praying silently, their hands clasped. A thundering of hooves beyond the castle walls sent them running.

The warriors gathered in the courtyard on horseback, ready and waiting. The archers snapped into action first. The whist of arrows sounded through the air. They never stopped loading and firing in rapid succession. Cries could be heard from outside the walls. Rebecca sat on her mount next to Edward. Every nerve in her body was taut and ready.

A battering ram thumped loudly on the main gate portcullis. It creaked in protest. Her sharp mind and ears became aware of a battering ram on the side gate. No archers stood above them. As Rebecca pointed, Edward could see the problem. He shouted for the archers to move, just as the side door splintered. The men at arms converged on the Kirkguards who entered.

A splintering noise across the courtyard announced the entry of more Kirkguards through the main gate. Rebecca and Edward rode for them. They fought hard to unseat the Kirkguard men. Cavenaugh clansmen with lances worked to clear the enemy from their horses. The MacCleary and Cavenaughs dismounted and the hand to hand fight began.

Rebecca fought a large man who tried to take her. He soon

breathed his last breath. The gates were quickly reinforced and the archers, dangerously low on arrows, alerted the clan. Kirkguard men scaled the walls. The archers picked up their swords and helped to stave them off.

One after the other fought her, each time gaining ground for the enemy clan and getting deeper into the castle. Rebecca fought for each breath. Still she took every chance she could to see Edward. The largest and most dangerous men assailed him. But none could outshine his passion and they fell. Nathaniel brought down a man at Rebecca's back.

"Watch your back, Lady Rebecca, I might not be there next time." He yelled to her, fear in his eyes.

She swung around to knock another Kirkguard off his feet. Keeping up her momentum, she finished him. She saw Edward outflanked by three, swinging to parry each one. Nathaniel caught her eye and they moved in to even the match. More MacCleary men fought other Kirkguards who would attack Edward and Rebecca. As in a game of chess, all pieces protected them, some falling.

Edward looked around as the path cleared for them. "Where is that damned Ruppert?" They followed after the enemies who passed them.

Bloodied men, everywhere. Rebecca refused to look at their faces. The strong smell of sweat and blood assailed her, making her dizzy. With a deep breath she met another man's sword forcefully. She lifted her shield, warding off a blow and thrust her sword just under her shield to wound the attacker. The dizziness overcame her. She went into an empty chamber to regain her strength.

Closing the door behind her, she slumped against the wall in the darkness. Finally, she caught her breath. Two men came into the room. She tried to hide in the shadows.

"Get a torch from the hall. I know she came in here."

Ruppert's voice shook her to her toes, and then rage took over. She held her sword up with a fury she had never felt before.

"What good fortune finds us alone to end this thing?"

Rebecca smiled her contempt.

"Good fortune, indeed. And would you finally bed with me?"

"Not ever." Rebecca advanced on him.

The other man walked into the room, the torch he held lit the dim chamber. Ruppert pulled a bow from behind his back and sent an arrow her way. She sliced it from the air with her sword, just before it hit her body. She felt a swish of air as another arrow missed her head.

"Put down the bow, and fight like a man." Rebecca wasn't so lucky with the next arrow. It found her side, grazing her flesh shallowly as it struck her armor. She leapt at him, swung her sword into the bow, splintering it in two.

Ruppert drew his sword, parrying her next blow.

Rebecca fought off dizziness again, and tried with all her might to land a mortal blow to Ruppert. She could hear the hounds being released. Galahad would find her. Ruppert parried her sword and made his way to the open chamber door. He slammed it with his foot. A strange passion lit his eyes.

"I will have you, Rebecca Kirkguard."

"I am not a Kirkguard!" She lunged—cutting his arm.

One thought echoed in Edward's mind. *Where is Rebecca?* He fought on, constantly defending his life. The dogs raged at the Kirkguards' heels. Galahad barked at him . . . and barked, and barked again. He tried to follow the dog, each time waylaid by another man. A Kirkguard swung at Galahad. The dog ducked and jumped into the man's face. The enemy dropped his sword and tried to get the dog off—screaming.

Edward got next to him and struck. Galahad let go and ran away from the fight, nose to the ground. The dog stopped, turned to Edward, barked, and turned to run on. Edward followed, some Kirkguards still on his heels. Clearly he was the target of the day. He looked to see the door that the dog stopped at before turning to fight the men.

Edward noticed Nathan and MacKey following his steps

closely as the fight thinned. The Cavenaughs continued to control the castle and led many Kirkguard men to the dungeons.

Nathan and MacKey took over fighting the men who stopped Edward from entering the chamber. His heart knew whom he would find. *Please God let her be alive.* When he finally opened the door he saw Rebecca and Ruppert fighting. She looked tired. Ruppert struck hard, over and over again.

Edward went to her aid. A man lunged at him from the side of the room. As Edward fought the man, he saw Rebecca lose concentration, almost suffering a wound. Then, using the parry Edward taught her, she nearly unsworded Ruppert.

The man who fought Edward was swift and strong. Ruppert had saved his best man for last. Edward's anger helped his fight. The red haze disappeared before him. He felt renewed with the thought that this was it. This would tell how happy or sad his future would be. They would win. He struggled to concentrate on his own fight, and see to Rebecca's safety as well.

Oh, how he wanted to face Ruppert. Galahad tormented Ruppert from behind, each time just barely being missed by his sword. A storm of footsteps approached the chamber.

All at once Rebecca unsworded Ruppert and brought her sword up for the fatal blow. Edward's adversary halted his attack, going to Ruppert's aid. Edward grabbed him from behind before he could put his sword through Rebecca.

The chamber door filled with the presence of the Stuart King. "Rebecca, stop the killing. Now! Make an example to the people of Scotland. Make a show of clan unification! Don't kill Laird Ruppert."

Rebecca heard Edward's curse and watched as he threw the Kirkguard to the floor, then came toward Ruppert with his sword ready. It took four of the king's men to subdue him. They dragged him to stand off to the side of King James.

She stood with her sword frozen in the air. Tasting the conquest of Ruppert. Every muscle in her body screamed at her to kill him. Run the sword through the filthy— Her heart constricted at the thought of a unified Scotland. No more killing. Freedom from the wars for the women and children. She cursed the king under her breath. Her own happiness wrestled with her loyalty to Scotland. She'd given her happiness up before. How could she do it again?

Rebecca turned her head to look at Edward, the pain of her predicament clearly written on his face. Her expression pleaded with him for help in her decision. He averted his gaze as if to prevent her from reading the answer in his eyes.

Her hand gripped the sword harder, making ready to swing.

TWENTY-THREE

Rebecca's tongue ran over her dried lips. Her arms strained to keep the sword ready. Ready to strike Ruppert. "This man holds no honor. He would not serve Scotland. He's the cause of all the fighting!"

"Let the court decide that." The King held his ground.

"I want this over with now, King James, I beg you . . ."

"No, Rebecca, I need you to do this—for Scotland. Put down your sword."

Rebecca's eyes teared. *No. This canna be.* She swung her sword away from Ruppert's body and it fell onto the floor with a clatter. Her anguished cry echoed though the chamber. She met Edward's eyes, feeling ashamed. His proud smile sent her fleeing for his arms. The guards released him.

"You see? She's an adulteress." Ruppert's voice contaminated the air.

Edward released Rebecca and reached for his sword. A flash behind Ruppert startled Rebecca. As if in slow motion she watched as Mavis ran from the shadows, her blade glittering in her hand. She slashed at Ruppert's neck, cutting his life flow. He fell to the floor. Rebecca watched in stunned silence.

Mavis faced King James. "Justice is done. We don't need a court to know that." She fell to her knees before the king, putting the knife to her own throat. She cut herself before Edward could stop her.

Rebecca ran to her and tried to stop the flow of blood.

Sobbing, she saw she couldn't save her. Edward gently guided her away from the bodies. The world spun around as he held her, wiping the blood from her face with his sleeve.

Rebecca pushed away from him to gaze around the room. Everyone stood in stunned silence. Only then did she notice that Nathaniel and her father stood at the chamber door. She watched MacKey remove his tartan and lay it over Mavis, honoring her, his feelings written painfully on his face.

The days followed full of sadness. A haze surrounded Rebecca. Edward gently supported her mood and she saw him try to deal with his own. They spoke quietly about nothing important and slept alone in the night.

The morning of the third day after the siege dawned with an aching beauty that begged Rebecca to celebrate all that life had to offer her. Her body blossomed with a pink glow and joy entered her being.

They still entertained King James, who offered Mavis's children residence in his court.

She dressed for morning meal. Every event in the castle held such formality with the king in residence. She chose her MacCleary and Cavenaugh plaid gown. Newly washed, it smelled fresh. She lifted the dress. Rose petals glided to the floor. Sarah had added her special touch. Picking up a petal, she brought it to her nose and breathed in its scent.

She put on her best belt. It glittered with a gold Celtic knot. Combing out her hair, she fashioned it in large plaits all along the side of her head with one large braid down her front, left side. It reached well past her waist and ended with soft curls under its binding.

Hose and boots followed as she hurried, not wanting to be late. She nearly skipped down the hall but held back because, after all, that would be unladylike. Her freedom of Ruppert flowed from her as she hummed her favorite ditty. She stopped to listen at Edward's door but heard nothing.

He'd been so distant lately. In fact everyone seemed to be

avoiding her. Had her mood been bad? Well, today she would make up for that. She danced down the stairway to the great hall. As she entered everyone got quiet. Odd. She smiled, feeling awkward and walked over to Edward. Why was no one talking?

When Rebecca caught sight of Edward it took her breath away. He wore a handsome waistcoat of black velvet with gold buttons, over a white shirt. His breeches, matching black velvet, ended just below his knees meeting MacCleary hose.

He stood and placed a kiss on her cheek. He knelt before her on one knee, taking her hand in his. She looked at the faces staring at her with wide smiles. Everyone was dressed in such finery, as if . . .

"Lady Rebecca, you're more lovely than this fair morning."

Rebecca nodded her pleasure and whispered, "Edward, what're you about?"

His grin looked full of mischief. "Would you do me the honor of becoming my wife? This very day?"

Rebecca nearly swooned. "This day?"

The clergyman piped in. "You have the church's blessing."

Rebecca nodded thanks to the clergyman.

"Be my wife." Edward gazed into her eyes, his full of love.

"Aye! Yes, Edward!" She put her arms around his shoulders and hugged his neck.

Edward's mouth found hers and they kissed amid the cheers of the clans. All at once her clan's ladies surrounded her.

"Stop—Don't touch m'lady. I'll wed her now. She doesn't need any adornment. This gown is perfect—give her back." Edward signaled with his hands, beckoning to them. As they parted from her, he lifted her into his arms and led a long procession of people to the church.

He carried her up the aisle of the small chapel amid cries of, "Laird Edward, that's not how it's done," and, "put the bride down." None of the cries came from the bride. Rebecca savored the wonder of the events to come, but her eyes never left Edward's beloved face.

He shrugged and told them all, "This is the way I'm doing it."

Rebecca laughed and cried, all at once. He showered her face with kisses. At the altar the clergyman waited, a little ruffled, but with a smile that looked like it would split his face. He laughed with Rebecca as she looked up at him.

The laughter sounded like music as Edward joined in.

"I've waited long enough. Marry us."

"Edward, you can put me down now."

"No." He hugged her closer.

"Edward, I would be standing when I vow to love and honor you for the rest of my life." Rebecca struggled to get down.

"Ach . . . all right." Edward released her gently to the floor.

Rebecca straightened her ruffled dress and looked up at Edward. He looked at her as if she were a goddess.

Without taking his eyes from her he spoke sternly to the clergyman. "Get on with it, man, before I draw my sword."

The man recited the marriage ceremony as they looked into each other's eyes. Rebecca thought her heart would burst with joy. Instead, the joy oozed out of her eyes as tears. Edward cradled her face with his hands and brushed his thumbs over her cheeks to wipe the moisture away.

"Are ye sad?" His voice sounded low and husky with emotion.

"No, my love, I overflow with happiness." She whispered back.

Edward smiled and looked at the clergyman for the first time. They spoke their vows strongly for all to hear. When the bride and groom kissed, the crowd raised a heartfelt cheer. A decade of war and feud ended. A lifetime of love began.

The midday meal turned into a wedding feast. And like the magic of the day it seemed like a dream. Edward presented heirlooms to her and adorned her with them. A jeweled necklace, bracelet, beautiful hairpiece and shimmering ring.

Rebecca worried over what to give him. Calling a steward, she whispered in his ear and he quickly departed.

"More mischief, my dear wife?" Edward grinned at her and winked.

"Aye, and you'll have a lifetime of it." She laughed as he groaned.

"I wouldn't have it any other way." He lifted her onto his lap, causing the wedding guests to yell encouragements.

King James rose and a hush fell over the hall. "To the happy couple, I award all the lands between the MacCleary and Cavenaugh castles."

Edward and Rebecca stood and bowed their thanks to the king. The hall filled with lightheartedness as everyone continued to celebrate.

Musicians began to play and people danced. Amid the festivities the dog keeper brought a young dog to Edward, Rebecca's gift. He accepted with glee and she promised to show him how to train the pup.

She looked deeply into Edward's eyes and wished that the people around them would vanish.

"Let's dance." Rebecca stood quickly, a glint of mystery in her eyes.

Edward took her by the hand and waist and they danced into the throng of people. As they moved by a doorway Rebecca took over the lead and guided him through it. Stopping the dance, he wrapped her tightly in his arms and kissed her deeply, his intent already large against her.

"No time to waste, my love." Breaking away, she led him to a wall. She pushed it and a secret panel opened. They escaped into an inner staircase and out to the upper hall. "They'll not disturb our bedding if they don't know we're gone."

Edward laughed heartily and carried her to his room. Laying her on the bed he teased, "I think I'm over tired, perhaps you would just hold me the day through." He turned from her.

"Not a chance!" Rebecca launched herself at him from the bed. She landed on his back and reached around to open his waistcoat. The soft velvet on her fingertips aroused her. She slid off of his back and moved to face him. His male incense engulfed her.

Edward untied her bodice, pushing her dress down her shoulders. Her bared breast rose with each breath she took. She waited for him to kiss her. His hands cupped her breasts and he kissed them. The pleasure of their love grew inside her. She worked at his belt, longing to see his splendid body. It had been such a long time.

His hands stopped her. "Sit on the bed," he ordered.

She complied. He could have said, "stand on your head," and she would have, without a care.

He undressed slowly in front of her. His eyes gleaming with the same hunger she struggled with. As his clothes fell to the floor she reached out to touch his golden body.

Playfully, he swept her hands away. "Don't touch."

She bit her lip and enjoyed the way his body moved to be free of his breeches and reveal his shaft in all its glory. Her breath caught in her throat. He stood there naked. Lifting her chin with his hand he brought her gaze back to his face.

It held such a satisfied expression, her heart soared, what a stunning face. She touched her finger to his thick brows and traced down his nose. With feather-like softness she let her finger outline his lips and the vertical ridges between his nose and lip.

He opened his mouth and nipped at her finger, sucking it into his mouth. She removed her finger with a laugh and his mouth molded to hers with hot passion. Every woman's part of her burned for him. Jumping from the bed, she pressed her body against him and realized, with frustration, that she was still half-dressed.

Her hands struggled to remove the clothing. He brushed them aside.

"Watch." He slowly undid her ties and buttons, letting each piece of clothing float down her body to the floor.

Everywhere his hands touched ignited with a heat that shot to her most secret parts. She breathed in the essence of them both and made the sparks turn to fire with each deep breath. The last piece of clothing fell to the floor. His hands traced her body starting at her neck, down to her shoulders and then to her breasts. Her peaks tightened and poked up against his fingers as he circled around them.

Then his hands moved down her sides to her stomach and around to her backside. He squeezed each cheek, lifting her toward his swollen shaft, moaning deeply. Putting her down, he continued with his hands, down the back of her legs and up the front.

His hands swept up her thighs. He parted the rose petal folds with his thumbs and found the bud within with his tongue. She melted against him. Standing again, he kissed her mouth softly.

"Ah . . . Edward." Reaching for his shaft, she caressed it. She knelt and kissed him, licking the tip of his manhood.

Edward lifted her to sit on the bed and stood on the wooden stair. He spread her legs, entering her. She rose to meet his thrusts. But it wasn't enough. Pulling away from him, she let out a cry of despair as they parted. Edward laughed at her and jumped onto the bed. She wrestled away from him, teasing them both.

He fell on top of her and entered her quickly and deeply. Her gasp made her pleasure heighten. She stopped his movement. He lay still inside her and caressed her face with his large hands. She started moving again slowly, enjoying the feelings.

Just as their passion reached its peak, she kissed his lips. He kissed her back deeply, and their bodies pulsed with the intensity of their love. He held her until their bodies quieted.

"Edward?"

"Huhm?" He lay on his side gazing at her.

"We're husband and wife!" She sat up straight in bed. "God save us!"

Edward startled at her words and looked at her in apparent alarm. She greeted his look with a witty smile. He made a noise of annoyance and gripped the pillow beneath his head.

"Edward, behave yourself. I just wanted to see if you were listening!" The pillow being swung into her face cut off her scream.

Edward turned serious. "All right, now, there's no time to play. We best get back to our wedding guests." He got off the bed, pointing his finger at her. "Don't you dare."

"Don't you trust me?" Rebecca scooted to the side of the bed and swung her legs over it, still gripping the pillow.

"Of course not, do you think I'm daft?" Edward laughed as he picked up his clothes on the floor. Watching her as he bent down to get them.

Just as his eyes left her to retrieve all of the clothing, she brought the pillow down forcefully behind his head.

"Daft you are." Rebecca rolled over with laughter.

In a fraction of time, she found herself stomach-down over his knees. She struggled to get to the floor. "Nooo, Edward! I must dress."

"What a shame to cover this pretty bottom."

"Let me down!" She struggled harder.

"Ah—but you didn't listen. Isn't it my duty as a husband to teach you to mind?" Edward sounded like he was enjoying himself.

Her hands found the bedpost and she pulled. "No—it's not!"

He gripped her tighter laughing at her efforts. "It's a good thing you're not so puny when it comes to swordplay."

"Edward!" The bottom of her foot swung up accidentally connecting with his face.

His hand reacted directly onto her backside.

"I didn't mean—"

"Neither did I." His deep laugh told her he lied.

Edward turned her around on his lap and kissed her outraged face, until she gave in to his arduous plea for peace. He whispered, "I love you."

"And I love you." Rebecca placed a small kiss on his nose and jumped to the floor.

They both dressed quickly. She wished they didn't have to. They slipped out to the passage, following it to the room.

"Shall we dance, dear wife?"

Edward's grin made her laugh. They danced back into the hall. Rebecca noticed that the atmosphere had become a little more raucous. Probably due to the French wine her father brought out for the occasion.

In one corner she could see the "new" Madeleine . . . in the arms of Malcolm, nearly kissing him in public. Rebecca looked away, hoping that Edward would not notice—too late.

He stormed over to his sister, Rebecca at his heels.

"Madeleine, let me bring you to your room."

"Ach, brother, leave me be. I've listened to you all my life. I won't let you bully me any further. Isn't that what you told me, Rebecca?"

Rebecca's mouth dropped open. Edward turned his ire toward her. She cringed outwardly. "You should listen to your brother before the wine causes you to do what you normally wouldn't." She gave Malcolm a stern glare. Circling, Madeleine she guided her toward her brother.

Edward gripped Madeleine's arm, taking her from the room. Then Rebecca set herself on Malcolm so he didn't get the wrong idea about Madeleine.

"Are you daft?" She punched his arm, causing him to look from the departing Madeleine to her.

"I—"

"Don't you dare try to compromise my husband's sister while she's in the spirits." She punched his arm again. "You'll have to make amends to Madeleine and her brother on the morrow. I suggest you get a bundle of flowers before you do, understand?" Her fist made contact again.

"Aye, Rebecca—don't punch my arm again, or I'll forget we're grown and take you down a notch or two."

"Oh, Malcolm, I'm scared." She resisted the urge to punch him again and smiled instead.

"Ach, Rebecca, I'll do as you ask. Do you think she's sweet on me?"

"Tread carefully, and she might have you. And remember, she is Laird Edward's sister and a very good friend of mine, as well."

This time Malcolm's hand stopped her fist from hitting his arm. "All right. All right! I hope that husband of yours knocks some manners into you." Malcolm laughed.

"I hope you won't hold your breath waiting for it!" She walked away feeling victorious.

The events of the day swirled through her head. She reached for a chalice of wine and laughed when she saw it was dented. Looking up she found herself surrounded by womenfolk.

They asked her how she endured the fighting and admired her strength. Although it made her feel proud, she was sure to tell them how distasteful the fighting was. When asked, she said that it's a good idea to learn to wield a sword for their own protection.

"Will you go on more raids, Lady Rebecca?" A young woman asked her.

"Nay, I think I've had enough of that."

"Have you now?" Edward stood behind her, his voice sounded surprised. He put his hand on her elbow. "The ladies are my witness. Should Lady Rebecca wish to go off and fight again I'm counting on you to remember her words."

The ladies nodded, clearly taken by Edward's charm and good looks. Edward led her gently away and up to their chambers. The crowd cheered and followed them up to the rooms.

"In which room will we rest, my love?" Edward looked into her eyes.

"Mine?" Rebecca could see sparks of emotion in his.

"Aye." They entered the room amid the crude shouts of the crowd.

Rebecca blanched.

"Come now, with your vocabulary that shouldn't shock you." Edward turned to the crowd and his expression silenced them.

The door closed and he pulled her gently into his arms. What is this talk of having enough of the fighting? Are you feeling ill?" His mouth quirked with humor.

Rebecca shrugged, but would not give up her secret yet. "I'm not ill."

"Don't think I've forgotten what you've taught my sister. You're lucky it's our wedding night." He lowered his mouth onto hers.

She could feel his kiss all the way to her toes. Her passion flared again. Raking her hands through his hair, her tongue fought with his to dominate their kiss.

Edward pulled her body roughly against his growing desire with one hand. The game continued. His other hand held the back of her head. Pulling her hair gently, he brought her head back to let him devour her mouth more fully. He tasted so good, her husband . . . the joy of that thought released a pulsing from the center of her being.

She pulled her mouth from his, silently beseeching him to take her. Her hands worked frantically to undo his breeches. This time he didn't stop her haste. He worked with the same fervor to remove her clothes.

Rebecca woke to the sweet songs of birds. The scent of roses filled the room. She searched for the source with her sleepy eyes and found a beautiful urn of roses sitting on her dresser. Had they been there the night before?

She looked over at the sleeping Edward. He looked peaceful. His mouth smiled in his sleep. The tousled hair on his pillow and across his forehead sent her blood pounding again. Memories of the night before made her dizzy.

She slipped out of bed and could feel a winsome soreness in every muscle. They had loved well the whole night through. Yet she didn't feel tired.

Walking over to the flowers, she breathed their scent in deeply. She plucked one of the many roses from the urn. Being careful not to stick herself—but there were no thorns. She quickly took all the roses in her arms. They'd been picked clean of every thorn.

She buried her face in the sweet mass of flowers. Her throat tightened with her joy and tears spilled from her eyes onto the roses. *Yes, Edward would see that her life was free of the thorns.*

"I'll try, my wild highland rose." Edward spoke as though he had read her thoughts. But she knew that they both remembered his words that day in the rose garden.

She brought the flowers with her and jumped onto the bed.

Her heart filled with love for Edward. They hugged with the flowers between them.

"As will I," she vowed.

The welcoming wall of the MacCleary castle shone proudly before Rebecca. The lazy rhythm of her horse lulled her and she savored the sight of it. Turning to Edward she met his eyes.

"Home." She smiled.

Edward smiled back and looked at the castle with pride. "It is a wonderful sight. Will you be happy here, Rebecca Mac-Cleary?" His tongue rolled over her new name in high style.

"Aye. As lady of this castle, I will serve it well."

"And what of her laird? Will you serve him well?" Edward's eyebrows rose.

"Aye, well enough. However, the laird must be aware of his lady's need for freedom. Will he serve me well?" She smiled without contempt.

"Aye, I'll worship your body with mine. I'll try not to ask you for anything that would quell your free spirit." Edward brought his horse closer to hers. Leaning over he kissed her lips lightly, sealing his promise.

"My thanks to you, Laird Edward MacCleary."

A clarion sounded their approach. Shortly after Edward's steward rode out to greet them.

"Greetings my laird and lady. Are you riding alone?" The graying man looked fondly at Edward.

"Aye, the army and ladies are a few hours behind us."

Rebecca blushed when she thought of their cave. They chose to travel together through the short cut. She smiled at the thought of their stops along the cave passages. They dismounted and followed the steward as he led their horses to the stable.

"You look well, Lady Rebecca. Welcome to your new home." Now the elderly man's admiration was for her.

Edward put his arm around Rebecca's shoulders as they walked. "Lady Madeleine and Gwen return with us. Some of the Cavenaugh men will also reside here to sharpen their sword skills. Will you see rooms are readied for them?"

Rebecca remembered the look of joy on Madeleine's face when Malcolm stepped forward to join them. Her parents had asked that Sarah stay behind, they needed her skills.

As the men talked, she though proudly of Gwen. Sarah had taken her under her wing and taught her the ways of herbs as she had Rebecca. Gwen would be a help with all the ailments and tending the herbal gardens. The future loomed brightly before her.

She would pray for peace, every day, peace in their land and peace for her restless spirit.

The MacCleary clan welcomed her royally with a banquet. The men sang King James's praises to Edward. He told them about the battles, and that King James was on his way to Kirkguard castle with his army to change their ways—or exile them.

The arrival of Nathaniel, Madeleine, Gwen, and the army sent more cheers through the hall. Minstrels sang beautiful love songs, and food aplenty filled the hall with the scents of home. In the castle walls a warmth and peace prevailed.

Edward reached under the table to rub Rebecca's leg, smoothing her gown. She smiled and nodded toward the door. He excused them both and in his true fashion, lifted her into his arms and carried her to their chamber.

The clan's cheers followed them up the stairs and then grew quiet. Rebecca breathed in the familiar scents of the castle and remembered the first time they walked this hall together. Edward's musk filled her senses. She sighed again.

"You've been very quiet and reflective since we got here. Is all well with you?"

"Aye . . . more than well." With a lilt of teasing in her voice, she looked deeply into his eyes. "I love you with all my life, Edward MacCleary."

Warmth filled his eyes and he kissed her while they walked

down the hall. Stopping by the master chamber he opened the door and carried her over the threshold.

"You're such a wonder, Edward." Rebecca breathed his name. "At times so gentle and romantic, and at times so harsh."

"Well balanced, don't you think?" He grinned down at her and laid her gently on the bed. He undid his belts.

"I wouldn't have you any other way." Rebecca suddenly felt shy. "And which will you be as a father?"

Edward stilled. "You don't mean?"

"Aye. I'm with your babe." She smiled timidly, hoping he would be glad.

A loud whoop filled the air and she was swept into his arms again and twirled around the room. He let her down before the fire and looked closely at her body. Turning her this way and that, he asked, "Where?"

"In here." She patted her still flat stomach.

He knelt in front of her kissing her stomach. Her eyes filled with tears.

"I'll be full of emotions, maybe hard to live with." Rebecca tried to stop her tears.

"What's new?" He shrugged playfully, still gazing up at her from his knees.

"Edward!" She laughed at his humor.

Then he grew serious. "I'll be a gentle father."

"I know." Rebecca knelt beside him and they embraced. She could feel the warmth of their love as it flowed between them and their unborn child.

ROMANCE FROM JO BEVERLY